The Unfinished Child

Theresa Shea

BRINDLE
& GLASS

Brindle & Glass Publishing Ltd.
brindleandglass.com

LIBRARY AND ARCHIVES CANADA CATALOGUING IN PUBLICATION
Shea, Theresa
The unfinished child / Theresa Shea.

Also issued in electronic format.
ISBN 978-1-927366-02-8

I. Title.

PS8637.H42U54 2013   C813'.6   C2012-907618-X

Editor: Lisa Martin DeMoor
Proofreader: Heather Sangster, Strong Finish
Design: Pete Kohut
Cover image: Bojan Sokolovic, istockphoto.com
Author photo: Catherine Burgess

Brindle & Glass is pleased to acknowledge the financial support for its publishing program from the Government of Canada through the Canada Book Fund, Canada Council for the Arts, and the Province of British Columbia through the British Columbia Arts Council and the Book Publishing Tax Credit.

MIX
Paper from
responsible sources
FSC
www.fsc.org   FSC® C016245

The interior pages of this book have been printed on 30% post-consumer recycled paper, processed chlorine free, and printed with vegetable-based inks.

2 3 4 5 17 16 15 14 13

For my children, Dashiell, Sadie Rain, and Levi

There is nothing more truly artistic than to love people.

—Vincent Van Gogh

ONE

1947

·

At five in the morning, Margaret felt her water break—as if a crystal had been shattered by a lone, high note. An invisible hand, or perhaps the unborn child's deft heel, flicked a switch and the floodgate opened. As the warm liquid rushed from her body she moved as quickly as her lumbering figure would allow from her reclined position on the couch, where she'd been elevating her feet to relieve the swelling in her ankles, to a standing position beside it. It's time, she thought calmly. Finally it's time.

After carefully preparing for months, she was ready. An overnight bag sat packed beside her dresser in the bedroom where her husband, Donald, slept soundly. The nursery was equipped with all the necessities—a crib with a shiny white finish, an oak rocking chair with a padded cushion tied onto two of the back rungs, and a multicoloured mobile hanging from the ceiling above the crib.

In the bathroom she removed her wet underwear and cotton nightgown and rinsed them in the sink. Then she washed her thighs with a warm cloth, wondering when the contractions would begin.

Start a pot of soup, her mother's voice echoed in her mind. That had been the only advice her mother had given her about labour. *Keep yourself busy. There's no knowing how long it will take, and you might as well pass the time by being useful.* Farm women like her mother believed that leisure was as unnatural as a two-headed calf. Sleep was the time to do nothing, she used to say, and from the time her feet touched the wooden floor in the morning until the time they lifted off that floor at bedtime, her mother didn't stop doing. Margaret watched her mother with a mixture of admiration and dread. The lines on her mother's face stemmed from irritation and fatigue, not laughter. And her dark hair, tucked into a scarf, was constantly covered. She could have been pretty if she'd tried, or if she'd cared, but she'd spent her entire life keeping busy.

Keeping busy was the one trait her mother had tried to pass on to her only daughter. To follow in her footsteps would mean living a life without joy.

Garlic sizzled in the hot oil, an unusual sound and smell for the early morning hour. Margaret sliced into an onion and cut quickly before her eyes teared from the pungent fumes. The carrot skins curled against the peeler and dropped onto the cutting board.

She thought of her mother, already up and working at the farm, and recalled the time she'd threatened to cut Margaret's hair off if she spent one more minute brushing it. She thought of her father, tight-lipped, dusty, and stoic. She thought of her brother, gamely hiding his affliction as he shyly put his arm around Ethel, the girl from the neighbouring farm. She thought of stones in her back. And she thought of Donald, her young husband, asleep still and not knowing that today was the day.

Thirty minutes later the first contraction tightened her belly into a shell as hard as a turtle's. Then the heat came and she felt as if her torso were roasting over a flame. She held her breath and stared at the hard, moving swell of her belly, and she was both amazed and afraid. This was it. There was no turning back. No saying she'd changed her mind.

The stories about childbirth she'd heard her mother and women friends talk about in corners and kitchens, with astonishing and descriptive details, sprang vividly to mind. Babies lodged inside birth canals. Forceps puncturing infant eyeballs. Infections and depressions. Detailed descriptions of the sounds and smells of new life ripping its way into the world. Her own mother's voice describing her inability to have more children after Margaret. *My labour was so hard that my insides ruptured after Margaret came out*, sounding both proud and aggrieved at the same time. No, this was it; even if she couldn't endure the pain, the pain would happen anyway. The labour would come, and the labour would go. That's how time worked; both the things you dreaded most and the things you wanted desperately came and went. Margaret knew that by this time tomorrow she'd be a mother, and all the events leading up to her child's birth would be behind her. She put her hands below her bulging belly and rocked herself gently. "Let's go, little one," she whispered, adopting a joyful tone, trying it out. "I can't wait to meet you."

Outside the kitchen window the eastern sky glowed a soft pink. It would be another warm day, sunny with blue skies and the threat of an evening thunderstorm if the heat built up throughout the day. A great prairie storm with a dramatic display of lights and sound, and the brownish surface of the river quickly rising, carrying sticks and twigs that turned in slow circles and snagged on the concrete bases of the High Level Bridge that spanned the waterway.

Margaret reached for the wooden spoon and stirred the blackening onions and garlic in the pot. Then she opened a jar of tomatoes and gripped it tightly as her body contracted again and the tomatoes rushed from the jar's smooth mouth.

By the time they arrived at the Misericordia Hospital, her body was a third-degree burn desperate for cool comfort. Margaret bit her lip and felt hot tears slide down her cheek as Donald helped her to the admitting desk, where the nurse recognized her panic, quickly put her into a wheelchair, and found someone to take her to a room. She was wheeled past a small population of pain and injury in the waiting room. Metallic smells and guttural moans assailed her senses. Life and death were intricately connected here, linked by an orderly's mop, each pull a bleached path that connected hope and fear to a long history of human struggle.

This is what delirium must feel like, Margaret thought as her mind bounced from one image to the next in the small pain-free moments. A kindly nurse put an ice chip in Margaret's mouth, and she sucked the cold shaving with silent thanks in the pale green delivery room.

Then the injection came and she welcomed the oblivion that followed.

Twilight sleep, they called it, even though she wasn't asleep. But she no longer felt her body, so the pain was entirely gone. Sweet Jesus. A voice from far away issued instructions. *Push.* She tried to obey but wasn't sure if her numb body listened.

Four seasons could have passed before she finally heard a small whimper. Had she made that noise? Or was someone crying?

There were sounds all around her. Hands on her body. Was someone knocking at the door? Answer the door.

Slowly she became more aware of her surroundings. She was in a hospital, that much she remembered. How long had she been here? Was Donald still outside pacing? Had the child been born?

She felt a hand on her wrist and opened her eyes to see a dark-haired nurse taking her pulse.

"What time is it?" she whispered hoarsely, licking her parched lips.

The nurse smiled. "It's just after nine o'clock."

"At night?"

"Yes. We're done now. You did great. The doctor will be back again any minute."

She opened her eyes again to Dr. Morrison's deep voice. He had long, shaggy sideburns that almost reached his chin, and big hands.

Soup on the stove. Did she turn it off?

Darkness.

"Margaret?"

Someone was shaking her. She opened her eyes and a wave of dizziness almost made her vomit. Donald's creased brow was before her; his eyes were wet and full. She smiled weakly as he squeezed her hand.

"The baby?"

"It's a girl," he said with relief. "We have a daughter."

The world tilted; everything was different.

"Where is she? Have you seen her?"

He shook his head. "No, not yet."

"I want to see her."

"Okay. She's in the nursery. They're just having a look at her, cleaning her up. They'll bring her in soon."

Margaret tried to sit up. Everything hurt. There was a burning sensation between her legs, a throbbing heat from where she'd been sewn up. She groaned with embarrassment when she realized someone had shaved between her legs.

The umbilical cord that had attached her to her baby had been cut, replaced by an invisible cord that tightened as the minutes passed. Where was her baby?

"When did they take her away?" she asked. "How long has it been?"

Donald's calm demeanour started to fade. "I'm not sure. The nurse came to get me just before I came in."

"Go find her," Margaret said. "Tell them I want to see her."

The minutes ticked by on the big round face of the clock over the door to the hallway as Margaret waited for her baby, and with each passing minute her sense of dread deepened. Donald returned and said they'd be bringing the baby soon, but when Dr. Morrison finally entered the room, he was empty-handed. Donald stood up and the two men shook hands, but there was something missing from their transaction. The doctor wasn't smiling. The crow's feet around his eyes were stark scars etched into tanned skin.

"You've delivered a baby girl," he said, scratching his right sideburn thoughtfully. "But I'm sorry to tell you that she is a mongoloid."

Margaret looked at her husband to see if he registered what the doctor had said. Donald was a city boy, born and raised. Unlike her, he'd never seen how nature can go horribly wrong. On the farm, she'd seen chickens hatched without feet. A calf born with its intestines spilling out of a hole in its side. A kitten with no eyeballs. Her father's gun was always ready and loaded to dispense with nature's accidents. Or sometimes he'd leave the gun and wring a neck with his strong, bare hands. But mongoloid? The word came as if spoken from a great distance through a thick fog.

"What does that mean?" she asked, repeating the word in her head as her brain began nonsensically to search out rhymes. *Mongoloid. Celluloid. Unemployed. Sigmund Freud.*

"It means your child will be sick a good deal and require special medical and nursing care, which cannot be given at home," he said. Then Dr. Morrison switched to autopilot, delivering blow after blow until the bruises quietly blossomed beneath the surface of her flesh. She didn't even remember delivering the child, and she had yet to lay eyes on it. She wasn't squeamish; farm women were practical to the bone. It was city people who talked too much without taking any action. Margaret knew first-hand that schooling didn't necessarily make a person smart. Or good. How could Margaret make up her own mind about the child without seeing her? "I would advise you not to

5

take the child home, or even see her, for that matter, as there's no sense becoming attached. To do so would make it even more difficult when the time comes to place her in an institution. Besides," he continued, glancing quickly at Donald, "the child will be difficult to feed, and you'll need to think of the larger picture: she will require a lot of time and money."

Dr. Morrison made eye contact with her husband again, and his tone took on a more paternal note. "You're young," he said, placing his hand on Margaret's shoulder. "I'm assuming you'll want to have more children, and this child will take time away from their normal development. Having a child who is so difficult will be a strain on your relationship with your husband and it will restrict your friendships."

The fog was thickening now. Dr. Morrison's face was hazy, his lips shone with saliva and moved in slow motion. Margaret locked her gaze onto his mouth, saw the once-white teeth now stained yellow from tobacco, and marvelled that his lips would not stop moving.

Should their daughter live, he continued, she would have the mental development of a three- to six-year-old. She would have no friends, never be allowed to go to school, never work, and would spend all her days at home with nothing to do. The humane thing was to put her in a place where she'd be housed with others who were just like her. Society's rejects. The retards, mongoloids, and imbeciles. Those weren't the doctor's exact words, but they could have been. But didn't Margaret herself feel like a reject most of her waking hours? A move to the city was almost like moving to another country. She didn't speak the same language as the women she met. Around Donald's family, with its comfortable money and polite conventions, she felt as if she had four arms, three legs, and stood ten feet tall. Maybe that's the kind of girl child Dr. Morrison saw, one ill at ease in a foreign land, stunned by her removal from her mother's warm body.

"The odds of you having another mongoloid child are slim," he went on, patting her shoulder as if she could now look forward to her next delivery. Then he smiled and made some quip about lightning never striking twice in the same place.

"I want to see my baby," she said.

Dr. Morrison's face grew stern. "I don't think . . ."

The invisible cord that tethered her to her child tightened. "I want to see her now."

The doctor fixed his gaze on Donald and shook his head almost imperceptibly. Margaret cleared her throat and Donald met her eyes. Her heart constricted. He was just a boy, really, sweet-natured and kind, used to being taken by the hand and safely guided through his days. He'd never learned how to push against someone in authority. Make waves in a still pond. There was fear in his eyes, and as he reached out to take her hand, she could see him waver between asking her to lead him and taking the lead himself. How quickly his first test as a father had come, before he'd had any time to get used to the role, before he'd even set eyes on the being he'd helped bring into the world. Margaret found she was holding her breath. What kind of man was he going to be?

"We need to see her," she said firmly. Donald nodded.

"I think you're making a mistake," Dr. Morrison said, "but if you must see her, please do so quickly. Believe me, it's for your own good."

The doctor left the room. Two minutes later a nurse arrived and placed the swaddled infant into Margaret's arms.

Margaret felt the weight of the child sink into her chest. If only she could absorb this child back into her body and hold her safely there. The warm flannel blanket against her skin radiated heat like a late winter sun in a blue sky reflecting off newly fallen snow. She closed her eyes against the brilliance and took a deep breath. Then, slowly, she peered down at her child, at the flawless skin on her baby's face, perfect as a newly ripened peach. Such relief. Her baby wasn't monstrous in the least. In fact, she didn't look that different at all. How could they possibly know she was a mongoloid?

The girl had thick, dark hair covering her scalp. Her chestnut eyes were slightly up-slanted, but they weren't dull in the least. A spark of life burnt within, just waiting to be fanned. Margaret's heart melted and broke at the same time. Was what Dr. Morrison said true? Was she to look at her baby with only the future in mind? Couldn't she mother her child in the present? Give her love and sustenance for just this day? Surely there was hope.

She continued to inspect her child. Maybe her nose was a bit flat, as if she didn't have a bridge, but maybe she just had a little nose that

7

would fill out in time. Hadn't Margaret spent endless childhood hours pulling the tip of her nose down to stretch it from its blunt roundness into a more dignified and lengthy line, with little result other than developing a bad habit of pulling at her face all the time.

Margaret placed the baby onto the coarse bedding that covered her outstretched legs and unwrapped the blanket. "Look, Donald. She's not missing anything." Ten toes, two dimpled knees, ten fingers, two ears, a tiny cleft in her small chin. The dread was fading now. Margaret lifted her baby to cradle her against her chest, but the child's arms fell slack like a rag doll's and her neck rolled perilously toward her shoulder blades.

"Careful," the nurse cautioned kindly. "Her muscle development isn't what it should be. She needs extra support, like this," and she put Margaret's hands not just beneath the baby's neck to cradle her head but also at the base of her shoulders to keep her arms from flopping too low.

Margaret raised the baby to her chest and held her. Then she lowered her face, placed her nose atop the baby's head, and breathed in the scent of her. She had never smelled a newborn before, but the infant smelled like she imagined a normal baby would smell—sweet, needy, and infinite.

Should their daughter live, the doctor had said. Did that mean she might die? Or was it a question he posed? *Should* she live? Was he asking if the small bundle of warmth in her arms should have a life? A small cry escaped from her throat. Oh, it was too much to take in. Yet this was her baby. This was the child she'd said she couldn't wait to meet, but now their meeting was all wrong. It was without joy. If Dr. Morrison had just given the baby to her without saying anything, she'd never have known something wasn't right. She'd have taken it home and let it sleep in its crib. She'd have nursed the baby in the rocking chair and watched the colourful mobile sway above the crib. Oh, why didn't he just let her love it and find out on her own?

The nurse returned with a bottle of formula and, once she had confirmed the doctor wasn't present, asked, "Did you want to try to feed her?"

Donald shifted nervously beside the bed. "Margaret . . ."

She waved away his fears, took the bottle, and placed it to her baby's lips. Milk dribbled down her daughter's cheek and filled the hollow of her ear. The baby sputtered and choked and began to cry even as her mouth opened for more fluid. Despite her efforts, Margaret couldn't quite direct the baby's mouth for proper suction to occur. She stared at her child, her little mongoloid, a defenceless infant who needed care. Extraordinary care, if what the doctor said was true. Extra-ordinary.

"It's not so bad," the nurse said softly, as if reading her mind. "I've seen far worse."

Margaret met the nurse's eyes. What was she trying to tell her?

Dr. Morrison returned to the room with a sheaf of papers in his hand. "Look these over," he said, handing them to Donald. Then he took the baby from Margaret's arms, handed her to the nurse, and nodded toward the door. "It's for the best," he repeated. "She'll get the special care she needs. Poplar Grove Provincial Training Centre. She'll be taken care of there. They even have a special ward just for mongoloids."

The door closed behind her baby.

The room emptied of life until just she and her husband remained.

The overhead lights shone like a spotlight onto the black type on the pages before her. A government-run institution for undesirables. All they had to do, according to the doctor, was sign at the bottom of the page and their troubles would disappear. Dr. Morrison said their baby would have the mental development of a three- to six-year-old, but people loved three- to six-year-olds, didn't they? Why hadn't he spoken about love?

Shame wrapped them in its dark cloak. "She's just a baby," Margaret cried. "It's not her fault."

Donald sat on the edge of the bed and rubbed her shoulder. Margaret took his hand and forced him to look at her. His eyes were wet and afraid, like a little boy who had hurt himself. In that small glance before he looked away, she saw his fear and his attempts to hide that fear so he could be strong, like a man should be. She saw his desire to take charge, to comfort and not need comforting himself, and as she witnessed his clumsy effort to shield her from his own fear, she loved him more and desperately hoped his decision would make him someone she could be proud of.

"It's not anybody's fault," he said. "If the doctor says Poplar Grove is the right place for her, then we have to trust him. Those places must exist for a reason."

"Did you see her? She was warm and sweet and—"

"Stop it, Margaret. I can't . . ." He stood up and walked to the dark window.

Margaret felt herself go cold. Did he think his mother might be outside in the parking lot, ready to tell him what to do? Was she standing by to heap more criticism on Margaret, in her muted way. *You tried, dear. Better luck next time. Don't use the dessert fork for the salad, dear.*

Donald looked so vulnerable that for a brief moment Margaret felt her heart constrict. He *had* chosen her; he'd stood up to his mother at least that one time.

Finally he turned and spoke. "I'm not a pioneer, Margaret," he said so quietly that she strained to hear. "I'm sorry to say that I'm not that brave."

She held out her hand. "Maybe we could learn to be brave together."

He turned back to the window and didn't respond. Against the dark pane, his face was reflected back to her, but she was unable to read the variety of emotions that played across his face. Finally, she saw his back gradually straighten and she knew what he had decided.

Hours later, when Margaret finally stopped crying, she and her husband signed the papers, but first they named their child. Carolyn, after her mother's sister who died of tuberculosis at thirteen. Jane, after Margaret's childhood friend. Carolyn Jane Harrington.

Donald gathered up the papers and tapped them on the table to line them properly. The death of expectation, that's what this was. They'd expected to take a baby home, and now . . .

"We'll try again," her husband said, wiping a tear from her cheek. Then he kissed her softly on the mouth and held her chin up to look into her eyes. "We'll be okay, won't we?"

Margaret smiled weakly and nodded, moving her hand to touch his unshaved cheek, gathering all her energy into that simple gesture to move them both forward.

It was worse than a funeral. Nine months of hope and a lifetime of regret. No ceremony, no finality. Her in-laws tried to be kind to her, but Margaret could read their true thoughts: if only their son had married someone from his own background . . . Sometimes Margaret caught her mother-in-law looking at her as if she wanted to wash her hands, as if Margaret was a piece of raw meat left out too long on the counter.

Nonetheless, her in-laws *did* try to be kind to her, for Donald's sake, and they repeated Dr. Morrison's words as if they'd written the script together. She was doing the right thing. She was young. She would have more babies, healthy babies that would feed and laugh and not be sick. Babies that people wouldn't turn away from. Babies that would give her something in return for all her hard work.

Three days after Carolyn's birth, Margaret left the hospital empty-handed save for a set of strict instructions prohibiting her from visiting her baby for at least six months and the mantra *It's for your own good* firmly lodged in her brain. Her breasts pushed sorely into her thin blouse. Her milk had let down and left large, round stains in the silk. What dress-up game was she playing? What had she been thinking when she'd packed that blouse? She was nothing but a childless mother, left to fend for herself with an ear always cocked to an empty distance.

The sun scalded her pale skin. She and Donald returned home, and Margaret saved her tears for the long hours when her husband was at work. Nothing happened naturally anymore. She switched from taking baths to having showers because she couldn't stand to look at her bloated and changed body, the bruises still so close to the surface. Her feather duster stirred up unwanted images of her baby crying and alone. Better to have put it in a burlap sack and thrown it into the creek than to be left thinking of it unloved and untended. Faceless and unwanted. She dusted the images away. And when her husband reached for her in the night, tender and seeking mercy, she feared what the outcome might be.

On a bitterly cold January night in a northern city, Elizabeth drove west toward a restaurant where her friend Marie had made dinner reservations. Christmas lights still decorated the avenue and many of its storefronts in an attempt to change retail statistics. Elizabeth drove carefully on the now-rutted streets and finally pulled to a meter at the curb. All day she'd been fighting the feeling that she was moving underwater and something awful was about to happen. How absurd. There was no running or standing water in Edmonton at this time of year—the North Saskatchewan River was jammed thick with ice. But travelling on ice could produce a similar fear of drowning, for at any moment the ice, thin in spots from the moving current below, might give way and she'd fall right through, gasp at the excruciating chill of the water, and succumb sweetly to hypothermia just like that father of a boy she'd known in school who had fallen through his pond while using a tractor to clear the snow from the hockey rink he'd built for his kids. The whole class had gone to the funeral.

A cold blast of icy wind sucked the air from Elizabeth's lungs as she stepped from the car outside the restaurant. Move, she told herself as the fingers of winter slipped beneath her collar. Just move.

Inside the restaurant, a young, pierced waitress in cowboy boots led her to a booth at the back, far from the drafty door, and brought her biscuits with a green jalapeno jelly. Elizabeth ordered a margarita. She wanted to lick the salt rim and imagine herself at the beach, a hot sun overhead, and pull the heat deep into her bones.

Elizabeth watched the waitress, who looked as if she could step outside in her fashionably ripped leggings and not even feel the cold. Elizabeth was well past putting fashion before comfort. In this weather, she enjoyed her wool-lined boots and the silk long johns she wore beneath her jeans, and while she admired the fashion of youth, she definitely preferred her sensible attire that made its own fashion state-ment. She picked up the menu and instinctively scanned it for errors. Her father was an English professor, and every time they went to a restaurant he woefully pointed out typos and misplaced apostrophes.

Elizabeth was in her late thirties, of average height, thin and long-waisted. Women her age followed her with their eyes when she entered and exited a room, their gazes openly envious of her slim ankles, her muscular calves, her flat stomach, and her breasts, still high and firm. Nobody wanted to know that Elizabeth didn't have to work to have that body. She was simply built that way.

Marie appeared suddenly and plunked down on the leather ban-quette on the opposite side of the booth. She unwrapped the long black scarf around her neck and apologized for being late. "The roads are awful," she said. "Barry got stuck in traffic coming home, and I didn't want to leave the girls alone."

The girls, Nicole and Sophia, were twelve and ten and miniature versions of Marie, with their dark hair curled tight as springs. Elizabeth loved those girls and often wished they were her own.

Elizabeth noted that Marie had put on weight again; her cheekbones were no longer identifiable. In the thirty years she'd known her, Marie's weight had continuously shifted. It was easy to tell when she wasn't happy.

"What's new?" Marie asked.

"I'm happy to be on this side of Christmas," she said. "Business was great. I had record sales in December." She saw the yellow roses arranged in decorative vases in her display cabinet. The tropical flowers sent direct from Hawaii. The spools of red and green velvet ribbons, and the sleigh-bells on each vase as an extra festive touch.

Marie nodded her head in agreement. "No matter how organized I am at Christmastime, it's still a lot of work to be in charge of all that holiday magic."

The noise level in the restaurant had increased. Elizabeth saw her friend's mouth moving but no longer listened to what she said.

Sometimes her joy in Marie's company was squashed by the weight of her longing.

"How's Ron?" Marie asked.

"He's good," Elizabeth answered, wincing inwardly. Once, when she'd said Ron was good, Marie had answered, *I know*. She'd meant it as a joke, but Elizabeth hadn't laughed.

"Don't look so guilty," Marie laughed. "It's water under the bridge. You guys were made for each other. It's not like I didn't try, right?"

Elizabeth had been in love exactly three times: at the ages of fourteen, seventeen, and twenty. Three times lucky, she had told Ron before she walked down the aisle in her pearl white dress with tight lace sleeves that showed off her lean arms, and before Marie walked down ahead of her, having finally forgiven her friend.

The waitress refilled their water glasses. Elizabeth drained her margarita. Marie ate fried chicken with potato hash. Obviously she was off her diet.

Marie talked about the girls' Christmas concert, their dance recital, their music accomplishments, and the many other things her children were involved in. Her hands waved in the air as she illustrated each point she was making and exaggerated her own feelings of being overwhelmed.

"What did we do when we were kids?" Elizabeth finally asked.

"We climbed trees," Marie said. "I'm not sure what we did in the winter. Climbed cold trees."

They laughed and talked about their favourite poplar tree at the playground, the one with limbs perfectly spaced like rungs to the sky. "That tree was as good as having an older sister," Marie said. "We were privy to all kinds of information up there, weren't we?"

They reminisced about how they'd arrive quietly at the playground and, when no one was watching, quickly scale the poplar's branches. Invisible in the thick foliage, they listened to the mothers' conversations on the park bench below. They heard irritations with husbands, doubts about whether love would last, worries about offspring. There was no end to the private details about people's lives, details that ten-year-old girls didn't need to know. Mysterious bleedings. Infidelities. Sexual escapades. They learned that the principal at school was having an affair with one of the students' fathers; the police had arrived at Sammy Trainor's house because he'd been caught shoplifting again; Lorie Jones had three little children and had just been diagnosed with breast cancer; Jane Bosney was being held back a grade at school.

The girls breathed softly and listened. Sometimes they pantomimed great shock and held their sides to keep their laughter from bursting free. The bark of the old tree was rough against their bare legs, but they felt nothing, so great was their desire to hear the salacious tidbits of gossip.

One afternoon black clouds blew in over the High Level Bridge. They travelled at great speed. When they finally let loose, the poplar tree, the girls' portal to an adult world, was blasted by a bolt of lightning.

"We played in the ravine too," Marie said. "But kids today don't run free like they did when we were kids."

"You were always trying to ditch me," Elizabeth said.

"That's because you never had any ideas of what to do." Marie laughed. "*Somebody* had to think of something. If I didn't run ahead, I wasn't sure that you'd follow."

Elizabeth smiled and let Marie continue.

"I do get overwhelmed at times with all the girls' activities, but they seem to enjoy them all, so . . ." Marie used her finger to wipe the final bit of whipped cream from her plate. "My weight's up again, in case you hadn't noticed."

Elizabeth nodded.

"It's hard to say no during the holidays," Marie continued. "And *some* people aren't as lucky as you."

Elizabeth was the same weight she'd been in university. But how lucky was she, really? Would Marie rather be thin and infertile?

"Barry got me a gym membership for Christmas," Marie said. "I tried to look pleased, but sheesh. That's not really a present, is it?"

They paid their bill and said their goodbyes. Elizabeth tightened the scarf around her neck and stepped into the bitter cold. Only clear skies could produce an arctic chill this severe. Clouds at least acted as an insulation.

She held her scarf over her nose to warm the air entering her lungs as she walked down the street, where restaurant windows remained garnished with mistletoe and painted snowflakes and wreaths with large red ribbons wrapped the glowing streetlamps.

Post-holiday blues. That's what she felt. And a growing irritation that Marie's unhappiness was limited to such an uncomplicated discontent with the numbers on her scale. Why did she let a five-pound weight gain measure her happiness? She reached her car, and the cold engine slowly turned over. Buckling her seat belt, Elizabeth checked her side mirror and waited for a break in traffic before pulling onto the avenue.

The new year stretched before her like an endless chore. She hadn't made any resolutions. She had given up trying to hope.

THREE

The cold front lowered itself over the city like a cloud fallen from the sky heavy with grief. There was a kind of beauty in the savage wildness of it. Unexposed skin was frostbitten in minutes. Church basements became emergency havens for the homeless when two youth were found dead on top of a sidewalk grate downtown. Children drew pictures on frosty windows with their fingernails as curlicues of ice fell from the glass. The birds wintering over fluffed their feathers, creating air pockets for extra insulation, and sheltered in the thick branches of hedges and spruce trees. Here and there abandoned snowmen decorated front yards, their fronts slowly yellowed by neighbourhood dogs.

"You don't ever listen, do you?" Marie said, staring at her husband. "Are you just going to pretend this isn't happening?"

Barry was reading a book in his recliner. A fire burned in the gas fireplace on the far wall of the family room, producing a welcome heat.

"I just can't believe this," Marie said from the couch. "I like our life. I don't want it to change." A whine had crept into her voice. She didn't want to be pregnant. She felt a momentous fatigue and envied her daughters, asleep upstairs, their uncomplicated, pre-menstrual lives. At twelve and ten years old, Nicole and Sophia were at the height of their girlhood powers. Marie remembered when her own breasts had just begun to develop. She had inhabited her body with an unreserved ease until she had had her first unrequited crush on a boy. Then that ease had abruptly vanished and was followed by a painful self-consciousness that had coloured the next ten to twenty years.

Outside, the winter wind howled. The cold snap was in its fifth day, frozen in place like a tongue on a metal pole. The night before, she had taken the garbage out to the curb and had stepped on an orange peel that lay frozen on the ground. It had shattered like glass.

"Plus, I'm too old to have another baby."

"Oh, for Christ's sake, Marie, you're *not* old," Barry said. He wasn't really listening.

"I'm thirty-nine! I'll be *forty* when the baby turns one!" she said. "I was *eighteen* when my mother turned forty, and I thought *she* was old." Marie reached up and ran a hand through her hair, fanning it out to look for grey strands that she could pluck from her head to illustrate her point.

Barry sighed loudly to be heard over the wind and placed his open book in his lap. Then he shrugged his shoulders as if the abrupt movement would dislodge his irritation and make it slip to the ground. He didn't appear the least bit interested in what she had to say.

"And the girls are getting so old," she continued.

It was his dismissive tone that irritated her; the way he acted as if she was being unreasonable. He'd never been that way in the early years of their marriage. Or maybe she'd just hung on his every word then. Familiarity had brought a sourness to their relationship; it was as if Barry no longer felt the need to impress her. He had a wife. He had kids. The wondering about who he'd marry had been over for some time. Now he thought nothing of passing gas freely.

"You know damn well they'd love to have a baby in the house."

Pins and needles began their stabbing exploration in her feet, and Marie carefully pulled her legs out from beneath her.

"And anyway," Barry said, "some people are just starting at forty. So what if you have another baby now?" Barry turned back to his book, content to let his words be the last on the subject.

Why did every conversation become adversarial—him against her? He looked so smug in his recliner, his chin jutting out like a snowplow pushing his point home.

She shifted on the couch and felt the leather crinkle beneath her thighs as she studied her husband. He was committed to routine. Barry hadn't changed his hairstyle in all the years she'd known him. He used the same shampoo, the same deodorant, and wore the same brand of shoes. Every morning he ate two pieces of toast, a bowl of Raisin Bran, drank a cup of coffee and a glass of orange juice. And he was superstitious too. Once, in the early years of their marriage, Marie had surprised him by buying a different brand of cereal. On the way to work that day he'd had a flat tire. He was convinced it was because his routine had been broken.

"You know what I think?" he said, licking the middle finger of his right hand to turn a page. "I think you're feeling guilty."

Guilty? She sifted through her brain. "About what?"

"About being pregnant again."

The first hint of jowls were forming in the thickening skin around his jaw line. He still had a full head of dark hair, sprinkled liberally with grey, but his hairline had recently begun to recede. Grandpa. That's what some people might think if they saw him pushing a stroller. Isn't it great that you're a grandpa?

"Why would I feel guilty about being pregnant? Stupid, yes, but guilty?"

"Be-*cause*," Barry said, drawing the word out as if what he were about to say was obvious. "Because Elizabeth's been trying for years and hasn't had any luck." He reached for his cup of tea and took a sip, almost triumphantly. "You get pregnant even when you're not trying."

A hot sensation started behind her belly button and gained heat and intensity as it rose to her brain.

"I can't believe you said that," she whispered.

He didn't reply.

How like him to start something and then back off, making it her problem. Marie took a sip of the tepid tea and tried to ignore his comment, tried to wipe it from her memory.

The wind continued to rage as the minutes passed and Marie built a case against her husband, stealing an occasional glance his way to see if he noticed. How effortlessly he moved from one minute to the next without dragging anything from the previous moment along with him. It would be enviable if she didn't find it so frustrating.

She picked up her book. *You get pregnant even when you're not trying.* Stop. Rewind. *You get pregnant even when you're not trying.* He made it sound like an intentional act, as if *he* had nothing to do with the process. And what right did he have to talk like this about her best friend? Was it bad *luck* that had kept Elizabeth from having a baby for all these years? And even if it *was* bad luck, didn't luck, good and bad, run out after a while? Three bad things were usually followed by three good things. If you believed that, then Elizabeth should have had some good luck by now. She should have had a baby. What did Barry know about guilt, anyway? He never second-guessed himself. He set a course of action and didn't deviate from his plan. So why was he seemingly calm about this new wrinkle in their lives? Had he even *thought* about it? Was it *fair* that Marie was pregnant again?

No, it wasn't fair, but she knew there was no such thing as capital-J justice. When she and Elizabeth had been in their early twenties, Elizabeth had often talked of how much fun they would have becoming parents together.

"I can see them now," Elizabeth had laughed. "Little girls with freckled faces who'll refuse to wear dresses and run around with bed-head." Her enthusiasm was infectious. It *would* be great. Their kids would grow up closer than sisters. And when Nicole was born, it seemed as if Marie was fulfilling a pre-ordained script, except that Elizabeth's pregnancy never followed. Twelve years had passed and Marie had had two children while Elizabeth had had none.

Back then, Elizabeth would flip her dark hair in a gesture of impatience. "We're still trying," she'd say. Marie didn't really want to think about them going hard at the sex, even though she was happy with Barry, because every now and then she couldn't help but feel a slight stirring when she remembered how she and Ron had enjoyed each other in bed.

But as the years went by and Elizabeth "failed" to conceive, "trying" changed to mean they were making trips to the fertility clinic. "No luck yet," Elizabeth always added.

Marie closed her novel, which was a simple tale of love and regret. She'd read two pages without taking in a word, while Barry remained engrossed in his book. Would he never notice her silence? If she stayed downstairs much longer, he would get to bed before she did. But that never happened, did it? She used his predictability to his advantage and always made it upstairs before he did.

She walked to the kitchen, rinsed her cup, and put it in the dishwasher. Upstairs, she quickly washed her face, applied cream with gentle upward strokes on the thinning skin around her eyes, and brushed her teeth. A few strands of grey hair stuck straight up like antennae from the part in the middle of her scalp. Grey hair and pregnancy. In Marie's world, the two did not go hand in hand. Back in her bedroom she undressed, slipped her flannel nightgown over her head, and climbed into bed. Above her nightstand, the frost on the window reminded her of the puffy white mould that grew on food left in the fridge too long. Marie closed her eyes and tried to slow her heart. She imagined the mountain ash swaying in the icy blasts of wind outside her window and wondered how, in these frigid temperatures, the branches didn't snap clean away from the trunk.

Finally, Barry quietly came upstairs. Marie regulated her breathing and pretended to be asleep. They had performed this scene so many times in their married life—she pretending to be asleep, and he pretending to believe she was sleeping. But maybe this time would be different. Maybe this time he would apologize for his remark and seek some kind of reconciliation. It wouldn't take much, just a light touch on the small of her back, or a brief kiss on her cheek. Just a small acknowledgment that this pregnancy was not simply hers to deal with, nor was it a way to measure her life against her best friend's. Why didn't he ever just say that she was doing a good job, that she was a good mother? But when he emerged from the bathroom he slid slowly into bed, careful not to bounce the mattress. Then he turned over, his limbs contained to his side of the bed, and within minutes began to snore.

Sometimes loneliness was a physical pain that was worse than any cramp or contraction she'd ever had. She fought the urge to get up and steal quietly down to the kitchen to make herself something to eat, just to take the edge off the dreadful ache of feeling isolated from people who were supposed to love her. Barry might as well be sleeping alone.

Their conversation had settled nothing; they had talked around the baby as if it wasn't there, but another baby had no place in her ordered life. It wasn't only Barry who loved his routines. His love of order had rubbed off on her too. Over the years, she had become a careful list maker, the kind of person who didn't wait for the ketchup to run out before buying another one. One look in her pantry confirmed the orderliness of her mind. She and Barry had life insurance, house insurance, car insurance, dental insurance, they even had disability insurance. Nothing would take them by surprise.

No, it wasn't right at all. She felt as if someone had gotten a hold of one of her lists without asking and added just one word: *baby*.

In the morning, Marie awoke to find the bed beside her empty. She glanced at the clock and was surprised to see it was an hour later than her usual time to rise. The chill coming off the wall confirmed that the cold snap continued.

She could just make out the sound of her husband's voice downstairs, but the words were lost in the clinking of cutlery on dishes. At the thought of food Marie's stomach heaved. She reached for the box of saltine crackers on her bedside table and slipped one from its crinkly sleeve. The coarse salt crystals dissolved instantly on her tongue, and soon her mouth was moist enough that she could even lick her chapped lips.

Laughter filtered up from downstairs, and she smiled as she pictured Sophia telling her older sister a joke. Or maybe the two girls were laughing as they tried to get their dad to solve a riddle.

She reached for another cracker and nibbled tiny bites, beginning with the corners and then working her way around the edges to form a neat and uniform circle. Crumbs spilled onto her chest and settled in the bony hollow between her breasts. She stared at the dried bits of cracker for a moment, and then at the stretch marks on her breasts, silver minnows that mapped the terrain of breastfeeding.

Her nipples were sore. Her breasts were tender to touch and felt heavy and fibrous. The obvious signs of pregnancy that she had once so eagerly courted she had recently tried to ignore.

More crumbs settled between her breasts. When her kids were small she had lived for years with crumbs and sand in the bed and the feeling that she would never again have clean sheets. Once, when Nicole was three and Sophia had just celebrated her first birthday, Elizabeth had dropped by after work. The house looked as if a bomb had gone off inside of a toy store. Dolls and stuffed animals and small plastic knick-knacks were strewn all over the floor, mixed up with the pots and pans that had been dragged from the kitchen cupboards. Marie felt the sting of inadequacy that had shadowed her since having children. Normally she kept a clean house. Even when Marie was a child, her mother had never had to tell her to clean her room. She knew it was useless to expect any kind of order when the kids were so young, but she couldn't stop caring about the mess. She tried to laugh it off, but she was exhausted. Her sleep-deprived eyes burned when she closed them tight. Her shoulder-length hair no longer had any shape or lustre. Her waist had yet to reappear from the pregnancies. Her skin felt dry, her breasts overused. Just the day before she had discovered that her nipples no longer pointed straight ahead as they once had. Now they drooped downward as if looking for lost coins. How sad. Her breasts had been lovely once.

In contrast, Elizabeth looked neat and crisp in her summer pantsuit and sandals. Elizabeth's dark hair had recently been streaked with golden highlights. Her toenails were freshly painted, her clothes weren't stained, and her breasts weren't leaking. Everything about her was proper and trim. When she stood up, her hips were high, narrow, and compact. She had the most shapely arms too, firm and muscular. When Marie raised her arms to point at something, she could feel the skin beneath her arms swinging from the bone. Batwings, someone had called them, and she'd hated that term with a passion. No, sleep-deprivation hadn't aged Elizabeth. She looked ready for anything. Marie looked forward to the possibility of an afternoon nap.

Sophia moved from Elizabeth's lap and flung herself at the box of crayons on the floor next to the table. Marie saw a look of longing cross her friend's face. Look at me! she wanted to shout. I haven't had a good night's sleep in three years, and I haven't showered in three days. I can't even remember if I brushed my teeth this morning. I'm not doing this well!

Just then, Elizabeth confided, "We're off to the clinic after this. Round one."

"Really? That's great." At least she thought it was. Was it?

"We've been waiting for over a year," she'd said. "Apparently Ron and I aren't the only ones having trouble populating the planet."

Marie had crossed her fingers and held them up for luck. She wracked her brain for something encouraging. "Good luck," she finally said. "Let me know how it goes."

The doorbell rang. "That'll be Ron," Elizabeth said, standing. "He dropped me off."

Before Marie knew it, Ron was inside her house, saying hi to the girls and kissing her cheek in a chaste greeting. She felt grubby and overweight under his gaze. If she'd known he was coming she would have showered and made an effort to look good. Marie wanted to cry for the lost opportunity and for the way Ron looked at Elizabeth with a mixture of passion and pride. Almost immediately he had his arm around her, as if he'd been off balance without her by his side.

Marie smiled ruefully at her younger, vainer self. She'd spent so much time wanting to tidy not just herself, but her house as well. And now her girls were well past the stage of crawling into her bed, day or night, trailing the playground and their last snack along with them. She'd gotten used to having clean sheets; was it wrong to be happy those days were gone? To not want to repeat them?

Barry was right—she did feel guilty. Why else wouldn't she have told Elizabeth at dinner the previous week that she'd missed her period? Those were conversations you had with your best friend. Instead, Marie had circled the baby and ordered dessert instead. She'd even licked the plate clean. If she'd been alone, she might have ordered another slice. It would be Elizabeth's fault if her weight was up again.

Or the baby's.

She did the math again. A late summer baby meant she'd be heavy and hot through July and August. She'd gain at least fifty pounds. Her ankles would swell. Sweat would bloom beneath her heavy breasts that would flagrantly flop onto her damp stomach. She'd been through two pregnancies; she knew exactly what to expect, and much of it wasn't in the least bit attractive.

Another cracker slowly softened on her tongue. Nicole would soon be thirteen; how embarrassing to have a pregnant mother. It was hard enough going through puberty; did Nicole need living proof of what lay ahead? A daily reminder that her parents were still *doing* it? Likely she would want a different mother. A slim mother. One who didn't so visibly flaunt her sexuality. Not a mother who lumbered about, swollen and sporting damp odours and fatigue. Marie could well remember her own thoughts about her mother when she was Nicole's age. How disgusted she'd been to know she'd come out from the small, dark space between her mother's legs.

Yet at times she'd also secretly admired her mother, who sometimes sang at the kitchen sink and who waited in the foyer to take her husband's coat and kiss his cheek when he returned home from work. There were sensuous secrets about her, and, for a time, she'd made becoming a woman attractive.

Now Elizabeth would fulfill that role for her girls. She'd stand straight and thin beside Marie's bulbousness. And who would be envious then? There had definitely been times when she'd envied the freedom of Elizabeth's childless life.

Marie pulled her knees to her chest beneath the duvet. No, it wasn't guilt she'd felt in those early days of mothering, it was envy. Still, she wouldn't trade her kids for anything.

Outside, the neighbours' dog barked. Winter had submerged the city into a prolonged darkness. It would be almost another hour before daylight. She surveyed the room. The sheets needed washing, the carpet vacuuming, and the dresser dusting. The girls needed new pants and more socks. Nicole's wrists were sticking out of the sleeves of her winter jacket. The fridge was almost empty. The kitchen floor needed to be scrubbed. The neighbours' dog howled to be let in. Tiny caps of snow fell from the red berries on the mountain ash outside of her window.

Marie closed her eyes. There was too much to do. Too many people depended upon her.

Downstairs at last, she kissed her girls and placed a hand on Barry's head, a conciliatory gesture that wiped clean the silence of the previous evening.

"Guess what?" the girls said in unison. "There's no school today!"

Marie looked at her husband. "Didn't you hear the phone ring?" he asked.

She shook her head.

"The school called after seven o'clock."

"A pipe broke," Nicole said.

Barry nodded toward the counter. "Coffee's on."

Marie raised a hand to her mouth. "I can't stomach it."

She ducked her head into the fridge and started making a grocery list. "I've got to nip to the store," she said. "I invited Elizabeth for lunch today."

"Oh yeah? What for?"

"The sooner I tell her, the better."

"Tell her what?" Nicole piped up.

"I wasn't talking to you, Miss Big Ears," Marie said, ruffling her daughter's hair.

The telephone rang as she kissed Barry goodbye. She ran back into the kitchen.

It was her sister, Frances.

Marie inwardly rolled her eyes and glanced at the clock. Frances was a lot of work. She did all the talking and Marie listened. Yes, her sister was exhausted. Yes, the baby had kept her up all night. Yes, she could understand why Frances wasn't taking Max out today, not in this deep freeze. Marie made all the right conciliatory sounds and agreed with everything Frances said. It was quicker that way.

"I can't drop by today," she finally said to her sister's invitation. "Elizabeth is coming for lunch."

"What's the occasion?" Frances asked.

"Why does everyone think there needs to be an occasion to see a friend? I just have some news to tell her, okay?"

"Okay, okay. Relax. What news?"

Marie juggled her options. "Promise you won't tell Mom?"

"Oh yeah, like Mom's the first person I go to," she said.

"I'm pregnant."

"Good one."

"No, I am."

"I thought you and Barry were done having kids."

She grimaced. It was like the grand inquisition with Frances, and Marie didn't feel like defending herself. "Yeah, well, so did I."

"So you forgot birth control, or what?"

"For God's sake, Frances. Do you think that's helpful?"

"Sorry. I'm just surprised is all; I was caught off guard."

"Well, you and me both," Marie said.

"So you're going to tell Elizabeth?"

"Yeah, I want to tell her before she guesses."

"Do you think she'll take it okay?" Frances asked.

"I'll find out," Marie said. "Look, I've got to get to the grocery store. We'll get together soon, okay? The girls would love to see Max."

She dressed quickly and herded the girls into the van. The garage door opened automatically behind her. Marie imagined Elizabeth's mouth, opened wide with joy, opened wide with anguish. Her stomach twisted tight with anxiety. She put the van in reverse and drove slowly down the icy street to the four-way stop at the corner.

FOUR

Across town in an old wartime bungalow with a rooftop covered in snow, Elizabeth stepped into the shower and slowly turned from side to side to allow the hot water to erase all of her goosebumps. Standing fully beneath the shower head, she felt the water make its own course through her hair, over her face, along the slow curve of her waist, and down the full length of her body until it reached the drain. Gradually the chill left her bones, and when the water's heat began to fade, she turned off the tap and stepped out into the steamy room, drying herself quickly before the chill returned, avoiding the full-length mirror that would reflect the uselessness of her body.

As a young girl, she had been obsessed with horses. She read every horse book she could find, collected horse statues, and took weekly lessons at a local stable. Her favourite riding horse was a one-eyed palomino named 10-10 (who'd lost an eye as a yearling due to an unfortunate run-in with a tree branch), and every Saturday morning she made sure to arrive early enough to claim him for the day. She wasn't bothered that in all of his gaits he moved with his neck slightly at an angle to adjust for his lack of vision because she loved all things wounded and their various imperfections. In grade school she'd envied a girl who broke her leg and had to hobble about on crutches. And she coveted the neighbour boy's large husky that had lost a leg in a car accident. Aptly named Tripod, the dog was easy to manage on a leash because of its affliction.

Despite her kindness to flawed things, she couldn't accept imperfection in herself. When she was twelve, she started to believe there was a hidden flaw in her: she hadn't been perfect at birth. That must explain why her mother had walked away as soon as the umbilical cord was cut. *Snip snip*—free at last! Her adoptive parents were wonderful, and she loved them, but deep in her cells she craved a unique heartbeat, a familiar voice, the rhythms and vibrations of the woman who'd provided her first real home.

By the time she was a young adult, she understood better that women made hard decisions sometimes. Like Sandy, a girl who often showed up at the church dances. When Sandy got pregnant at sixteen, Elizabeth was as surprised as everybody else. Sandy was just an ordinary girl, not too bright, not too pretty. Then she disappeared for a while, and the following year at school, she didn't have a baby. Nobody referred to the incident, at least not to her face; only the Grade 12 boys snickered when she walked by. Elizabeth almost told Sandy that she'd been adopted, to reassure her that her baby would be okay. But she didn't because she knew there was another baby out there now who one day might hunger for its real mother. Plus, what Elizabeth really wanted to ask was if Sandy regretted letting that little bit of herself slip away. And she was afraid Sandy might say no.

Then Ron came along—funny, optimistic Ron—and he made her laugh at her superhuman attempts to be perfect.

Elizabeth had first met him at a party, which would have been nice if he hadn't been Marie's new boyfriend at the time.

The French expression is le coup de foudre—a bolt of lightning, an act of God—which translates in English to love at first sight. And it felt like that, a sudden and searing heat. Elizabeth held his gaze a fraction longer than necessary and then backed away, embarrassed. Ron had immediately put his arm around Marie for balance. All night Elizabeth couldn't help staring at him when she thought he wasn't looking. But on more than one occasion their eyes locked.

And then the telephone calls and Marie's sobbing voice on the other end trying to describe the breakup. "I don't know what happened."

Months later, Elizabeth's phone rang. It was Ron. Was she seeing anyone? If not, would she like to have dinner?

If only he hadn't gone out with Marie! She'd thought about him often and remembered that heady feeling when her eyes had locked with his. She'd never been so instantly attracted to a man before. Ron knew that it was awkward, he said as much on the phone, but he also said he hadn't been able to stop thinking about her. Could they go out just once? He convinced her that it was possible they'd both imagined the attraction. Yes—she'd see him once, let him down easy, and Marie would never have to know. But when he drove her home after dinner he'd parked around the corner from her house because she was still living at home then, and she'd stayed in his car for hours until they couldn't see out of the windows because of the steam before she stumbled home, thick-lipped and weak with desire. It took her weeks to have the necessary conversation with Marie. And it took weeks again for Marie to get over the idea that Elizabeth had stolen her boyfriend. When she finally did forgive Elizabeth, it was with the unspoken belief that Elizabeth had overstepped some line of friendship and was lucky to have Marie's forgiveness.

Elizabeth squeezed the excess water from her hair with a towel and tried to remember the last time Ron had made her laugh. Their dreams hadn't quite come true. Only after they'd married had her greatest flaw revealed itself—an inability to bear children. You didn't get to use crutches for that, and there was no special infertility sign that she could hang from her rear-view mirror to explain why her backseat wasn't filled with crumbs and government-approved baby seats.

In the bedroom, a feeble light pressed against the white sheers on the south window facing the backyard. It was a deceptive winter light, almost bluish, as if it had succeeded at the ultimate challenge of freezing itself. It could be eight o'clock in the morning, or it could be noon.

Elizabeth pulled on her silk long johns and blue jeans before finding a turtleneck and sweater. She'd told her staff at the flower shop not to expect her this morning. Business was always slow in the period after Christmas and before Valentine's Day, and even more so when customers worried about their flowers freezing before they could get them safely to their cars and then home. It was a good time to take a little break.

In the kitchen she saw the remains of yesterday's coffee in the pot and realized Ron hadn't made himself a fresh cup before going to work. He always said her coffee tasted so much better.

She ground some coffee and put on a fresh pot before heading to the bathroom to dry her hair. Bloodshot and swollen eyes stared back at her from the mirror. The small pocket of skin beneath her eyes was puffy and criss-crossed with spidery lines. She pursed her mouth in concern and then stared at the pleats that circled her lips. How quickly aging crept up on a body. At least the copper streaks in her hair made her complexion not so pale. She mixed some foundation and moisturizer in the palm of her hand and smoothed the lotion into her face with gentle strokes. She didn't feel like wearing her contacts, so she placed dark-rimmed glasses on the bridge of her nose, hoping they would conceal some of the puffiness around her eyes. Finally, she tucked her shoulder-length hair behind her ears and stretched to her full height. Ron still found her to be beautiful, or at least he said so from time to time, but she suspected he tried to bolster her self-image by paying her compliments to offset the years of negative self-image she'd suffered through with all the side effects of fertility drugs.

When she was thirty-one, and they'd been trying to get pregnant for five years already, she'd finally called the fertility clinic to set up an appointment. From the start, Ron said he'd follow her lead, but he also let her know he was already happy, without kids. He loved the life they already had; he wasn't looking ahead to the future one with kids that he didn't know. "I'm a teacher," he'd remind her. "I get my kid fix during the day." Well, no kids were coming into her flower shop. Could Ron really be happy with or without children?

It annoyed her that it seemed so easy for him, but in fairness, he'd done things that he hadn't expected to do.

"You have a twenty percent chance of getting pregnant," the clinic doctor had said optimistically on their first visit. Elizabeth had immediately burst into tears.

"Those aren't bad odds," Ron had comforted, stroking her hand.

But all Elizabeth heard was that four women failed for every one who succeeded. Four women cried their eyes out for every one who threw a party. She had never won anything in her life, and after years of trying to get pregnant naturally, she wasn't feeling the least bit lucky.

They'd start with intrauterine insemination; it cost less than in vitro fertilization and required lower doses of fertility drugs. No egg retrieval was required because the sperm, carefully prepared in the laboratory, was inserted directly into the uterus. Elizabeth admired the science behind it all. They filled her uterus with an abundance of fast-swimming sperm energetically poised to penetrate the eggs that were lined up like buttons on a blouse waiting to be done up.

But Elizabeth had bled on the fifteenth of the month. Okay, she told herself, that was the practice run. It was always easier the second time around. There would be no surprises. She made sure to eat well. To exercise and get sufficient sleep.

Two rounds later, she still wasn't pregnant. So she rolled up her sleeves and turned to the in vitro.

At one of their appointments the doctor gave them a small box filled with ampoules of liquid that would induce ovulation. *For intramuscular injections*, the small print on the box read. *To be injected deep into a large muscle.*

"You need to get the needle straight into the muscle," the doctor had instructed, and Ron had paled visibly. He hated needles.

"What happens if I miss?"

"You won't miss if you go slowly. Don't try to rush."

The men moved behind Elizabeth in the small examination room. She bent over the table, as instructed.

"But there must be nerves in there," Ron said. "What if I hit a nerve?"

Elizabeth slowed her breathing. She wanted him to sound confident, but his hesitant tone led her to imagine her leg collapsing beneath her, nerve damage, partial paralysis.

"Just watch closely," the doctor said. "You'll get the hang of it after the first few injections."

She tried not to flinch when she felt the sharp prick of the needle burrowing into her backside.

"It's okay, Ron," she lied, massaging her behind as she straightened. "It's not so bad."

He didn't look convinced. "Look," he said to the doctor. "If I'm going to do this at home, with nobody around to help me, I need more than just watching you give one needle. There must be something else . . ."

Elizabeth looked at the ampoules cradled seven to a box. She would take home two boxes. Ron would give her one injection a day for the next two weeks. The clear fluid would heat her ovaries to a low boil. She pictured him as a fertility superhero dressed in a red and white latex suit, holding a syringe in both hands with clear liquid spurting from the needles. She saw a scientist's lab, her reproductive organs hovering over a Bunsen burner's blue flame.

On a normal menstrual cycle, one egg would drop from her fallopian tubes. With this artificial stimulation, her body would drop as many as two dozen. Two years of eggs condensed into one month. Twenty-four cycles in one. Twenty-four chances to get some high-quality eggs to remove, fertilize, and re-insert. It was dizzying.

"Nobody likes giving needles," the doctor replied, "even me. But here's a little trick that might help at home." He asked Elizabeth to pull her underwear up, then turn around and rest her elbows again on the examining table. "I'm going to lift your gown now for a moment. I hope these aren't your favourite underwear," he added. Then he took a blue felt pen and drew a circle over the spot where the needle should go in. "Cut this circle out when you get home," he said to Ron, "and make your wife wear them each time you give an injection. That should help you feel better about getting it into the muscle."

There had been so many needles along the way, and so many drugs. Follicle-stimulating hormones with names that sounded like they should be administered to cattle, except that the word *human* was thrown in sometimes. Some days Ron's superhero image evaporated and he became, instead, a mad scientist pulling syringes from his laboratory holsters.

Timing was everything. Ultrasounds determined the maturity of the eggs in their fluid-filled follicles. Elizabeth imagined setting a gigantic egg timer at home on her kitchen counter to log the hours before her eggs were collected. Then the timer was set again and Ron pleasured himself to produce sperm. Then his juice was mixed with her eggs. Three to five days later, the embryos were returned to her womb. Then the two-week wait for the ultrasound that would reveal if any of the eggs had stuck.

Simple—wasn't it? Petri dishes. Microscopes. Latex gloves. Cramps.

And sometimes nausea, dizziness, hot flashes, headaches, acne, weight gain, bloating, and pelvic inflammation. At every step the doctors announced the statistics and asked if she wanted to continue. Over time, she was numbed by the details: *Your chances decrease with each treatment cycle. Twenty-five percent of IVF pregnancies miscarry. Multiple pregnancies are a possibility.*

"Yes," she always replied. "Yes, I'm willing to go on," or, "Yes, I understand the risks and I'm willing to try that." Ron was always there to squeeze her hand in support. She would do everything she could and beat the odds.

After each in vitro cycle she rested and pampered herself for the two weeks leading to the ultrasound. And on that day, she and Ron would show up holding hands like high school kids on a date. Such a brave face they put on. And then the disappointment when the technician looked for some small sac suctioned like a snail to her uterine wall and found nothing but a Vacancy sign again and again. Once, after two failed attempts, and knowing the odds were declining with each cycle, she and Ron decided to implant five fertilized eggs—five!—knowing that multiple births could be a factor. Still nothing.

Unexplained infertility. That's what the experts determined after all the tests she had endured, all the pills, blood tests, ultrasounds, injections, and urine samples. Unexplained infertility. The experts had no idea why she didn't conceive.

Elizabeth poured herself a cup of coffee and went to the fridge to get some cream. Magnets held pictures on the fridge door of her and Ron in happy moments: at Christmas smiling in front of their tree, Ron with his perfectly straight, cavity-free teeth and fabulous grin, his arm draped casually over her shoulder. On their friend's boat at Pigeon Lake. Next to the stage at Shakespeare in the Park. Her eyes roamed over the photos and stopped at one that Marie had taken of her daughters. It was a couple of years old now. Sophia had recently lost some teeth, and her pink tongue poked through the gaps in her smile. Nicole stood beside her, engaged in an equally funny grin, her fingers hooked into the sides of her mouth and pulling wide. She took a big gulp of coffee and burned her mouth. When she was finally able to swallow, the scald continued down her throat.

She was turning forty this year. For whatever arbitrary reason, forty felt like a firm transition point—either have children *before* turning forty, or don't have them at all. Elizabeth had been on the verge of talking with Ron about a trial separation at least three times during the weekend, but she couldn't speak the words out loud. *I just need some time to myself.* It wasn't his fault they hadn't had a child; she couldn't blame him. But how had it happened that making the life she wanted was all up to her?

On Sunday they'd cancelled their plans to go cross-country skiing at Elk Island Park because of the high wind chill. It was the perfect time to start the conversation. They spent the entire afternoon at home, catching up on household chores, but still she stayed quiet. She couldn't remember the last time they had just hung around the house together. She'd made sure to keep herself busy because she preferred not to have time in which to think. It didn't do any good. One of the women in her infertility support group had summed it up perfectly: "My head is like a bad neighbourhood," she'd said. "I shouldn't be in it alone." Elizabeth had laughed along with the rest of the women in the room, but it was true, wasn't it? She shouldn't be in her head alone.

It had been over a year since her last treatment, and she missed some of the women she'd become close to. Audrey had been fun. "If you think your brain feeds you negative messages," she'd said, "you should hear my mom. *Be patient, Audrey,*" she mimicked. "*Remember poor Abraham and Sarah.*"

Abraham and Sarah?

Audrey nodded. "Yep, they're in the bible—the first couple plagued with infertility. They were married and childless for seventy years, but they kept their faith." At this point she lapsed into her old lady's voice and shook a crooked finger at her listeners. "And when Abraham was one hundred years old and Sarah was ninety, their son, Isaac, was born!"

A sad laughter filled the room. All the women were done with being patient.

"My mother's been quite wonderful," Elizabeth said. "But she does question the lengths I'm going to. More than once she's said, 'You can change your mind, you know.' She means well when she talks about adoption. I mean, I was adopted, but I wish she'd just support me one hundred percent."

She was one of the older women in the support group. One gal, Jennifer, was twenty-five, the same age Elizabeth had been when she'd gotten married. The woman's youth made her feel negligent, like she hadn't paid enough attention to her predicament. But she and Ron hadn't wanted children right away, and by the time she'd thrown away her birth control pills she was already twenty-eight. If she'd started earlier, like Jennifer, might things have gone differently?

Some of the women had been together for years, bonded by their own failures to conceive. Others, the lucky ones, like Audrey, who'd had healthy twin boys, disappeared into the much-sought-after chaos of mothering.

But Elizabeth wasn't one of the lucky ones, and after seven years of treatment, the emotional toll was eventually too great. She finally admitted defeat.

She hurriedly made the bed and threw some clothes into the hamper. Thank goodness for the luncheon date at Marie's. She needed a destination, but suddenly she was late. All that useless standing around in the shower hadn't helped at all. Before lunch she had an appointment to view an apartment she'd seen advertised in the weekend paper; the price was right, and it was within walking distance to her downtown shop. If she was serious about leaving, she would need her own place to live. She was just going to look. But if she did leave, she wanted to move as far from her life in the suburbs as possible. Far away from the baby strollers and playgrounds and girl scouts and ice rinks and soccer fields and trick-or-treaters and anything remotely connected to what she couldn't have.

FIVE

1940

Margaret was fifteen years old in the summer of 1940, and even though the long years of drought had finally ended, on hot days she could still feel dust crunching between her teeth like tiny shards of glass. Impending doom, some called it. But it certainly wasn't right to have endured and survived the long years of drought and then to go directly into another war. A few years of peace and prosperity was all they'd have needed to erase the deep memories of hardship. Bumper crops of wheat golden in the fields. Corn that grew fat on the stalk. New equipment. Straggling out of debt. Just a few good years to stop taking it all so personally.

Instead, that summer her brother, Johnny, sliced off four fingers on his left hand while trying to fix the thresher for the upcoming harvest. Their father wasn't home that day; he'd taken the truck to help Mr. Boyko on the neighbouring farm. Johnny came stumbling in, already pale from loss of blood, and their mother quickly took charge. "Get the wagon," she commanded, "and bring it to the front." Farm injuries were just another chore to add to her endless list of things to do. Gutting chickens would have to wait.

Margaret drove the four miles to town as quickly as the road allowed while her mother crouched in the back, holding Johnny close for comfort and absorbing the shocks from the road with her body. Margaret would always remember the image of her mother, black skirt spread out over the wagon floor, rocking on her heels over the hard bumps, her arms firmly around her first-born and only son.

The sun had already passed over the midday mark and was slowly making its way toward the western horizon. When they pulled up in front of the doctor's office their horse, Anvil, was lathered in sweat, his neck slicked an oily black, and Johnny's face was white as the full moon. The towel wadded around his hand was soaked through with blood and dripped a trail from the wagon into the house. Dr. Jenkins had just returned from delivering a baby. They were lucky to catch him, said his lanky son, Stuart. He stood by and watched his father sever Johnny's mangled fingers from his hand with a sharp blade and stretch the ragged skin into a flap that he sewed over the swollen palm.

"It's a good thing you kept your thumb out," Dr. Jenkins told Johnny as he stitched the flesh together. "That thumb will come in handy. You'll be able to use that hand for something, anyway."

Johnny's numb face didn't register a thing.

Stuart Jenkins held the light for his father. He threaded the needle and he held the light. He glanced at Margaret, seated across the room from him, and smiled. She'd never seen teeth so white and straight before, and she couldn't stop herself from staring.

When Margaret was a little girl, the creek that ran through their property had seemed like a small river. Her father would sometimes bring her to a spot by the cottonwoods he'd planted as a shelterbelt to keep the soil in the open fields from drifting away in the wind. "One day you'll have shade here," he'd tell her. "Cottonwoods grow like weeds. And like children," he added as an afterthought. "You kids grow like corn in the night." Margaret fixated on the *belt* in *shelterbelt* and imagined what one might look like holding up a pair of pants.

It was two weeks after Johnny's accident, and the water in the creek had been reduced to a small trickle, insistent but inconsequential. The midday sun beat directly onto Margaret's dark hair, searing her scalp where her hair was parted. She could feel the freckles on her arms and face rising to meet the sun. Johnny had gone into town again with her parents to have the doctor examine the mound of flesh where his fingers used to be. An infection had been sidestepped, but often when she looked at Johnny, she saw the way he grit his teeth to keep the pain at bay. Exhaustion was etched into every expression and movement he made. Margaret had even more work to do with Johnny healing in the house, but now, with her family gone, the house stood empty. It was a rare moment, and she couldn't resist the urge to sit by the creek to cool herself, if even for a few minutes. She'd be sure to work extra fast at cleaning the chicken coop to make up for the lost time.

It was a short distance from the house to the creek. In the cotton-wood's shade the temperature was at least five degrees cooler. She removed her shoes and socks and stretched her toes into the cool water. The wind lifted the loose hair around her face and she tucked the errant strands behind her ears while she wiggled her toes. She closed her eyes and tried to hear the heat waves rising from the earth in the way that yeast raises bread. No. She couldn't hear it. Just wind, the sound of grass rustling against itself, and a drone of insects. Somewhere nearby a snake rustled through the dry grass. A pebble turned and rolled. And another. She swivelled her head and he was there. Stuart. The doctor's son. Quickly she reached for her socks and shoes.

"What's your hurry?" he asked. Dark red hair cropped close. Large hands too white to be farm hands. Pants pressed from his mother's iron. She'd never known a boy who wore pressed pants. It wasn't right here, like church clothes worn to muck out the barn.

"What's your hurry?" he repeated, moving closer. His head blocked the light and for a moment his silhouette was outlined in black as if his body had swallowed the sun. When he moved again the sun was released and he stood beside her. "How's Johnny?"

"He's fine," she said, rushing to get her shoes done up. "He's up at the house," she lied. "Did you want to see him?"

She tried to stand but he put a firm hand on her shoulder and lowered his body beside her.

"I like your hair," he said. "It's beautiful." He had a phony voice, sing-song, like he was trying to convince her that he liked her. She moved her head to one side as his fingers parted and combed through her hair. "It's nice to be alone here, isn't it?" He smiled and rested his hand on her knee.

Margaret tried to stand again but Stuart wrapped his hand around her wrist. "My mother's waiting for me," she said. "I have to go, she'll be looking for me."

"No one's home," he said. "I know your folks are in town with Johnny to see my father. I left the house when they came in."

She felt the dust drying on her bare arms, melting and disappearing into her damp skin like snowflakes on an outstretched tongue. Why was Stuart Jenkins here? Aloof and untouchable he was, thinking better of himself than the country kids. Eighteen going on thirty and off to study medicine in the fall. Even though he was three years older, she'd seen him in school. Everyone knew everyone in Mayburn. Plus, all the girls talked about him. Stuart this and Stuart that. The one most likely to get a girl to the big city. Dogs didn't like Stuart Jenkins and took a wide path around him, but none of the other girls seemed to notice. They all believed catching a ride on his coattails could only be good. He was going places, and most of the girls wanted to go places too.

But she was a country girl, and he barely gave the *town* girls the time of day. Why was he here? She had chores to do, and here she was in the middle of the afternoon trying to cool herself at the creek. How disgusted her mother would be to see her daughter dangling her toes in the cool water and enjoying herself in the middle of the day.

"I have to go."

Stuart reached out a hand and stroked her cheek. His fingernails were square and clean, his palms white. "I've always wanted to do that," he said.

She closed her eyes to his lie. If she didn't see him, maybe he'd go away. She would become invisible, cast no shadow, and fade into the sand-coloured stones at her feet.

She felt the warmth of his breath on her cheek as he leaned closer. It only added to the heat of the day, scorching the fine hair along her jawbone and down her neck. Maybe he would go away if she kept still. Invisible and still. His breathing grew quicker, his hand moved with greater determination, and still she maintained her silence, closing her eyes to the picture that God must see from above.

"Lie back," Stuart said, and he pushed her down.

His hand was on the hem of her dress. She tried to push it away, but he was persistent. He wasn't going to go away, and she wasn't disappearing. For a town boy unused to physical labour, he had surprising strength.

Grasshoppers whirred in the fields around her. The creek's small trickle could barely be heard. Stones pushed deep into her back from the weight of Stuart's body on hers. She turned her head sideways. A short distance away her house shimmered in the heat, rising like a mirage. The cottonwoods strained deep into the earth and pulled hard for moisture.

Shelterbelt, she thought. There was no shelter here.

SIX

1983

When Marie was twenty, the year that Elizabeth started to go out with Ron, she gained ten pounds. Food had always been a great comfort to her. During the long, lazy, hot summer afternoons when Elizabeth was at the stables and Marie was left to wander on her own, she'd stroll over to the Dairy Dell and buy a large cup of soft chocolate ice cream, her surrogate friend all that summer. It came in a tall white Styrofoam cup, swirls of thick, cold chocolate coiled around and around and around in the cup and ending at the top with a delicate curlicue flip. She'd find a shady spot under a tree and slowly spoon the creamy coolness into her mouth. If she was patient, she could make the contents last up to half an hour.

She was drawn to sweets and salty things when she was a child, and to fats and breads when she got older. It was the romantic combination of being happily alone and feeding her extreme loneliness. There wasn't really any other way to explain her need to eat. Betrayal was certainly a trigger.

She thought back to her earlier conversation.

"For God's sake, Elizabeth, I slept with him!"

"I know," Elizabeth apologized.

"No, you don't!" Oh, she hurt. Her toes curled with the pain that tightened right up her spine.

"I'm sorry, Marie. He only phoned me a month ago."

"*Only* a month ago? You waited an entire month to tell me?"

"No, no. I mean, you guys hadn't been together for a while. You'd already broken up."

"You mean *he'd* already broken up. *I* was still very much interested." Marie was shaking with anger. She wanted to throw something, break something in two. She looked around her and shook her head. Elizabeth was smart to tell her in a public place. The university pizzeria was busy, as usual. And the music was getting louder as the evening progressed. Maybe she'd smash things when she got home. Maybe she'd clear her shelf above her dresser of nail polish and hair accessories with one big sweep of her arm.

"I didn't want this to happen, Marie. You have to believe me."

Marie nodded her head as if something had become suddenly clear and set her mouth in a firm line. "Yeah, un-hunh."

"I'm telling the truth!"

A stain of resentment had spread out between them. They were both breathing heavily, as if they'd run up a steep hill.

They understood that this was a turning point in their relationship; what direction would they take?

Marie knew she had it in her power to ask Elizabeth to give Ron up. She could cause her friend great pain and then help her to get over it, just like Elizabeth had tried to help her to get over Ron in the first place. Before she decided she wanted him for herself.

What to do?

Her stomach felt empty. Should she take, or should she give?

"What a cliché," she finally said, feigning indifference. "My best friend stealing my boyfriend."

"You should know me well enough to know that I didn't intentionally set out to hurt you. It just happened, okay? And I'm telling you about it because it matters to me that we stay friends. Do you think I wanted this to happen?"

"Well, you have hurt me, intentionally or not."

The extra weight gathered in her waistline and protruded in a soft roll over the top of her jeans.

She ate because Ron was now with her best friend.

She ate because Ron had seen her naked, and he'd fondled the cellulite on her thighs as if he'd discovered a rare artefact. And then shortly afterwards he'd stopped calling.

She ate because at night she dreamed of the two of them together and saw Ron removing Elizabeth's clothes, one piece at a time, slowly and with immense delight.

She ate her way through the hurt until one day she didn't need to eat over it anymore. The pain had passed, and she could talk to Elizabeth again without faking her affection. She could honestly wish them both well.

And she could meet the eyes of the man at the gym who'd been watching her. The one who showed up on alternate days, always at the same time. He wasn't as tall as Ron, or as slender, but there was a take-charge quality about him that she admired. He moved from one workout machine to the next in fifteen-minute intervals like clockwork. And when he was done with the machines, he pulled on a lightweight black knee brace (the result of an old soccer injury, she would later learn) and did some laps around the track.

She started to run when he did, knowing that if he came up behind her he'd see the way her rump jiggled in her tight black workout pants. He'd know that she carried some weight on her bones, that she wasn't some naturally thin woman. She was at the heaviest weight she'd ever been when he smiled at her after his run; if he thought she was attractive at that weight, then there was hope.

Marie made sure to be at the gym when Barry was there. She smiled when he caught her eye. She made it clear that she was interested in talking with him. She laughed at his jokes. He picked up on her cues and asked her out for a drink. Oh, she'd been so lonely.

Later, when they had married and the children had come and her life seemed to be spinning out of control with the chaos of parenting, she scolded Barry as if he were her third child. He raised his voice too much with the children. He didn't laugh with them enough. He needed to loosen up. He was out of the house all day—he didn't have any excuse for being impatient.

But she did.

If he'd known her well enough then to read between the lines, he'd have known she was talking about herself. *She* was impatient. *She* didn't laugh enough with the children. *She* needed to loosen up, not fatten up. Had he noticed that she'd put on weight?

In the early years, when the children were babies, there had been some winters when they hadn't gone outside for days at a time because of cold snaps that had stubbornly parked over the city for weeks on end. And if she did go out, by the time she got all their winter gear on and was sweating herself, they would play outside for ten minutes and then cry to come inside again. Yes, there had been plenty of bad parenting moments. Teething. Diaper rashes. The constant squabbling between the siblings. Some days it seemed as if the walls had closed in and the world had simply shrunk to the size of her bathroom. She remembered grabbing one of the girls once and shaking her hard before throwing her on the bed. Blind rage. The kind where you stand outside of yourself and know full well that you shouldn't be doing what you're doing but you just can't stop.

And then a little child would sidle up beside her and say, "I'm sorry, Mommy," as if her anger could disappear just like that. Oh, to be a child and move from emotions so rapidly! It took Marie time to let go of her anger. Sometimes a lot of time.

But she had worked hard to develop her patience. She did it for her children because she wanted to be a good mother. And she had gotten better. The work had paid off.

But she still had dreams sometimes. And she'd wake in a cold sweat because she knew she had it in her, the ability to abuse something that was less powerful than herself.

SEVEN

1999

In her thirty-sixth year, when Elizabeth had embryos inside her and was waiting to discover if one had eagerly put down roots, she walked into a downtown mall and passed a store that had baby clothes on sale. Dozens of matching sleepers and overalls hung from the ceiling on invisible wires. Primary colours screamed their existence. Elizabeth slowed as she passed a rack at the store's entrance. She fingered a little pink sleeper that swung from a miniature hanger. It was plush and cozy. And such tiny feet on it! She pulled it from the rack and smiled at the little plastic strawberries used for buttons. Instinctively, she reached for her wallet and walked to the counter.

"Is it a gift?" the salesclerk asked as she wrapped the outfit in white tissue paper.

"No."

The clerk smiled knowingly. "It's your first, isn't it? New mothers are always the shy ones."

Elizabeth smiled. Her neck was hot and itchy. She left the store swiftly, the weight in the plastic bag as light as a bird.

At home she emptied a small drawer in the big wooden wardrobe and gently slid the sleeper inside. Its pink perfectness pleased her.

The following month, Elizabeth added a small crocheted tie-dyed hat and a white cotton undershirt that snapped at the crotch. Sometimes, if Ron went out at night, she would lay the clothes and hat out on the bed and busy herself by putting them in different positions.

Thus began her monthly ritual of buying something new and stashing it away. She shopped at different stores so she wouldn't be recognized. Too soon, the sleepers began to pile up in the drawer. Did she have too many pink? Maybe she needed to add more blue sleepers. Or maybe twins were hovering somewhere on the outer edge of her aura, patiently waiting for her to get the right combination of colours.

Or triplets! Two boys and a girl? Two girls and a boy? One of each? How was she to know? Hadn't she read somewhere that children choose their parents? What more did she need to do to be chosen?

The sleepers piled up. After a few months, she realized she could not keep the baby clothes at home. It was bad luck, a reminder of her previous month's failure. So she began to dispose of the sleepers in the dumpster behind her shop, where she and her staff threw the remains of flowers that were past their prime.

One afternoon, she stepped out into the back alley with a small pail of flower clippings and stems. It was early July. Dark clouds snagged in the high branches of the old elms on the side avenue. She had already lifted her pail into the air, where it hovered over the garbage inside, when she heard some muttering and paused, afraid that someone might be lying inside the garbage bin. But the noise came from the other side. Elizabeth stared over the bin's lip and saw the man foraging through a pile of garbage on the ground that he'd removed from the dumpster. He droned to himself, a steady humming that never changed pitch. His long black hair was matted together in greasy clumps. His running shoes, once white, were a dull grey without laces. They were at least two sizes too big for his feet, and they gaped open and flapped as he moved methodically around the navy metal dumpster.

The shop door swung closed loudly behind her and the man looked up, caught in the act. The whites of his eyes were the brightest spot on his face. Held in his filthy, scavenging hands was a tiny pink sleeper, its toes hanging empty and lifeless. Elizabeth's stomach heaved. "Get the hell out of here!" she yelled. Her body shook with the intensity of her rage. The man dropped the sleeper and took off. She quickly retrieved it and held it tightly to her chest. I'm losing my mind, she thought. Mascara ran down her face in a thin black trail.

EIGHT

2002

Marie busied herself making a new recipe for tuna salad from the cookbook Frances had given to her for Christmas. It seemed to be the easiest recipe in the book. Too many of them called for ingredients she had never heard of before. Umeboshi paste, hijike, tempeh, seitan. Even if she knew what these ingredients were, she had no idea where to find them.

"I know you guys aren't vegetarians," Frances had said when Marie opened the gift, "but it's got some fish recipes in it." Marie hadn't had the heart to say she was hoping to get another *Best of Bridge*, something with some traditional meat recipes in it, or perhaps some new ideas for how to jazz up meat loaf or pork chops. Curry wasn't really to her taste. "Cinnamon, dill, celery, slivered almonds . . ." It would be satisfying to tell Frances she'd made something from the book.

Nicole and Sophia pulled all the ingredients from the cupboards to make Elizabeth's favourite cookies. Already the countertop was coated in a light dusting of flour. The girls bumped against her as they raced to the refrigerator for a carton of eggs. Marie swallowed a wave of irritation. It was hard to watch her kids make such a mess. They rarely put things back where they found them, despite her constant reminders.

She watched them crack two eggs into the mixing bowl. Then they got their fingers in there and began pulling out the stray shells. It was too late to ask if they'd washed their hands. Marie bit her tongue when Sophia aimed the mouth of a full bottle of vanilla into a tiny measuring spoon. Miraculously she didn't spill a drop.

Her stomach growled and she remembered she hadn't eaten anything besides the crackers that morning in bed. Despite her hunger, she could think of nothing that would sit safely in her stomach.

The tuna rested in a stainless steel bowl on the counter. Accompanying the acrid scent of fish was the tinny smell of the empty cans that had recently housed the fish. Marie swallowed hard and breathed deeply through her mouth. Fish. She wouldn't be able to escape the smell now. She hated this stage of pregnancy, when every scent was magnified a thousand times over. Even if she went upstairs and shut herself in the bathroom, the room farthest from the kitchen, the smell of tuna would find her there.

Tiny wisps of snow fell from the tree branches outside the kitchen window, dropping to the tree's base, where a flock of sparrows had left their forked tracks. Marie stared out at the shimmering snow's surface and reminded herself that it was still minus thirty outside; it was hard to reconcile the abundance of sunshine with such frigid temperatures.

The doorbell rang promptly at noon. "She's here," Sophia shouted, trying to get to the door before Nicole. They yanked it open and pulled Elizabeth, laughing, into the house.

"What are you doing home? Isn't today a school day?" she asked.

"A pipe burst," Nicole replied. "And it flooded the whole school!"

"We made your favourite cookies," Sophia interrupted.

"*Sophia!*" Nicole whined. "It was supposed to be a surprise!"

"Oh, but I *am* surprised," Elizabeth said, diffusing the situation. "I'm surprised you're home *and* I'm surprised you made my favourite cookies. Chocolate chip walnut, right?"

"I'll take your coat." Marie laughed, rolling her eyes as the girls raced back to the kitchen. "Who knew a water main would break? Hopefully they'll busy themselves after lunch."

"Oh, that's fine," Elizabeth said. "You know I love to see them."

"I know," Marie replied. "But I also love *not* to see them sometimes! Come on in. The coffee's on."

Marie followed Elizabeth into the kitchen, noting how snugly her jeans hugged her slight form.

"I'm glad you're here," she said as she handed Elizabeth a cup of coffee. "The days go by so fast. I can't believe it's already been a week since we had supper. I swear I wake up and it's Monday, and I go to bed and it's Friday." Marie paused to take a breath, conscious that she was talking too fast. It was a bad habit she'd developed since having kids—the belief that if she talked quickly she might finish a thought before being interrupted. "You look great," she continued. "I like your hair all one length like that."

"Slow down." Elizabeth laughed. "You're making me nervous. And, yes, I just got it cut last week."

"Well, it suits you. You look very stylish. As usual."

Marie envied Elizabeth's ability to wear straight-legged jeans without looking like she'd been poured into them. Too many women wore them who shouldn't. When she and Elizabeth were teenagers they'd developed their own code for assessing women's clothes. If one of them spied someone in an unflattering outfit, she'd surreptitiously elbow the other and quietly say, *Somebody lied to her.*

"And I like your sweater," Marie added.

A brief silence followed. The girls had gone downstairs with a cookie in each hand. Instinctively, Marie cocked one ear to listen. "Are you hungry?" she asked. "Frances gave me a new cookbook, and I made some wacky tuna recipe out of it. I hope you'll like it."

Elizabeth smiled knowingly. "Still trying to change you, is she?"

"Always," Marie said as she nodded. "Nobody knows how to do things like Frances."

"It must be hard being right all the time," Elizabeth said.

"I wouldn't know."

"No, me neither." Elizabeth picked up her coffee and moved to the sitting area beside the kitchen. The leather loveseat sighed softly when she sat down.

"I'll put the fire on," Marie said. "This weather makes it impossible to heat the house." She walked to the fireplace and flicked a switch. Flames immediately appeared around the logs.

Marie nervously searched for a topic of conversation. She never used to have to fill in the silences because there had never *been* any. Best friends were always comfortable together, even if they didn't tell each other the truth all the time. Some things just had to be overlooked and forgiven, for the sake of friendship.

No friendship was ever entirely equal—Marie knew that. In all relationships, someone always had the upper hand. In the early years, Marie had been the one in charge; later, though, when boys became interesting, things flipped. She had never told Elizabeth how much it had stung to see the way men's eyes always slid quickly over Marie's plump figure to linger on Elizabeth's lean yet shapely one. In university, when they'd walk into a bar, Marie had seen the raw hopefulness in men's eyes when they saw Elizabeth, and she'd also seen the shadow of disappointment when they saw her tagging along behind, even though she pulled in her stomach and stood straight to make herself look slimmer. It was hard to be second fiddle all the time, to be the one men settled for but didn't really seek out. It certainly hadn't helped when Elizabeth had ended up with Ron.

But Marie had sucked it up because that's what friends do. Isn't it? Every friendship had its small jealousies and irritations. And sometimes the tables turned and the person who'd always been doing the envying was suddenly the one who was envied. It happened that way when Marie had her children. Then it was Elizabeth's turn to suck it up.

"Aren't you having any coffee?" Elizabeth asked.

"No, not now." Marie dropped her gaze and felt her friend's eyes studying her.

"You look kind of tired. Are you sleeping well?" Elizabeth asked. "You've got circles around your eyes. How's work?"

"Work's fine." Marie shrugged. "You know, the same old stuff. I'm sure you don't want to hear about accounting. I certainly don't." She had completed a course by correspondence, working on it when the girls were in school. It certainly wasn't a passion of hers. In truth, she'd never really had a strong desire to do anything. Not like her sister, for example, who had always been driven and already had two degrees.

Having children had freed her from finding the perfect career. What a relief that had been. But even when her kids were small, the idea that she would be expected to go back to work one day was a black cloud on the horizon.

Now, sitting with her third child growing inside of her, she wondered if she could buy another ten years at home with this baby. By then she'd be forty-nine, almost ready to retire. The thought did not bring much relief.

"Are you okay, Marie?"

Marie startled. How beautiful Elizabeth looked with her dark hair fanned gently off of her face, her lipstick perfectly highlighting her complexion. No wonder the boys had always been drawn to her.

"Yeah, I'm fine. Sorry, I was somewhere else there for a minute." She leaned back and put her feet up on the coffee table. Sunlight filtered in from the kitchen window illuminating the wood floor in wide shafts. The clock ticked loudly on the wall above the sink where the smell of tuna hung like fog over the countertops.

"I was just sitting here thinking that you look a bit piqued," Elizabeth said. "A bit green around the gills, if you know what I mean. It seems to me that I've seen that look on you before."

Marie made eye contact before quickly looking away.

"Are you *sure* you're feeling okay?"

Marie nodded again.

"Look at me."

Marie lifted her chin to be examined.

"I've got a funny feeling something's going on here," Elizabeth said. "And from the look of things, I'm going to take a wild guess." She gave Marie the once-over with her eyes. "You're pregnant, aren't you?"

The air escaped from Marie's lungs. *It was an accident*, she wanted to say. *I didn't do it on purpose.*

"And you're not even bloated or bruised from trying." Elizabeth shook her head. "Lucky you."

"I'm sorry, Elizabeth," she whispered.

Elizabeth turned away and stared outside the sliding glass door to where sparrows flitted in and out of the densely gnarled hedge.

"What are you sorry about?"

I'm sorry it's not you. "I don't know. I'm just feeling like I've messed up." Marie splayed her hands out onto her thighs. "I think I'm a little old for an unplanned pregnancy, don't you?"

They sat quietly for a moment. From downstairs came the sound of the television and the girls' laughter.

"Remember when you found out you were pregnant with Sophia and I'd been trying for two years to get pregnant, without any luck?"

Marie nodded. A cloud passed before the sun and the room fell into shadows.

"And do you remember what you said? You said, 'Am I going to have to stop seeing you for nine months?' As if we could have gone nine days without seeing each other!"

Marie smiled weakly. But something *had* changed once she'd had the girls. They still talked on the phone regularly, but sometimes months went by and they didn't see each other. "I'm sorry," she repeated. "I can't help it. It's just not fair. I know you've always been happy for me, but I can't help thinking that it should be you."

The sun came out again and the room grew to twice its size.

"When's the baby due?" Elizabeth asked.

"Late August, early September."

The phone rang. Relieved, Marie jumped to her feet and ran across the kitchen to the desk against the far wall.

"Sorry," she said, returning a minute later. "That was Frances. Again. She says to say hi."

"How's she doing?"

"Well, you know Frances. She says she's fine, but I don't think she'd tell me otherwise. I think she's finding it a challenge being home alone all day with Max, especially since Craig is back at work full-time. As you know, Frances likes to be in control, and one thing being a mother teaches you is how little control you really have. If you don't like a job, you can quit. If you're unhappy in your marriage, you can get a divorce. But you can't walk away from your kids. Once you have them, you're stuck with them." Marie ended abruptly, suddenly self-conscious. Her friend looked ready to bolt from the house.

"Not *stuck* exactly but . . ." She'd done it now—delivered a double blow to Elizabeth. Upper cut one—her birth mother had given her up. Kidney blow two—she'd never had her own children. "Lunch should be ready," she said hurriedly, hoping to hide her gaffes.

She felt lighter now; her breath came more easily. What a relief that Elizabeth had guessed. How much easier than trying to find the right words.

She sliced thick pieces of bread from the whole loaf and set them aside on the cutting board. Bickering voices rose from downstairs and become more shrill. *Mom!* Marie walked over and closed the door to the basement. Let them fight their own battles, she thought.

"How's Ron?" she asked.

Elizabeth pulled out one of the stools next to the island and sat down. "Well . . . funny you should ask." Then she told Marie that she'd signed a lease on a downtown apartment that morning.

"I'm not looking for any advice," she added. "I have no idea if I'm doing the right thing or not. Who knows, maybe I'm even making more of a mess of things. All I know is that I just need some time on my own to figure out what I should do with the next phase of my life."

Marie buried her face in the refrigerator to hide her shock. Thirty years of friendship! Is this what it resulted in? Neither of them had *ever* made any big decisions without consulting the other first. Yet Elizabeth was leaving her husband and had signed a lease on an apartment? She blinked back tears as she mashed the tuna onto the bread before adding sliced tomatoes and lettuce.

"And wait until you see the view! I think that's why I took the apartment, because it looks south, over the river valley. Right now the river's frozen, of course, but it'll be especially lovely in the fall when the leaves are turning. And I'll be able to walk to work. That'll be nice. It's only about twelve blocks."

"How's Ron handling this?"

"I haven't told him yet."

"You haven't *told* him?"

Elizabeth winced. "I know. I wanted to tell him yesterday, but I just couldn't. I don't want to hurt him," she added, "but I just can't stay in that house right now."

"But you love that house. You've worked hard to fix it up. What's changed?"

"I worked hard to get it ready for a family. It was supposed to be a *family* home."

"Can't you and Ron be a family?"

"We're a couple, not a family. There's a huge piece missing, and sometimes I feel like that house just mocks me. It's an old house. Who knows how many babies might have been born in it. Healthy babies. Happy babies. Stupid, isn't it? Anyway, I'll tell Ron. Probably tonight. Signing that lease certainly gives me the incentive."

Marie tried to imagine how he'd take the news. She hadn't seen him in some time, mostly because she didn't see as much of Elizabeth anymore either.

"Well, I guess there's no more putting it off," she said.

Elizabeth didn't appear to register the pain in Marie's voice; she had returned to the sliding doors and was once again staring into the backyard. Her figure was a dark skeleton in the full sunlight. "The apartment's empty right now, so I can start moving in any time."

Marie called Nicole and Sophia for lunch, and they pounded up the stairs like a herd of elephants to see who could get to the table first.

She had set the table herself, taking great care to make it look lovely. A navy blue tablecloth dotted with yellow stars and planets hung halfway to the floor. Yellow cloth napkins lay over each plate. A glass pitcher filled with iced tea sat in the centre of the table.

"Aren't we lucky?" Elizabeth said as she took a seat. "While the wind gusts outside, we're inside having a summer picnic!"

The girls grinned widely. Nicole ran off and returned to the table wearing a sun hat and sunglasses. "Remember not to go swimming for at least an hour after lunch!" She laughed.

"And watch out for sharks!" Sophia added.

"It's not the ocean, stupid," Nicole said. "We're at a lake."

"How do *you* know? We could be at the ocean! Are we at the ocean, Mom, or at a lake?"

Marie was only half listening. The girls laughed so easily with Elizabeth. Her own role too often involved nagging the kids to do the things they were supposed to do, like homework and chores. She *tried* to have fun with them, to be light, but lately her timing was off. She took small bites of her sandwich and chewed each one until it was pulp in her mouth. She wished she could lie down.

Elizabeth asked the girls about school and their friends. She seemed to know about the latest videos they'd watched. Marie was thankful that she didn't mention her impending move. Nicole and Sophia would be envious of her downtown apartment with a view.

And then suddenly it was two o'clock and Elizabeth needed to leave. She turned down dessert because she was full, so the girls filled a container with cookies for her to take home.

"Can you take us to a movie soon, Auntie Elizabeth?" Sophia asked as she followed her to the foyer.

Elizabeth pulled her winter coat on and slipped into her fur-lined boots. "I sure can. You guys let me know which one and when, okay?"

The two women smiled at each other across the children.

"Will you call me soon?" Marie asked. "I'd like to help, if I can. Packing, shopping—whatever you need. Just let me know. Okay?"

Elizabeth nodded. "You bet. Thanks for lunch. Take care of yourself. And say hi to Frances for me."

A gust of cold air entered the house when Elizabeth slipped through the door. It swirled around Marie's bare ankles in tight circles and then spread out low over the tiles before gusting into the four corners.

The children disappeared downstairs again.

Marie walked to the front window and watched her friend's car as it backed down the driveway.

She had her hand up to wave, but Elizabeth never looked back.

NINE

Elizabeth's vision blurred as she put the car in gear. A block from Marie's house she pulled to the curb, put her forehead on the steering wheel, and wept. Her life was falling apart, and her friend was having another baby. Marie didn't even sound like she *wanted* another baby. And how smug she'd been, waiting for Elizabeth to guess her condition. *I'm sorry. It should be you.*

She slammed her hand down on the steering wheel and winced from the pain. Damned right it should be me, she thought.

And what was all the crap about not walking away from your kids? Did Marie think that made her a better person? What about all those women out there, including herself, who *didn't* have kids, by choice or not? Marie made it sound like they were all missing out on ways to become better people, but Elizabeth knew that life threw people all kinds of situations in which they had the opportunity to grow. Marie needed to get out more; she needed to get her head out of her own sense of perfection.

As her rage slowly decreased, Elizabeth recalled the look on Marie's face when Elizabeth had told her she was leaving Ron. Marie had crawled inside her shell immediately to nurse her pain. But she didn't need to clear every decision about her life with Marie. And she certainly wasn't going to apologize for shocking her. The history of their friendship was that Elizabeth *always* apologized and made things right in their friendship. She worked *far* harder at it than Marie did, ever since Ron. But not today. Oh no. Something had come over her when she'd heard the reproach in Marie's voice, and it was the desire to cause her pain. Why? Because Marie had just pulled a baby from a hat. Well, Elizabeth had some tricks up her sleeve too.

She reached into her purse for some tissue and blew her nose, checking in the rear-view mirror to see if her makeup had smudged. Something foul had lurched up inside her. She stared into her own eyes and knew she didn't want to be this way. She couldn't go on falling apart without warning, or lashing out. Plus, there were more tears ahead. Maybe she should have talked to Ron before signing a lease. Now it looked so premeditated. But it *was* premeditated. She'd been thinking about it for months. She blew her nose again. Maybe what she needed was to call her mom. Yes. That would help. Elizabeth drew in a deep breath, put the car in gear, and headed home.

"Hi, sweetie!" Her mother always sounded so happy when Elizabeth called, as if she'd just received good news that she wanted to share.

"How's Victoria treating you?" Elizabeth asked. Her parents had moved there when her father retired from teaching.

"Well, it's raining, as usual. But the view of the inner harbour is always lovely. And I see you've been having some cold weather."

"That's an understatement." She laughed.

"What's up?" Her mother always got quickly to the point.

"Are you sitting down?"

"Should I be?"

"You might want to."

She could hear movement on the other end of the line as her mother followed instructions.

"Okay, I'm ready."

"I signed a lease on an apartment this morning. It's empty right now so I can start moving in right away."

"Are you selling your house?"

"No. I'm moving by myself."

"By yourself? What about Ron?"

"I'm hoping he'll stay in the house."

"Wait a minute now. Slow down. This is going too fast for me. What's going on, Lizzie? You're leaving Ron? Why now?"

That was a good question. She couldn't say for sure why now, this exact month, after being married for fifteen years. "I don't really know. I just feel like I've been in some kind of holding pattern and I've got to get out of it. My life's not what I wanted it to be, Mom, and I don't know what to do." She could feel the tears building inside as she confessed her fears to her mother.

"Oh, honey, I think it's called growing up. We don't often get the lives we imagined we'd have when we were children. I know I didn't. I'd have had six children if given the chance. That's what I'd hoped for, but I didn't quit living because I only had you. Far from it, in fact. You brought lots of excitement into our lives. Didn't you want to be a dancer and a veterinarian?"

Elizabeth laughed. "Marie wanted to be a dancer, and a writer too, I think. I wanted to be a veterinarian."

"And look at you both. Neither one of you is doing what you dreamed of when you were children."

"What I really wanted to be was a mother. A veterinarian and a mother. Marie at least got to be a mother. And more. I just found out today that she's pregnant again."

"Ah, so that's it. You're feeling sorry for yourself again, are you? Lizzie, Ron is one of the best things to ever happen to you. Don't throw him away because you didn't get something else you wanted. He certainly helped you try to have kids, didn't he? If I remember correctly he did a lot of things he wasn't so sure about because you wanted him to. And I still don't understand why you've never tried the adoption route. It certainly made me happy. I got you."

"Yeah, you got a child nobody else wanted. I don't want a baby who is abandoned by its mother."

"Elizabeth! What's come over you?"

Elizabeth had never spoken those words before, let alone to her mother, but she'd thought them a million times. Everybody was different, after all. Just because she couldn't get over her mother giving her away at birth didn't mean that she didn't appreciate her adoptive parents. Maybe she'd even had a better life because she was adopted, but that didn't erase the fact that her *real* mother hadn't wanted her in the first place. Elizabeth knew it was a lovely gesture to raise a child as if it was your own, but she wanted to raise her *own* child, not one that some agency had finally approved them for after analyzing her and Ron's lives with a magnifying glass to ferret out anomalies.

But now she could see where her single-minded determination might possibly have let her down. She'd thought persistence was the solution. Never quitting. The old *If at first you don't succeed, try, try again*. And again. And again. And then let the years go by until you really don't feel like you're young enough anymore to deal with a baby. That's where being strong-willed had gotten her. "I'm glad you got me, Mom," she finally said, "'cause I got you."

"Darn rights you did!" Her mother laughed. "And you're not getting rid of me."

No, this mother wasn't going to leave her. Not like the mother she'd never known, the one she couldn't help but think about from time to time, especially on her birthday. Was she still alive? Possibly living on the next block? Had her mother been one of those young girls who'd quietly disappeared for a few months, like so many girls in the sixties who'd been sent to a fictitious aunt in the east?

"Why don't you come for a visit, Lizzie, before you make up your mind? Your dad and I would be happy to have you. Actually"—she lowered her voice to a whisper—"your dad could use a break. He's been working too hard on his next book."

"That's because he's not marking papers anymore." Elizabeth laughed. "He's finally got time to do his own work." All throughout her childhood her father had had ink-stained hands from correcting his students' ideas about Victorian literature.

"And don't worry," she added, "we'd be sure to give you some time on your own to think things through."

"That's a nice offer, Mom, but I've made up my mind. I'm going to talk with Ron tonight and we'll sort out the details. I'll call you later, okay?"

"I won't say anything to your father until I hear more. Okay? I love you, honey."

"I love you too, Mom. And Mom?"

"Yes?"

"Don't worry. I'm going to be okay."

Elizabeth waited until Ron finished eating dinner before pouring a fresh cup of coffee for them both and sitting back down at the table. Ron looked at her expectantly. Normally she cleared the table and did the dishes right away.

"Can we talk?" she asked.

"Uh-oh. You look serious. Is something wrong?"

"Yes and no."

"Well, don't keep me in suspense. Shoot."

Elizabeth took a deep breath for courage. "I signed a lease on an apartment this morning. It's empty right now so I can take possession anytime." That didn't come out right. She'd jumped right to the conclusion without setting it up properly.

She saw the hurt and confusion in his eyes. He stared at her until she dropped her gaze. Maybe that wasn't the best way to start, coming out of the blue like that.

"I wanted to tell you earlier," she rushed on, "but I didn't know how."

"I don't understand what's going. You want to move *out*? By yourself?"

She nodded.

He raised both hands in the air in a sign of helplessness. "Why?"

"Please don't get angry, Ron. It's not like I've been thinking about it for years. I'm not even sure I can explain except to say I'm not living the life I thought I'd be living at this stage of my life. I need a change." She reached across the table and took his hand. It felt warm and soft in her own, comfortable as a worn glove. "There's nothing wrong with you. It's me."

"Oh, that's convenient," Ron said. "Blame it on yourself so I don't have to feel bad. That's good. Look, we've been through some stressful times. I know that, and they haven't exactly been easy for me either. But I thought we'd done okay. I don't see why—"

She put her finger to her lips to silence him. "All I ever wanted was to be a mother, and last year, when we finally decided to stop the treatments, I had to let go of that dream. So here I am," she laughed weakly, "thirty-nine and I don't know what I want to be when I grow up."

"Be whoever you want to be," he said. "Grab hold of something else. God, you're free to do that now. Aren't you even a tiny bit relieved that we're not in a holding pattern anymore? For a long time it felt like all we did was sit around and wait for some doctor to tell us good news. It was hard."

"Really? You never told me that."

"I didn't come right out and say it, but I certainly let you know that I was okay with the life we already had." Then his voice softened. "And I still am."

Elizabeth smiled and gave his hand a squeeze. "You truly are one of the nicest men on the planet."

He grinned. "I try, but I'm not sure that helps me sometimes."

"Don't get mad at what I'm going to say. Okay? There are days when I can't help thinking if you'd been with someone else you'd have a brood of kids by now. And I love the picture of you with a child on your shoulders."

"That's *your* picture of how you think I should live. What about mine? I don't feel sorry for myself that I'm not hanging out at playgrounds. Would I have done it if we'd had a child? Sure, but do I pine for it? No, I don't because it's not as if we didn't try. That would have been worse, to have wondered if maybe we *could* have had a baby. But we gave it our best shot, no pun intended." He held his hand up and mimed squirting juice out of a syringe.

"It's not funny," she said sulkily.

"Okay, okay. Look, maybe it's time to talk about adopting again; we never explored that avenue like we could have."

"I knew you were going to say that. You sound just like my mom."

Even before their first trip to the clinic Ron had proposed adoption. But Elizabeth didn't want to raise a child who might one day search for its real parents. Plus, medical advancements in the fertility field had done wonders to help women like her. She was convinced the experts would help her too.

"I wanted to be a mother ten years ago," she whispered. "Who knows how long we'd have to wait before we'd get a baby."

"Maybe late is better than never."

"I just need some time on my own," she repeated. Even to her the words sounded like an excuse, but she was tired of being consoled. Tired of how understanding Ron always was. *It doesn't matter*, he'd said after one failed attempt to conceive. *We still have each other*. She'd grown to hate his attempts to comfort her because it *did* matter. It mattered a lot! She knew he was trying to be helpful, but the nicer he tried to be, the more she resented his understanding.

"What can I say?" Ron finally said, pushing his chair back from the table. "I don't want you to go. I think we've made a good life for ourselves. And we've certainly done everything to bring a baby into our lives. Everything except adoption. *You* were adopted, and things worked out. I don't understand why you're so resistant to at least giving it a try."

"It doesn't make sense, does it? All I can say is it's strange not knowing if I have brothers or sisters or aunts and uncles. I often find myself walking down a busy sidewalk and seeing someone who reminds me of me. Then I start to wonder if maybe we're related. Then I realize that there could be this whole big family out there that might be waiting to welcome me into it. Ever since I was twelve and my mom told me I was adopted, from that moment on I felt like there was someplace I was supposed to be, but no one had given me a map."

"You could have tried to find out more."

"I know. But I was afraid of hurting my parents. Every time I mentioned wanting to find my mother, they'd cook up some excuse to delay my going to the registry. It finally dawned on me that they didn't want me to go, so I just sort of left it alone."

Her head hurt. She'd never tried so fully to explain herself, and she realized that even now the explanation didn't come close to describing her sense of dislocation. Ron rubbed her hand gently.

"Maybe you're not meant to find out," he said. "Maybe it's okay not to know."

She smiled sadly and nodded. A list of rebuttals found their way to the tip of her tongue, but she stopped herself from speaking.

The conversation felt finished. Everything had been said. "Oh, by the way," she added, "I had lunch with Marie today. And guess what?"

"What?" Ron tried to look interested. Did he ever think about Marie and remember their romantic times together? His lips had kissed hers. Their hands had undressed each other. He'd taken her to his bed. At times like this it annoyed Elizabeth that Ron had once been intimate with her best friend.

"She's pregnant."

The news sucked the air out of the room. Elizabeth watched him closely.

"Good for her," he said, taking his cold coffee to the sink. "But I don't wish it was me."

"Ron?"

He turned and looked at her, hopeful and sad.

"I'm still leaving."

"What can I say?" he asked, his arms spread wide, taking in the room and the house and the years they'd spent together. "What can I say? I don't want you to go."

A few minutes later Ron disappeared downstairs to mark student assignments. Elizabeth stood at the sink and rinsed the dinner dishes. Then she took a warm cloth and wiped the counters and the kitchen table. She was surprised to not feel a greater relief now that the conversation was over. Instead, she felt annoyed. Why hadn't Ron put up more of a fight? She had steeled herself to have a lengthy conversation, but it had ended in less than fifteen minutes. Fifteen years of marriage disintegrating in a short conversation on a frigid winter evening. Maybe that's what she'd remember in the years to come, the wind howling, the ice crystals shimmering, the furnace kicking on again and again. Being housebound. *What can I say?* he had asked. But in the end he had said nothing but the obvious, *I don't want you to go*, and disappeared into the basement.

The evening wore on. By bedtime the temperature had dropped to minus forty with wind chill. Ice fog hung in thick clouds beneath the street lamps. *Stay inside if you can*, weather announcers warned. *Exposed flesh will become frostbitten in seconds.* Elizabeth sat at the kitchen table and made a list of things she'd need for her new apartment. Were there blinds on the windows? Did the kitchen have a double sink? What colour were the bathroom tiles? It was almost as if she hadn't been there at all. In truth, her thoughts kept returning to Marie and the baby that was growing in her belly. Could she possibly fake her way through another baby shower? Marie had said she knew Elizabeth would be happy for her. Well, she was wrong. She wasn't happy at all. Maybe their friendship had run its course.

Finally it was bedtime, and Elizabeth and Ron, shy now with each other, slept side by side, their thighs lightly touching in the middle of the bed.

TEN

1947

Six months passed without a word from anybody at Poplar Grove. Every day Margaret thought about Carolyn, her little child that she'd wrapped up tight in a pink flannel blanket to keep her warm and safe when she'd let her go. Christmas lights decorated city hall and the legislature grounds, and all around her people prepared for holiday festivities.

She was free to visit now, but she was afraid. An entire building, like a deserted island, filled with castaways and a baby who didn't know her own mother. She had only held Carolyn once, and she'd been so tiny. Had that moment been imprinted on the child's brain? Was she patiently waiting for her mother to return?

Margaret tried to act as if everything was normal. She put up a Christmas tree and hung two stockings on the mantel. Neither she nor Donald mentioned the missing third stocking. They also didn't mention the new baby growing within her because they'd learned the danger of becoming excited too soon. This new baby grew in a mother who held her breath. In a mother who held joy at bay, who looked full into the sun until she felt her eyes burn. Who returned to an old childhood habit of pulling nervously at her nose as if she could control her fate by altering her appearance.

Six months of silence in which she was supposed to forget and move on. Act as if nothing had happened. That's what her mother had finally said when she gleaned the truth about what the doctor's son had done to Margaret. But before that, she'd used strong words to berate her daughter, who'd been discovered in bed in the middle of the afternoon. *How did she think a farm would run? Did she think they had hired hands? Did she think at all?* Then she'd noticed her child's red-rimmed eyes, saw the shame and devastation therein, and suspicion lodged in her gut. They'd passed that boy on the way home from Doc Jenkins's. She stood rock still for some time. Margaret could see her mother's mind racing to process the situation. Then she sat on the corner of the bed, her voice low and un-tender. "Don't you dare breathe a word of this to your father. To *anyone*! Do you understand me?" She reached out a claw hand and shook Margaret's arm. "Am I right in what I'm thinking?"

Margaret's mind raced with confusion. Could there be anything worse? She nodded and fell to crying again.

"You clean yourself up and get back to the chores immediately, you understand? This never happened."

She'd seen him once in town, after that day on the farm. She'd turned the corner from the post office and there he was, sitting in the shade outside the general store, sipping a cold soda straight from the bottle, looking cool as could be in a linen shirt white as a gauze over a wound. Her heart teemed with a mixture of panic, dread, anger, and hope. It was the latter that turned her stomach the most. The hope. For deep down, a part of her hoped he'd notice her, be kind to her, offer to buy her a soda and make everything right. It wasn't too late for him to somehow make amends, to make what happened at the creekbed a moment of insanity from which he'd begged forgiveness. He would be a gentleman after all and acknowledge his fault. He would be good to her parents. They would have a proper life together.

But Stuart Jenkins had sipped his cold drink and smiled with his perfect teeth. He'd looked right through her.

This was the boy who had stood over her and buckled his belt. "Remember," he'd said. "You never once told me to stop."

In her mind she'd been screaming, but out loud she hadn't made a sound.

She never visited the creek again.

But six months of not loving her daughter was a greater shame even than this. What kind of a mother was she? She'd lived through the years on the farm when the rain never came and her parents lost the ability to laugh. She knew that a body didn't just bounce back when times suddenly got better, just like the ruts in a road didn't disappear when the weather improved.

In spite of her terror that another pregnancy would result in a similar shame, she allowed her husband to love her. She'd picked this man. She'd walked self-consciously down the aisle at the church Donald's parents had been married in, wearing a white dress chosen by her mother-in-law. She'd said, "I do." So when he slid beneath the covers and reached for her, she fulfilled her duty. It wasn't long before her belly gently swelled with her second child, yet her thoughts remained on Carolyn.

One year, almost to the day, after kissing her daughter goodbye, she delivered a healthy baby boy. They named him James, after his paternal grandfather. And Donald, after his father. James Donald Harrington. And when she placed her nose to the infant's head, the spice cabinet swung wide open again.

Dr. Morrison was all smiles when he congratulated her. "What did I tell you?" he said, as if the earth had righted itself at his suggestion. "What did I tell you?"

It was only after she brought her infant son home and experienced his constant need to drain her breasts every two hours that she began to fear for her first-born child. Baby James demanded her constant care. Hold me. Rock me. Feed me. Change me. Hold me. Rock me. Feed me. Change me. Who was holding Carolyn? Who was feeding and loving her girl? The bathroom mirror did not answer her questions. Instead, it reflected back the image of a young mother—exhausted, uncertain, proud, afraid. Guilty. When she looked closer, stretching so her face almost touched the glass, she saw it in the lines marking her forehead and surrounding her blue eyes—guilt. A caught-in-the-act, split-second reflection that disappeared as soon as she noted its presence. A woman leaving a child in a basket on the stairs, ringing the bell and running.

But still she didn't pick up the phone, and nobody from Poplar Grove did either. Would they call if Carolyn died? Was no news good news?

Eighteen months after James's arrival, Margaret gave birth to another daughter, Rebecca Constance Harrington. She weighed eight pounds even and brought a flood of pink into their home—booties, hats, blankets. Like her brother, she, too, required much care and attention, and Carolyn remained a ghostly presence in Margaret's peripheral vision, the shadow in the corner of every room she entered, the echo that came back louder than the soft query sent into the midnight air.

Then, as if overnight, Margaret fell into a deep depression. Her husband stood by helplessly and watched his wife's industrious, farm-girl nature dissolve into lethargy and darkness. Margaret gave in to the crushing weight of grief and the knowledge that she, herself, was motherless. Her brother, Johnny, had married Ethel Boyko from the neighbouring farm. They now had two boys. Margaret's mother baked fresh bread for them and delivered eggs fresh from the coop. Women from the community also dropped by with offerings because that's what they did in Mayburn. But Margaret was alone in the city. She wasn't really a part of any community, so no one dropped off meals or offered to mind a child. Life here was built on an etiquette guide she'd never read. She was as alone in her rocking chair while nursing her child in the middle of the night as she was while feeding her in the middle of the day. A person could go crazy from loneliness.

Donald took time off work when his wife failed to get out of bed one morning despite the children's cries. She didn't eat, she stopped bathing, and her beauty faded like fresh-cut flowers without water. If she was lucky, she slept for three-hour stretches. More often than not, she wandered the house at night, staring out the window into the winter darkness, aware that there was something she should be doing but having no clue as to what that might be.

The winter of 1950 was a terrible one for Margaret. Donald would bring the children into her bed and sit with her, hoping their small faces, their absolute need, would jar the melancholy from her bones. They were beautiful children. She could see that, but her heart was unmoved, and the new silence she inhabited hardened into stone. What right had she to love and be loved? When Margaret had left the farm, her mother's dry-eyed goodbye could not hide that she welcomed the separation. But it wasn't natural. Not natural at all.

Just as it wasn't natural to give up a child. Margaret could not live anymore with not knowing that child's fate. How far was it to Poplar Grove? The depression clawed at her attempts to connect to her life. If ever she could get away . . .

Just one visit to be sure she was being taken care of. To see how her hair had grown in, to hear her laugh.

One morning the light returned and her heart became right-sized again. There was no explaining the transition. Depression came; depression went. Margaret returned to her duties with a raw gratitude. How good it was to feel again. To see her children and know that she loved them. Yet it was clear to her now that if she was going to hold on to her slim wedge of sanity, she would have to rescue Carolyn by a great act of imagination. She would dream a life for her, one surrounded by stuffed animals and light. Pancakes and syrup. Birdsong and flowers. By a profound act of concentration, she would float her child on a cloud toward a place of lemonade and fresh-cut lawns. Toward a playground with enough swings for every child.

In 1951, when James was three and Rebecca was a year and a half old, Margaret finally found the courage to step onto the asylum bus and make her first visit to Poplar Grove to verify that her daughter was indeed receiving the special care she needed. Four years had passed since she and Donald had signed the institutionalization papers and handed over their child.

It was a Wednesday. It was summer. Donald wouldn't be home until five-thirty. Margaret arranged for a babysitter, her neighbour's live-in mother-in-law, and carefully kept her plans to herself. "I'm going shopping," she said.

The asylum bus. That wasn't its official name, but someone on the phone at Poplar Grove had called it that. "The asylum bus leaves twice a day from the south terminal on the first and fifteenth of every month," the voice that had answered the phone said. "It'll bring you here and take you right back after an hour." Then the anonymous woman had laughed as if Margaret had told her a joke, but she hadn't. "Just between you and me," the woman added, "an hour's enough!"

The bus pulled out of the terminal right at the scheduled time. From the bus window Margaret saw a dark bank of clouds gathering on the eastern horizon. She'd left laundry on the line and silently hoped it wouldn't rain. She turned her gaze to the single red rose lying in her lap. It was her favourite flower. She imagined meeting Carolyn and extending her hand to the little four-year-old who would look upon her with curious chestnut eyes, without understanding that the woman before her had abandoned her and been too cowardly to visit. Margaret didn't think about the thorns on the rose's stem because this girl was special, wasn't she, so maybe normal rules didn't apply.

The bus headed directly to the highway from the transit terminal. Margaret realized that she did not know the way. Someone else had delivered her child to Poplar Grove. But who? Donald? No, he couldn't have. He would have told her. Wouldn't he? How had they never discussed it?

The bus gathered speed as it merged onto the highway and left the southernmost suburbs of the city behind. Almost immediately the landscape changed and the cramped houses buttressed against one another on small city lots gave way to a vast openness of country fields. Margaret felt her eyes relax as her sightlines lengthened in the open country. Most of the fields had been tilled and planted, but a few horses and cows could be seen grazing in the occasional fallow field. Her father and brother would be out in the fields this very moment. Her mother, as Wednesdays were wash days, was likely hanging laundry.

There were half a dozen adult passengers on the bus and two babies, yet nobody spoke, let alone made eye contact, despite their all having the same destination. Under normal circumstances Margaret might have drawn someone into conversation by commenting on the weather. *This is my first visit*, she wanted to confess. *What's it like? How bad is it? Did I do the right thing?*

Margaret noted the growing distance between the city and her first-born child. Ten minutes passed. Was there no place for a child like hers within the city limits? Then the bus turned from the tarmac onto a gravel road. And the gravel road disappeared from the highway, and then, finally, the bus turned up a rutted driveway beside a stand of poplars and Margaret held her breath.

From the outside Poplar Grove looked like a private boarding school. The red brick building was three storeys high and had a wide front porch that ran almost the entire length of it. The bus pulled right up to the front door and came to an abrupt stop.

"One hour 'til departure," the driver called out and promptly turned off the ignition and unfurled a newspaper. Margaret found the sudden quiet unnerving. She looked around her, not sure what to do next. Clearly some of the other passengers had made this trip before. They immediately got off the bus and made their way single file up the front stairs to the main door. Margaret stood and followed slowly behind them.

Six wooden stairs painted grey took her to the porch. There, she hesitated. The rest of the passengers had already gone inside. The front door was heavy. She needed to use both hands to swing the wooden door open. Then she walked thirteen more steps over a worn brown carpet to the front desk.

A woman sat behind it, talking on the phone. Margaret waited to be noticed. Even though the sun shone brightly outside, the lobby was underlit and dreary. She cleared her throat and the heavy-set matron looked up over her wire-rimmed glasses with a furrowed brow. Patience was not present in her demeanour.

Margaret's voice shook. "I'm here to visit Carolyn Harrington."

"First visit?"

"Yes."

"Wait here." The woman heaved herself to her feet and shuffled down a dimly lit corridor.

Margaret's heart was beating at an alarming rate. What was taking so long? Was the staff giving her daughter a quick bath to make her presentable? Changing her clothes? Brushing her hair? Why had there been no children playing outside on such a lovely afternoon?

Finally the receptionist returned with an oily-haired orderly who nodded at Margaret and turned on his heels. That was her cue to follow.

When the heavy metal door to Ward B, building number 2, slid open, the stench almost brought Margaret to her knees. Stepping into the thickly fouled air she instinctively lifted the silk scarf wrapped around her neck and covered her nose and mouth with it, certain that the poison in the air would penetrate the soft pink tissues of her lungs and burrow deep like a sharp splinter.

"This way," the orderly said, putting his hand on the small of her back.

Margaret felt the heat of his hand through her cotton blouse and imagined it left a dark stain that ran down to her hemline. Filth every-where, and he was a part of it.

The hallway was painted an institutional green—dull except for the shiny spots where some liquid, she didn't dare imagine what (certainly not bleach), had splashed against the baseboards and up to waist level, leaving intricate paisley-like dots and splotches in the flat paint.

A steady moaning came from the end of the corridor, drowning the sound of her low heels clicking on the grey linoleum floor. She jumped when a piercing scream rent the air behind her, followed immediately by a dull thud like a watermelon dropped from a height and then silence. She kept her eyes focused straight ahead, allowing what happened in her peripheral vision to stay blurred. A doorway opened suddenly on her right. She jumped and gazed into a crowded room of bodies. Many were lying on the floor. Half were partially dressed.

She kept moving, stunned by her surroundings. Tears stung her eyes, and she rubbed them roughly to keep herself from breaking down. She and Donald had been far too trusting. What *was* this place? Nothing but a trap for forgotten people. No matter what they called it—a school, or training centre. Nothing worth learning happened here, only things worth forgetting. Poplar Grove. She snorted. Such a name was more suited for a lakeside resort. No name could possibly mask the horror of this place. Margaret felt a quiet rage building within. She had signed papers based on a name! A fault in nomenclature! Purgatory's Place was a far more apt name. Or Hell's Haven. Why hide the truth?

The sound of children crying pressed in from all sides. The orderly led her through a maze of locked doors, disinfected hallways, and crowded wards until, finally, they arrived at her daughter's ward.

Margaret could smell her own armpits in the mix of ripe body odours. She felt as if she'd left the civilized world where she operated instinctively and entered a place where the everyday code of conduct no longer applied. How else to explain the assault on her senses? The sounds were magnified, horrific, and not always identifiable. The smells were heady and putrid. The sights, rude and vulgar. Her feet kept moving as she narrowed her vision to reduce her disgust at the surroundings. To think that she'd showered and put on makeup to make a good impression! To think that her doctor had recommended this place. How had she not come first, with Donald, to be sure their daughter would be well cared for here? How trusting they'd been, taking pen in hand and signing away their daughter's life without even making a visit.

The orderly stopped beside a crib in which a small child lay curled into the corner. He rattled the bars and the girl jumped and rolled her head sideways to have a look. She had dull brown eyes, flat as pennies and equally inexpressive. Margaret looked away for a moment, hoping to see something better, but the crib beside Carolyn's was filled with two small babies who appeared in desperate need of a bath.

"That's her," the orderly's husky voice interrupted. "I'll be back for you in fifteen minutes."

Margaret stared at his retreating back with panic. Fifteen minutes? What was she supposed to do here? She felt the rose in her hand and realized how inappropriate the gift was. This child, although older than her two at home, was younger in so many ways. She seemed barely able to sit up on her own. Margaret watched mutely as Carolyn struggled to shift her balance. When she finally reached an upright position, balanced solidly on her bum, her head lolled to one side as if someone had put a heavy barrette in her hair and unbalanced her. Drool ran from her slack mouth and down her chin, yet the child made no effort to wipe it away. Although she was four years old, she was still in a diaper, and from the looks of the brown stains on her bare upper thighs, she'd been wearing it for some time.

Margaret took it all in and almost buckled under the weight of her shame. She shouldn't have come. The life she'd tried to imagine for her daughter, the one with goodness and light, was non-existent. No one brought ice cream cones to these children. No one made them laugh. It was better to have imagined Carolyn well taken care of and happy. She glanced around the room. There must have been forty cribs all told, positioned in rows with narrow walkways between them, and all of them were full. The age range appeared to be infants right up to ages six or eight. It was hard to accurately say because the children looked so small in the cavernous room with its high ceilings. How cold it must be in the winter, she thought, gazing at the old, tall windows high up on the walls.

She felt something touch her arm and instinctively pulled away before realizing it was Carolyn's hand reaching through the crib bars. Margaret looked at her child and experienced a host of emotions. Revulsion was one of them. Gaining steadily, however, was a fierce and immense compassion. This was her child. She reached out and took Carolyn's small hand in her own and saw that her nails were overgrown and broken.

Margaret made a mental note to bring nail clippers next time. If there was a next time.

The child kept reaching, and soon Margaret realized she was after the rose. Margaret pulled the stem off and handed the flower head to Carolyn. For a moment her daughter sat motionless, absorbed by the newness of the soft petals in her palm, thin as a layer of skin pulled from a sunburned shoulder. Then she lifted the flower to her mouth and began to chew.

The bus trip home felt twice as long as the initial drive to Poplar Grove. Margaret rested her forehead against the cool window and stared flatly out at the tilled farm fields that now looked ravaged. She saw a falcon dive low over the ground and pull up with something struggling in its claws; she could relate to the small animal caught in a grip far stronger than its own. She could relate to the struggle and the shock.

Something had been set into motion four years ago, and she had gone along with it, trusting that the doctors knew best. After all she'd been through, she should have known not to be so trusting. Look at the boy Doc Jenkins had raised. Obviously the good doctor knew nothing about children. And Dr. Morrison too. She hadn't even asked him if he had kids. What kind of a father would he be if he thought Poplar Grove was any kind of a place for a child? His words echoed in her mind, *It's for her own good*. Rage simmered in her bloodstream. She had been completely misled.

The bus turned off the highway and headed to the south terminal. She couldn't tell Donald what she'd found—their tiny, undernourished daughter, still in diapers, left to rot in a crib. Abandoned, really, in a foul place where there was no love. Thank God she'd come without telling Donald. What would Donald think if he saw this? No. She would never tell him what she'd discovered. She had to protect him from knowing more about this horrific place. She had to shower the grime of that place from her skin.

She needed to hold James and Rebecca in her arms. Maybe, if she tried, she could forget this visit entirely.

ELEVEN

2002

January, the coldest month of the year, came to an end. The hours of daylight slowly began to extend—but even so, the city's inhabitants walked in a dreamlike state, fearful that the dark season of cold and snow would never end. The calendar days passed, but the snow continued to fall.

Winter, with its extended hours of darkness, is the season for sleeping. Windows stay closed; snow muffles the neighbourhood noise. Marie didn't often have difficulty sleeping, but on this cold, late-January night, she woke with her heart hammering. She sat upright in bed and listened. Had one of her daughters called out? She strained her ears and waited. Nothing.

Disoriented, she lay down again and closed her eyes. Then the dream came back to her. In it, her newborn was fully swaddled. She couldn't tell if it was a boy or a girl. All she knew was that it was hers to care for and she'd forgotten it somewhere. At the store? The bus stop? No—the beach! Down the steep cement stairs to the waterfront she ran to find her baby resting on a huge piece of driftwood. It was a pebbled beach, and the small stones kept pulling at Marie's feet so, despite great effort, she never got any closer to her child. She could hear the baby's thin cry and she dug harder for traction. She flailed and dug and flailed some more.

And then she woke up.

She'd had these dreams before, with her girls; she'd wake with her breasts hard and leaking and walk barefoot to find them quietly sleeping in their rooms. But this time there was no baby to check on in the room next door.

Barry snored quietly beside her, the duvet tucked beneath his sleeping form. Shadows of naked tree limbs moved rhythmically on the bedroom ceiling from the light cast by the lamppost at the sidewalk's edge. Aside from the usual household noises—the furnace softly humming, the alarm clock clicking as the numbers turned over on the bedside table—the house was quiet. It was too early for the neighbours' dog to begin his customary howling. And it was a weekday, too early for anyone to be up and too late for anyone not to have gone to bed.

Marie stared at the shadows on the ceiling and tried to calm her pounding heart. She wasn't even at the quickening phase yet, when she could detect fetal movement, so how could she check on her baby?

Maybe there was something wrong with it. She'd been lucky to have two healthy children, but she was older now. Her doctor would stamp a big fat RISK on her file when she went in with the news. She worried the thought, turning it over and looking at it from every angle, until it became a premonition. Her foreboding became a certainty. The hunch a reality.

There is something wrong with my baby.

Shortly after four she heard Mr. Jantz's car start up when he left for the bakery. Then a long silence punctuated by a car idling along the avenue as the morning's paper was delivered.

She climbed quietly out of bed and walked to the window. Snow had fallen in the night and was still falling. Thick flakes floated heavily to the ground. The neighbourhood glowed as if under a fresh coat of paint.

The mountain ash stood in stark contrast to the blanket of whiteness, its red berries delectable treats for the waxwings that visited by the hundreds, cooing and trilling and leaving a trail of red droppings in their wake.

She returned to bed and stared once again at the ceiling. The shadow of naked tree branches was gone now. She thought of the Dutch elms in the city, seasonally engaged in a fight against disease. She thought of her baby possibly warring against its own cells. She thought of her mother, eating sparingly and watching her figure under a hot Arizona sun. She thought of her father, teeing off with other white-haired men after a long career in an unfulfilling job that paid the household bills. She thought about what to make for breakfast. She thought of Elizabeth packing her belongings and carving out a single life.

Finally, at five-thirty, she reached out and shook Barry's arm. She rolled closer to him and curled her body against his warmth.

"Barry," she whispered. "Are you awake?"

"Hmm."

"Wake up. I need to talk to you."

"What time is it?" He squinted into the dark and ran his tongue over his chapped lips.

"This is serious, Barry," she said. "I need you to listen."

"Okay, okay. I'm awake." He rolled onto his side and propped himself on one elbow. His right cheek was deeply lined with pillow creases. White flakes of saliva had dried onto his bottom lip. "Okay," he said again, suppressing a yawn. "I'm listening."

"I think there's something wrong with the baby." She put her hands over her face to stifle her sobs.

"What are you talking about?"

"Something woke me up and suddenly I had this feeling that something's wrong."

He looked dazed. "Are you in pain?"

"No, it's nothing physical. I mean, it *is* physical, but there's nothing specific that happened. I just feel it, that there's something wrong."

Barry sat upright in bed and let the covers slide from his bare chest. He rubbed at his eyes. "Jesus, Marie. What do you mean by wrong?"

Marie couldn't pinpoint the problem. It was free-floating and unidentifiable.

"I don't know. I just know something's not right."

Goosebumps formed on Barry's arms. Marie drew him back under the covers and rested her head on his chest. His heart beat a strong rhythm. He put his arm around her and held her close.

"How far along are you?"

He should know this, she thought. He shouldn't leave it all up to me.

"I'm not exactly sure. If this had been planned, I'd know, but I'm guessing it's eight weeks. Give or take a little."

They lay quietly together. A car drove by, its headlights straffing the bedroom ceiling.

"You should call Dr. Cuthbert."

"And tell her what? That I'm pregnant?"

"No, tell her you think there's something wrong. Maybe she could run a test or something."

Marie didn't respond. She knew it was too early for tests.

"But there's no sense getting worked up about this. We don't have any real evidence to say we should be concerned," Barry added.

"Other than I never had this feeling with the other pregnancies."

She cast her mind back to the early years of having an infant. Changing soiled diapers and walking with a crying baby seemed like a lifetime ago. Nicole had been such an easy baby; she'd just nursed and slept for the first few months of her life. And two years later, when Sophia was born, they realized just how lucky they'd been. Suddenly, when she was ten days old, Sophia started to cry. At first, Marie assumed she had eaten something she shouldn't have, and that the offending food had worked its way into her breast milk. But the crying didn't stop. Day and night Sophia cried, her face red and scrunched up, her legs kicking in anger and pain. A week went by. And then another. Dr. Cuthbert shook her head in sympathy. *We don't know what causes colic, exactly, but we do know that it usually ends at the three-month mark. Give or take a few days.* She and Barry had gone home and marked a big red X on the calendar on a date three months down the road. Then they continued to take turns passing the screaming baby.

It had been the longest three months of her life. When Barry left for work in the morning, Marie cried because she was afraid she might harm the baby. She remembered holding Nicole in her arms, tears streaming down her own cheeks, while Sophia screamed in another room. And she remembered how mad she was that no one in her family offered to help. Frances, still single at the time, was busy at university and never thought to drop by and relieve her sister. Her brother, Joe, was already married and had two kids of his own. She didn't expect any help from him. Or from her father, for that matter, who was in his final years of working and preparing for retirement. But she was very disappointed that her mother never stepped in to offer a hand. Mothers were supposed to *mother*, but Fay had made it abundantly clear that she'd already done her parenting. It was unspoken, but she had raised three children, with little help from her husband, or anyone else for that matter, and her job was done. Finally she was free to travel and do things for herself.

Elizabeth had been the only one to show up with a meal.

No, the baby stage wasn't easy. Seen in the distance it loomed like Everest.

"We need to talk," Marie said, glancing at the clock. "Do you know what you want?"

"I was slowly getting used to the idea of having a baby in the house again. But if there's something wrong with it . . ." He hesitated. "If you said you didn't want this baby, then I'd say don't have it."

Tears stung her eyes. "And if *you* said you really didn't want another baby, then I'd say the same thing. Or at least I *would* have, but it's a bit late now, isn't it?"

Barry had closed his eyes. The whiskery half of his face had disappeared into the shadows.

"Remember how easy it was with Nicole?" she said. "We couldn't wait to have a baby."

Barry smiled and nodded.

"And it was the same with Sophia."

"We wanted Nicole to have a sibling," he said.

"Yeah, someone to talk about her parents with. But maybe now, if we're both so ambivalent, then maybe we're not supposed to have another child."

"Being ambivalent doesn't mean we won't love it," Barry said.

"I know," Marie said, but she was older now. She didn't have as much energy. And she was scared now too.

Barry laughed softly. "We've jumped rather quickly into imagining ourselves with a disabled child."

"It's not funny." She bristled as she stepped out of bed. "Anyway, it's not like we're *deciding* whether or not to get pregnant. That part's already done." She had always been so careful in her life. What insurance would cover this? Genetic mutation insurance? Fear of having an imperfect child insurance? Your life has been wrecked insurance?

She shivered in the chill air. She felt caught in someone else's life, having the kind of conversation that teenaged lovers have when they discover an unwanted pregnancy. But she was almost forty; she wasn't supposed to be talking about aborting a child. She pulled her robe on and knotted the sash at her waist. She already had two children. And she loved her husband. Good people didn't talk about terminating pregnancies under such conditions, did they?

It was still dark. She felt Barry's eyes follow her across the room.

"You'd better hurry up," she said over her shoulder. "We're running a bit late."

"Will you call the doctor?" he asked.

She turned back to the bed. Barry sat with his knees drawn up, his eyes deep hollows in his face. He looked like a child ready to spit up in a bowl. She walked back to him and placed her palm on his forehead. His arms circled around her waist.

"I'll phone later."

She knew there was little a doctor could tell her now. But maybe he was right. The doctor should be informed at each step.

Downstairs at last, Marie scrambled some eggs for her daughters and set out the cereal, toast, coffee, and juice for Barry's breakfast. Then she made cheese sandwiches and put them in Ziploc bags inside the girls' brown paper sacs. She added an apple to each bag, two homemade cookies, and a juice box.

The girls zipped up their winter coats, and she kissed them good-bye. The fresh snow muffled the sounds of their boots and the cars driving slowly by on the unplowed road. The snow continued to fall. At the front window she watched Nicole and Sophia make tracks in the unmarked snow. They walked a large circle in the yard and then started to cut across it as if to make a maze. Marie looked at her watch and tapped on the window. She gestured toward the corner. The girls stared at her for a moment and then stepped out onto the freshly shovelled sidewalk before walking down the middle of the road to the corner. A group of kids already stood there waiting, throwing snowballs and making snow angels.

The sky was grey and low. Snow swirled from its murky depths. The naked elm trees looked as if they were single-handedly keeping the sky from falling.

Minutes later, the school bus pulled to a stop at the corner. The kids automatically lined up, their snowsuits bright as gumdrops. Then the bus and the children soundlessly disappeared.

Marie returned to the kitchen and began her morning cleanup. This was the favourite part of her day, when the house was completely empty and she could return things to their proper place and remove every fingerprint from every surface. She rinsed the dishes and loaded them into the dishwasher. With a fresh dishcloth she wiped the counters and the table. She sprayed the toaster with Windex and heard her sister's voice, "Is that the same toaster you got at your wedding? It looks brand new." Or, "Hey, Marie, I see a fingerprint on your toaster." She said it as if it were a criticism, as if nobody else in the world took good care of their possessions. Marie stood back to survey her work. She was pleased to be in control of the standards in her own home. It had been a long time coming. Growing up she'd had to battle against her sister's slothful ways. Cleaning the kitchen together had been unbearable. Frances always wanted to wash instead of dry the dishes. So Marie would wait, towel in hand, and Frances would plow through the dirty pile as if the house was on fire. Dish after dish filled the drying rack, all with some kind of crud left on them. Marie would refuse to dry them if they were dirty, and Frances would refuse to wash them again after a second rinse. "It's good enough!" she'd hiss through clenched teeth, and then she'd drain the sink and leave the greasy residue to set into a hard crust.

When the kitchen was clean and a load of laundry was in the wash, Marie phoned the doctor's office and made an appointment. Then she phoned Barry.

She could picture him in his office on the twenty-first floor, the phone cradled against his shoulder. His window faced south and overlooked the river valley. It was a lovely view. South of the river were four glass pyramids, the Muttart Conservatory, that squatted like giant icebergs pushed up from the river's depths. Farther still and toward the east, billows of smoke from the tall stacks at Refinery Row would obscure his view of Sherwood Park. To the west, the High Level Bridge spanned the river like a long line of boxcars shunted together. Beyond it, the varied buildings of the university huddled along the south banks.

"I've made a doctor's appointment for late Friday afternoon. Can you come with me?"

"What time?"

"Four o'clock."

"Do you want me to?"

"If you don't want to come, just say so."

What Barry really wanted to know was if his presence was necessary. Was it just another appointment or would she find anything out? Despite her irritation, she didn't want to hang up on him.

The backs of her hands had blue veins on them, thick as earthworms. She had aged imperceptibly. While sleeping, while sweeping the floor. She pictured her husband slumped heavily in his chair at work, his jowls pushing out from his freshly starched collar.

The premonition tapped her on the shoulder. She turned to find an empty room.

She walked to the sliding glass doors that led to the backyard. The children's snow fort had collapsed onto one side. February and its drabness stretched out before her.

I want it to be spring, she thought. I want the trees to bud and the robins to sing.

An airplane crossed the sky like a zipper parting the clouds.

Not a spot of colour anywhere she looked.

TWELVE
1963

Why this orderly insisted on leading her was baffling. She knew the way by heart—the map had been permanently seared into her memory. Carolyn was sixteen now, and Margaret had been visiting for twelve years. Once a month, predictable as her own cycle, she nodded wordlessly to the driver of the asylum bus, stepped up the narrow stairs, and avoided eye contact with the other passengers. Sometime during her early visits to Poplar Grove her reflexes had dulled to the abuse and misery she witnessed around her because she knew that she didn't really have other options. To raise her voice against the injustices would sooner or later involve her husband and children; she'd kept her secret for too long, and Carolyn still needed a home.

The air grew thicker with each step that brought her closer to the mongoloids, housed in the west wing. To see them all together at the same time was to witness a macabre family reunion, so much did they resemble one another, with their broad faces, slanted eyes, and thick wrestler's necks. Nothing made her daughter stand out in this crowd. Carolyn, who could feed and dress herself, was as much a societal reject as the rest of them. She more resembled the other mongoloids than she did her flesh-and-blood brother and sister. In fact, when Margaret looked deep into her first-born daughter's eyes, cupping Carolyn's dimpled chin in her hand and gripping hard to keep eye contact, she saw no hint of her own genetic makeup or that of her husband's. Nothing. If she hadn't birthed the child herself, suffering through the long contractions until her body released the six and a half pounds of sadness, she'd have in good faith denied all familial ties.

Her first visit a dozen years ago had been the hardest, and it appeared to Margaret that the conditions inside Poplar Grove had improved modestly over time. Or perhaps she had lost the ability to be shocked. Still, as she followed the male orderly down an endless yet familiar hallway and through another locked door, she couldn't help but notice how the stench intensified. She could be a seagull at the dump, diving quick and hard for any scrap of spoiled food. Or a crow diving for shiny bits of treasure. What did she dive for here? A smile? Maybe what she dived for was reconciliation. If Margaret could love and accept her damaged daughter, maybe it would erase the pain of having been abandoned by her own mother. It wasn't her fault she'd gone to the creek that day. Her mother was wrong about that. Stuart Jenkins would have found her in the chicken coop, in the barn, or in the garden. She knew that now. Margaret had never considered bringing her other children to visit. It was unthinkable. James and Rebecca were teenagers now too, and it was impossible to imagine springing the news of a mongoloid sister on them.

No, Carolyn had been forgotten by everyone but her, and Margaret wanted it to stay that way.

The orderly gestured toward the corner of the overcrowded room, then retraced his heavy steps down the dark hall. Margaret would let herself out, as she always did.

In the cavernous room Carolyn sat on a wooden bench facing a blank grey wall. Completely immobile, she could have been cast in cement. She stared intently at the wall, as if waiting for an image to appear. The Virgin Mary? Jesus? The other mongoloids were either staring, pacing, or rocking. Carolyn's hands rested upturned in her lap. Red creases scarred her wrists, but at least today her hands weren't restricted and she was fully clothed, unlike some of the women in plain view who appeared to enjoy the coolness of the linoleum on their nakedness, exploring their bodies without shame. Margaret was repulsed and dug deep within herself to find that place where love resided. But, oh, how she would love to spray the room down with a hose and cleanse all the unwashed bodies and urine and feces that stained the floor. That and grab a pair of scissors to take the mats out of the patients' hair. But they would never be clean. None of them, so steeped were they in daily filth. To see just one of them at a time wouldn't be so bad, but a room full of filthy, guttural mongoloids was almost too much to bear.

"Carolyn?" she said quietly as she drew near her motionless daughter. "It's me."

The girl turned her head and stared. Slowly a light went on in her eyes and she began her inarticulate mumbling, of which Margaret could make little sense. It was no wonder her daughter hadn't learned to speak—in all of her visits over the years Margaret had never seen anyone talk to her daughter. If the staff didn't talk to Carolyn, how could she have ever learned to talk to them?

Margaret wiped the saliva from around her daughter's mouth and allowed herself to be hugged briefly before pushing Carolyn firmly away. "None of that now," she said. Her daughter wanted to touch her at all times. Even now, at sixteen, she'd easily climb into her mother's lap if allowed, no matter that her stout body was no match for her mother's slim one.

Carolyn reached for her mother's outstretched hand and took the single red rose gently from her grasp. She had learned over the years to watch out for the thorns. She lifted the flower to her nose and inhaled deeply. Then she turned and began pulling her mother toward the hallway.

"Yes," Margaret said, "we'll go outside."

It was their ritual, when the weather was fair. From the eagerness with which Carolyn pulled her toward the door Margaret suspected that she didn't get outside much, if at all, and she loved being outside. She especially adored watching the birds and, when summer arrived, touching the roses that grew in a flowerbed next to their favourite bench.

It was Monday. Her other children were in school until three-thirty. The bus back to the city left in an hour. Sunshine would do Carolyn good.

Another attendant stationed at the locked door to the courtyard let them outside, where the fresh air seemed even sweeter because of the stark contrast. May could be a beautiful month, and if you could see beyond the shoddy chickenwire fence that surrounded the courtyard and acted as a deterrent from venturing afar, you could believe the open fields nearby led to freedom.

Carolyn shuffled along on her flat feet in sneakers without laces. Her grey buttonless shirt fit snugly over her midriff and a flash of skin showed between the bottom of her shirt and the black elasticized waistband on her pants. It looked as if her clothes had been shrunk in the dryer by a lazy laundress who'd equated smaller clothes with less work.

They walked toward the bench beneath the poplar tree with its lime-green leaves fresh from the buds. Margaret sat upwind from Carolyn and noted a splotchy patch around her collar, a flush that disappeared down into her shirt. It couldn't be a heat rash at this time of year. Bedbugs? No, the rash wouldn't be so isolated. An allergy, maybe? Perhaps new laundry detergent in the clothes or sheets, although only God knew how infrequently the laundry was done—probably the day before visiting day. She looked once again at the shrunken shirt that her daughter was wearing and then suspicion focused her gaze. Something had changed. Carolyn's hands rested in her lap, palms up, but even her lap seemed different. Smaller. Less spacious. Her cheeks were flushed and her fingers were puffy. And the girl's bosom was expansive.

Slowly the pieces fit together to make a picture Margaret didn't want to see. A picture so fantastic as to not be real. Surely the signs would have been visible the previous month. How had she not noticed?

No. It can't be. She shook her head fiercely as her eyes raked her daughter's body. Who had done this to her?

She leaned over and retched on the base of the tree. Her daughter was supposed to be safe here. Safe!

She wiped her mouth with a tissue and hauled Carolyn to her feet. Margaret had voiced her fear about pregnancy to the doctors when Carolyn started menstruating, but they'd brushed her concerns away, saying it could never happen. Mongoloids were unfinished children, they said. Their organs were only partially developed at birth. She'd been assured that no child could possibly grow in a body that was unfinished. Well, obviously the doctors were wrong!

Margaret dragged Carolyn's sluggish body behind her, pulling hard to hurry her along, and stabbed at the buzzer beside the door to the building.

"Open up!" she screamed, banging with the palm of her free hand.

The orderly who had led her through the hallways opened the door. This time Margaret noted his unshaven face and sallow skin, his long and dirty fingernails. He appeared almost as unwashed as the patients, and when he smiled his teeth were a putrid yellow, stained, no doubt, from years of chewing tobacco. She couldn't help but notice his thin brown leather belt, the end of which flopped softly from years of usage. Margaret felt a current of disgust jolt her to the core. What had they called these kind of orderlies? Bug-house bums, yes, unemployed workers without skills who had drifted along the tides of the Great Depression, floating from one institution to another. Filth! She'd seen his type before, preying on the disadvantaged.

Dragging Carolyn from the orderly's deceitful eyes she felt a cry build in intensity as she sped toward the office of the director of the institute, Dr. Maclean. "No!" she hissed with as much force as she could muster. "*No!*"

Carolyn's hand was hot in her own. She continued to pull her along. Her sweet child. It wasn't her fault she'd been born this way. And to have this happen to her! Margaret bit her lower lip so hard that she tasted blood. Who could do this? What deviously warped individual could take advantage of a damaged child? Dr. Maclean was one of the newer doctors, one who actually seemed to take an interest in his patients. She arrived at his door and quickly wiped her face before bursting in, not bothering to knock. The doctor looked up from his files, startled by the sudden disruption.

Margaret pushed Carolyn in front of her and pointed. "What is this?" Her voice sounded shrill and accusing. "How do you explain this?"

The doctor looked at Carolyn, and Margaret could tell he was trying to recall her name. Her daughter could be any one of them, for all he knew. They all looked alike, with their greasy crewcut hair. He turned his gaze to the girl's midriff, as directed, and Margaret saw him note the gentle swell that pushed outward, the breasts that appeared heavy and full. He stood up and approached her.

"Mrs. . . . ."

"Harrington."

"Yes." He nodded, then turned Carolyn sideways to view her protruding midsection. "It's uncanny," he whispered.

"Look at how the weight gain is isolated to her midriff," Margaret said. The initial panic was over and a calm had descended over her, if you could call it that, for her leg began to tremble so violently that she had to sit down.

"Yes," he agreed, "but let's not be hasty. I've never heard of such a case before. Perhaps it is a tumour. Mongoloids are certainly prone to illness and disease. I don't want to jump to conclusions. It may not be as it appears."

Already she began to think of her real family, the daughter and son she'd taught to care for themselves. The children who brought home good grades and played the piano and knew right from wrong. The children who bathed themselves and emerged from steamy bathrooms smelling sweet and fresh. They'd have pot roast for dinner, with potatoes and carrots, all simmered together in a large black roasting pan, just like her mother used to make. Maybe she'd bake a cake—double chocolate, their favourite, and buy vanilla ice cream on the way home. Yes, they'd have a quiet evening at home—maybe play a board game or watch a movie. Carolyn was in the doctor's care now. He seemed like a good man, although he was very young, probably not even thirty. A decade her junior. But at least he was clean-shaven and wearing a tie. He was about the only bright spot in this place, the only person she felt comfortable leaving her daughter with. She could go home now. Yes. Home. She rubbed her hands together, wishing she could lather them with a strong soap.

Having regained her composure, she stood, indicating the end of their unscheduled meeting.

"You and your people have created this situation and now you're going to have to deal with it," she said, working hard to keep her voice from trembling. "The board of directors will have something to say about this, I'm sure." Even as the words left her mouth she knew how preposterous they were. To raise any fuss would mean involving her husband and children.

Dr. Maclean nodded. "You're absolutely right. The board members will have to know. They will want a full report."

Margaret's knees buckled, and she sat heavily in the chair. Another doctor involved in her life. He would believe he knew what was best, and he'd never admit that people of his profession had created the situation to begin with. Would Dr. Maclean and his colleagues explain away the situation? Her mother's words came back to her. *It's a woman's lot in life to bear the shame.* But why should it be? Why didn't men carry the burden of their own bad behaviours?

She stood quickly. Black spots swam before her eyes, and she felt a light loss of sensation from the neck down as she fell forward, senseless, to the ground.

On Friday afternoon, Marie and her husband sat side by side in the doctor's waiting room, six floors up from the sidewalk. More than a dozen chairs were set in a rectangle, in the middle of which stood a low table covered in magazines and newspapers.

A woman seated in the corner coughed without covering her mouth. Beside her, a mother cradled a young boy in her lap and tried to keep him from scratching the red rash that covered one side of his face. Marie breathed shallowly and reminded herself to wash her hands once she'd left. She reached for the stack of reading material on the table. A story headline on the cover of a cheap tabloid caught her attention: MOTHER SAVES SON'S SPERM. A picture showed a dark-haired woman in her late thirties holding a test tube.

"Look at this!" she said, elbowing Barry in the arm. "This woman's son died of cancer, but before he died she had him leave some sperm at a sperm bank. She plans to one day buy a donor egg, have it fertilized *by her son's sperm*, and then implant it into her womb! Can you imagine? She'll be giving birth to her own grandchild!"

"Is that even legal?" Barry asked.

Marie snorted and shook her head. God, the situations some people got into.

The air in the waiting room was suddenly close. Marie inhaled slowly to steady herself. Barry had his nose in the sports page. He didn't notice that there were too many people in the small room. Or that the sun was too bright.

Like in Arizona. Her mother had phoned from there the day before.

"How's everything in Edmonton?" she'd shouted, as if the phone couldn't carry her voice over that distance.

"Fine," Marie replied. "Everything's fine here."

"And the girls?"

"They're fine too. You and Dad have missed some pretty cold weather. It's just warmed up in the last few days. Now we're getting snow."

Fay loved to hear how they'd escaped a deep freeze. They talked for a while about the dangers of black ice on the roads.

"Have you seen Frances lately?"

"She's coming over on Friday. Max sure is cute. He just nurses and smiles all the time."

"Well, he should smile! He gets everything he wants!" Fay said. Then she lowered her voice. "I don't think your sister is very happy with me right now."

Marie pretended to be surprised. "Why?"

"Well, she was complaining about not getting any sleep, saying how exhausted she was, so I told her to let Max cry it out. I said he'd get used to it, and so would she."

Marie winced.

"And I also said Max should be sleeping in a crib in his own room."

"What did she say to that?"

Fay sighed. "She said that parenting had changed since you guys were young. But nobody ever called Social Services on me! If you want to know what *I* think, *I* think that women weren't meant to start having kids at thirty-five. They try too hard to do everything perfectly. I think it was a blessing that my friends and I had kids when we were so young. We didn't know any better. We never jumped to attention the second one of our babies cried. Nowadays mothers get up in the middle of the night and scramble eggs for their kids if they want them! Can you imagine? Thankfully we were too young to know how to do things *perfectly*. I didn't tell Frances that though. Your father wouldn't let me."

Any desire Marie had had to tell her mother about the pregnancy disappeared. "She's just trying to do her best, Mom," Marie said. "She just wants your support." *We basically raised ourselves*, she wanted to say, *because you were always too busy to listen. You never listened.*

"Well, how do you support someone who never asks for help?"

Marie wanted to tell her mother that she should show up without waiting to be asked, or just drop off a meal every now and then. People often needed help the most when they were the least able to ask for it.

She clenched the phone in her hands. The words *I'm pregnant* almost came out of her mouth. She tried to imagine her mother's response. *For crying out loud; you're no spring chicken.*

"Did you get my postcard yet?" Fay asked.

"No, maybe tomorrow."

"Well, take care. Tell the girls that we say hi."

"I will," Marie said. "Give my love to Dad."

The phone went dead in her hand.

Marie reached for her purse and pulled a cracker from a Ziploc bag. Lately her nausea extended throughout the entire day.

The phone rang at regular intervals at the front desk. Five women in matching pale green uniforms pulled files and answered the calls that never stopped. From down the hall wafted the smell of disinfectant. The woman in the corner had another coughing fit. She still didn't cover her mouth. Marie shifted in her seat and closed her eyes. Someone in the room was wearing too much perfume.

She turned her attention to her husband. A late afternoon shadow covered his cheeks. By the morning, his whiskers would have broken cleanly through the thick skin on the lower half of his face and neck. Then he'd do what he always did: bang his electric shaver against his fist to empty the old whiskers into the toilet bowl. After he shaved, he'd forget to flush the toilet, even though she'd asked him to a million times, and all his whiskers would cling to the side of the porcelain bowl like metal filings to a magnet and she would have to get the brush out and scour it clean.

Barry read on, unaware that he was the object of her scrutiny. She felt the beginning of a resentment searching for a resting place in her chest. For a brief moment she wished he wasn't with her. It would be nice to be alone.

Finally, the receptionist called Marie's name. She and Barry followed one of the doctor's assistants down the hall to an examination room.

The room wasn't much bigger than a walk-in closet and held the usual equipment—an examination table with a disposable sheet of white paper on top and stirrups at the end, a blood pressure sleeve and pump, and a glass jar full of cotton swabs that sat next to the stainless steel sink.

It was all so predictable. How many times had she seen the poster with diagrams of the inner nose, illustrating various nasal conditions?

Barry stepped onto the scale next to the table and frowned. There was no way she was going to check her own weight. She already felt a bad mood coming on.

Marie heard someone outside pull her chart from the door rack. A few seconds later, Dr. Cuthbert walked in, smiling.

"Hi, Marie," she said and then turned back to her file to search quickly for her husband's name.

"Barry," he said, shaking her hand.

"Ah, yes," the doctor replied. "It's been a while, Barry. Since the birth of your youngest, I think. When was that?" She consulted her chart again and laughed. "Ten years already! How are your girls doing?"

"I'm pregnant," Marie blurted.

The doctor waited for Marie to proceed.

"I know this is going to sound strange," she said, instinctively moving her hand to her belly, "but I woke up a few nights ago convinced that something is wrong with the baby."

The doctor nodded. "Premonitions aren't unusual," she said. "Lots of mothers have them, but they're also not accurate assessments of a baby's condition."

"This wasn't a planned pregnancy," Marie added. "And now we want to know more about the baby's health before we make any decisions."

Barry listened while Marie and the doctor spoke, nodding occasionally to show his support.

"Well," Dr. Cuthbert said, referring again to her chart. "You're thirty-nine, correct? The standard genetic counselling we give suggests that women thirty-five and over have amniocentesis. Just to be safe. As I'm sure you know, maternal age plays a role in chromosomal abnormalities." She paused to write a quick note in Marie's file. "If you're concerned about the baby and want to know more about its health, the most accurate test we have right now is amniocentesis."

The doctor looked at the calendar. "What I'll do today is schedule you for an ultrasound. Are you sure about your dates?"

Marie shook her head. "Not entirely, no."

"Okay. At the ultrasound we can take some measurements and get a better idea of your due date. An ultrasound at eleven to twelve weeks will give us the best results, and we can also at that time look for some soft markers of Down syndrome. If you decide to have amniocentesis, you'll have to wait until at least your sixteenth week of pregnancy, to be safe." She jotted a few notes in her chart. "We could do a pre-screening blood test too, if you like, but the amnio gives us much more reliable information. Any questions?"

Marie and Barry shook their heads.

"Well then," she added brightly, "let's proceed with the ultrasound for now, and, if you like, I'll schedule you for amnio in about two months."

Dr. Cuthbert's file snapped shut. She repeated that Marie's intuition didn't confirm any abnormalities and then started for the door.

"Excuse me," Barry said. "Do you mean we won't have any idea of our baby's condition for another eight weeks?"

The doctor nodded. "The ultrasound will give us a preliminary idea of the baby's condition. However, unless there is some obvious physical deformity, we'll have to wait for the amniocentesis results, yes."

The afternoon sun had already slipped behind the University Hospital when they left the doctor's office.

A white Jetta drove slowly by in the bumper-to-bumper flow and honked its horn.

"Hey, there's Elizabeth," Marie said, waving.

"Oh, great," Barry said. "Bring on the guilt."

Marie's mood altered instantly, as if someone had touched a dial and switched it from medium—moderate contentment—to low—irritability. She felt the click and immediately her perception changed. She'd only just stepped out of the heated building, but already her feet felt cold. Why hadn't Barry parked underground, like she'd asked him to? He could at least have left early and warmed the car. She hated winter. Hated having to gather the scarves, sweaters, mittens, hats, and jackets that were necessary to keep warm. Hated how her kids routinely lost gloves and expected new ones to magically appear. She clumped heavily along the shovelled sidewalk in her winter boots. With each boot fall she felt a greater burden on her shoulders, and a mammoth fatigue lodged in her bones. The sound echoed off the building and rode the wind around her. She walked past a store window and was startled by her reflection. She looked like her sister, with a hate-on for the world.

Suddenly she realized she was mad at everyone: her husband, her mother, her sister. Even Elizabeth, who hadn't called since she'd moved. She hadn't even pulled over to the curb to say hi. Instead, she'd honked and waved, as if that was as good as a visit.

She hurried to the car and waited impatiently for Barry to open the door.

Barry eased the car into rush hour traffic.

"I'm sick of this," he said, gripping the steering wheel tightly with both hands. "One wrong word and you clam up."

She stared straight ahead, her lips a hard blue line.

"It's like walking on eggshells with you. You act as if you're the only one worried about the baby. But I've been thinking about it too, you know. Christ, I can't go anywhere these days without seeing someone in a wheelchair and wondering if that's what our future holds." He paused and added, "We're not in competition, you know."

Fifteen minutes later their garage door opened and Barry eased the car into the small space between her van and the toboggans lying against the garage wall.

Marie remained in the passenger seat and watched his back disappear. The garage door closed automatically. A few minutes later, the overhead light clicked off. How long would she have to sit in the garage before he worried that she might freeze to death and come out and check on her? Obviously he didn't care that she was angry. She sat in darkness and breathed through her mouth to avoid the industrial smells of gasoline and oil. As her eyes adjusted to the dark she saw the outlines of her children's bicycles hanging from hooks in the rafters like the carcasses of deer.

It wasn't long before the chill began to creep into her bones. Barry probably wouldn't notice she was still outside until six o'clock, when dinner wasn't on the table. They always ate at six o'clock sharp. Barry liked it that way. She did too, most of the time. It only bothered her when she was mad at him, then she blamed him for all kinds of things, like making her adhere to a random schedule that he made appear fixed. In reality, it was good to have dinner ready for six. The girls knew their homework needed to be done by then, and it gave Marie a firm deadline to prepare for.

The cold was now a scarf at her neck. She shivered and gave herself a hug. What she didn't need right now was to get sick. She had enough to think about without losing a few days in bed. The light came on when she opened the car door. She quickly stepped into the darkness and slammed the door behind her.

The house smelled wonderful when she walked in. She'd forgotten that she'd asked Frances to be at the house when the girls came home from school. It was good to have an icebreaker.

In the kitchen two cooling racks sat on the counter beside the sink, lined with chocolate chip cookies. The sink was full of mixing bowls and measuring cups. Flour dusted the counters. A bag of sugar rested on its side, tiny granules of white crystals spilled out like tropical sand. A pound of partially used butter sat slowly melting in its wrapper.

Frances sat on the loveseat nursing Max.

Marie ran some hot water into the sink and began to clean the mess that Frances and the girls had left. "What snack did you make? Grilled cheese?"

Frances nodded. "How was the doctor's?"

"Fine," Marie said.

"Well, what did she say?" Frances persisted.

"She scheduled me for an ultrasound in a couple of weeks and for an amnio in two months."

"Why is she scheduling you for amnio?"

"It's standard procedure," Marie said. "They suggest it for all women over thirty-five."

"Who's they?" Frances asked cynically. "The doctors? Or all the people who make money from scaring perfectly healthy women?"

Marie felt the hair on the back of her neck prickle. She heard the anger in Frances's voice and remembered, too late, that her sister, not quite two years younger, had been thirty-six when Max was born. She would have had the same choices presented to her.

"You do know," Frances continued, "that your chances of having a child with something wrong with it are the same as your chances of miscarrying from having amnio?"

Marie immersed her hands up to her elbows into the hot soapy water and closed her eyes. She wished Frances would shut up for a change and stop trotting out her facts and figures, especially when nobody asked for her opinion.

"Do you want to stay for dinner?"

Her hands swept the bottom of the sink.

"Did the doctor tell you that?" Frances persisted. "That your risk of miscarrying is the same as your risk of having something be wrong with your child?"

To be fair, Frances knew nothing about her premonition. "But those risks are both low, aren't they?" Marie said. "So why not find out if there's a problem?"

"Why don't you at least call my midwife? She's great. She—"

"Your midwife won't be able to fix anything that might be wrong, Frances."

"I didn't say she could. I'm just saying that if you go looking for trouble, you'll find it."

Marie rinsed the frying pan and the stainless steel bowls and stacked them on the drying rack beside the sink. Frances really was a know-it-all. The day after Max was born, she was a sudden expert on childbirth, and on home birth in particular.

Would Frances have been so exuberant if some emergency had forced her to be moved to the hospital? Probably not. She was still on her post-birth high, so Marie had overlooked that her sister was indirectly criticizing her own decisions to have her kids in the hospital. But what she didn't tell Frances was that she *liked* being in the hospital; she *liked* being surrounded by equipment that beeped and buzzed and let her know at all times what her baby's heart rate was; she even *liked* having the student doctors come in because she was contributing to the medical care and well-being of future women.

Unlike Frances, Marie didn't think that hospitals were barbaric places to give birth in. On the contrary, she found the idea of having a baby at home, without the possibility of drugs, to be unthinkable. Crazy even. Why endure all that pain if you didn't have to? Of *course* women in the old days gave birth at home all the time, aided by midwives or local doctors, but many of them had died too. And back then they also washed their clothes by hand, burned wood to keep warm, hauled water, did all of their own baking, killed their own chickens, used an outhouse, and read by candlelight. She didn't see Frances depriving herself of any other modern conveniences.

Marie pulled the plug in the sink and listened to the water gurgle its quick descent. "Look, Frances, Barry and I have talked about it, and we've decided to have the test. So I'd appreciate if you didn't conjure up any statistics on how it's unsafe."

Frances draped a receiving blanket over her shoulder and burped Max. She leaned against the counter where Marie chopped vegetables for her pasta sauce. "I'm only trying to help. Hospitals and tests are for sick people. You're pregnant, not sick. Those tests will just screw with your brain. I know a woman who had one of those blood tests done, the alphafetaprotein or whatever it's called. She figured she was healthy; why not let them have a look at her blood? But the test came back saying she had a higher risk of having a baby with Down syndrome. A one in 294 chance or something ridiculous like that, and when she did the math she figured out that was half a percent! And for that her pregnancy was ruined."

Marie kept her gaze low and continued her chopping. What about the couples who found out something *was* wrong and were able to make informed decisions? Did they count?

"My midwife says—"

"Look," Marie interrupted. "I already told you that Barry and I have talked about it," she said, her voice shaking, "and we've decided to have the test."

The two sisters stared at each other. The vegetables sizzled in the frying pan. Max grabbed a fistful of his mother's hair. The radio droned on in the background.

Frances finally averted her gaze and sat down at the kitchen table. "I'm only trying to help."

Marie heard the self-pity in her sister's voice and wanted to scream. "I didn't mean to snap your head off. I'm just a little worried right now." She picked up a cookie and walked toward her sister, extending it as an offering of peace.

"Mom says to say hi, by the way. She called yesterday."

"Yeah, well, hi back. She never calls me."

"That's because she loves me more," Marie said. They laughed, fully aware of the truth in her joke.

"Have you told her yet that you're pregnant?"

"No, not yet. I'm going to wait until the test comes back before I do."

"You're going to wait two months?"

"Frances, we're not sure we want this baby, okay? Until we decide, I'm not telling Mom or Dad anything."

"That's probably wise," she said. They both remembered Fay's response to the abortion Frances had when she was seventeen. It was the first time Marie had ever seen her mother cry. But she'd made all the arrangements and drove Frances there herself. She never did learn who the father was because Frances wouldn't tell her. There was a price to pay after all for not listening to your children. They didn't suddenly start talking to you when things got bad, just like a person didn't run a marathon without first training. Marie knew that Frances had secretly appreciated that neither parent had asked too many questions, but she'd resented having to include Fay in her life at all. If she could have arranged the abortion herself and not told her mother, she would have, but she was a minor; she had to have an adult with her for the hospital to perform the procedure.

Marie added red peppers and mushrooms to the mixture in the frying pan. Then she put a big pot of water on the stove to boil.

Nicole and Sophia came running into the kitchen. "Hi, Mom," they said. "What's for dinner?"

Marie opened her arms for a hug. She kissed both girls on the head and glanced up at the clock. Almost six o'clock. Barry would be wandering in at any moment, ready to eat. Well, supper would be a bit late today. Hopefully it wouldn't wreck his entire evening.

She hugged her daughters again and asked them to set the table.

"What did you do in school today?" she asked.

Their noncommittal responses echoed softly off the walls.

It happened so quickly that Dr. Maclean wasn't prepared for the patient's mother to tumble headlong from the chair onto the floor. He rushed to her side and took her pulse, but she quickly came to and was determined to leave immediately.

"Rest for a moment," he said and helped her to her chair. He poured a glass of water and handed it to her. "Drink this."

She drank deeply, as if she'd been parched for days.

Carolyn, meanwhile, had found the couch and had slumped into its corner.

"I'm sorry," Mrs. Harrington said, smoothing her dark hair in an attempt to restore some order. "This is more than a shock. I can't quite . . ." She removed a handkerchief from her purse and dabbed at her eyes and nose. "How did this happen?" she moaned, gesturing with her hands around the room and at her daughter, who had nodded off. "None of this was supposed to happen!"

Dr. Maclean understood intuitively that she was talking about the big picture of her life. She wasn't supposed to have had a child with Down syndrome, she wasn't supposed to spend an afternoon a month in a place like Poplar Grove, and she certainly wasn't supposed to discover that her mongoloid daughter was pregnant. He himself didn't want to dwell on the possibilities of how that pregnancy had occurred, or on the possibility of what that pregnancy might produce. The doctor had small children of his own at home; he remembered how his wife had worried when she was pregnant, largely because he'd made the mistake of bringing her to Poplar Grove when he accepted the job. He had wanted Joanne to be able to imagine him in his work setting when he was gone for nine hours a day. But all she took in was the room lined with cribs housing damaged babies. So many in one place made the odds of it happening to her seem that much greater.

"I have to go now," Mrs. Harrington said, standing more steadily this time and moving toward the door.

Dr. Maclean put his hand on her arm. "I must repeat that this might not be what it seems. To my knowledge, mongoloid pregnancies are not possible."

"Forgive me, Dr. Maclean, but I am sick to death of doctors' so-called knowledge." She glanced at her watch.

"The bus doesn't leave for another ten minutes. Why not sit and rest a moment to steady yourself."

She ignored his comment and removed a pair of white gloves from her purse before meticulously pulling each finger firmly into place.

"Goodbye, doctor."

He nodded. "Once again I ask you, please, don't jump—"

She held a gloved hand up to silence him. Such a large gesture for a petite woman. Yet one that suggested she could be formidable if pushed. He noticed the cut of her clothes, and her well-coiffed hair. All the more surprising, then, that she was able to visit Poplar Grove at all. For if ever there was squalor, it could surely be found here.

Mrs. Harrington nodded her official goodbye, took a long look at her daughter, and then marched deliberately down the hallway. Her posture was erect, almost regal, as she walked out the front door and down the steps to where the asylum bus waited.

Dr. Maclean closed his office door. What was he supposed to do now? He looked at Carolyn. In her slouched position she looked so obviously pregnant that he couldn't believe he hadn't noticed earlier. She could be as much as five to eight months along. But all the literature maintained that mongoloids weren't able to bear children. He'd had no cause to look for pregnancy in a population in which it wasn't supposed to occur.

But what if the literature was wrong? What kind of child would she produce?

He watched as Carolyn stirred and stared at the closed door. She made some incomprehensible sounds that were slurred by her thick tongue. If only she could tell him what had happened.

He stepped toward her and gently touched her arm. Pointing to her belly he asked, "Who did this to you?"

Carolyn's chin dipped forward until it rested on her chest.

Taking her hand, he placed it on her swollen stomach and asked again, "Who did this to you?"

The girl pulled back as if she'd touched a burning surface. "Un uh," she mumbled, shaking her head. "Un uh."

Was she even capable of connecting the two events? Sex and pregnancy? He couldn't expect her to understand she had a baby growing inside of her.

He grabbed the stethoscope from his desk drawer and approached the young girl, rubbing the end in his hands to warm it. "I'm just going to have a listen now . . ." She pushed his hand away as he lifted the edge of her shirt. "It's okay. Just a quick listen."

There it was. He shook his head in disbelief at the sound travelling through the stethoscope. Another heartbeat, clear as a bell. She was at least seven months along.

Dr. Maclean moved quickly toward the row of metal filing cabinets along the opposite wall. He pulled open a drawer and muttered distractedly to himself before removing a file. Then he opened another drawer and repeated the process before carrying his findings to his desk.

He opened the first file. "Carolyn Jane Harrington," he read out loud, glancing again at the patient before him. Born at the Misericordia Hospital on June 15, 1947. The attending physician, Dr. Morrison, provided the standard counselling and suggested immediate institutionalization. He and the parents subsequently signed the appropriate paperwork for the infant's confinement at Poplar Grove Provincial Training Centre.

The doctor continued to flip through the papers, reading the various comments of other doctors over the years. "The patient is delayed in nearly all of her milestones." "The patient did not walk until age five." "The patient was not completely toilet-trained until age eight." "The patient is extremely dull-witted." The doctor threw the file to the corner of his desk, disgusted by the useless information it held. He could be reading about any of the 967 patients under lock and key. There was nothing unique about Carolyn.

Until now.

He reached for the other file and flipped carefully through the papers inside until he found a mimeographed copy of an article that had been published in a recent issue of an obstetrics journal. Scanning quickly, he finally came to a passage that caught his attention. *One of the characteristic deficiencies of mongoloids is in sexual development. Next to nothing is known about the reproductive powers in mongols, since the majority of patients succumb to some acute illness or to congenital heart disease and thus do not reach reproductive age.* He nodded and recalled the many deaths at Poplar Grove and its large cemetery that constantly pushed against its borders.

The majority of those who survive the first years of life are committed to institutions for the feeble-minded, which precludes any possibility of reproducing offspring . . . although one could well imagine that this would not be absolutely impossible in mongols of both sexes with a higher grade of intelligence and good physical development.

The latter part of the sentence appeared suddenly as if printed in bold red letters . . . *one could well imagine that this would not be absolutely impossible* . . . He snapped the file closed. Across the room, Carolyn had drifted back to sleep. He stared at her face, took in the short nose with the broad nasal bridge; the thickened, averted lower lip; the open mouth with the protruding tongue; the dark, matted hair framing her round face. When had someone last put a comb through her hair? And what about the man who'd done this to her? Was it at all possible that Carolyn might have been a willing participant? Or was it yet another example of her being roughly treated and abused? Dr. Maclean shook his head in dismay. Hadn't he turned a blind eye from time to time when he'd seen a patient being roughly treated? And why? Because even he, a professional in charge of helping these patients, sometimes leaned on the convenient belief that they didn't really know what was happening to them anyway.

He rummaged through his desk and pulled out a black notebook. He cracked the spine, turned to the first page, and wrote the date.

May 16, 1963
A remarkable event has occurred of which I'm trying to make sense. Today one of my patients' mothers stormed

into my office with her daughter in tow. The cause of her rage was not immediately clear to me, but when she explained herself more fully I understood. It appears the girl is pregnant. What is remarkable here is that she's not one of the regular mental defectives (who are healthy in body but not in mind), most of whom, I believe, if they've reached sexual maturity, have been sterilized. In this case, Carolyn is a sixteen-year-old mongoloid who, after my examination, appears to be into her seventh month of pregnancy.

I will search for other cases, but to my immediate knowledge I do not know of other female mongoloids who have become pregnant. One article from an obstetrics journal published in 1960 did mention, however, that in terms of the reproductive powers of mongoloids with good physical development, one could well imagine that pregnancy would not be absolutely impossible.

Whether or not Carolyn will deliver a child remains to be seen. If she does carry to term, I can only assume that the child will also be a mongoloid.

He stopped writing and shifted his attention to a name and number on the Rolodex. With trepidation Dr. Maclean picked up the phone and dialled the board chair.

"Dr. Stallworthy? It's Michael Maclean. Of Poplar Grove. I think we have a rather unfortunate situation here."

In her chair, Carolyn's head slowly tilted to the side as she entered a deeper phase of sleep. The fabric covering her belly stretched taut. A red rose, whose stem she clutched tightly in her left hand, lay wilted in her lap.

FIFTEEN
2002

Elizabeth took the elevator up to her new apartment and changed from her work clothes into a pair of sweats and a T-shirt. Then she uncorked a bottle of red wine. TGIF, she thought. The red liquid gurgled from the bottle's mouth and reminded her of the rock fountains she sold at work, the ones designed to make you think you were sitting beside a babbling brook, a half-clad Buddha at your side.

She dropped heavily onto her new couch and brought the thin-lipped glass to her mouth. The wine was dry and made her pucker. She put her feet up onto the low-slung coffee table. It was also new. So was the dark brown leather chair that matched the couch, the glass-topped end tables, and the burgundy lamps with the gold leaves embossed on them.

Despite the February chill outside, it was hot in her apartment. She could grow orchids in it. She couldn't remember the last time she'd been able to walk around in bare feet and a T-shirt in her own home in winter. Her house had always been drafty; to keep it warm would have cost a fortune.

She opened the patio door a crack to let in some cool air. The winter sun had already set, but the eastern skyline remained lit with a soft pink glow that hinted at the coming spring thaw.

"If you're dead set on living by yourself," Ron had said, "then *you* stay in the house and I'll find a place of my own. The house is more yours than mine anyway."

He was right about that. She'd made all the decisions that had turned the old and impersonal wartime bungalow into something warm and unique to them. She had done everything she could to make the house a home, everything but fill it with children. It was supposed to be the starter house that would grow too small for them, but the kids never came. She'd sent out hundreds of invitations and prayers, but not one child had come to play.

How did Marie get so lucky? The thought came out of nowhere. Another sip of wine fuelled her self-pity. Pregnant again. Oops! And so sorry about it too. Boohoo. *I'm sorry, Elizabeth. It's just not fair.* She hated the way Marie's forehead had scrunched up, the way her eyes oozed pity. How hypocritical because what Marie really wanted was to be comforted. She was like a little baby caught doing something wrong, a baby who was desperate to be picked up and forgiven. It brought out a perverse desire in Elizabeth to say something cutting, to chastise Marie for her stupidity.

"I know you've always been happy for me," Marie had said. Ha. She didn't know her very well then, did she? There had been times when she'd wanted to slap Marie for being so lucky. Slap her hard. Her and any other pregnant woman parading around town with her belly button poking out like a third eye or with children in tow. Oh, yes, she'd had her share of envy all right, of sleepless nights, crying quietly to herself so as not to waken Ron. Elizabeth had never needed anyone to feel sorry for her; she'd had enough self-pity to last a lifetime.

Laughter in the hallway interrupted her thoughts as a group of people passed her door on the way to the elevator. Their laughter was spontaneous and yet staged, and there was something carefree in their banter. They sounded young and enthusiastic. They weren't in the midst of trying to pick up the pieces of their lives and imagine a new future.

Elizabeth tried to imagine going out with a bunch of friends but couldn't. Who *were* her close friends, anyway? Besides Marie, did she have any? All her energy had been focused on her business, on her marriage, and on trying to get pregnant. All those years when she should have been having fun and making friends were lost. Her life had narrowed to attaining one goal. Clearly, it had been too much to ask for.

The hallway became suddenly quiet once the elevator doors closed. Restless, Elizabeth turned the television off and walked to the sliding glass doors. The city was particularly beautiful at night from the vantage point of the twelfth floor. All those lights shining like living stars, the frozen river a serrated blade slicing the city in two. She stared to the south, trying to pinpoint her old neighbourhood. What was Ron doing right now? Staring to the north?

An ambulance rushed over the Low Level Bridge, lights flashing, siren blaring.

Elizabeth took another sip of wine and stared at the sky where she saw the first real star glittering in isolation. By reflex, she recited the childhood poem.

> Star light, star bright
> The first star I see tonight
> I wish I may, I wish I might
> Have this wish I wish tonight!

Nothing ever came from wishing on stars. There was no magician in her life to wave a magic wand. The doctors with all their needles and transducers had failed to make the impossible possible. She closed the balcony door and went to fill her glass. The bottle was empty. She opened another bottle and smiled when she remembered how her mother had always cautioned her about drinking to excess. *A girl can be taken advantage of without even knowing it.* There had to be more to that story. What had her mother not told her? Was she speaking from personal experience? Was this some clue to Elizabeth's birth mother's situation?

She sat back down on the couch and closed her eyes. Memories came unbidden. Breaking her arm falling off a horse when she was fourteen. Visiting Marie in the hospital after Nicole was born. That awful lunch with Ron.

She was thirty-two and they were celebrating her birthday at the Upper Crust restaurant. The sun was high in the mid-afternoon sky, the wind calm. They chose a spot outside on the patio. She smiled at Ron and squeezed his hand over the small, round table that separated them. She couldn't remember the last time she'd felt so happy. Everything was perfect—the day, the restaurant, the sun shining down, the colourful wildflowers stretching up, up, up in the large pots on the patio—cosmos, black-eyed Susans, wild flax, yarrow. There was nowhere else they'd rather be. They studied the menu carefully and ordered rich appetizers and an expensive bottle of wine and sat back to enjoy the crowds walking past the restaurant.

Then the pregnant woman walked by.

Her helium-filled belly pushed against her sundress and cast Elizabeth in shadow. The woman was holding hands with a blond girl who looked to be about three. The girl's hair was pulled into two pigtails that stuck straight out from the sides of her head. She held an ice cream cone in one hand, and her mouth and chin were covered in chocolate. The mother bent down onto one knee, carefully lowering her weight, and wiped her daughter's mouth, smiling. Then she took the cone and, with her own tongue, cleaned up the ice cream dripping down the side and pushed the scoop more securely into the cone. Elizabeth stared at the intimate act, the pregnant woman bowed on one knee, her saliva merging with her daughter's, the girl's upturned and trusting face. Suddenly the only sounds she heard came from the playground across the street. The chains squeaking on the swings, the thud of children's feet as they hit the slide, the shouts, the laughter. She couldn't take all that laughter. Unable to compose herself, she got up and went to the car.

Ron got their food to go.

Poor Ron. She really had been a lot of work at times. He'd danced around her unpredictable emotions more than once.

Another group of people moved down the hallway outside her apartment door. Elizabeth hadn't realized when she moved into the building how many young people lived in it. Times had changed. When she was twenty, the suburbs were all she had known.

Cigarette smoke drifted under her door and into her living room, invisibly filling the empty space around her as if a guest had suddenly departed. But of course she'd had no guest. She had no friends except Marie, who didn't need her because she had a family. Imagine that— having a family. Marie had gotten everything she'd ever wanted. All those wishes *she*'d made on stars had come true. She had a *real* family. Not like the make-believe one Elizabeth had imagined when she played house as a child. And even *that* had ended. One year they were too old to play house and too old, even, to play with dolls.

It had been Marie's idea to dispose of the dolls. Elizabeth held a mouthful of wine in her cheeks until her tongue turned numb. Why had she always listened to Marie? The girl who had enjoyed pulling the legs off of daddy-long-legs.

Come on, Marie had cajoled, convincing Elizabeth to carry her favourite doll down to the creek. Marie's ratty doll Mitsy was already missing an arm, so what did she care about setting it free? She skipped across the open field and down the gravel path that led to the wooden footbridge. *Come on!*

It had been rainy the previous week and the creek ran high. Marie climbed onto the railing and leaned her body over the dark water rushing below; Mitsy dangled perilously from her hands.

"Ready?" Marie asked.

Elizabeth remained quiet. She felt a sudden pang for Moxie, the doll that had heard so many of her childhood secrets. She loved its frilled dress, its hard plastic limbs, its blue eyes that opened and closed depending on whether it was standing up or lying down. Most thirteen-year-old girls didn't play with dolls anymore, but that didn't mean she had to get rid of it. Couldn't she just keep it in her closet? Or in a box under her bed?

"Are you ready?" Marie asked again, more insistent this time.

Elizabeth clutched her doll to her chest. M & M: Mitsy and Moxie. No, she wasn't ready.

"Come on," Marie said. "We agreed. We're too old for dolls, right?"

Was thirteen too old? She nodded.

"Okay, then. Come on. It's just a doll. Follow me."

One final kiss, one last whisper into a shell-shaped ear. Then they counted to three and the dolls arced into the air and splashed lightly into the creek. They bobbed momentarily to the surface before racing away with the current, smiles frozen on their plastic faces, blue marbled eyes shuttered by thick black lashes. They bounced from rock to rock as the current sent them downstream and the water tried to penetrate their waxen hair.

So vivid was the memory of being a child again that her next sip of wine tasted like grass and sunshine. She missed that doll. Sweet Moxie. They had shared a bed for years; she didn't deserve to be cast away. Why had she listened to Marie?

Maybe the clouds had parted for a split second and God had peered down at her that August afternoon and seen a heartless girl throwing her dolly away. And maybe the clouds came together again and blocked His view before he had a chance to see that Marie was there too. It had been her idea! And maybe at that moment God touched the eggs inside of her that were jockeying for position, deciding in which order they would fall for the next forty-odd years. And maybe He had touched each one and taken the light out of them, leaving dark, dry husks behind.

The phone rang. Elizabeth rushed unsteadily to the kitchen.

"Hello?"

"Uh, is Fred there?"

"I'm sorry, you must—"

The phone went dead in her hand. Something in her deflated. She poured another glass of wine and sloshed half of it onto the counter.

The carpet felt good under her bare feet, cushy and deep. She spread her toes and flexed her feet, restless for something to do. She turned the television on and flipped through the channels. Nothing interested her. She stood and began pacing again. On the wall behind her kitchen table, she'd hung some black and white photos of herself and some friends in their first year of university. In one, she and Marie stood side by side on the roof of Gillian's house. That had been a good party. Marie's hair had been long then, pulled back into a bushy ponytail. In those days, her own hair had hung straight and silky down the middle of her back. Funny to think that Marie had once envied how straight her hair was because Elizabeth would have loved to have had some of Marie's curls.

Marie. Pregnant again. And with two lovely girls already. Sometimes she wished she could drop Marie as a friend and start fresh. But it was too late for that now. Her whole life was twined with Marie's. She couldn't simply transplant herself without doing serious damage. Then again, it didn't seem that either one of them was taking great care to keep their friendship alive and thriving. Somewhere along the way they had both stopped watering it.

She looked at her watch. It was almost ten o'clock. Impulsively she moved to the kitchen, picked up the phone, and dialled Marie's number. She'd just say hi, how are you? What are your plans for the weekend? They'd talk like they used to, quickly, with no pauses between words, rushing to get the next thought out. Maybe she'd invite Marie and the girls over to see her new apartment. She'd bake muffins, buy some good coffee and some juice for the kids. Maybe Nicole and Sophia could even have a sleepover.

The machine picked up on the fourth ring. Elizabeth heard Sophia's small voice through the receiver: "If you would like to leave a message for Barry, Marie, Nicole, or Sophia, please do so after the tone."

She hung up.

Pregnant again. Without all the pokes and prods and drugs and hopes and disappointments that had plagued her own numerous attempts to conceive.

The black cordless phone sat beside the bottle of wine. She thought about phoning Marie. Then she remembered she'd already tried.

She rocked back and forth. All she wanted was for someone to hold her and tell her everything would be okay. Ron would comfort her. Ron would listen. Would he be home? It had been two weeks since she'd moved out, and she'd asked him not to phone until the newness of their separation had worn off. But it was her rule, so she could break it.

Dear Ron. The warmth started in her abdomen and slowly spread throughout her body. When they were first dating, Ron had gone to Vancouver to help his uncle with some renovations, and Elizabeth had taken the train to visit him there. They hadn't seen each other in almost a month. It was a nineteen-hour trip, and the train had arrived at eight in the morning. Ron stood waiting patiently on the platform, an umbrella sheltering him from the rain. He was wearing a suit and tie. "What's the occasion?" she'd joked. He kissed her and smiled. Then she realized that he'd dressed up for her. She was the occasion.

Elizabeth reached for the wine bottle and was surprised to find that it too was empty. How had she managed to drink both bottles?

She dialled the familiar number. One ring. Two rings. Three rings. She pressed the phone hard against her ear and listened to the echo of her heart beating loudly. "Pick up the phone," she whispered, rocking back and forth, her lips parted, her mouth dry.

On the seventh ring she realized that Ron hadn't re-set the answering machine. She'd taken her own voice off the machine when she left, leaving him concise instructions of how to put his own message on.

The phone kept ringing. Every time she was about to hang up, she saw him fumbling for his keys, rushing for the phone.

Finally, she hung up. She'd been the one to leave. Of course he'd be out on a Friday night. What had she expected?

Elizabeth looked around the room and saw two sliding glass doors. Two television sets. Two coffee tables. Her stomach flipped.

Unsteady on her feet, she made her way to the bathroom. A couple of Tylenol might keep the inevitable hangover at bay. And maybe some toast for the stomach, but just as she was about to put two slices of bread into the toaster, she spotted mould growing alongside the crust. She threw the bag in the garbage and went through the cupboards. She needed something that would be kind to her stomach, but she found nothing, not even a box of crackers.

She staggered back to the bedroom and flopped face first onto the bed. How pathetic could she be? It was a good thing Marie hadn't been home to answer the phone. And, oh, God, she'd phoned Ron, hadn't she? Thankfully he hadn't been home either. She'd have made a fool of herself for sure. *I miss you. Can you come over?* But where had he been? Who might he have been out with? She closed her eyes and pictured him in his faded blue jeans with the black shirt that she loved. He had kept in good shape over the years. She felt the warmth of old memories, the rekindling of a passion that had almost been extinguished over time. Maybe there was a hot coal under all that ash. Maybe, if she remembered the early years, the good times, she could fan it back into existence. She needed to remember his hands before they held the syringes. Love came and went, after all. It took work; it wasn't always steady and true. Maybe she could get it back.

She thought about how his cheeks dimpled when he smiled, how warm his hands were on her body. They'd met eighteen years ago—almost half her life. He'd encouraged her to open her own business, and he was proud of her. *I'm your number one fan,* he always said. Starting over with a new man would entail her finding someone who had the qualities that Ron already had. Maybe giving up the idea of having a baby didn't really mean throwing out her marriage too.

The room began to spin. She rolled onto her back and tried to pinpoint a spot on the ceiling to stop the room from moving, but to no avail. She'd just have to wait it out and try not to vomit in the process. She groaned when the dizziness became almost too much to bear. When would it end? When would the oblivion come?

Margaret stared at the freshly tilled fields outside the asylum bus window. How much cheerier they looked when she was heading home. In the months to come canola would brighten the landscape with its bright yellow blossoms. Or mustard. Last year the farmer had planted corn. But what did it matter? She would never recognize beauty again, just like her brother, Johnny, would never grow new fingers. Some things couldn't be fixed. Like Carolyn. Pregnant. The shock was in realizing that her situation could become worse.

For twelve years Margaret had been riding this bus, trying to believe her visits mattered and that she could make something right from this terrible circumstance. How naïve she'd been. A person could not put a child in a place like that and then pretend that showing up made any kind of a difference. Once a month she brought her daughter a rose and, in good weather, took her outside. She was there one day out of thirty. Twelve days in a year. For the other 353 days, Carolyn was obviously defenceless. Prey for vultures. Margaret grit her teeth. Without moving, she seemed to stagger.

The bus window felt cool against her forehead. Her mouth tasted sour, as if she hadn't brushed her teeth in a week. She closed her eyes and once again felt the stones press into her back under a cloudless sky. She saw her farmhouse hazy in the heat, felt Stuart's body heavy upon her. *See you around.* That's what he'd said when he righted himself. He'd never said he was sorry. Not that that would have made it better, but just to hear an apology might have lessened her pain.

A tear fell onto the window ledge. She hadn't escaped after all. She'd left Mayburn because she suspected her mother's shame had turned into loathing; her mother wouldn't look at her anymore. In her eyes, Margaret was the country girl who'd let that privileged boy take what he wanted. And what if he came back? What if he'd told his friends?

Her mother, grey by the time she was thirty, couldn't stand that some people got away with taking things that weren't theirs to take, but she also knew that to confront the issue would tear her husband apart. So her normally curt replies to her daughter were replaced by stony silences. As time passed and the silence between them continued, it became obvious to Margaret that her mother would rather be alone than have her daughter nearby.

Margaret told others she needed more than what a small farming community could offer. Edmonton in the year 1943 was an attractive place to a country girl. Margaret knew she could live a decent life there and have some independence despite the constant talk of war that dominated most conversations. She was already used to the long, hard winters, and she never tired of taking the streetcar around the city, enjoying an anonymity that she'd never known before.

Donald Harrington was a real estate broker. He ate at the same small restaurant across from the teachers college, where Margaret sometimes treated herself to a bowl of soup and a slice of bread and where she ended up working on the weekends because they were short-staffed and she needed the extra money.

She didn't notice him at first because he was quiet and minded his own business, not like some of the young men who immediately assumed a warm familiarity simply because she put food in front of them. No, Donald was courteous and polite at all times, and he tipped generously. One day, his tip was almost equal to the cost of his meal. As he was leaving the restaurant, she ran after him.

"Excuse me, sir, but you've left too much money." She extended her hand with his change.

He refused to take it. "Please, it's for you. The meal was delicious, and I enjoyed it." He smiled and she took a step back when she noted his perfect teeth. Then he nodded his head and put his hat on before taking his leave.

When he came in the next time, she watched him more closely. Once again he was alone and sat with the newspaper spread on the table beside him. His shoes were polished and the cuffs and collar of his shirt were starched and clean. His dark hair was closely cropped with a clean part down the left side of his scalp, and he was clean-shaven. His cheeks were blemished with either acne or chicken pox scars that looked like shallow caves above his whiskered jaw. When she took his order she noted how blue his eyes looked in the sunlight that streamed through the large front window.

Soon she began to look for his tall, lean frame, and he didn't disappoint her. One Saturday evening, the dark storm clouds that had gathered throughout the afternoon opened to release a heavy downpour just as she was leaving work. Donald offered to walk her to her rooming house. She shyly accepted.

Donald was a city boy, born and raised. His father was a senior banker at the Toronto Dominion and his mother was his father's full-time hostess, managing their social calendar. They were middle-upper class, believing themselves to be more upper than middle, and Margaret's humble origins made her feel awkward around them. It was almost as if they spoke another language from the one she was fluent in.

Margaret left teachers college six months into her tenure when she married Donald. With that one move, Margaret Galloway became Margaret Harrington, and when she took her husband's name she felt confident that she'd left Mayburn and Stuart Jenkins far behind. By saying, "I do," she boxed her childhood nightmare, put a sturdy lid on it, and finally was able to store it away.

Or so she had thought.

The asylum bus ground its gears as it entered the city limits and slowed for a red light. Margaret removed her white gloves and dabbed at her eyes with a tissue. Once again she saw her fifteen-year-old self, silent and unmoving. Then that girl's body changed and turned into Carolyn's. Margaret pulled the cord for the next stop. She was still miles away from her home, but she felt ready to vomit. She needed some fresh air to rid her clothes of the scent of that place.

When her feet hit the pavement she set a brisk pace. What could she do with her anger? She'd been silent for so long. Donald was a good father. He was adored by James and Rebecca, and he adored them in kind. He had become the man she'd wanted him to be—honest and good. Patient with the children. Talking about Carolyn would be like detonating a bomb in their quiet cul-de-sac. Especially now, given the circumstances.

A baby. Would that child be her responsibility too?

The scent of lilacs was heavy in the air. Another season of growth was ahead, but all Margaret could think about was the young child growing within her daughter's body, awkward and bent, like her father's failed attempt to graft two different kinds of apple saplings. Down syndrome and pregnancy—she shivered involuntarily. Nothing good could come of it.

Her low heels rang loudly on the sidewalk as she increased her pace until she was almost running. Not all injustices could be brushed aside, she knew that. But they couldn't all be spoken either. She needed to be careful. She'd succumbed to darkness once before, and she wasn't sure that she'd be graced with another recovery. In truth, she was scared to death by the image of her unwashed and uncaring self hiding from the world beneath the sheets. She'd abandoned one child in her life, what on earth would she do with that child's baby?

SEVENTEEN

Dr. Maclean clasped the pen tightly in his hand and bent over the notebook on his desk. The light outside was fading, so he switched on the desk lamp and moved to the edge of his seat and began to write.

> Carolyn Jane Harrington, age sixteen, went into labour spontaneously on July 10, 1963. A low cervical Caesarean section was performed under spinal anaesthesia and a five pound, two ounce, apparently normal, female infant was delivered. Pomeroy sterilization was performed.
>
> The mother is a mongoloid and the father is unknown.
>
> Dr. Cooper of the Pediatric Department of the University of Alberta had been forewarned of our situation and was eager to be involved in the case. He was immediately called upon and was on hand to aid in the delivery. You can imagine our surprise to discover that the infant appears to be normal. Further testing over time will determine the extent of her mental capacity.

He stopped writing because to continue would mean going on at length. For now, all he needed to record was the birth. Carolyn had come through the procedure without incident and her sterilization meant another pregnancy would be out of the question. The infant had been taken to a special room for observation. Both he and Dr. Cooper had agreed that it would be detrimental to her survival to place her with the other infants in the main ward. He looked around the book-lined shelves of his office. Took in the dull light coming in from the small window. Everything felt shabby now. The board's quick fix to Carolyn's situation was to make sure she could never get pregnant again. *What? She was never sterilized?* The board's response to the investigation into the identity of the baby's father, which had turned up nothing, was to ask if the family would press charges. They might have well said, *Can we sweep it under the rug?* For all Dr. Maclean knew, that man was still working here.

And so was he.

Because of his need to take care of his family. Because of his fatigue at the idea of finding something new. But other doctors made moves in similar situations. Why was he still here? Had he thought he'd make a difference?

He checked his watch and saw it was late. His wife would be expecting him soon. The desk lamp was hot when he reached to turn it off, and he pulled away quickly as he felt the burn. Sucking gently on his hand to relieve the sting, he grabbed his coat and locked the office door behind him.

In the hallway he realized he wanted to see the infant once more before leaving for the night. She was being kept in a room down the corridor from the reception desk. His footsteps echoed loudly in the quiet entranceway. As he got closer, he heard the sound of a newborn's cry coming from the child's room. When he opened the door he found the room deserted save for the infant in the crib. Her face was purple and she'd kicked the blankets off of her. Dr. Maclean looked around in anger. When would someone have come? He saw an empty bottle by the sink and a canister of formula on the counter. Without delay he ran the water to make it warm and quickly read the instructions before measuring the appropriate amount of powder into the bottle.

He was sweating now, unnerved by the baby's constant cries and enraged that no nurse had tended the child's distress. He lifted the cuff of his shirt and sprinkled formula onto his inner wrist as he'd seen his own wife do. It seemed to be the right temperature.

The baby's body felt hot to his touch. He put her onto his shoulder and tried to soothe her. Then he cradled her in the crook of his arm and placed the rubber nipple to her mouth. She gasped and choked and then, tasting the milk, began to suck deeply, stopping only to take a few extra breaths to calm her distressed breathing.

Dr. Maclean gazed at her tiny mouth and the small fingers of one hand firmly formed into a fist. This was no place for a child. Not just this child, but any child. Suddenly the cruelty of the place threatened to engulf him. The glaring contrast of having an apparently healthy baby here shone a spotlight on the faulty logic of the benefits of warehousing these people away. Who really believed in the benefits of this place?

Since discovering Carolyn's pregnancy, he'd read everything he could get his hands on regarding Down syndrome and reproduction. He'd discovered that the *real* reason there'd been no mongoloid pregnancies before was that few mongoloid females reached a healthy reproductive age. It wasn't, in fact, because they were unfinished children. In 1947, for example, the year Carolyn came to Poplar Grove, twenty-eight other mongoloid infants were also institutionalized. Of the twenty-nine, twenty-two had died by the time they were eight years old. Only seven were still alive. The following year, 1948, an additional eighteen mongoloids were institutionalized, and only five of those were still alive. The number of unadorned white headstones that lined the graveyard on the grounds was a clear accounting system that marked the many deaths.

In fact, the very high infant mortality rate of mongoloids who had been institutionalized was staggering. The life expectancy had risen from twelve years in 1949 to sixteen years in 1963, but still, that was if they survived the first five years of neglect and didn't succumb to respiratory infections. Heart defects were never surgically corrected. Even now heart defects were too often seen as nature's way of ending such a life quickly.

The introduction of antibiotics had certainly helped more children to survive the early years. One day someone must have had the bright idea that a mongoloid life might be worth preserving. God knows why, given the bleak lives most of them led behind locked doors. As far as Dr. Maclean could see, their days consisted of nothing except wait-ing—waiting for meals, waiting for the day to end. Not all the patients at Poplar Grove were mongoloids, only approximately thirty percent, but the other mental defectives lived similar lives of quiet hopelessness, un-bathed and unattended. The stench and chronic bickering over small possessions would depress even the most able-minded individual.

The baby finished the bottle and gradually became limp in his arms. He placed her gently into her crib, noting that her sleeper was soaked through with urine. Then he set off down the hallway in search of a nurse. The sound of a television came from the staff room and

Dr. Maclean followed the noise. Inside, a nurse was sitting in a chair, her feet resting on the chair beside her, eating a sandwich. He didn't recognize this nurse and cleared his throat to alert her of his presence. She glanced his way and then returned her gaze to the television.

"I'm on my break," she said. "They told me when I started that I could take a half-hour dinner break."

Her frizzy grey hair was pinned haphazardly behind her ears, and he noted that her ankles were swollen beneath her transparent stockings. She had a washed-out look to her as if she'd been on her feet for days and only just found a place to rest. He judged her to be somewhere in her late fifties or early sixties and felt sure she wouldn't last long in her position.

"Nurse . . ."

"Langford," she offered. "Alice Langford."

"Nurse Langford, there's an infant in Room 5 who is in need of a change. I found her unfed and in a state of distress."

"Room 5? What's a baby doing in Room 5?"

"Do you mean to tell me no one told you to look in on her?"

Throughout the entire conversation Nurse Langford kept her eyes on the television. "Nope. It's the first I've heard of it."

He threw his hands in the air to register his disgust. "Just see to it that she's cared for," he said angrily. "If I come in tomorrow morning and she's not clean and fed, you'll be looking for a new position. Have I made myself clear?"

Clean and fed? What new standards was he asking of the staff? He raced to the front door and breathed in the summer air with relief. Gravel crunched under his shoes as he walked briskly to the parking lot. The red brick building of Poplar Grove was a dark shadow behind him, a nightmare from which he couldn't quite wake. That child should not be here, he thought. No child should be here. His arms felt empty because his instincts told him he should take the infant home.

Not now, he told himself. In the morning he would write to Mrs. Harrington and inform her that her daughter had given birth. The sooner that child was removed from Poplar Grove the better.

After the children had finally gone to bed and the nighttime kisses had been exchanged, Marie put the kettle on for tea. Fluorescent lights glared from the kitchen ceiling. Beside the sink, the dishwasher churned noisily. She put two teabags in a teapot and ran a cloth over the counter-top as she waited for the kettle to boil. Barry walked into the room behind her. She could feel his gaze upon her and wondered what he saw. Had he noticed the greying roots that were now starting to appear in her once-dark hair? Was he comparing her figure today with the one that had first caught his attention almost twenty years earlier? Probably not. He was not critical of her in the same way that she was of him.

She kept her back to him and scrubbed the sink, pretending not to know he was there. Out of the corner of her eye she saw his dark reflection in the window above the sink. Her hands kept moving. She wasn't ready to face her husband yet. Her anger had disappeared as the evening wore on, replaced, as usual, with regret for how unfair she was to him. It had been helpful to have Frances at the house when they'd returned from the doctor's office. She had stayed for dinner and gradually the ice had thawed between Marie and her husband as Frances voiced one opinion after another on issues ranging from agriculture and drought to interest rates and UN policies. She knew all kinds of things about large issues, but when it came to the day-to-day things, she was quite clueless. Ask her how much a loaf of bread cost, and she'd give you a blank look as if it was an irrelevant piece of information. The only information she retained was the kind she thought would impress people. To her, knowing the cost of groceries was pathetically domestic and reeked of failed feminism. But that might change, Marie thought, now that Frances had a child. She'd have to have food on hand at home sometimes. She couldn't just keep opting out. Marie shook her head: All that education, and Frances never seemed to apply it to daily living.

The kettle finally whistled.

"Would you like a cup of tea?" she asked Barry.

"Please."

"Come and sit down," she said. "I can't talk to you when you're pacing like that."

Barry's chair scraped along the wood floor. She'd asked him a million times not to drag the chairs because it scratched the wood. But he was on edge. She didn't need to pick another fight now.

"What are we going to do about the baby?" he asked.

What he really meant was what was *she* going to do about the baby. Barry had always left all domestic decisions to Marie; for him, this would be just another thing that he'd hope she'd take care of. But she wasn't going to take care of it all herself. No.

She took a sip of tea. Licorice. Black licorice. She had eaten pounds of it as a kid. Summer and long, sticky black ropes sprinkled with sand. She stirred in a spoonful of honey.

"Isn't it kind of soon to be talking about it?" she said. "We can't really make any decisions until we know if there's something wrong because if we were to end the pregnancy now, would we be deciding not to have another child because we really didn't *want* one, or because we were afraid it wasn't well?"

"I don't see what difference that would make," Barry replied.

"But could you live without knowing?"

"Not knowing what?" he said. "Whether it was sick or well? You already said you think there's something wrong with the baby. I swear every time I got in my car today I had a bloody DATS van shadowing me. Am I supposed to get prepared or something?"

"But what if I'm wrong?"

He threw his hands in air.

The dishwasher moved to its next cycle. Water gushed loudly into the drain.

"What do you mean, what if you're wrong?"

"A premonition is just a *feeling*," Marie said. "It isn't necessarily accurate."

The phone rang. In the stillness it sounded like an alarm going off. Marie started; the phone rarely rang after nine o'clock at night.

"Let the machine get it," Barry said. "It's probably just Frances with another bit of wisdom to dispense."

The phone continued to ring. Finally, the answering machine picked up, but all they heard was a dial tone. It would bug her all night now, wondering who had phoned.

"It can't have been important," Barry said. "So we get the tests done and then we decide."

"Maybe we should decide now whether we want a baby or not."

"What difference does it make if we decide now or later?"

She stared at her husband in disbelief. "Well, first of all, I'll be pregnant for that much longer, and it'll be harder to terminate if we decide to go that route. And second of all, having an abortion means you don't want a child. *Any* child. Terminating a pregnancy after finding out something's wrong means you don't want an *imperfect* child. There's a *huge* difference." Her voice had risen. "Having a baby isn't like buying a house. You don't get to pick the colour of your baby's hair like you do the fixtures in your bathroom or the paint for your walls."

"Shhh," he hissed. "Don't get so worked up. I don't want to argue about this. I just want to find out what we both want."

Marie forced herself to remain seated. "Are you saying you're okay to have this baby, no matter what?"

"No, I'm not saying that. Don't put words into my mouth. What if it needs constant care?" he asked. "Is that fair to the girls?"

"Other people do it."

"Other people do lots of things that we don't do, so don't make me the bad guy, Marie. You're the one who started all this. I'd have been fine to have another baby if you hadn't told me something was wrong with it."

"You've got to be kidding me." Marie threw her hands up in complete surrender. "Has the Barry I married been replaced with another man?" He didn't do anything spontaneously. This was the man who hadn't changed his brand of cereal for twenty years. The man who never deviated from routine. And wasn't it this very quality in him, his desire to know the outcome before taking any action, that had made her, over the years, less spontaneous and more restrained in the things she did?

It didn't seem fair that he was looking at her now as if she were the one who was unwilling to be daring.

"I thought you'd be first in line for testing. I've seen you read the last pages of a book to find out what's going to happen before you even start! How can you say that you wished you didn't know?"

"Because I never would have thought something might be wrong. The other two pregnancies were fine, why wouldn't this one be fine too?"

"Oh, so it's my fault?" Marie asked, her voice rising.

The dishwasher finished its cycle and the room fell into a hushed silence.

Marie pictured the small writing on the calendar, three weeks away, that marked the date of her ultrasound appointment. Barry was right. The waiting was going to kill them both. Maybe she'd miscarry before then and solve everything. That was the body's natural way of eliminating embryos that weren't healthy. She moved from hope to guilt in two seconds. That was no solution to wish for. If it happened, okay, but to wish for it . . . Plus, that little baby was probably suctioned on for dear life. Literally. Nothing would jar it from its home.

Barry pushed his chair back and nodded toward the stairs. "Come on to bed." He squeezed her shoulder as he walked by.

She placed the palm of one hand on her belly. Her own heartbeat pulsed back. It was too late now for a normal pregnancy. She sat for some time lost in thought. Finally, she picked up the teapot and cup and carried them to the sink. Then she unloaded the dishwasher and ran a cloth over the table and countertops.

At the doorway she stopped for a quick survey. The floor had been swept. The counters were clean. The sink was empty and the stainless steel shining. Everything was in its proper place, ready for the morning. Everything except her old life, the one that was safe and good.

She turned off the light and followed her husband up the stairs.

NINETEEN

Three weeks passed. The days gradually lengthened. March was around the corner and spring and optimism were in the air.

In the doctor's waiting room Marie sat perched on the edge of her seat, her bladder so full that she could concentrate on little else. She squeezed her thighs together and covered her lap with her purse so she could clutch her crotch discreetly.

She'd been told to drink eight cups of water before her appointment because, as the receptionist had told her, a full bladder lifts the womb and gives a better picture of the baby.

Marie had nodded. She'd been through this procedure twice before. But this time she'd drunk so much water that the baby must be floating around her heart. She rocked back and forth to distract herself.

"Think of something else," Barry said, patting her on the knee.

"I'm trying to!"

She focused on the carpet. The tables. The chairs. The fluorescent lights in the ceiling.

Half a dozen other pregnant women sat in stockinged feet reading magazines. None of them appeared to be in as much discomfort. One woman wore a long-sleeved shirt with a picture of Mickey Mouse on it. DISNEYLAND, the shirt screamed. Frances would love that. Long ago she'd vowed never to be caught dead in Disneyland, let alone pay to advertise for them. But she'd see. She'd take Max one day. He'd beg and plead and she'd give in because she loved him. Nicole and Sophia had sure enjoyed their trip. She had too.

Finally they called Marie's name and a nurse led her to a small cubicle, handed her a white paper gown, and asked her to undress.

Marie clutched at herself again and danced from one foot to the other, turning this way and that, contorting and clenching her muscles to stop the flow of urine that begged to be released. She had never in her life undressed when her bladder was so full without being able to relieve herself. After two pregnancies, her muscular control wasn't quite what it used to be. Thankfully, the nurse appeared as soon as she was finished and led her down a hallway lined with doors.

The room was not much larger than her pantry at home, just big enough to house the examination table and a small desk upon which a computer sat. The lights were dim. Everything looked grey or black beneath the low ceiling. To distract herself, she began to count the holes in one of the false panels directly over her head. The door opened suddenly and the technician appeared. She was a young woman, in her late twenties. A thick chestnut ponytail divided her shoulder blades. Small, dark-rimmed glasses perched on the top of her nose. She said hello and took a moment to examine Marie's file. What was in it? Marie MacPherson. Aged thirty-nine. Mother of two. No allergies. Broke a collarbone skiing when nineteen. Accidentally pregnant. Old. Scared.

Marie lay on her back and undid the sash that held her gown closed. She flinched when the technician applied a cold gel to her bare belly and ran a transducer in small circles over her swell.

"You drank too much water," she said immediately. "You'll have to go to the bathroom and let half out."

Marie snorted, certain it was a joke, but the technician had already turned away. So she closed her gown, gingerly descended from the table, and almost ran down the hall to the bathroom. Holding it in was virtually impossible now that she had permission to actually go to the bathroom. She barely made it to the toilet and, with great muscular control, emptied her bladder of half its contents. The relief was immense.

She climbed onto the examination table again, and the technician picked up the transducer and paused for a moment, suspending it in the air. It was sleek and long and slightly rounded at the bottom. It reminded Marie of one of those hand-held soup mixers, the ones you submerged right into the pot to puree your vegetables. The technician put cold jelly onto Marie's belly again and moved the transducer in wide sweeps before zeroing in on the right spot. Then she positioned herself behind the computer with its glowing screen.

Tap, tap, tap went the technician's fingers as she connected a shape with an organ, another with a limb, moving from one image to the next. *Tap, tap, tap.* Her fingers moved from the keyboard to the transducer.

She focused on the spine, the heart, the brain. She isolated the limbs. *Tap, tap, tap.* Sound waves bounced off Marie's baby and were projected onto the screen. The technician scrutinized the images, her lips pursed in concentration. Instinctively, Marie trusted her. Sometimes a person had that effect. Sometimes you just met somebody and you knew right away that you could leave your children with her.

"This might sound kind of strange," Marie said, "but can you please take extra care to see if everything's okay? I've had a terrible feeling for some time now that something's wrong with the baby."

The technician nodded. "Mothers are incredibly intuitive when it comes to their own babies. I'll just take a good close look," she said. "But ultrasounds can't show you everything; they can often pick up neural tube defects, like spina bifida, and they can pick up obvious problems like missing limbs and, depending when the ultrasound is done, heart defects and other organ problems. But what they can't do is detect most chromosomal disorders. There might be what we call some 'soft' indicators, but amniocentesis is really the test you need for that." She paused and examined an image closer. *Tap, tap, tap. Tap, tap, tap.*

After a few more minutes, the technician rose. "Okay," she said. "I'll call your husband in now." The air in the small, dark room rushed about when the door opened and closed.

A moment later, Barry sat beside her and watched the image of his baby on the screen. At first, everything looked blurry, non-descript.

"Here is the baby's spine," the technician said.

A tiny string of pearls floated up from the cloudy depths and ran up to join with the baby's head. How like a fish spine, Marie thought, so fossil-like and tidy.

"And here's the heart."

On the screen it looked the size of an olive. Inside the tiny skull cavity a shadow indicated a brain cushioned like a bird in a nest. The baby had all of its limbs and organs. Marie could tell that Barry had entered the room expecting the worst, but now she saw relief relax his features. There was nothing obviously monstrous about the baby. It didn't have two heads, or eight arms, or no arms at all. The brain wasn't growing independently outside the skull. The baby seemed to be okay.

In the car, Barry pulled out of the medical building's underground parkade. They both squinted when they hit the full sunshine. He turned right and drove along a road that was lined with old houses and new condominiums. "I feel like celebrating," he said, and reached over and gave Marie's hand a squeeze. "Let's go for lunch."

Marie stared straight ahead. She saw her baby's chalky image on the screen. Everything *seemed* okay, but her dread hadn't lifted.

It wasn't noon yet. She felt the heat from the sun through the windshield.

"Marie?" Barry said, squeezing her thigh. "Did you hear me?"

She turned toward him. He was leaning forward over the steering wheel, smiling at her.

"I'm sorry, what did you say?"

Barry swerved to miss a pothole. "I said, don't you feel relieved?"

She quelled the impulse to lie. "I'll feel relieved when we get the amnio results back."

"That's a month away!" The car jerked forward. "I don't get it, Marie. You never worried like this when you were pregnant before."

"I never had a feeling that something was *wrong* before, otherwise I'd probably have wanted more information then too."

"More information," he said derisively and tapped his fingers impatiently on the steering wheel. Then his voice softened. "Look, we've been lucky twice before. Why don't we just go for it?"

Marie wavered. Maybe if she allowed herself to believe in *his* belief, then everything would be okay. "So, let me make sure I understand you. You want me to cancel the amnio appointment. We'll just go for it, like you said. And we'll take what we get. If there's something wrong with the baby, we'll deal with it when it happens." It would feel good to be reckless for a change, to live boldly and without fear.

Barry braked at the next intersection and squinted into the sun.

Marie saw the baby's little olive heart beating. She saw its tiny hands curled into fists and knew that when they opened they'd have all their digits. The ultrasound hadn't shown any obvious abnormalities, and the technician had used the male pronoun when she pointed out the baby's bladder. Was it a boy, or was she just using "he" as a generic pronoun? Still, as Barry slowly manoeuvred the car down the back streets of

Garneau, she pictured a fair-haired boy with a thick-lipped smile and upturned eyes, a gentle boy who loved to throw a ball for his dog. She could handle that part. The baby. The boy, assuming it was one. But her son would age. And as he aged, his disability would become more visible. He'd be less loveable to strangers as puberty thickened his neck and he developed hairs and body odours.

And who would come to his birthday parties? Kids with Down syndrome were integrated into public school now. Would the "normal" kids from his class ever come? Or just kids like him? Marie had seen the Special Olympics on television; all those volunteers helping the athletes couldn't be involved simply to look good. But if she was honest with herself, she'd admit that she felt sorry for them and everyone else whose lives were touched by that one child. Yet she admired them too.

And if she and Barry had a child who wasn't quite right, people would feel sorry for them too. They'd be "poor Barry" and "poor Marie." How would they handle that, the double takes from strangers? It made her mad just thinking about it. And who would care for their son when she and Barry were gone? Nicole and Sophia? How would they feel, once they were adults, when they learned that their parents could have known in advance about the Down syndrome?

Marie repeated her question, more softly this time. "Do you want me to cancel the amnio?"

"I don't know," Barry said, a tone of defeat in his voice. "What are the odds that he'll have something like Down syndrome?"

They were speeding south now. The windshield was speckled with grime from the melting snow. She looked around her. The entire city was in need of a good wash. A two-day downpour would do the trick. But it was too early for that. February rains meant freezing rain, thin sheets of ice covering everything, a hazard to drivers and pedestrians alike. Old people, in particular, with hips brittle as dried wishbones.

"It doesn't matter what the odds are," she responded. "If it happens to us, it's one hundred percent."

TWENTY

1963

It was mid-July, and Margaret looked forward to having her children home from school during the holidays. James would be fifteen in a week, and Rebecca was already thirteen and a half. The children were more interested in their friends now than they were in their parents, but Margaret was determined that they'd have a nice summer holiday together. If Donald agreed, they'd take the train from Edmonton to Montreal. She'd never been to Montreal before.

The sun was high in the cloudless sky. Donald had put the screen door up again over the weekend so Margaret could open the door without letting bugs in. She enjoyed having the windows and doors open and feeling the cross draft in the kitchen, the room in which she spent the most time. What she loved most about her kitchen was the window over the sink. Every woman needed a window above her sink, one with a long sightline that could take her away from the never-ending domestic tasks.

The doorbell rang and Margaret dried her hands on a dishtowel as she walked to the front door. A postman stood on the front stoop with a letter in his hand. He extended a pen and a piece of paper on a clipboard. "Sign here, please."

"What is it?"

"A registered letter, ma'am. I just need your signature here."

He pointed to a line on the page, and she signed. Then he handed an official looking letter to her and told her to have a nice day.

The blood rushed from her face. In her trembling hands Margaret held a creamy beige envelope with the Poplar Grove Provincial Training Centre return address in the upper left corner. What if Donald or one of her children had been home when the letter arrived? She hadn't heard anything from that place in almost sixteen years, and suddenly a registered letter. She closed and then locked the front door.

Margaret, in the weeks since her last visit to see Carolyn, had found it necessary to go over it all in her head, as though this dreadful process of repetition could somehow alter the events. But she could not now, weeks later, remember it all; there were particular images that stayed with her—the red flush on her daughter's neck, the slip of white skin that showed above her elastic waistband, the look of surprise on Dr. Maclean's face. And waking suddenly on the couch in the pale afternoon light.

She'd only missed one of her monthly visits to Poplar Grove. Was Dr. Maclean checking up on her? She'd left Carolyn in his care. It was up to him and his staff to fix the mess that place had caused. Now that Margaret knew how bad things could be there, she couldn't go back. Over the years she had resigned herself to the stench and neglect, but to know that some person had done this to her daughter? No. That couldn't be reconciled in *any* world in which a loving God was supposed to be present.

The letter brought the familiar feeling of impending doom that she'd been trying to shake since Carolyn's birth.

She returned to the kitchen and sat down, placing the letter on the table before her. The stone of anger that had once been jagged and rough had been smoothed to perfection over the years. It sat like a polished worry bead in her gut and she worked it over and over and over again.

With shaking hands she opened the envelope.

July 12, 1963

Dear Mrs. Harrington,

I am writing to inform you that on July 10, your daughter Carolyn gave birth to an apparently normal baby girl. To my knowledge, this is the first case of a healthy child being born to a mongoloid, although I may be mistaken. Your granddaughter weighed five pounds, two ounces at birth and has a good appetite. We have separated her from her mother and are keeping her under close observation. As you are her lawful guardian, we await further instructions as to the placement of the child. Obviously, she may go home with you.

However, if you wish her to be placed elsewhere, you must inform us of this decision. It is my hope that you do so in a timely manner. Believe me when I say that Poplar Grove is not a viable option for the child. I look forward to discussing this matter with you at your earliest convenience.

Yours sincerely,

Dr. Michael Maclean

Margaret put the letter on the table and held her head in both hands. A granddaughter. Another tie to the past that she was trying to run from. Would the pain never stop? Would it go on, year after year like newspaper stories on wars and natural disasters?

An apparently normal baby girl? How was that possible?

She paced the kitchen floor. Who could she talk to? She wanted someone to take care of her, tell her what to do, tell her it would be okay. But she was alone at the helm of a disastrous journey. Never in her life had someone stood in her corner, rooting for her all the way. Someone who loved her no matter what. A mother who looked past her own resentments to see a daughter in need. Mayburn was only four hours from the city, but it might as well have been a country away. Her parents' lives were still dictated by the farm. And in her mother's world there was no room for self-pity. Pick yourself up, dust yourself off, and get back to work. She'd forgotten about Carolyn as soon as she heard the baby was a mongoloid. The silence on the end of the party line was deafening. Who might be listening in? But maybe that stopped her from saying, *Did you want your father to get the gun?*

No one from her family ever came to the city. Once she'd left the town, her ties had been cut. *Margaret's too good for us*, they might as well have said. Their not coming to her wedding made clear their estrangement. But Margaret had also been relieved. Her mother next to Mrs. Harrington? Calloused hands next to white gloves? Even now, twenty years later, Margaret had trouble believing she had lived a childhood with parents and a brother. Its abrupt ending made it all feel like a lie. Even now, twenty years later, she found it difficult to believe that her family experienced emotions as strong as her own. They were oxen, steadily plodding through their days. No peaks. No valleys. Nothing like this. Surely nothing as dramatic as this.

She glanced at the clock over the stove. She had two hours before her children came home, enough time to get to the post office and back. And with the decision came action. She would not visit. She had been cut from her own family, and she had survived. She could cut too. If she refused to see the baby, her heart could not be moved. Dr. Maclean would never understand her decision, and she had no intention of filling in the history that might make him understand. Still . . . she hesitated for a moment. A little girl. Five pounds, two ounces. Tiny fingers and big, trusting eyes. This was another turning point in her life. She stood at an intersection, and whatever road she'd take would have grave ramifications for the rest of her life. Was this her second chance to do the right thing? To break the silence of Carolyn's existence? If she didn't have Donald, James, and Rebecca to think about then she could be brave. But she *did* have them, and she was not about to destroy their lives by dredging up the past. They would never trust her again if she pulled her past into her present. She had made a commitment to this silence.

Her pen flowed smoothly over the page. She slipped the letter into an envelope and copied the address onto the front. Now it was two o'clock. She'd have to hurry if she wanted to stop at the store too.

A week passed. Seven days of slush and thaw and sun and flurries. Marie's appetite returned, along with her energy, but sleeping still proved to be a problem. Always in early pregnancy she suffered from insomnia. This time was no exception. At four o'clock she woke up and was unable to get back to sleep.

It was March now. Lying in bed the previous night, she had lain her palm flat on her belly and felt her uterus extended like a hard stone from the surrounding softness. Usually small as a kiwi, it was now the size of a large grapefruit. Already it had expanded beneath her skin to reach almost to her belly button. Obviously her body had done this stretching before. Marie felt she was twice the size that she'd been with Nicole. At thirteen weeks she was having difficulty zipping up her jeans. That hadn't happened with her first pregnancy until she was at least seventeen weeks.

The baby was growing inside of her, oblivious to the uncertainties that plagued its parents' waking hours. It existed. It was feeding from her.

At five o'clock, she quietly made her way downstairs to the kitchen. The noise from the coffee grinder sounded like a wrecking ball in the still-quiet house, but everyone slept on. It would be another two hours before Nicole and Sophia reluctantly rolled out of bed, sleep crusted in the corners of their eyes, hoping it was Saturday and they didn't have to go to school.

She poured the water into the coffeepot, flicked the on switch, and sat at the table to wait. It was Wednesday, her day off. Her shopping day. She could make a list and get a head start on things. Normally the idea of getting her pantry and fridge organized excited her, but this morning she sat idle at the table, occasionally lifting her coffee to her mouth.

Daylight was still an hour away, but the days *were* getting longer.

She heard the shower upstairs and glanced at the clock. Barry was right on schedule. Maybe she'd surprise her girls and make blueberry pancakes for them. She opened the refrigerator and pulled out a carton of eggs and some milk.

The shower turned off. She removed a box of Raisin Bran from the cupboard, put on a fresh pot of coffee for Barry, and set a place at the table for him before turning back to the mix the pancake batter.

A few moments later, Barry kissed her cheek and wordlessly helped himself to a cup of coffee. Then she heard light footsteps descending the stairs.

"What's for breakfast?" Nicole asked as she rounded the corner.

"Good morning," Marie said.

"What's for breakfast?"

"*Good morning, Mom, nice to see you*," Marie said with an exaggerated sweetness.

Nicole mumbled a good morning and sat down. Sophia arrived a minute later, her hair a tangled mess.

"Not pancakes," Nicole said with disgust.

Marie tried to ignore her daughter's surliness. "I thought you liked pancakes."

"Not on a school day," Nicole whined. "They're too sweet. My mouth is sticky until lunchtime."

"I'll eat hers," Sophia piped in.

Nicole stood and grabbed a bowl from the cupboard. She helped herself to some cereal.

Peace descended immediately when Barry and the girls left. Marie stood at the front window and watched her daughters standing amid a group of children at the street corner. Marie liked to watch her kids come and go, and at such times she tried to pretend they weren't her children in order to see them as other people might see them. Often when she looked at them she thought of herself and Elizabeth as children: two dark-haired girls standing closely together. Only in this case, two years separated her girls and part of their closeness came from a natural blood bond. Nicole intuitively watched over her younger sister. She had been doing it for years. They hadn't chosen each other as Marie and Elizabeth had done all those summers ago when they found themselves at a playground looking for a friend.

She lingered at the front window until the school bus disappeared around the corner. It worried her that lately she enjoyed her children more when they weren't around. Grey clouds hung low in the sky. In the middle of the front yard a thick crust of ice was all that remained from the maze the girls had made after Christmas. Clumps of dried berries littered the ground beneath the mountain ash tree. The bits of lawn she could see were brown and in need of a good raking. Many of last fall's leaves were rotting in clumps along the perimeter of the flowerbeds. She had meant to tidy the yard before winter, but an early snowfall had caught her off guard.

The window was cool against her forehead. A furniture delivery van sped down the street and stirred up the grit and dirt that lay beside the curb. A moment later, a gold minivan followed. She stepped back from the window and the white sheer curtains fell back into place. She had seven hours to herself before her children returned home. Maybe Elizabeth would be free for lunch.

She went upstairs to get dressed. She'd sound casual, *Hey, Lizzie, are you free for lunch?* Or, *I'm coming downtown. Can I buy you lunch?* That didn't sound too needy, did it?

She pulled on a pair of jeans, surprised to find herself rehearsing a call to her best friend. Elizabeth used to rely on her, but she hadn't even asked for help moving, and she'd been in her new place for almost two weeks and still hadn't invited her over. In fact, they hadn't talked since the day Elizabeth had been over for lunch. How was that possible? Marie was beginning to have the feeling that there was a big party going on somewhere and her name had been left off the guest list.

Elizabeth used to need her, and Marie enjoyed being needed. Maybe she'd even enjoyed being envied.

She deferred the call until later.

By nine-thirty, Marie was ready to go. She backed the van down the driveway and into the street. A light breeze moved the branches of the pine tree in the neighbours' yard. They swayed in a gentle rhythm, as if inhaling and exhaling. A skiff of snow fell slowly to the ground. It was hard to believe that somewhere behind the greyness a brilliant sun waited for its turn to shine.

She drove as if on autopilot. Occasionally, Marie noticed her surroundings and was surprised to see the distance she'd already gone. She was thankful not to have had an accident given that she barely noted the blocks she was passing. She continued north, thinking she was heading to the grocery store. Traffic was steady. Soon she was in Frances's Strathcona neighbourhood of coffee shops and cafés. She passed the low brick building that housed the farmers' market on her left. Before she knew it she was going down Scona Road and crossing the Low Level Bridge. She gazed at a high-rise perched on the riverbank. It was the colour of sandstone and had balconies facing the valley. That's where Elizabeth lives now, she thought, and felt a momentary pang for her single life long ago, when the only person's day she planned was her own.

The next thing she knew, she was pulling into the parkade beneath the downtown library. Minutes later she was standing before a computer terminal. Under subject, she typed *Down syndrome*. Immediately, as if the person before her had been searching the same topic, a screen full of references appeared. *Newborn Babies and Down Syndrome. Down Syndrome Today. Everything You Need to Know About Down Syndrome. Down Syndrome: The First Year. How Children Learn. From Institution to Integration. Becoming an Advocate for Your Down Syndrome Child.* She scrolled up and down the screen and jotted down call numbers on a recipe card in a thin, dark scrawl.

Subject: Amniocentesis. See genetic testing.

Subject: Genetic Testing. See Human chromosome abnormalities.

When her index card was full, Marie moved tentatively to the stacks. Was she tempting fate by educating herself about Down syndrome? She scanned the spines of the books and felt new fears as a host of other maladies presented themselves: cerebral palsy, childhood leukemia, spina bifida, autism.

It doesn't hurt to know, a voice inside her said. She breathed deeply: dust, paper, mould.

It was still early, and the library was quiet. Only three people sat at the dozen or so tables that occupied the Quiet Zone. A librarian pushed a squeaky wooden cart laden with books down the aisles.

Grey light filtered in through the tall windows on the outside walls. A dishevelled man with dark, greasy hair and flapping running shoes wandered over to a chair in the corner and dropped his weight into it. He began a conversation with himself.

Marie picked up a book and gazed at the cover. A young girl was swinging on a swing. Her blond hair was pulled into two braids that were fastened with pink ribbons. She wore a frilly dress. Her mouth was open wide in laughter, and her teeth were sharp and crowded. She wore thick glasses. Her small hands clutched tightly at the chains that held the swing to the metal set. The picture caught her in mid-swing.

From Institution to Integration. She turned the book over, read the back cover, and noted with interest that the author was a local doctor.

Marie opened the book and began to read.

> Kids with Down syndrome are kids first. Thankfully, these children are no longer automatically condemned to institutions where, segregated from society, often ignored, and given little education, they fulfilled the low expectation held for them. Today, babies born with Down syndrome are more likely to be raised in their own loving home environment which, by contrast, helps them to be integrated into the everyday communities which will nurture and guide them as they move through all the physical changes of adolescence and into adulthood.

Marie stopped reading and flipped to the chapter on newborns. She read of parents' initial disappointment in discovering their child was not "normal," and the grief and anger that often followed. *How will we tell people? Will my child reach adulthood? And if so, who will care for him when we're gone?* She read of the gradual acceptance that followed when the parents began to focus on their baby's tiny features and their soft, soft skin. She read of the improved educational opportunities, the better health care practices, and the new laws designed to protect these children. She read that some cultures in the world had no word for babies with this condition.

Facts and figures jumped out at her. Trisomy 21. The babies have one extra chromosome. It occurs evenly in boys and girls. The babies tend to have low muscle tone and slightly irregular facial features. They have smaller than normal heads. Their eyes may appear to slant upward. They have mental retardation.

Marie closed her eyes for a moment and willed herself to continue. *The degree of mental retardation varies tremendously*, she read. *Your baby WILL learn. A normal IQ is 70–130. Most children with Down syndrome score in the moderate to mild retardation range, with IQs of 40–70.*

She picked up another book of personal stories and read of women who had decided to keep their babies and who had never looked back. Stories of personal triumph and joy. She also read of women who had terminated their pregnancies when a positive test for Down syndrome returned. *It's a lose–lose situation*, one woman confided. *It's like choosing between being stabbed or being shot. Either way, the pain is immense.*

She read of ethicists who believed that, once a fetus could survive on its own, at roughly twenty-four weeks, it should have the same right to life enjoyed by any human being. She read of surveys that showed seventy-five percent of people in Canada and the US believe that legal abortion is acceptable in cases where the fetus has an abnormality. She read and she sifted, skimming just enough information to learn something while simultaneously remaining aloof from the potential reality.

Her stomach growled. Suddenly the room brightened. Marie looked up. The sun had burned through the clouds and was shining in the tall, south-facing windows. A thick coating of dust on the window revealed a winter of neglect.

She thought of Nicole and Sophia, healthy and happy. But what about tomorrow or the days after? If something happened to one of her girls now, nothing would ever stop her love. Having a healthy baby was not a guarantee that it would have good health and fortune for life.

She'd be damned if she did and damned if she didn't. The stack of books sat before her, thick with human experiences. The weight of their burdens was stifling. She stood up quickly and put her coat on. The word trisomy rolled off her tongue, familiar in its rhythm. Try-so-me-fa-sol-la-ti-do. It was contagious, the small syllables that felt fun in her mouth. Try-so-me-fall-so-let-me-go.

She crossed the carpeted floor and dust rose in small bursts from beneath her feet. It danced in the shafts of sunlight and then gradually settled once again on the many flat surfaces.

What had she accomplished here? Nothing. She needed to go shopping. She would load her cart with all their necessities then return home and line the canned goods evenly on the pantry shelf. Lunch with Elizabeth no longer looked attractive. She was tired of being the one who always called first. She had her family to keep her busy; maybe she didn't really need Elizabeth that much anyway.

TWENTY-TWO

Elizabeth awoke on Saturday at home in her apartment with nothing on her calendar. She made oatmeal with wheat germ and toasted sunflower seeds for breakfast and enjoyed the contrast of textures and the way the brown sugar melted into a dark glaze that swirled on top of the white milk. The presentation was beautiful, almost like a well-designed floral arrangement.

This weekend was already better than the last one, when she'd woken Saturday morning with the worst hangover of her life. Her mouth had felt like someone had stuffed it full of cotton balls while she'd slept, and her pulse beat like a giant drum in her head. The last time she'd been so hungover had been in university, when Gillian had invited some friends to spend the night at her parents' cabin at Pigeon Lake. She and Marie had gone without knowing that Gillian had opened it up to a much larger crowd. It was a loud party. People had skinny dipped late into the night. A window was broken. The bathroom the next morning looked as if food poisoning had blown through the guest population. She and Marie both drank too much and basically fell asleep in the chairs they'd last been sitting in before oblivion overtook them.

But what Elizabeth most recalled as she put her breakfast bowl in the dishwasher and ran some hot water into the pot to soak was the similar feeling of hunger/nausea that persisted throughout the day. She and Marie had groaned from morning to mid-afternoon until they finally started to feel human again.

Marie. Elizabeth hadn't called her since moving into her new place. It had been hectic, getting packed and then getting organized in the apartment. Marie could have helped, but Elizabeth had wanted to be alone. It felt cathartic to build a new life without someone giving her advice on where she should put her furniture. But Marie was probably upset that she hadn't called yet. Thankfully she hadn't picked up that night Elizabeth had phoned when she was drunk. Elizabeth probably would have ended up crying at some point and getting all maudlin about Marie's pregnancy. Would Marie have felt vindicated that Elizabeth had made the wrong decision in moving out?

Elizabeth caught herself. Was Marie really that keen on seeing her best friend fail?

She picked up the phone and dialled Marie's number.

"Hi! I was hoping to catch you at home."

"Elizabeth!"

Marie truly sounded pleased. And a bit relieved.

"I'm sorry I haven't called," Elizabeth began. "Things have been kind of hectic lately."

"I know, with me too."

"Look, this is late notice, but I was wondering if you and the girls could come over this afternoon to see my new place. I'll pick up some snacks. It'd be nice. What do you think?"

"That would be great. The girls should be on their way home. Barry took them to their swimming lessons this morning. But I know they'll be delighted to come."

"Excellent! How about two-thirty?"

"Sounds good. Just give me your apartment number again, in case I can't find it. Can I bring anything?"

"No. Just yourselves. You'll be my first guests."

TWENTY-THREE

After Elizabeth's call, Marie hung up and returned to her weekend cleaning ritual. Saturday was bed sheets and bathrooms. She heated the chicken noodle soup that she'd made that morning. That, together with a grilled cheese sandwich, would keep her girls going until dinner. She glanced at her watch again and increased the flame under the pot. The girls would be so excited to visit Elizabeth's new place. Nicole in particular. She felt a pang of jealousy. Nicole was never that excited to see *her*, but she sure did idolize Elizabeth.

The soup bubbled in the pot. She gave it a stir and turned the flame down low. The sandwiches were ready to go into the frying pan as soon as the kids got home.

She filled the sink in the main floor bathroom with hot water and lemony liquid soap and put on some rubber gloves. Now that she thought about it, she realized Nicole hadn't expressed much interest in her of late, except when she wanted something, like food or money. Marie knew she shouldn't take it personally, but it was hard not to.

Just the other night she had felt an unsettling presence while doing the dishes and had turned to find Nicole's darkly appraising eyes making an inventory of her body, measuring and judging.

"What are you doing?" she'd asked. "Admiring my bum?"

Nicole had rolled her eyes. "Hardly."

There'd been a time when Nicole had picked out clothes for her. "Wear a dress, Mommy, the blue one." Or, if Marie was wearing a vest, then Nicole would find hers and put it on too. It was sweet and seemed to foreshadow the years ahead when Nicole would be older and ask for her advice on things. But maybe that period of wanting to be like her mother was already gone. Maybe that had been it, when she was six and adoring and filled with admiration for her mother. "You're so pretty, Mommy."

Marie had been shopping at Southgate one day and seen one of Nicole's best friends, Jody, outside the library. She'd been talking to a boy with long hair that covered one of his eyes. His jeans were ripped at both knees. He looked like trouble. And Marie had experienced a surge of hope that the girl might not be as good as everyone believed her to be. Then she'd felt an equal dose of guilt for wishing someone's child might become one of the "wrong" crowd.

That's why it was so easy to stay friends with Elizabeth. Her childlessness meant there wasn't any competition around the children. Marie hated how when other mothers bragged about their children's music awards or sports accomplishments that she, too, felt the impulse to trot out her daughters' accomplishments as if she were reading from a stellar and lively resume. But it was so hard just to listen without adding something about her own children. Maybe she was too competitive. Or maybe she was just insecure.

She finished scrubbing the bathroom floor and tucked a wisp of hair behind her ear. The girls would adore Elizabeth's new place. A high-rise! An elevator to the twelfth floor! A balcony with a view! Coming home afterwards would be torturous. *I wish we could live there*, they would whine, completely overlooking the fact that Elizabeth lived there alone.

The toilet bowl glistened.

Elizabeth didn't know to keep quiet about the pregnancy. How could she tell Elizabeth that she wasn't entirely sure if she wanted this baby?

Marie heard the door to the house open from the garage. She stored the rubber gloves in the cabinet beneath the sink and went into the kitchen. Nicole and Sophia came in, their hair damp and clinging to their cheeks.

"What's for lunch?" Sophia asked.

"How was swimming?"

"Good. What's for lunch?"

Marie turned on the burner beneath the sandwiches and told the girls to put their wet stuff in the laundry basket.

"Something smells good," Barry said as he walked in.

"It's chicken vegetable soup."

"Not again!" Nicole's mouth formed the shape of disgust.

"When was the last time I made it, huh? You tell me that."

Nicole looked surprised but didn't answer.

"Sheesh, someone got up on the wrong side of the bed," Barry said, and Marie hated him at that moment.

She put a bowl of soup in front of Nicole. "Sorry I snapped, sweetie, but I thought you liked chicken soup."

"I do. I just don't feel like having any today."

It was hard not to mimic her response. *I just don't feel like having any today.* One day she'd have her own kids and feel a similar frustration when they suddenly stopped liking something or complained about the food placed before them. She almost said as much but then decided not to. "Well at least eat your grilled cheese, please."

Just a grain of gratitude from time to time would be nice, she thought, a small nod to acknowledge her hard work.

Sophia bounced into the kitchen again and sat down at her place. "Yum, grilled cheese. Can I have some ketchup, please?"

How could one child be so easy to please and another be so difficult? Marie put the ketchup in front of Sophia and ruffled her damp hair.

"What are we doing this afternoon? Can I have a friend over?" Sophia asked.

Barry searched the refrigerator for pickles and olives.

"Are you sticking around the house this afternoon?" Marie asked her husband.

He nodded. "Golf's on later."

"Why don't we ever do anything interesting?" Nicole asked.

Marie ignored her. "Let me talk to your father alone for a few minutes to figure out what our afternoon will look like."

"Why can't you talk in front of us?" Nicole asked.

"Because I'd prefer to have some privacy."

"How is that different from whispering?" Nicole added. "You always say it's not polite to whisper."

"Just a few minutes, please."

She took Barry's hand and led him out of the room.

"What was that about?" Barry asked.

Marie shook her head. "I don't know. I'm feeling out of sorts. Elizabeth called and invited me and the girls over this afternoon to see her new place."

"That's nice. You haven't seen her in a while."

"But it's *not*. The girls are going to go over there and be totally in love with her apartment with the balcony and the view."

"I don't know about that," Barry interrupted. "They've been to my office before and it has the same view."

"But you don't *live* there. I feel like Nicole doesn't want to be around me these days, and she *adores* Elizabeth. Plus," she continued, "the girls don't know about the pregnancy, and I haven't told Elizabeth that I'm worried about the baby's health."

"Why don't you just go alone?"

She paused. "What do you mean?"

"Don't take the girls. Tell Elizabeth that they had other plans."

"But I already said we'd come."

"Well tell her that *I* made plans that you didn't know about."

Marie felt a glimmer of relief. "I don't know . . ."

"If you go alone you can talk to her about the baby. It probably wouldn't hurt to have someone else to talk to."

Sophia bounced out of the kitchen. "Finished yet?"

Marie nodded. "I'm going out to do some shopping."

"Can I come?"

"Maybe next time," Marie said. "I've got a bunch of errands to do."

"I could help." Sophia's bright eyes took on a tinge of pleading.

"I need some time to myself, honey."

"But you've been alone all *morning*. Why can't I come?"

Marie wavered slightly and smiled at her youngest. "Next time," she said and watched both corners of her daughter's mouth turn down. "I promise."

"Hey sweet-pea, go ahead and call a friend if you want," Barry added. "I'll be around all afternoon."

From the doorway, Nicole stared at her mother, then slowly turned away.

The neighbourhood felt eerily quiet for a Saturday afternoon. No children played outside. The blinds in the front windows of most of the houses were closed. So, too, were all the garage doors. It was the in-between season—too early yet for yard work and gardening and too late for any winter play. In the next few weeks the city's street cleaners would come and remove all the gravel and sand that hugged the curbs alongside every street. Until then, the air would remain gritty with winter silt.

She put her blinker on and turned north on the main road flanked by an endless variety of stores and merged into the slow-moving traffic. She stopped at a plant store and bought a large rubber tree in a dark blue ceramic pot. She hadn't intended to spend so much on Elizabeth's housewarming present.

As she loaded it into the back of the van, she practised some excuses to explain the girls' absence. *I forgot they had a birthday party.* No, that wouldn't work. Elizabeth knew how organized she was. *I was hoping we could have a chance to talk alone.* But she'd missed her chance to say that when Elizabeth had called. If only she hadn't accepted the invitation so quickly.

Too soon she found herself crossing the Low Level Bridge. In the river below, large chunks of ice broke steadily from the ice dams along the shore and merged into the brown waters moving sluggishly on the invisible current. She kept left and rounded the bend to her friend's new home.

The high-rise stood at the base of the hill, a tall magnet for winter grime. An intricate wooden boardwalk of stairs and sidewalks traversed the hill in a series of switchbacks that led up to the downtown core. She smiled as she recalled Sophia once asking why they called it downtown when you had to go up to get there.

She parked in a visitors parking stall and stepped out of the van. Grit and dust spiralled in the wind.

The plant was heavy. She balanced it on her thigh and closed the side door. Then she hoisted it higher in her arms and walked into the building.

Elizabeth buzzed her in. Marie dragged the plant into the turquoise and pink lobby and toward the two black elevators. Now that she was here, she almost wished she'd brought the girls along. So far the building was nothing to brag about.

The doors opened on the twelfth floor and Marie hoisted the plant one last time. A gold-plated sign on the wall facing the elevators listed the apartment numbers. She turned left for 1208.

At the end of the hallway a door opened and Elizabeth stepped out, illuminated by the light spilling into the hall from her apartment.

The distance between the two women shrank with each step Marie took. She shifted the plant in front of her to block her face. Her arms ached. Her stomach felt suddenly light.

"Where are the girls?" Elizabeth asked.

Marie avoided eye contact and groaned as she put the plant down inside. "Whew, that was heavy!" She dusted her hands on her pants. "They didn't feel like coming. They stayed up late last night to finish a movie, so they were exhausted after swimming. But they said to say hi and asked if they could come next time." She was explaining too much but couldn't stop. "Plus, Sophia had sort of planned to have a friend over. She hadn't told *me* though; she'd cleared it with Barry."

Elizabeth nodded and took Marie's coat.

"They wanted me to get you a really big plant. Easy for them to say! I was the one who had to carry it."

Elizabeth looked dubious, as if she didn't quite believe her. Marie wondered why she just hadn't told her the truth: *I wanted to talk about the baby. I'm afraid that Nicole will love you more.* No, she couldn't say that last bit.

"Where do you want it?"

Together they lifted the plant and placed it in a patch of sunlight by the sliding glass door. The mid-afternoon sun shone brightly through the window.

"That looks lovely," Elizabeth said. "Thank you. And thank the girls too. Who is Sophia's lucky friend?"

Marie opened her mouth but nothing came out.

"You said she was having a friend over."

"Oh, yes. Her friend of the week is Stephanie."

"Does she live in your neighbourhood?"

"Yes, not far at all."

"That's good," Elizabeth smiled. "So Barry didn't have to go and get her?"

"No, she walked." Marie turned to hide the flush in her cheeks. "This place looks great. Can I have a tour?"

"Well, there's not much to see. This is the living room." Elizabeth lifted her right arm horizontally and swept it slowly around the room. Then she walked briskly toward the hall. "And in here is the bedroom."

A double bed stood in the middle of the room, covered with a patchwork quilt and at least a dozen throw pillows of assorted colours. Against the wall was a dresser made from polished steel; its drawers were old wooden Coke crates. Some cast iron hooks on the walls held Elizabeth's scarves and accessories. She had removed the closet doors and hung a bead curtain instead. Elizabeth had a great decorating sense. Nicole would have loved this.

"The bathroom is over here," Elizabeth went on, retracing her steps. "And this is the kitchen and dining room."

The table was set for four. China plates with delicate pink flowers and gold rims were set beside pink linen napkins upon which sat small silver forks and spoons. A crystal vase of colourful gerbera daisies served as the centrepiece, the sharp pinks, yellows, oranges, and reds like a sudden burst of summer. On a silver tray beside the vase was an assortment of goodies: banana bread cut into triangles, plum-sized scones with jam and cream, delicate rectangles of mille feuille, and bite-sized lemon squares. Chilling in a silver bucket at the table's edge were four cans of Italian soda.

"Oh, Elizabeth," she said. "I'm so sorry. If I had known you were going to go to this much trouble I'd have insisted the girls come with me."

Elizabeth shrugged. "It doesn't matter. I suppose it'll give us more of a chance to visit. I hope you're hungry!" She went into the kitchen and returned with a carafe of coffee. "I made decaf," she said and gestured toward Marie's belly. "I figured you'd be off caffeine."

Marie nodded. She moved toward the sliding glass doors and stepped onto the balcony while Elizabeth poured the coffee. Sure enough, the view was lovely. It was breezy at this height, and cool. She walked to the railing and rested her elbows on it. The ground was a long way down. She started when Elizabeth appeared suddenly beside her with two coffee mugs in her hands.

"Beautiful, isn't it?"

Marie nodded and took the coffee.

"The ice is finally coming off the river," she added. "Believe it or not, I think spring is on the way."

"I hope so. It was a long winter."

They stared quietly out at the valley. It was too early yet for any signs of green, but the belt of naked black trees along the river offered its own kind of beauty.

Marie nodded to the distance. "Those trees wouldn't have given much of a hiding place, would they?" She shook her head. "I still can't believe some of the stuff we heard when we were up that tree. I wonder whatever happened to that principal. Remember? The one who ended up with that girl's dad?"

"I have no idea. I've always wondered about that girl who flunked first grade. Jane something-or-other. Imagine flunking first grade. What would that do for your self-esteem?"

They went back inside, and this time Marie noticed the furniture. The leather couch and matching chair. The low-slung coffee table made from some kind of acid-washed metal. Everything was new.

"Do you like it?"

Elizabeth might as well have punched Marie in the stomach. She hadn't consulted her on any of this. Normally they would have gone shopping together. What had happened to their friendship? She wrapped her arms around her middle and rocked imperceptibly.

"Yes, it's fine," she lied. "I can see you've spent some time decorating."

"Oh, just a bit here and there," Elizabeth said dismissively.

Marie noticed pictures hanging on the kitchen wall. She walked closer and peered at the black and white images. "I haven't seen this in a while." In one photo she was twenty years younger and twenty pounds lighter.

"Whose roof are we standing on?" Marie asked.

"That was Gillian's."

"God, I haven't thought about her in years." Only part of that was true. She *didn't* think of Gillian, but she often remembered the party she'd had at Pigeon Lake. Marie had passed out on the couch. When she woke up the next morning with a wicked hangover, she'd groped her way to the bathroom and tried to overlook the pools of vomit in the bathtub. How could people be so disgusting?

"Whatever happened to Gillian, anyway?"

"I don't know. I bumped into her at Southgate about ten years ago. She was with two of her kids. I think she had four already at that time."

Gillian had been religious, yet she'd thrown some wild parties.

"I guess she could have had four more by now," Elizabeth said, reading her thoughts. She sat down. "Help yourself."

Marie put one of everything onto a small china dish.

"How are you feeling, anyway?" Elizabeth asked.

Terrible. Terrible and terrified. "Better now. Now that the first trimester is done, the morning sickness is over, and I'm not so exhausted as I was."

"That's good."

"My doctor's scheduled me for a routine amnio next week. Apparently being pregnant at thirty-nine means I'm a bit of a 'risk.'"

"Sometimes I think doctors just like sticking needles into people. I know I was a pincushion for more than a few years."

Marie remembered the bruises that covered Elizabeth's stomach. The hair that had sprouted on her chin. How at one point she'd been so bloated she looked like she'd been on an eating binge with Marie.

They sampled their pastries in silence. *Tell her you're afraid.* The chair creaked as Marie shifted. She remembered its newness.

"Have you talked to Ron lately?"

"No, I told him not to call for a while, but I was feeling so lonely one night that I tried him anyway. And can you believe it, the bugger wasn't home! He hadn't reset the machine either, even though I'd left him instructions. I must have let it ring a hundred times before I finally gave up."

Marie pictured Elizabeth staring out over the darkened valley, the phone at her ear and nobody answering on the other end.

"Do you miss him?"

Elizabeth shrugged. "It's hard to say. Do I miss *him* or do I just need to get used to being alone?"

"Well, you guys have been through a lot. Maybe some time apart will help you know whether or not you should be together."

"That's what I'm hoping. Lately I've been feeling fond of him. I'm remembering our early days when we were just getting to know each other."

"Apparently Frances bumped into him at the farmers' market," Marie said. "She was *really* mad that I hadn't told her you guys had split up. She felt like an idiot when she asked him what was new."

They laughed, imagining the look on Frances's face.

"Then she interrogated me. She wanted to know if you were seeing someone else. She said you'd better watch out because probably all the single teachers at his school are lining up for him. 'Trolling,' I think was her exact word."

"Well, she's probably right. But I think I confused the vultures when I sent Ron some flowers for Valentine's Day. I sent them to the school."

"That's sweet." They were courting again, Marie thought, and she pushed away the jealousy that she was beginning to revisit.

"It gets better; the next day he sent me some flowers at work."

Marie laughed, imagining a delivery person delivering flowers to a flower shop. She watched Elizabeth lick her finger and dab at the crumbs on her plate. She was wearing a short-sleeved shirt and Marie admired the sculpted cut of her upper arm.

"I sense there's more to this story."

"Maybe . . . We'll see. We haven't actually seen each other yet. We've written a couple of letters."

"Letters?"

"Yeah, you know, paper and pen . . ."

"Of course I know," Marie said. "How did that start?"

Elizabeth shrugged. "I was missing him one night, and I decided to write down some of the sweeter memories I had of us together. I didn't write much, but it felt nice to remember them. And then I figured, What the hell, why not put a stamp on it and send it to him? Maybe he'd enjoy remembering those times too."

"And?"

"And a week later I got a letter from him."

"I *love* that!"

"Yeah, me too. You know, when I first left I wondered if I was just punishing him for not getting me pregnant. It was almost like I had no one to blame, so I decided to blame him."

"Well, it's not like you'd been wanting to leave for a long time or anything," Marie said.

"Actually, I'd been thinking about it for a couple of years."

Marie put her coffee down abruptly.

"Oh, for God's sake. Don't take it so personally, Marie. This isn't about you, okay? It's not like you call me every day. You're busy. You've got your family and now you're working part-time." Elizabeth shrugged. "You probably would have said the same thing as my mom: *Don't leave him, he's the best thing to ever happen to you.*"

Marie picked up a lemon square. A dusting of icing sugar covered the filling that sat on a thin pastry crust. She bit into it. It was sweet and tart at the same time and melted on her tongue like a snowflake.

"I wouldn't have seen it as complaining," Marie said. "It's natural that people go through trying times in their relationships. It doesn't mean they've made a mistake necessarily. Barry and I have certainly had our ups and downs."

"I know," Elizabeth interrupted. "It's just . . ."

"What?"

"Oh, I don't know." Elizabeth shrugged.

"No, tell me. What?"

"You don't tell me everything that goes on in your life, do you?" Elizabeth said firmly.

"The big stuff I do," Marie said. *Tell her now.*

"Well I'll try harder to keep you informed," Elizabeth promised. "Really, I will."

Marie opened her mouth. "I was downtown the other day, and I almost called you for lunch. I was at the library and . . ."

"Oh, that would have been nice," Elizabeth said, "but I've started going to the gym again at lunch. I do yoga three times a week and I row on the other days." She held up her taut arms and showed her muscles. "I realized that I'd stopped taking care of myself, so I'm trying to eat better and exercise more. Plus," she added, "it helps pass the time. Speaking of which"—she gestured toward Marie's belly— "the time's getting closer, huh? Nicole and Sophia will be great big sisters. I remember Nicole once telling me that she'd love for you to have another baby."

"Really?" Marie said. "When was that?"

"Oh, a few years ago. She'd asked me why I didn't have any kids of my own. I told her that I really wanted one but was having some problems getting pregnant." Elizabeth laughed. "Do you know what she said?"

Marie shook her head.

"She said, 'Maybe my mom could have one for you.' Wasn't that sweet?"

Marie smiled. "Nicole's always been fond of you."

"Speaking of Nicole, what would you say if I asked her to work part-time at the shop this summer?"

Marie imagined Nicole's delight.

"I could use her for a few hours every Saturday. And I'd teach her how to cut flowers and make arrangements."

"She'd love that."

"And I'm sure she'd love some pocket money too. It's still a few months away. Do you want to ask her, or should I phone?"

"Why don't you call? I won't mention it. It'd mean more to her if you called."

Marie looked at her watch. "I'd better get going," she said.

Elizabeth filled a small box with leftover goodies. "Take these home, and tell the girls I'll have them over soon."

Marie dropped her eyes and thanked her.

"When is your amnio appointment again?"

"Next week."

"I'll put it on my calendar to be sure to send you good vibes."

"Thanks." She looked down at the box in her hand so Elizabeth wouldn't see the tears that had filled her eyes.

"And thanks for the plant."

"You're welcome."

Marie put on her jacket and hugged her friend goodbye. She felt Elizabeth's eyes on her all the way down the hallway. She waved once more when the elevator arrived, then she stepped inside, eager for the doors to close.

TWENTY-FOUR

Elizabeth watched Marie walk down the dimly lit hallway. If she hadn't been watching, she felt sure Marie would have burst into a run. She waved again, and then Marie disappeared into the elevator.

The deadbolt slid into place. *The kids didn't feel like coming.* Marie had never been a very good liar.

Outside on the balcony, she watched Marie exit the building and walk toward her van, cradling the box of pastries in her hand. The van backed out, merged into the southbound traffic, and disappeared over the bridge.

Every time Elizabeth had tried to talk about the baby, Marie had changed the subject. She wondered why.

The front of her building was now in shade, but the sun continued to shine on the floodplains alongside the river. At the park to the south a dozen players warmed up at the baseball diamond. On the still-brown grass the white ball could have been the last snowball of the year. She found herself watching a lean, dark-haired figure in right field who had a similar stride to Ron's.

Two months had passed without either one of them calling, and as the days passed she realized the extent of her loss. She'd be behind the counter at work and think he was in the store. Her heart would flutter wildly for a moment until she realized it was someone else. How ironic. When she had moved out she hadn't expected to be the one disappointed.

She gazed out at the valley again. Joggers, cyclists, and dog walkers dotted the trails. The day hadn't turned out as she'd planned. Instead of it being an exuberant housewarming party, Marie's visit had tinged the afternoon with sadness. She thought about phoning Marie's house and telling the girls she was sorry they hadn't been able to come. Marie would arrive home and find two angry daughters waiting.

A more mature response would be to wait until Marie was ready to unburden herself with whatever it was that was bothering her. In all fairness, she could understand Marie's hesitation in talking about the baby with her. But if she was patient, Marie would come to her. She always did.

Inside, she finished clearing away the dishes. Then she wiped the table, found a clean sheet of paper, and sat down.

Dear Ron, she began.

> Another weekend without you. I was just out on my balcony catching the last of the day's sunshine when I saw a handful of men playing baseball in the field by the old brick school (did you know that was once a home for unwed mothers? It was run by nuns, I think). Of course I thought of you immediately (because of the baseball, not the nuns). I guess you'll be happy to know that even when you're not here my thoughts easily turn toward you. Animal magnetism you'd probably say. Right? Grrrrr. But I was thinking about your eye–hand coordination (or lack thereof)! Remember that grounder you stopped with your jaw? I was so happy that you hadn't lost any teeth because you've got a beautiful smile.
>
> But enough about your good looks. I know I was the one to put an embargo on face-to-face visits, but at this very moment I'm thinking that was a really stupid idea. I deserve a failing grade for that one.
>
> I miss you, Ron. These months alone have helped me to understand some things. Like how I haven't appreciated you enough. Like how you're the best friend I've ever had.

She stopped writing. It was true, wasn't it? Ron *was* her best friend. How had she not seen that before?

> I also don't think you fully understand how crazy I was. I never did tell you about the baby clothes I used to buy and

hide all over the house. Mostly they were infant sleepers, clothes so tiny you could hardly believe they'd even fit a baby. They were like the shucked-off shells of beetles that I'd find when I was a kid. Or abandoned turtle shells. I got into the habit of buying them because I thought it might increase my chances of getting pregnant. Even as I write this I feel stupid, but it made sense to me at the time, which just goes to show how crazy I'd become.

I think it was the terrycloth material that really set me off. I just loved the soft nubby texture of those sleepers. They reminded me of my favourite pair of pyjamas when I was about seven or eight years old—a pair of one-piece purple velour pjs with attached feet. The bottoms of the feet were made out of a slippery white material, and I loved how I could run and slide across the kitchen floor. Finally I grew too tall and my toes started to poke out of the enclosed feet, so I cut them off and had my mom stitch a seam at the bottom of the pantlegs so they wouldn't unravel. God I loved those pyjamas! When I rubbed the velour one way the purple became light, and when I rubbed it the other way it turned dark. I used to flatten out the material all in one direction and then use it like a chalk board to write things on.

Those were good days. Maybe by buying the terrycloth sleepers I was trying to capture some of that happiness for our child, the one we would have together.

The light had waned in the small apartment. Elizabeth stopped writing and cleared the remaining dishes from the table. She welcomed the coming darkness, for then she could go to bed, place the flat of her hand on the empty pillow beside her, and imagine Ron's warm body beside her.

That's enough for now. I'm going to bed. I really wish you were here.
Love, your Lizzie

She reread the letter. Much still needed to be said, but it was a start, wasn't it? She could write another letter. And another. And maybe if he wrote back, between the two of them, they could remember enough reasons to piece their marriage back together again.

TWENTY-FIVE

April arrived with cool spring rains. The squirrels and the blue jays vied for peanuts at the feeder in Marie's backyard. The robins' return added a splash of much-needed colour to the branches of the pine trees. Spring cleaning began.

Marie woke up. The neighbours' dog began to bark. That was a good omen; the day was starting as any other. Except Barry had taken the day off. He'd risen and showered early. "I can't sleep anyway," he'd said. "You might as well stay in bed. I'll get breakfast for the girls."

In less than two hours, a doctor would stick a long needle through her tautly stretched abdomen. A long needle, hollow like a quill, that would gently sip some of her amniotic fluid. Or puncture her like a balloon; there was always that possibility. She tried not to dwell on that part. She pictured a large glass vial slowly filling with bubbling liquid, smoke rising from the experiment, bells ringing, electrical currents running between two conductors, and a hunchbacked man shuffling from one experiment to another, his knuckles hairy and bloated as he reached for a vial. She'd always been afraid of needles. It wasn't too late to change her mind.

Barry called for her.

Dr. Cuthbert had warned that many women experienced cramping after the procedure. She suggested that someone be with her to drive her home.

"What about the possibility of miscarrying?" Marie had asked, remembering her sister's ominous words. "How will I know if the cramping is normal or if it's the beginning of a miscarriage?"

"Well, let me start by saying that your chances of miscarrying are low," Dr. Cuthbert reassured her. "However, miscarriages can occur, and they're most likely to happen in the first twenty-four to forty-eight hours. So take it easy for a few days. Put your feet up if you can, and if you find yourself bleeding at all, come in right away to see me."

Mis-carry. Such a stupid word. What happened to your baby? Oh, I took my eye off the ball. I fumbled the pass.

Then she realized that miscarry rhymed with trisomy. *Tri-so-me-fall-so-let-me-go.*

Downstairs at last, Marie had a quick cup of decaf and some toast. Then she put Nicole and Sophia's lunches together.

"How come you're driving us to school today?" Sophia asked. "Why isn't Daddy going to work?"

"I have a doctor's appointment," Marie said.

"Is Dad going with you?" Nicole asked.

"Yes, he is. Now come on, let's get our shoes on."

"Why is he going with you?" Nicole persisted.

Marie looked into her daughter's face. How mature she looked with her knit brow and her small, pursed lips. She wondered if it was every eldest child's burden to carry the weight of her parents' happiness on her shoulders.

"He's coming with me because I asked him to."

Nicole studied her mother. Her eyes lingered on her abdomen. "Mom?"

"We have to hurry, Nicole. What is it?"

"Are you going to have a baby?"

Marie froze. *Not yet,* she pleaded. *I only need another two weeks.* She met her daughter's eyes and wavered. Then she knelt down and pulled her into a tight embrace. "Yes," she whispered. "I am."

Nicole pulled her face away and beamed. "Really?"

Marie nodded and wiped a tear from her cheek.

"When?"

"Not until the end of summer. We've got a ways to go yet."

Then Nicole's face clouded. "Why is Daddy going with you to the doctor? Is everything okay?"

"Don't worry, sweetie. We are just going to make sure everything's fine."

Sophia came into the kitchen, ready to put her lunch into her backpack.

"Guess what, Sophia?" Nicole said. "You get to be a big sister after all! Mom's going to have a baby!"

The girls squealed and jumped up and down, surprising Marie

with their instant ability to access happiness. She realized how muted everything had been lately.

"Can I come to the doctor's office too?" Sophia asked.

"Not today, honey. Just Mommy and Daddy are going. You need to go to school. Come on, grab your school bag."

Barry had pulled the car out into the driveway, and Marie could hear him revving the engine. The sky was a blunt, shark grey, and a light mist was falling. She ushered her children out the front door, their backpacks dragging like stubby tails, then she hurried after them to the car.

"Daddy, Daddy, we know!" Sophia shouted when she jumped in the car.

Nicole beamed. "We can't wait!"

Barry looked questioningly at Marie, and she shrugged her shoulders to convey her innocence.

"I knew it," Nicole said. "I knew Mom was putting on weight, but I wasn't quite sure about the baby until you said you were going to the doctor's office. That's when I guessed." She was immensely pleased with herself.

"Can the baby sleep in my room when it's born?" Sophia asked.

Nicole's face suddenly registered horror. "I'm not going to have to share a room with Sophia, am I?"

"What?" Sophia whined. "Am I going to lose my room? It's not fair."

"Just hold your horses," Barry said as he backed down the driveway. "One step at a time. Nobody's going to lose a room, okay?"

The doctor used ultrasound images to make sure the needle didn't puncture the baby. That baby didn't burst, Marie didn't burst. Afterwards, Barry carefully helped her to the car.

They buckled up silently. Barry's hands splayed wide on the steering wheel. Outside of the parkade a light rain misted the windshield.

"First we wait almost a month for an ultrasound," Barry said, "and then we wait two months for amnio. And now we're *still* waiting."

Marie reached out and stroked his cheek lightly. "Hang in there," she said. "We're in the home stretch."

Barry brought her hand to his lips. "How're you feeling?"

"My abdomen's a bit tight. But the doctor told me to expect that. I think I'll spend the afternoon in bed until the girls get home. I'm glad they don't have dance today."

"I wish Nicole hadn't guessed," Barry said. "What if we don't get good news? Then what do we tell the girls?"

"That depends on what we decide," she replied.

Barry pulled into their driveway. "Wait there." He rushed to her side of the car and helped her out.

Marie stood slowly before stretching to her full height. Barry took her elbow and placed his hand firmly on the small of her back as he directed her up the stairs and into the front door.

"I'm okay." Marie laughed. "I'm not going to break."

"You can't be too careful," he said and placed his palm gently on her abdomen.

She must have fallen asleep because the doorbell startled her from a dream. She gingerly made her way down the stairs, cradling her pelvis as if she were carrying her daughter's fishbowl.

A man stood on the porch holding some wrapped flowers. The rain had turned to a light snow. "Marie MacPherson?"

"Yes." She reached for the colourfully wrapped bundle and smiled. She hadn't expected Barry to be so sweet.

She carried the flowers to the kitchen and removed a crystal vase from the cupboard over the fridge. Then she unwrapped the paper: a dozen red tulips. *Here's to good news!* the card read. *Elizabeth.*

Good old Elizabeth.

She had sent her tulips once before. They were the perfect apology flower, she maintained, because she thought of them as "two lips" meeting in a kiss. Then, she was apologizing for stealing Marie's boyfriend. Well, not stealing, per se, but the flowers had been a definite peace offering. And the card had repeated Elizabeth's case: *I never dated him when he was with you! Honest!*

Elizabeth knew that tulips were Marie's favourite flower.

Marie cut the stems and placed the vase on the table in the front foyer. The flowers were beautiful, especially since the morning rain had turned to snow.

She opened the front door to check the mail. Across the street, tiny green shoots pushed up through the thin dusting of snow on the neighbours' lawn. The small poplar trees that lined the block still stood naked. It would be almost another month before they'd be covered in leaf again.

A robin landed at the base of the pine tree in her neighbours' yard. It cocked its head and stared briefly with an unblinking eye. She'd read somewhere that a robin's hearing was so sophisticated it could actually hear worms moving beneath the grass. That's why it sat so still at times, its head cocked to one side, its ear pointing down to the moist ground—it was listening for the worm's slow meandering as it tunnelled through the densely packed earth.

The robin resumed its hunt, hopping on spindly legs toward the leaf mulch at the base of the hedge.

Marie saw her baby on the screen again, saw its head tilted to the side, and imagined its tightly cupped ears listening, listening to the snow falling.

Dr. Maclean sat at his desk and stared out the window to the open field. Empty. Always empty. Not even cows or horses to break the monotony or to add some life. The children were never let out to play here, and there was never any laughter.

And given the situation with Carolyn, Dr. Maclean now understood that there was an uglier side to Poplar Grove than even he could have imagined. He saw dark, secret tunnels winding far below the building's surface and shadows that darted furtively in and out of hidden doorways. He imagined his own babies at home, safe with his wife, who would meet with her friends and their children in neighbourhood parks to pass the time and allow the children to play.

How long could he stay here now that the faults of Poplar Grove were so glaring? He couldn't possibly defend the place against Mrs. Harrington's rage because he shared her convictions that something awful had happened here. Carolyn had not been cared for, despite her still being alive. She had beaten the odds and *stayed* alive, and look where it had gotten her.

The doctor raised a hand to his mouth and began to gnaw at his fingertips. He had just started to bite his nails again. It was a habit his wife despised, yet he took great comfort in manually paring down the nails. Such a personal act it was. He'd never seen someone bite someone else's nails to the quick.

It was still early, but he stood up and stared out the window. The asylum bus would arrive just after lunch. Perhaps Mrs. Harrington would be on it. Perhaps this day would bring an answer to the baby's future. Dr. Maclean could not explain his anxiety at keeping the infant at Poplar Grove. She was healthy and whole. She couldn't possibly thrive here. And that glaring recognition caused him to extrapolate the condition of care to *all* of the inhabitants. *No one* could thrive here.

Poplar Grove was a dead zone, a place where humans struggled to live while those around them hoped they would die. How could any parent or relative suffer anything but despair at visiting a child here?

And to think that he was one of the people who apparently condoned this treatment. Carolyn's pregnancy exposed the darkest side of human nature: the predatory desire to prey on weakness. Had she been raped? Could it possibly have been consensual? And if not, who else under his charge might have suffered similar indignities?

His mouth moved to the next finger, and he chewed firmly to strip away the nail tips.

Shortly after eleven o'clock, the front desk receptionist brought in a stack of mail. On the top of the pile was a letter in an unfamiliar script. He reached for it immediately and read the return address. Mrs. Donald Harrington. He pounded his fist on the desk. She wasn't going to come! He'd sent the letter five days ago and was expecting her to visit any time now. Instantly, he knew he'd made a grave error. Why hadn't he looked up her address and visited in person? He could have told her about the child and reassured her that the baby appeared to be perfectly fine. He wanted to get the child out of this place. Get it someplace where she would receive love and attention. He'd offered to take the child home, but the board members had voted against it. He ripped open the letter and began to read.

> July 15, 1963
> Dear Dr. Maclean,
> Thank you for your letter dated July 12. I appreciate your desire to keep me informed, and I truly believe that you have the infant's best interest at heart. I am both moved and reassured by your genuine display of kindness and I want to take this opportunity to thank you.
> However, I cannot impress upon you the emotional pain I've experienced by placing a mongoloid child in an institution. For the past dozen years I have visited faithfully to alleviate the guilt I suffered in leaving my baby to be raised by strangers even though every instinct in my body told me to bring her home. Over and again

I was told it was the best thing for her, that she would be taken care of, and more of the same such nonsense. I see now that nothing could be further from the truth. I also see now that people like Carolyn are at the mercy of predators and are defenceless against them. Where there should be good stewardship, there is cunning deceit. I am alone in knowing that I could not protect my daughter from life's cruel humiliations. I agreed to put her in Poplar Grove to lock her away from the brutal workings of a society in which she has no place; instead, I inadvertently left her to the lions. Indeed, by the time it occurred to me that she required protection it was too late.

You may have noticed that I have not visited Carolyn since discovering she was pregnant. Likely you think me an unmoving, judgmental, and unforgiving woman, but you would be incorrect in this assessment. There are more details to this situation than you can begin to imagine, and it is too late for me to rectify the past. Consequently, I must continue to focus on the present and the future of my immediate family. It pains me to confess that my husband believes Carolyn to be deceased and my children do not know of her existence. While this now seems like a grave omission, I cannot rewrite our family history. Or, rather, I will not.

However, the child is entirely innocent and should not suffer, unique though her existence may be. Hence I implore you to see that she be placed in a loving home, and I will sign whatever papers are required. As you made no mention of Carolyn's condition in the letter, I shall assume that she came through the labour in good health.

I shall drop in at your office when I next visit Carolyn, although I cannot say exactly when that might be.
With gratitude and regret,
Margaret Harrington

Dr. Maclean let the letter fall onto his desk. She was not coming to take the child. She was not coming.

Yet could he blame her? He felt the sting of her rebuke yet knew she was right. Poplar Grove had not kept her daughter safe, despite the assurances she'd been given when she handed over her infant child. How could he begin to understand what she might feel now?

He recognized the futility of trying to change her mind. She had suffered enough harm already. Now it was his job to ensure that the child be removed quickly from this place. He remembered the weight of the baby in his arms, her rosebud mouth sucking hungrily at the formula he'd so quickly thrown together. She could easily die here. In the days since her birth, he was the only one to visit her for reasons other than fulfilling the basic necessities. Without his attention, the child would receive no affection. No one would talk to the infant, tickle her cheeks. Try to elicit a smile. The early days were so crucial in a child's development. It had been proven. And now Dr. Maclean understood that the early days were crucial for *all* children, not just the healthy ones.

And as this new realization filled his consciousness, he was ashamed that this obvious insight had not occurred to him earlier.

He picked up the phone and dialled Dr. Stallworthy's number. It was up to the board to decide the next move, but he would encourage them to place the child in proper care until such time that she could be adopted. He would make sure that move happened.

Marie's father picked up on the fourth ring, and she was surprised. "Dad?"

"No, it's Pierre Trudeau. Who did you think was going to answer?"

She laughed. It was an old family joke. Fay had had a crush on the former prime minister for years. If someone didn't leave a message on the machine, or hung up when they answered, then they got into the habit of saying it must have been Pierre.

"You never answer the phone."

"I do when your mother's yelling at me from the bathroom."

"Well, how are you, Dad? I haven't talked to you in a while."

"I'm ready to come home. We're leaving next week. Hopefully we've missed all the bad weather up there."

They talked about the weather, about his golf game, about his hip that'd been bothering him more lately. Marie enjoyed the familiarity and comfort of his voice.

She'd been a little girl once, and he'd tucked her into bed at night and kissed the tip of her nose. *How much do I love you?* he'd ask.

BIG, she'd shout, and they'd both spread their arms as wide as they could to show how great their love was. Her eyes filled with tears as she remembered that. They hadn't said that in a long time.

Daddy? Can I tell you something?

"Here's your mom now."

"Hi, Marie. I *told* your father it was worth answering the phone sometimes."

Marie laughed. "I'm phoning with some news. I wanted to tell you before the girls spilled the beans."

A note of suspicion crept into Fay's voice. "Good news or bad news? Now my heart's racing. Should I sit down?"

"I don't know. Maybe."

"Oh, God," Fay said and lowered her voice. "Don't tell me. You're pregnant."

Marie swallowed hard. Why did her mother always look for the negative in every situation?

"Marie?"

"I'm here."

"You're pregnant." A statement.

"I am," Marie responded lightly. "You're going to be grandparents again."

There was a pause on the other end of the line. "I thought you were finished," Fay said. "The girls are already in school, and you're working. When did you decide to start over again? Is this because Frances has Max?"

"This has nothing to do with Frances, Mom. And we're actually happy about it. The girls are happy too."

"Of course they are. Their lives won't change that much."

Frances would have hung up by now. Frances, whose motto throughout childhood, whenever Fay had trotted out her martyr routine, had been, *I didn't ask to be born.*

"I just thought you might like to know."

Marie heard Fay whisper something to her husband. When she came back on the line her voice had softened. "Your father says to say congratulations."

It was hard to hold in her tears. When she was a girl, she had stepped on a rusty wire in a construction site that she wasn't supposed to be playing in. Elizabeth had run to Marie's house to tell one of her parents that she was hurt. The whole time Marie waited, the wire sticking half into her foot, she didn't cry. But as soon as she saw her dad come running, the father who loved her and looked afraid, the tears flowed. It was safe to cry then.

"We'll be home soon, Marie," her mother said. "Until then, take care of yourself."

I don't want to take care of myself. I want someone to do that for me. She nodded. "Okay, Mom. I'll try."

Margaret signed the necessary papers releasing Carolyn's child for adoption and sent them back to Dr. Maclean by registered mail. No, she did not want to see the child (or Carolyn, for that matter). Yes, she understood Dr. Maclean's urgency in wanting to place the child.

Margaret couldn't help but dwell on the irony of the situation. She had signed papers to put her own daughter in "care," and now she was signing papers to get her granddaughter *out* of the very place she'd been persuaded to put her daughter into. A doctor sixteen years earlier had assured her it was for her baby's own good, and now a doctor was making a strong case that Poplar Grove was no place for a child. Once again she cursed her naïveté and Donald's eager willingness to forget. Once again she regretted her impulse to live in the past and Donald's ability to put the past in a shoebox on the top shelf of the closet, tucked into the back corner. He knew it was there somewhere, but he was fine never actually going to look for it.

She hadn't been able to care for Carolyn, but at least the infant would find a good home where she would be loved. Dr. Maclean had assured her of that, and although she had no reason to trust any doctor's word at this point, she felt she could believe him.

The months passed quickly, and Margaret missed two more of her regular visits to Poplar Grove. But it was summertime, and she was enjoying the time with her family. The train trip to Montreal had been a great adventure. Margaret had insisted that they splurge and purchase first-class tickets for the cross-country journey. Donald, always conservative in his spending, had mildly objected to the extravagance, but she'd persuaded him and he'd finally agreed. The only drawback for the children was leaving their ten-year-old golden retriever, upon whom they lavished their affection. But once arrangements had been made for his care, even they got into the appropriately festive mood.

So Margaret didn't visit Carolyn in July. And when she returned in August, she reasoned that summer was almost over, and her garden and flowerbeds required tending.

Then it was September, and as the visiting day approached, she fell ill with the stomach flu. Even as she emptied the contents of her stomach into the toilet bowl, she was relieved not to make the trip. She was a thirty-seven-year-old grandmother, and nobody in her family knew but her. She felt old. Keeping secrets weighed upon a body. Sometimes, she noticed she was bent over as if someone had delivered a heavy blow to her abdomen. When she caught her reflection in a mirror or shop window and saw herself bent and hunched over, she'd stretch to her full height, unround her shoulders, and gain four inches in stature.

When October arrived, she reasoned that, since she hadn't visited Carolyn since May, what did another month matter? In November it was too cold. When December arrived, she focused on decorating the house for Christmas. In the new year she understood that mounting the steps of the asylum bus repulsed her so much that she needed time to prepare herself for the abuse her senses would have upon re-entering Poplar Grove. She'd been away too long. She'd have to relearn how to turn a blind eye to the overcrowding and unbearable filth and stench. It would be like visiting for the first time all over again, but at least then she'd been ignorant of what that place really was like. But now she knew.

So the months passed and Margaret bent a little more with each passing day, plagued by the stone of shame in her belly that she could do nothing but polish. Shame for not visiting. Shame for thinking that the man who had fathered Carolyn's child might still be visiting her. Shame for not taking action.

Sometimes as she lay awake in the early morning hours listening to the steady breathing of her husband sleeping beside her, she imagined waking Donald and telling him the truth. How did that expression go? A problem shared is a problem halved? Oh—to have someone take some of the burden from her! Carolyn was his daughter too, didn't he have a right to know? But now the situation was even worse. *Yes, Donald. Our first-born daughter is still alive. Oh, and by the way, she's had a daughter of her own. Isn't that lovely? We're grandparents now! No, I don't know who the father is. Actually, I don't even know where the baby is now because I agreed to have her adopted. Oh, but don't worry. I'm sure the doctor's found her a good home.*

The pit she'd dug got bigger by the second. How had one visit, years ago, led to all of this?

James had erased Donald's grief—a healthy son, that was more like it—and he'd moved quickly forward, trying to draw Margaret along in his slipstream. But James had only *increased* Margaret's grief. She hadn't been able to forget Carolyn.

Often, the nights were dark and lonely, but Donald wasn't as strong as he pretended to be. Despite his success in real estate (he owned many properties, in addition to all the sales he supervised), he still yearned for the approval of his parents. When he clinched a seemingly impossible deal, or when he won some prestigious award, he would phone his father. Margaret cringed each time, for his parents would never say what Donald wanted to hear. Or, if they did, he wouldn't believe them. *We're proud of you, son. We're glad you're our boy.*

It was Margaret's job to protect him so that James and Rebecca would not see him crumble.

So she held her tongue. It was not her place to make him revisit his heartache or to add something more to it.

Silence.

More silence.

TWENTY-NINE
2002

Elizabeth came home from work and immediately went to the row of mailboxes on the far wall of the lobby; she felt an old anxiety when she turned the key. But nestled inside was a thin envelope bearing her name. She recognized Ron's handwriting right away. Clutching it to her chest, she raced to the elevators and felt light in the knees as she thought about Ron's nose at the nape of her neck, his warm breath stirring the delicate hairs above her collar line and around her collarbones. And sometimes he'd let his lips linger briefly, just enough to send a shiver up her spine. Oh . . .

Elizabeth got to her apartment as fast as she could. Finally she was on the couch and opening the letter that still had the faint whiff of her husband clinging to it—a sweet mingling of aftershave and sweat.

Ron must have replied immediately to her letter for it to get to her so fast.

> Dear Elizabeth,
>
> Thank you for your letter. It's nice to come home and, as my dad used to say, "find something in the old hollow tree." Usually it's just bills and flyers in the mailbox, so I was particularly pleased to find some variety.
>
> You asked what's new. Well, aside from my wife moving out of the house two months ago and leaving me to fend for myself, not much at all. Because you requested it, I did finally put a new message on the answering machine. I'm not sure it was at all necessary as people who want to reach me will just keep trying. It's not like the phone rings off the hook. In fact, now when I come home and find that no one has called I feel sort of depressed. Not having a machine was better

because I could imagine that I'd missed calls.

But seriously, aside from the cavernous hole that your absence has made in my life, not much has changed. Things at school are pretty much the same. No one likes the new principal, so staff morale is lower than usual. But the basketball team is doing well and we hope to clinch a top spot in the upcoming tournament.

You know, I'm not nearly as oblivious as you think I am. Your confession that you'd been hiding baby sleepers wasn't at all necessary as I'd known about that for some time. On more than one occasion, probably while looking for a particular piece of clothing, I found sleepers tucked into the back of dresser drawers. At first I thought you might be pregnant, but as the days passed and you didn't say anything I began to wonder what was going on. Then one day I stood in the bedroom doorway without your knowing I was there. I watched you take out a little sleeper, place it flat on the bed, and then lay your hand ever so gently upon it. That was when I began to really understand the extent of your longing and loss. Over time the sleepers disappeared. I figured you'd talk to me about it sometime, but you never did. Until your letter.

Lizzie, I may not have said enough to comfort you. I just wanted to fix things somehow and didn't have any idea what to do. I can't tell you how hard it is to watch the person you love not get what she wants despite her doing everything in her power to make it happen. I've always admired your great determination and perseverance, but I'll admit there were times when I wished you'd concede defeat and turn your sights to something else. Maybe I should have told you that. You're not the only one who has kept things to herself.

Now I've got a memory of us to share. Remember the time we hiked the Skyline Trail in Jasper? Your feet were a mass of blisters because you insisted on wearing the new hiking boots that you thought you'd broken in enough. And because your feet hurt so much, while you were tender-footing it across a creek you ended up slipping off a log. You and your pack both landed in the water and got soaked. Luckily you weren't carrying both sleeping bags! But it turned out okay. We hung yours from a tree to help it dry, and that night I invited you into my sleeping bag. Those mummy-bags were definitely not made for two, but we managed, didn't we? What heat we threw off that night!

I've always loved you, Lizzie, and I still do. Say the word and I'm there. Ron

Elizabeth reread the letter three times before letting it rest in her lap. Then she wiped the tears from her cheeks. He'd known about the sleepers and hadn't said a word. How could he not have said anything? Then again, what *could* he have said that wouldn't have made her angry? He'd tried being supportive and that hadn't gotten him anywhere.

She stopped suddenly when she realized where her thoughts were going. Why wasn't she thinking about the fun they'd had on their hiking trip in Jasper instead of their failed clinic visits? Why did she always focus on what she *didn't* have? No wonder she was alone, she thought as she looked around her apartment. She certainly didn't want to be with herself. Why would anyone else?

Ron would. He said as much in his letter. Despite all she'd put him through, he still wanted her. *Say the word and I'm there.*

"The word," she said out loud and smiled. "The word." She swivelled her head. Where was he?

He was at home, in their house, waiting. He was used to that. For almost ten years their lives had been put on hold; they'd been stuck in an endless loop of one test and procedure followed by another and then a wait. Needles. Paper gowns. Sweat. Cramps. Ultrasounds. Pain. Tears. She needed to stop remembering the failures. Or put a new spin on them. Ron wasn't the bad guy, he'd done everything. Once, she had been told to make an appointment with a fertility specialist at a specific time during her monthly cycle. The appointment was to be preceded by a week of sexual abstinence, and she was to arrive at the doctor's office a prescribed number of hours after intercourse. Her appointment had been for three o'clock, so Ron had left school early that day to be home in time to have sex.

How undignified it all had been. How utterly exposed she had felt, like a butterfly with its wings pinned flat to a board. She remembered the doctor returning to the examination room. "I'm sorry to say that, although there should have been, there was no evidence of live sperm in the cervical environment."

"But that's not possible. I came here immediately . . ."

"We'll have to repeat the test," the doctor interrupted. "You have what is called an 'inhospitable cervical environment.'" Elizabeth's heart sank. Inhospitable. Like she didn't know how to throw a good party.

She looked down at the letter in her lap, at Ron's controlled penmanship, and she understood she didn't want the next ten years to be anything like what she'd just lived through. She closed her eyes and breathed deeply. There was Ron at the stove, flipping a grilled cheese sandwich, barefoot, unshaven, hungry, and lonely. And here she was, thinking of him, wanting to be with him. After almost two months she'd had enough. Invite him for dinner. Now.

For once she didn't stop to question herself. Instead, she picked up the phone and dialled the most familiar number she knew.

And now he was on his way over and she was preparing her body for his visit—showering and shaving her legs and underarms. Taking a pumice stone to her heels. Putting a dab of his favourite perfume at the base of her neck. Blow-drying her hair. Adding a light touch of foundation below her eyes.

When she was finished, Elizabeth walked to the balcony and looked at the night traffic coming into the city from the south, looking for a particular set of headlights cutting through the darkness. She glanced at the river's dark shadow. In another month it would be ice-free and flowing with spring runoff. But for now ice pans drifted silently down the middle of the river, the northern version of lily pads, while the banks remained hidden by ice. People could be like that too, she thought. They could suddenly expose a part of themselves you'd never known about, or reveal plans that surprised you. Elizabeth had certainly done that to Ron, many times. "Will you come with me?" she remembered asking him when their fertility doctor suggested they go to group counselling. Ron hadn't been interested. He said counselling was for people who had problems in their lives, and, aside from not being able to have kids, they didn't have any problems. But Elizabeth had persisted. So he went with her. For support, he said. As it turned out, he seemed to get more from the sessions than she did.

That first night, the counsellor separated the men and women into two groups. Ron had arched his eyebrows cynically when he marched away with the other men. Afterwards, however, he talked with some relief about what they'd shared.

"Give me PMS any day," a sandy-haired man in his early forties had joked. "That's nothing compared to the mood swings from the drugs my wife is on."

"I hear ya," another man had added. "There should be safe houses out there for men whose wives are on fertility drugs."

Ron told her he'd laughed along with them, surprised that he wasn't the only one caught in some bizarre cycle of emotions. Listening to the others, he said he felt as if he'd been walking around for years with his belt too tight and had suddenly been given permission to loosen it and breathe. He'd been all smiles and full of jokes when the evening ended.

"Did you exchange phone numbers?" Elizabeth had asked sarcastically because her session hadn't made her feel any better at all.

In fact, she'd come away emotionally drained, the skin around her nose and eyes sensitive because of all the tissue she'd gone through. Again.

She was supposed to be working on acceptance. She was supposed to learn to let go, to move on, to forgive herself.

The buzzer rang.

Ron was in the elevator, coming to her apartment.

Then she was welcoming him inside, kissing him shyly on his whiskered cheek, and giving him a tour.

Elizabeth could not stop the foolish happiness she felt in his presence.

In the kitchen she poured them both a glass of wine. He stood behind her, his body like a second skin that had lifted off. He didn't touch her but her flesh tingled as if he had lighted on every surface.

And finally, the familiarity of his lips. His hands drawing every note from her body. Too long. It had been far too long.

In the morning Elizabeth's feet padded soundlessly over the plush carpet to the kitchen. She pulled some eggs, cheese, green onions, a red pepper, and some broccoli from the fridge and began preparing an omelette. The eggs cracked neatly against the sharp metal edge of the mixing bowl. She inserted her thumbs into the thin shells and spread them open. Dark yellow yolks hovered for a moment, and then dropped intact. She whisked them into a frothy foam and cut some vegetables. Then she sliced a thick piece of butter from the block and watched it sizzle in the frying pan before pouring the egg mixture in.

A few minutes later, Ron came up behind her and wrapped his arms around her waist. She turned and kissed him, taking her time, enjoying the feel of his body against her. "I've worked up an appetite." She grinned.

Ron loosened the sash on her robe and slid his hands inside.

"Mmm. Smells good."

The noonday sun shone in the balcony doors. A thick shaft of yellow light fell across the living room floor.

They ate quickly and in silence, scraping their plates clean and pouring fresh coffees to take with them to the couch. Elizabeth pressed her back into Ron's chest. His chin rested lightly on her head. They sat in silence for a few moments, comfortable in each other's presence. A car alarm went off on the street below, high-pitched as a siren. The sound reverberated off the building and echoed down the valley.

Elizabeth twisted her wedding ring on her finger. "I don't even want to think about trying to get pregnant," she said, suddenly serious. "If it happens, it happens. But no more trying, okay? I'm done with any more disappointment."

Dust danced in the sun's shaft. The thick hairs on Ron's arm glowed in the light. A door slammed in the hallway and Elizabeth heard laughter. It sounded fresh and optimistic.

"When are you coming home?" Ron asked.

The world opened up. She could be happy; they could be happy. Just as they were now. Ron stroked the side of her cheek. She leaned her face into his warm palm. She didn't need anything else.

Her mind wandered. She tried to tune in, to see where it had gone. A thought circled about as if on a carousel, becoming louder at times and then dropping to a whisper before gaining volume again. She strained to hear what the familiar voice was saying. Try again, it said. Maybe this time will be different.

Elizabeth closed her eyes. Would it never go away? She wiped the tear away before Ron could notice. Then she slipped from his grasp and stared outside at the valley.

"What are you thinking?" Ron asked.

"I'm thinking it's such a beautiful day we should go for a walk." She turned back toward the couch and smiled.

"I'm thinking I should help you start packing," he said.

He stood and opened his arms, and Elizabeth walked directly into them.

THIRTY

MARCH 12, 1967

This morning, Carolyn Harrington died of cardio-respiratory complications, four months shy of her twentieth birthday. As is the custom at Poplar Grove, her body will be buried in the graveyard on the grounds.

The time of death is estimated at 3:30 AM. The nurse doing the morning rounds discovered Carolyn in her bed at 7:00 AM, curled into the fetal position. Her body was removed and an autopsy was performed.

Had I known her time was so near, I would have held a vigil by her bedside so she would not have died alone. I could have told her that she'd brought love into the world. I could have told her that her daughter, now four years old, is a vivacious and precocious child who was adopted by loving parents and who will live freely in the world from which she herself had been barred.

I could have told her many things, but beyond an intuitive knowledge that she was safe with me, she would not have understood. Carolyn never acquired speech.

So I am deeply grieved that I was never able to convey my gratitude to Carolyn. Had our paths not crossed, my vision would never have been elevated above the metal grate of the most pedestrian curb. Had she not produced a "normal" child, I'm not convinced the stark contrast of her own existence would have been so tragically apparent. To the unseeing, her life was better lived in hiding. To me, her life was larger than most.

Dr. Maclean wiped his eyes and closed the notebook. He heard his own ragged breath in the quiet room and sought a course of action. A door slammed down the hallway. He heard the intermittent drip of a leaking faucet at his sink.

Out in the wild expanse of fields, unnoticed, the snow very slowly softened. And in the white expanse the poplar's bark was darkened by the winter melt.

In his office, Dr. Maclean heard the sound of geese flying overhead in the late afternoon sky, and suddenly the unhappiness of Poplar Grove was a burden too great for him to handle.

And with this realization came a sudden clarity: Carolyn had held him here, but now his ties to Poplar Grove could be severed. Electrified by this buoyant sense of freedom and possibility, he signed Carolyn's death certificate and put it in his out box.

Then he pulled a blank piece of paper out of his desk drawer and began to write.

> March 12, 1967
> Dear Mrs. Harrington,
> It is with profound sadness that I inform you that your daughter, Carolyn, died this morning of cardio-respiratory complications. Simply put, her already compromised heart was further damaged by her pregnancy. I hope you find some solace, however, in knowing that she appears to have died peacefully in her sleep. As is the custom here, she will be buried in the graveyard on the grounds. I myself will see to the details.
> I am deeply grieved that we never had the opportunity to discuss Carolyn's case further after the discovery of her condition. I blame myself, in part, for not trying harder to convey the particulars of the case to you. However, as promised, the infant was adopted into a good home, and I continue to follow her progress. She is a four-year-old bundle of enthusiasm and joy, and she has brought much happiness to her adoptive parents.
> I shall be leaving Poplar Grove in a short time to embark on a new field of inquiry dealing with Down

syndrome, an interest ignited by the role your daughter has played in my medical journey.

Should you wish to contact me, I am sure that all mail will be forwarded to my next address.

Respectfully yours,

Dr. Michael Maclean

He signed the letter, slid it into an envelope, and licked the back flap. Then he found Carolyn's file and wrote Mrs. Harrington's address on the front. Adrenalin flooded his body. Finally he was taking some kind of action and focusing on work that would make him feel proud of his efforts. He put the letter on top of the signed death certificate in his out box, picked up his coat, and left his office. Although it was not yet officially spring, the sun's rays reflected a gentle heat. Dr. Maclean raised his face to the sun and closed his eyes. A red canvas appeared behind his closed lids, and on it he saw a map of his future begin to take shape.

The next day he hand-delivered his resignation to Dr. Stallworthy, whose private practice was in Glenora, one of the wealthier neighbourhoods in Edmonton. His reception area was lavishly furnished. A large saltwater fish tank was inset into one wall. Dr. Maclean walked over and gazed at the impressive display of vibrantly coloured fish inside—black angelfish, yellow and orange fish with stripes and antennae and bulging eyes. It was both marvellous and sad to watch them swim around and around with no hope of travelling any great distance. What was it, he wondered, that made humans want to capture and cage creatures for display?

After a short time he was escorted into Dr. Stallworthy's office and waited for what felt like hours. It wasn't as if he hadn't made an appointment, he thought with irritation as he glanced at his watch, eager to be done here. He just wanted the visit to be over. Dr. Stallworthy wasn't his favourite person to deal with. He was too . . . what? Condescending? Arrogant?

The door opened and Dr. Stallworthy entered, drying his hands on a cloth towel that he dumped into a canvas laundry bag beside the door.

"Dr. Maclean!" he said cheerfully, reaching out a meaty hand to shake. "To what do I owe the pleasure of this visit?"

His hand was cold and damp. Dr. Maclean resisted the urge to wipe his hand on his pants. Instead, he held out an envelope. "I've come to give you this," he said.

Dr. Stallworthy took the envelope and put on his reading glasses to see the letter inside. He read quietly to himself, at one point almost snorting with derision. Then he put the letter back into the envelope, removed his glasses, and rested his hands over his girth. "May I ask why now?"

"It's been four years, sir," he replied. "I received my appointment right out of medical school and was unsure at that time if this was a field of work I'd be interested in."

"And you've found it's not to your liking?"

"On the contrary, sir, I've found it to be eye-opening, to say the least."

"But your resignation suggests . . ."

Dr. Maclean cleared his throat and chose his words carefully. "I'm not convinced, sir, that housing hundreds of mental defectives in the same place is good for them or for their families. After all, it's not as if their conditions are contagious. There is no medical emergency that requires them to be so segregated from society."

Dr. Stallworthy smiled thinly. He wasn't an old man, maybe just forty-five or so, but he carried himself with a false aplomb as if he were holding court to conduct business that was somehow beneath him. "I see," he said, nodding. "A Liberal, eh? Gone to the other side, have you? You think Johnny and Susie drooling on the front lawns of suburbia would be an improvement? Shall we send some home with you? I'm sure your neighbours would be thrilled. Or how about we enrol them at your son's local school?"

"With all due respect, sir," he replied, "given your position on the board, I'd have expected a more charitable view. When was the last time you visited Poplar Grove?"

Dr. Stallworthy cast his eyes up, as if scanning the insides of his brain. Then he carefully examined his cuticles, taking the time to polish the diamond ring on his wedding finger.

"I'm there five days a week," Dr. Maclean continued. "I see how the place works, or doesn't work, almost every day. Most dogs are treated better than the people inside."

"I've never particularly liked dogs," Dr. Stallworthy replied dismissively.

Another nail in your coffin, Dr. Maclean thought. "This might be news to you," he continued, "but the stench and filth you likely have witnessed isn't an aberration. It's a chronic condition." He went on, asking if the board was aware that one poorly trained orderly at Poplar Grove was responsible for upward of twenty to thirty patients. He spoke about patients who couldn't feed themselves having feeding tubes inserted simply because there weren't enough capable bodies on hand to spend the twenty minutes it would take to get food into their mouths. Overworked orderlies produced cruel attendants, and cruel attendants took it out on the most defenceless. He'd seen enough. Didn't he remember what happened to Carolyn Harrington? Poplar Grove didn't *care* for people; it warehoused them.

"Are you finished yet?" Dr. Stallworthy said.

He nodded, breathless and weak.

Dr. Stallworthy gave a patronizing smile. "How old are you?"

"I'm thirty-two."

His lips drew back disdainfully as he continued. "And already you can see a better way of doing things?"

"A different way, yes." And he outlined the exciting new ideas for transitioning patients into group homes. When Dr. Stallworthy remained silent, he hurried on to describe the radical notion of allowing babies born with Down syndrome to be raised within their own families. Times were changing, he insisted, and there was a growing debate among doctors, social workers, and families that questioned the logic of automatic institutionalization of mongoloids. Of particular interest to him was an article by a New York doctor who had conducted a study comparing the development of children with Down syndrome who were reared in the home with those reared in institutions. His findings had been more than convincing—all those who were raised at home had higher mental and social ages than those in the out-of-home group. It seemed so obvious, yet the study and ideas of possible integration were met with much resistance.

"A new way of thinking won't happen overnight," he continued. "I know that. But it *will* happen. Not just for the children born with Down syndrome, but other conditions as well." He wasn't even sure that all the patients in Poplar Grove actually belonged there. Twisted bodies didn't necessarily mean deficient minds. In his four years of residency, he'd seen at least a dozen patients who'd appeared to be housed there for no other reason than someone had put them there when they were children.

Dr. Stallworthy's eyes had glazed over long before he finished talking. "There is no need to continue," he finally interrupted. "I accept your resignation, and I'm sure the rest of the board will agree. If I remember correctly," he went on, "when we hired you we weren't looking for a visionary."

"No, that wasn't in my job description, but I'll take your observations as a compliment," Dr. Maclean said.

He reached for his hat and overcoat and felt his chest swell with happiness and pride. It had been a long time since he had felt so good.

It happened something like this: the day finally arrived when Marie's results would come back from the lab. Dr. Cuthbert said she'd phone right after lunch with the news. Barry came home early from work. The phone rang. Marie gave the phone to her husband, holding it out as if it was something dead.

That's what she remembered. Not that the baby did a slow roll inside her and her stomach lifted to accommodate the movement. Not that she'd put too much salt in the soup. Not that the poplar trees outside her front window had large waxen leaves curled into their bud-like shells, just waiting to bloom. Not that the daffodils on the kitchen table were orbs of bright yellow light.

And then somehow she was in the car and in the last moments of not knowing, of still being able to convince herself that everything might be okay. For despite her foreboding and the darkness and uncertainty it had wrapped her days in, she still believed, at the core of her being, that she might have imagined it all. It was funny, really, how the mind could entertain two such drastic thoughts simultaneously—*There is something wrong with the baby* and *Everything will be okay*.

They took the elevator to the sixth floor. The receptionist led them directly to Dr. Cuthbert's personal office.

"She'll be right with you," the receptionist said, and Marie stared hard into her face to catch a glimpse of their future, but she found nothing to remark upon. She sat down and reached for Barry's hand again and gave it a tight squeeze.

A moment later Dr. Cuthbert walked briskly into the room, her stethoscope swinging at her chest. "Thanks for coming in so promptly," she said and reached across her desk for a file. Opening it, she stared at the information inside before slowly raising her eyes to look directly at Marie. "The tests results came in this morning." She folded her hands onto her desk. "I'm sorry to say that the baby has Down syndrome."

Marie listened to the words that left the doctor's mouth; she understood each one, and her heart didn't even miss a beat. After all, she had known, hadn't she? She had tried to convince herself otherwise, but she had known all along.

The doctor's phone rang, but she didn't pick it up. "I know this isn't the news you were hoping for," she said kindly, "but the prospects today are much brighter for these children than they were in the past."

"Are you sure that there hasn't been some mistake?" Barry asked.

The doctor shook her head.

"How accurate is this test, anyway?" he asked.

"About ninety-eight percent," the doctor replied.

Barry looked out the window and nodded. "So now what?"

"Well, there are a number of options, and I'll give you a referral for counselling if you would like more help in making your decision." Then she spoke with deliberate care.

For starters, they could continue with the pregnancy and have the child. Or, as with any pregnancy, adoption was also an option. There were agencies that specialized in the adoption of special-needs children. Finally, they had the option to terminate the pregnancy. However, if this were the route they chose, for obvious reasons they would have to make that decision as soon as possible.

"Do you have any questions?" the doctor asked gently.

Is there a cure for regret? Marie stayed quiet.

"Is it a boy or a girl?" Barry asked.

Before Marie could voice an objection, the doctor spoke.

"It's a girl."

Sugar and spice.

Barry nodded and sat quietly for a moment. "If we decide not to have the baby, what kind of procedure are we looking at? I mean, is it dangerous?"

Marie almost laughed out loud. Is it dangerous? For who? Her or the baby? Certainly for one of them it would be.

An appointment would be made for Marie at the hospital. Depending on the time of day the procedure was performed, she might stay overnight. She would be induced and go through labour. The doctor gave a few more details.

"I'm sorry," she said again.

Marie nodded, strangely comforted by the sympathy.

"Please let me know," the doctor continued, "as soon as you make your decision. Then we'll know what course to take next. And if there's anything I can do, or if you have any more questions, don't hesitate to call."

Barry stood up and shook the doctor's hand once more. "Thank you," he said. "We appreciate your help."

Marie rose slowly from her chair. She nodded to the doctor as well, and then wordlessly made her way to the door.

They drove home in silence. Nicole and Sophia returned home from school, like on any other day, and Marie didn't cry. Barry decided they should all go out for pizza, and they let the girls drink as many glasses of the bottomless pop as they wanted.

Back at home, Barry helped the girls with their homework. Then they all watched some television. Marie held together through it all— the meal, the homework, the TV, the bedtime rituals.

And then, finally, they went to bed, lay side by side, on their backs, and stared up at the ceiling. There was something about not looking directly at the other person that enabled them to be honest. They had used this technique over the years when they were experiencing some difficulty in their relationship. They didn't make eye contact; they didn't get hung up on the other person's gestures or facial mannerisms. They were just two voices in the dark. Two lovers staring up at the stars.

"So now we know," Marie said.

Barry reached for her hand. "When I was a kid, I thought that once you were an adult you had it made. You knew right from wrong, and you just did the right thing. There was no indecision, just action." He stroked her hand gently with his thumb. "I remember honestly believing that adults didn't make mistakes."

The furnace kicked on and the curtains across the room danced lightly in the circulating air.

"When it comes down to it," Barry continued, "I guess we have two choices."

Marie felt tears roll down her cheek. Maybe she needed to be strong for Barry until she could be strong for herself. They couldn't both fall apart at the same time.

She tried to steady her voice. "That makes it sound so simple, like we can just flip a coin or something. What do you want?"

"I want us to be happy again, and I don't want to have to make the decision."

"Nobody is going to make it for us."

"I know," he said. "You don't have to state the obvious."

She didn't reply.

"I don't have an endless reserve of patience and kindness," Barry went on. "I'm not comfortable around people with disabilities. I never know if I'm supposed to help or something."

"It's different when it's your own child," she said.

"Yeah, it hurts more."

Neither one of them had anything to say for a few moments.

"I read somewhere that living a comfortable life means you're not growing," Marie said.

"I'm not sure I buy that," Barry said. "What's wrong with being comfortable?"

"Well, maybe having this baby would help you grow in some way, maybe . . ."

"I don't *want* to grow," he snapped. "I don't want this 'challenge,' or whatever you want to call it. I just don't. I'm not strong enough."

"Do you think other people are? Huh? Do you think anyone says, *Down syndrome? Sure. I can handle that. I'm strong enough.*"

More silence.

"What if I had it anyway?" she whispered.

Barry tensed beside her. "Don't do this, Marie," Barry said. "We've got to stay together on this. We're a team, aren't we?"

Marie began to cry. "I just can't imagine what we'll tell the girls. They're so looking forward to the birth."

She could tell Barry had switched into fixing mode. "We'll tell them that something was wrong with the baby and that it died. That'll be the truth, so we won't even be lying."

"Oh, great. That'll make it okay then."

Marie shifted positions. The baby kicked and she started to cry again.

A little girl. She had preferred the distance of not knowing, but now she could name the child; she could imagine her more fully. A soft moan escaped from her lips.

A girl.

Terminate. Procedure. The doctor had given them all the details; in fact, they had learned more than they had wanted to know. Marie hadn't known, for example, that if she terminated the pregnancy she would still have to go through labour to give birth. But how stupid could she be? Obviously the baby had to come out somehow. She should have asked what the procedure was *before* she'd had the amniocentesis. Might that have changed her mind? She'd already been through two labours, but they had been joyous occasions. How could this one be anything but tragic? There would be no reward for the pain. Nothing to look forward to after her body emptied itself of its burden.

Barry took her in his arms. He ran his hand along her back, using his fingertips to slowly trace the outline of each vertebra along her spine. He started at the curve in her neck and followed each ridge and hollow down to her waist as if she were his rosary and he was saying his prayers.

Her belly pressed into his own. The baby let go a barrage of kicks, performing Morse code on his belly, trying hard to get a message to his heart.

Dr. Maclean pulled the chart from the rack outside the examination room and looked at the file. He smiled immediately. Behind the closed door, Elizabeth was waiting to have her booster shots. He opened the door and stepped inside, smiling at the girl and her mother.

"Hello, Elizabeth," he said warmly. "What brings you in today? A frog in your throat? A bug in your ear?" He knew she was getting a bit old for his childish humour, but he persisted nonetheless. She blushed a deep crimson and turned to her mother for help. "Oh," he said, following her gaze. "You've come in because there's something wrong with your mother?"

Mrs. Crewes laughed and gave her daughter's knee a squeeze. "Just the usual, doc. Check under the hood and put some air in the tires."

He smiled and filled a vial with clear liquid before rubbing a cotton swab of alcohol over Elizabeth's upper arm. "You're twelve now, are you?" he asked, diverting her attention while inserting the needle. She flinched and nodded.

"If you have a moment, doctor, when you're finished," Mrs. Crewes said, "I was wondering if I could have a quick word with you."

"Certainly." He rubbed Elizabeth's arm briskly where he'd removed the needle.

"Lizzie," said Mrs. Crewe, "how about I get you in a few minutes in the waiting room?"

Elizabeth nodded and exited the room.

Mrs. Crewes was normally vivacious and talkative, but today she looked ill at ease.

"Is there something wrong?" he asked.

"No, nothing in particular. I just wanted to let you know that I'll be taking Elizabeth to another doctor from now on. She's growing up, you know, and she's becoming self-conscious having a male doctor. But she's also been asking a lot of questions lately, like why she's the only healthy child in your waiting room, and I must admit that it's become rather obvious that she's out of place here. To be honest, I'm not able to justify why we see you anymore."

He nodded. "Frankly, I'm surprised I've been able to see her for so long. Especially after I moved my offices here into the children's hospital." Parents with healthy children, as well as the children themselves, often had a hard time witnessing first-hand how nature can deform and punish a body. Bald heads. Tubes and wheelchairs. Sometimes it was too much for them.

"In truth, there's really no need for me to see her anymore, other than my own personal attachment. It's been apparent for years that she's an entirely normal and healthy child born under highly unusual circumstances."

"Unusual circumstances is somewhat of an understatement," Mrs. Crewes said. "I'm concerned that when Elizabeth turns eighteen she'll be able to access her adoption records. I haven't told her anything about her mother, and I'm not sure I ever will, but what if she finds out and wants to meet her?"

He motioned Mrs. Crewes toward the door. "Let's discuss this in my office, shall we?"

He led her down the hall and offered her the seat by his desk.

"Elizabeth's mother died eight years ago, in March 1967," he said. "Her heart had been weakened further by the pregnancy and birth. So there is no possibility of Elizabeth meeting her birth mother."

"I'm sorry to hear that," Mrs. Crewes said. "Although I must admit that it's somewhat of a relief to know that her birth mother won't make any attempts to contact her."

"Even if she'd lived, she would have been incapable of doing so. Her level of functioning was not high."

"What about other family?"

"Carolyn's birth mother might still be alive, and if I remember correctly, she had two additional children who were healthy. I can't provide any more information even if I wanted to because places like Poplar Grove didn't require the parents of patients to keep up-to-date records. The majority of babies with Down syndrome who were institutionalized didn't live much past the toddler years, and those who did were basically forgotten."

"So you think Elizabeth has at least an aunt and uncle then?"

"Yes. However, given what I know of the family situation, I would be very surprised if they knew of her existence."

"Her father remains unknown?"

Dr. Maclean nodded.

"Perhaps you can answer this question for me. When Elizabeth decides to have children, will she have a greater risk of having a baby with Down syndrome?"

"No, I don't believe so. However, as Elizabeth's case is highly uncommon and we don't have other cases to compare it with, we cannot rule out entirely the possibility that she might have a higher likelihood. There is a small percentage of people who carry an actual Down syndrome gene. I know one woman who had two children with Down syndrome. After her first child was born, we determined that she carried the gene and had a fifty percent chance of having another child with Down syndrome. Which is exactly what happened. But infertility is not a likelihood at all."

"Thank you, doctor," she said. "As this is likely our last visit, I thought now would be a good time to ask some questions about her family." She paused. "Also, I'm embarrassed to admit that Elizabeth doesn't know she's adopted. My husband and I just never got around to telling her. There didn't seem to be any need. And if no one will come looking for her when she's eighteen, then maybe she never needs to know."

"I think I can say with some confidence that no family members will be looking for her."

Mrs. Crewes thanked him for his time and advice over the years.

"However, the longer you go without telling her, the more unlikely it is that you ever will. But that's a personal decision, obviously, and it's not my place to advise you on that decision."

"Yes, I know." She grimaced. "It feels deceitful not telling her, but I never meant to keep it from her. The time just passed; of course, there's no sense in telling a *baby* about its history, and by the time it feels right, so many years have passed that if feels almost wrong to bring it up. I·

should have told her when she was much younger, but I missed that opportunity. Maybe saying goodbye to you is the impetus I need," she added with great determination. "Perhaps I'll tell her as soon as I leave here today."

"No time like the present, as they say. And by the way, I have kept a journal of Elizabeth's case. I think she might one day benefit from its contents or, at the very least, be intrigued by them. I will hold it for her, until she's ready. When she starts asking more questions or attempts to find out more about her adoption, please tell her to come and see me."

Mrs. Crewes thanked him again and shook his hand warmly.

And then she left.

The office door closed behind her. Dr. Maclean sat at his desk and felt a heavy sadness in saying goodbye to Elizabeth. He pulled the notebook from the top shelf and jotted down the details of his final visit with her. He probably wouldn't see her again until she turned eighteen and gained access to her adoption records. Only then were her parents likely to tell her about the notebook.

THIRTY-THREE

Elizabeth had convinced her mother to find a new doctor. Her chest was beginning to develop and she'd started wearing a training bra. Seeing Dr. Maclean, who had known her since she was a baby, was like getting naked in front of her father. She didn't want either man to see the tender lumps of flesh on her chest that were growing into breasts. And she was tired of being the only normal child in the waiting room. It made no sense to keep going, so they'd made one final visit to say goodbye.

When they left his office, Elizabeth realized immediately that something had changed. Her mother was quiet in the elevator. Was she sorry to say goodbye? She wasn't usually sentimental. "Don't worry, Mom," she said, reaching to hold her mother's hand. "We'll find another doctor. There must be lots of doctors in the city. You have one; maybe I could see him."

Her mother squeezed her hand. "I'm not worried, Lizzie, I'm just a little nervous right now."

"About what?"

They were outside the hospital now and the sun was warm on her face. She squinted at the sudden brightness.

"Let's go over here," her mother said, pulling her toward a small rock garden adjacent to the entranceway. "There's something I need to tell you."

Elizabeth followed, curious about the sudden change in her mother's mood. Had she done something wrong? She scanned through the past few days but came up blank. She'd done her chores without too much complaining, she wasn't behind in her school work.

Her mother headed for a wooden bench next to a small pond.

"Shouldn't I be getting back to school?" she asked.

"No. It's already two o'clock; you can have the rest of the afternoon off." Her mother patted the bench beside her.

A plump woman in sandals pushed a young boy in a wheelchair to the hospital's entrance. He was wearing an Oilers ball cap.

"Is something wrong?" Elizabeth asked.

"No, honey, nothing's wrong. There's just something I want to tell you that I've maybe kept to myself for too long." Her mother's eyes filled with tears, and she reached into her purse for a tissue.

Elizabeth felt panic grow in her stomach. Her mother was sick. Or her father was, terribly sick. Or they were moving. She'd be leaving Marie and her other friends behind and be the new kid at school, going into junior high. It had to be something horrible.

"Just tell me, Mom."

Her mother laughed weakly and wiped at her eyes. "Oh, Lizzie. This is hard for me. Be patient." Then she took a deep breath and continued: "I should have told you a long time ago. Your father and I love you very much, honey. I hope you know that."

"You're not getting divorced, are you?"

Her mother laughed again and seemed to gain courage. "No, we're fine. It's not that. What I'm trying to say is that we really wanted to have children together, and we tried for years, but nothing happened."

"What do you mean 'nothing happened'? You got me, didn't you?"

"Lizzie, you're the best thing that ever happened to us. And the day we brought you home was the best day of my life."

What was her mother getting at? Why didn't she just *say* it?

"Just tell me."

"You were six months old when we first met you at the adoption agency. We fell in love with you immediately and were lucky enough to bring you home."

The sun hid behind a cloud and cast the bench in shadow.

"I'm adopted?"

Her mother nodded. "I never meant to keep it from you," she rushed on, placing her hand on Elizabeth's knee. "It just never seemed like the right time. We wanted you so much, and you've brought so much love into our lives." She stopped and peered closely at her daughter. "Lizzie?"

"I don't know what to say," she said, looking up at her mother.

A silence fell between them. A little sparrow landed on a stone at the edge of the pond and quickly scanned the surroundings before hopping into the shallow water and plunging its breast beneath the surface.

"I know you'll have questions once the surprise wears off," her mother said gently, "and your father and I will be happy to answer them for you."

Adopted? That explained some things, like how no one ever said she looked like either one of her parents. She glanced up at the woman seated beside her who had a long, straight nose while Elizabeth's was short and tended toward the pug side. The woman beside her, whose skin was liberally sprinkled with freckles while Elizabeth's was a blank canvas. Then she thought of her father, tall and lean, who joked that he spent a good portion of his time in the Victorian Age while maintaining a life in the present. Not her real father?

The news settled into her bones. Her mother loved her; she knew that. Did it matter if she wasn't actually her real flesh and blood?

"Did you name me?" she asked.

Her mother smiled, surprised by the question. "Yes. We did."

"But what was I called for the first six months?"

"You weren't given a name. The agency knew the adoptive family would want to name you."

Elizabeth nodded slowly, trying to track the questions racing in her mind. Nameless for six months. Why had it taken so long for someone to adopt her?

"My grandmother's name was Elizabeth and I'd always wanted to name my daughter that. And Rose, well . . ." she paused. "One of the few things I learned about your birth mother was that she loved roses."

Elizabeth smiled and nodded slowly. "That feels kind of special." She sat with that for a moment. "What else do you know?"

"Very little, except she was very young when she had you, just sixteen, and she wasn't able to care for you. That's why we've been seeing Dr. Maclean all this time. He was one of the attending physicians at your birth."

"Do you know what she looked like?" What colour was her hair? Her eyes?

"No, I never saw her."

Elizabeth stared at the pond. "Why did it take so long for someone to adopt me?"

Her mother shook her head. "I don't know all the answers myself," she admitted. "But what I know is that we wanted you from the second we saw you. Your dad and I have never agreed on something so fully in our lives."

Elizabeth smiled as her mother reached out, took her hand, and brought it to her mouth for a kiss. "Are you okay?"

Was she okay? Elizabeth nodded. Maybe when it sank in more she'd have more questions, but for now she was okay.

Rain fell from slate grey clouds. Although it was late morning, the sky had not lightened at all. Elizabeth watched the many coloured umbrellas bob up and down Jasper Avenue and knew her sales would be good for the day; people bought more flowers when it rained. When the phone rang, she was pleased to hear Marie's voice on the other end of the line.

"Are you busy today?" Marie asked. "Any chance we can have coffee?"

Elizabeth quickly checked her order book next to the till. "Can it be later, like, say, two o'clock?"

"That would be great. Thanks for taking the time. I know you're probably busy."

"We're all busy, aren't we? If you can't make time for friends . . ."

"Yeah, yeah, who *can* you make time for."

"The usual spot?"

"Sounds good," Marie replied. "My treat."

At one forty-five Elizabeth left the front of her flower shop and disappeared into her office. The sound of water gurgling in the small rock garden beside her desk was briefly comforting. She sat for a moment and closed her eyes, feeling the tension in her shoulders and neck. She had too much to do. It had crept up on her and now she felt overwhelmed. She made a couple of quick calls before putting on her jacket and grabbing her umbrella. The coffee shop was only a block away, but the rain was falling steadily again and the wind had picked up.

As soon as she stepped out of her office the bell over the door rang and a man slowly entered the shop. His head was bare, and thin white strands of hair were combed over a scalp thickly covered with liver spots.

Elizabeth called out a greeting and helped him fold his umbrella.

"Miserable day out there," he said as he thanked her.

Every Tuesday afternoon, like clockwork, he bought flowers for his wife, who was in the Alzheimer's ward at the General Hospital across the street. She loved flowers, he said, and he wanted to surround her with beauty in her final days.

"Has it been a week already?" she asked.

"Yes, it has. Can you believe it? The roses have wilted again, so it's time to freshen them up."

Elizabeth took her jacket off and moved to the display cooler. "What would you like this week?"

"A few red roses, if you have them."

"We just got a fresh shipment in from California this morning," she said. "Come and have a look."

He tried to straighten to his full height as he walked toward her, but his back remained rounded at the shoulders. In the past six months since he'd been a regular customer, his condition had deteriorated. Likely it was some degenerative bone disorder, and soon he'd be close to bent in half. Whatever condition he had, though, it was preferable to his wife's.

"How's your wife doing?" she asked as she picked out the best roses from the bunch.

"Oh, she's seen better days. Her mind wanders so much now. Some days she knows me, and some days she doesn't. But the not-knowing-me days are increasing."

"That must be hard."

"Yes, it is, but I guess I'm kind of used to it now," he said. "It's been a gradual process for me, watching her decline, because I see her every day. But my daughter is coming to town, and she'll notice a big change. I just hope Margaret recognizes her at least once. That would be nice."

"Where does your daughter live?"

"In Montreal. She moved there years ago and she never left. We took a trip there by train when she was younger and she fell in love with the place. She's a doctor, married a nice man, and raised a couple of children."

Elizabeth wrapped a half-dozen red roses in paper and took them to the counter. As always, she gave him a large discount. If he ever came when she wasn't in the store, she'd told him to tell the staff that he got the Elizabeth Special. Otherwise he'd be shocked by the true price of roses.

"How long have you been married?" she asked.

"Almost fifty-six years."

"Child bride, was she?" Elizabeth teased.

"You bet. I knew if I didn't make a move someone else would real quick."

Elizabeth smiled. "Well, it seems to me that you both got someone good."

"That was in the 1940s," he continued. "Over fifty years ago. Sadly, my mother never really liked her too much. That caused my wife some difficulties. She tried so hard, but my mother wasn't an easy woman." He pulled a handkerchief from his jacket pocket and wiped at his eyes, their blueness dulled by tears. "Damn these eyes, they're always running these days." He shook his head with resignation. "Age creeps up on you. But in your mind you're never really caught up. I'd say I'm about twenty years behind my body. People see an eighty-year-old man before them, but I feel like a sixty-year-old looking out."

Elizabeth walked him to the door and held his flowers while he opened his umbrella.

"Stay dry," she said. "See you next week!"

"I hope so."

Elizabeth watched him shuffle to the corner and wait for the light. When he'd safely crossed the street she returned to the counter and grabbed her coat.

"I'm going out for a bit," she told the young woman who worked for her. "I won't be gone long. If there's an emergency, I'm just down at the café."

Outside, she breathed in the smell of wet asphalt that always reminded her of childhood and collecting worms on the sidewalks. The temperature was milder than it had been in the morning, and Elizabeth welcomed the spring rains that helped to wash away the grime from the long winter months.

Jasper Avenue was busy with buses and cars and pedestrians. Elizabeth walked to the corner and waited at the red light. A gust of wind nearly ripped her umbrella from her hand, blowing rain into her face. A panhandler approached her, his palm open, cupping a small pool of water. "Not today," she said to him as she breezed by.

"When?" his voice called from behind her. "If not today, when?"

She hurried on, embarrassed. He was probably used to people like her, people who liked to act as if they were generous. Not today. As if she had given yesterday and would give again tomorrow. She hurried on, noting how much the neighbourhood had changed. When she'd first leased her store ten years earlier, the old railway yards were still there—big, open land, a developer's gold mine. Then the yards sold, the tracks were ripped up, the old black iron bridge that had spanned the avenue for decades was dismantled, and much of the land was turned into parking lots for the large stores that went in. The business district had been promised higher density apartments and condos, corner stores, restaurants, coffee shops, open-air markets, and independent bookstores. But the final product was a diluted version of the walkable and artsy neighbourhood that was supposed to enhance the area and draw more students to the new college campus nearby.

An ambulance turned quickly at the corner and headed toward the hospital emergency ward. Distracted, Elizabeth stepped into a puddle alongside the curb and cursed, annoyed with herself for not paying closer attention. She was rushing too much, that's why she was so scattered. She wished she had more time to get organized and relax. But it was good that Marie had called. She would always make time for her, even if it did throw her afternoon off kilter. She sighed. Marie must have some news. Maybe she was pregnant with twins. That'd be her luck.

The café was spacious and warm and smelled of freshly ground coffee and damp garments. Behind the counter, two young women wore matching shirts; one of them was busy steaming milk for a slope-shouldered man standing at the counter.

Elizabeth shook the rain from her umbrella and scanned the shop. No Marie. Then she noticed a loveseat near the back wall that faced a fireplace. She walked to it, took off her coat, and sat down, drawing the warmth from the artificial fire into her dampened bones.

Two minutes later Marie came rushing in, breathless. "I'm sorry I'm late," she said, shaking the water from her hair. "I had to circle the block three times. I didn't want to park farther away because I forgot to bring an umbrella." She wiped her cheek with the back of one hand. "It's really coming down out there!" she added.

"I just got here myself," Elizabeth said.

"What would you like?" Marie asked. "It's on me."

"Oh no. You bought last time."

"It doesn't matter. I invited you, so it's my treat. I insist."

Elizabeth gave her order and watched Marie walk to the counter. Her belly was taut and round and strained at the thin cotton sweater that covered it. What must it feel like, to have a baby grow inside you? All the skin and organs, limbs and digits, eyelashes and hair. It truly was miraculous. And to feel a baby kick, inside your own flesh!

Marie returned with a steaming latte and a mug of herbal tea.

Elizabeth smiled. "Remember when you were pregnant with Nicole and your mother told you to put a bandage over your belly button to keep it from sticking out?"

Marie laughed. "Yes, it poked out like a hard thumb. My mom said it looked like I was constantly hitchhiking." They laughed. "That was just one of the great pieces of advice my mother gave me."

"I always liked your mom," Elizabeth said. "She held down the fort pretty well."

A dull heat came from the orangey-blue flames in the fireplace. Elizabeth stared at her wind-swept friend. When had they both become middle-aged?

"Thanks for coming," Marie finally said. "You probably have a million things to do."

"I *always* have a million things to do, but sometimes it's good to have a reason to take a break. I should thank *you* instead."

Marie smiled and looked away. She opened her mouth as if to say something and then stared into her teacup.

"I have some news," Elizabeth said, smiling shyly. "Ron and I are back together again."

"Really? That's great!" Marie said. "When did that happen?"

"Last week. Remember how I said we were exchanging letters? Well, he's pretty eloquent when he puts pen to paper. His letters were lovely, full of funny memories of the times we shared. I could just tell how much he loves me, and I realized I missed him. So I called and invited him over. It seemed like the right thing to do." She smiled and winked. "I gave him the tour of my apartment, but he seemed most interested in the bedroom."

It felt good to laugh together.

"I moved my stuff back home on the weekend, well, the stuff that fit, anyway—I've got some furniture to get rid of. But don't worry," she added, "I would have told you soon. I've been crazy busy at work, and you've had your own stuff you're going through. Speaking of which, how are you feeling?" She stared at Marie's belly. "Have you heard anything yet?"

Elizabeth saw a shadow cross the surface of her face before Marie bowed her head and struggled to hide it.

"Are you okay?"

Marie looked up, her eyes pooled with tears. "No," she said quietly. "I'm not." She shook her head. "We got the test results back. The baby has Down syndrome."

Elizabeth felt her lungs empty of air. "Oh, Marie. I'm so sorry."

"We just found out yesterday. I still can't believe it. I find myself thinking that the doctor's office is going to phone any minute and tell us they made a mistake, but another part of me knows that it's true." She reached inside her purse for a tissue and wiped the tears from her face. Then she leaned closer to Elizabeth. "About three months ago I woke up in the middle of the night with a horrible feeling that something was wrong with the baby. I couldn't even explain it; it was just a feeling. The funny thing is, it was my idea to have the amnio because I thought that Barry would want to know. He's always been so careful about things, you know, planning in advance to be sure things go the way he wants them to. Nothing happens spontaneously with him. But then out of the blue Barry tells me that he'd have been fine just going ahead with the pregnancy *without* knowing!" She shook her head. "I was completely shocked, and annoyed if you want to know the truth. I mean, *I've* become more careful over the years of being with him, so in a way my having the testing done was really because of *his* wariness about new situations."

Marie's hair had fallen in front of her face and she tried to tuck it behind her ears to reduce the wildness produced by the rain. "Barry doesn't understand that pregnancy has changed, even in the short time since we had the girls. People can find out so much now, and if everybody else wants to know the sex of their child before it's born, it's harder not to know yourself. And the same goes for the testing. How can you not have amnio if you know the test will reassure you that your baby's fine? Isn't it a good thing to know in advance if something's wrong?" She blew her nose, and her shoulders slumped. "I know we would have found out sooner or later, and maybe in the long run it's better to know now, but even as I say that I feel sick. I'm not talking about whether or not to take my dog to the pound, I'm talking about my child."

Elizabeth reached across the table and squeezed her friend's hand mutely. She searched for some consoling words. "I don't know what to tell you," she finally said.

Marie put her head in her hands and sat quietly for a moment. "You know, I've handled everything that's come my way so far, and I've managed to do okay, give or take gaining twenty pounds." She laughed weakly. "Mostly that's because I haven't known what's coming. Can you imagine if you woke up each day knowing exactly what would happen to you? At five o'clock I'll be in a car accident. After lunch I'm going to fall outside the school and break my ankle. Or worse, Nicole will be hit by a car; Sophia will pour boiling water on herself in the kitchen. Barry will have a major heart attack and be found slumped over his desk."

Elizabeth imagined her own scenario. Lying on an examination table, her feet in the stirrups. *The implanted eggs will not take.*

"But I just bumble along, you know?" Marie continued. "I handle things when they happen. But not this time. I got scared and I wanted to know. I wanted to know that my child would be healthy before I'd even met it. The tests are there, and it's so hard not to have them. I know this is going to sound like I'm romanticizing the past, but I envy our mothers that they didn't have to decide whether to know or not. They just got pregnant and then waited to see what they got. They didn't know if they were having a boy or girl. All they knew was they were having a baby. And if it had something wrong with it, they dealt with it. There was no deciding if the baby was good enough or not. They waited nine months and kept their fingers crossed." She stopped to catch her breath. "But now I'm wondering if we're wired to know in advance. I don't think we are. Can you imagine asking someone in advance if they're ready to welcome a disabled child into their lives? They'd probably all say the same thing: I couldn't do it, I'm not strong enough. But you rise to the occasion. We all do. We do what we have to do when we have to do it. We show up. There's something good about showing up, isn't there?"

The question hung unanswered in the air. After a minute, Elizabeth reached across the table and gave Marie's hand a squeeze. "So now what?"

"So now Barry and I have this awful decision to make." Her voice broke. She shredded the tissue in her hand and squeezed her eyes shut. "I feel like we're damned if we do and damned if we don't," she whispered. "And I don't know what we'll tell the girls. They're so excited about having a baby around again. Nicole was really hoping for a baby brother. Oh, and that's another thing. We found out that the baby's a girl. I didn't want to know, but Barry asked."

The door to the coffee shop banged open, assisted by the wind, and a large group of office workers scurried inside. Soon, the sound of milk being steamed filled the shop.

Elizabeth leaned closer to be heard over the noise. "Do you have to decide right away? You only found out yesterday. Maybe if you sleep on it a while you'll have a better idea what to do."

Marie shook her head. "The doctor said we don't have much time. I'm already well into my fourth month. The sooner we make the decision the better." She wiped her nose and folded what was left of the tissue into a ball. "I feel like such an idiot. I mean, *lots* of women think something might be wrong with their baby, but not all of them have a damaged child. The doctor told me what the process would be, but it was like I was numb because I wasn't prepared at all for having to make this decision." She took a deep breath to compose herself. When she spoke again, the panic had left her voice. "I think if I'd never had kids it would be an easier decision."

Elizabeth nodded automatically. But did Marie mean that a childless person would have an easier time aborting a baby? That was ridiculous. And insulting. She wanted to correct Marie's misconception. She wanted to tell her about the time she had seen the mouse caught in a trap on the landing of her basement steps, its head twisted to one side by the gold bar that pinned its neck, its long tail stretched out like the root from a garden vegetable. She wanted to tell Marie how she had recoiled immediately, and then, despite her disgust, how she'd turned to look at it again, the soft grey underbelly.

And then it had moved.

The entire belly had heaved. The fur rippled and bulged. Then it was quiet again. She wanted to tell Marie how she had raced upstairs and closed the door, sick to her stomach for having killed a mother mouse with its babies still alive inside her!

Marie continued. "It gets worse. The baby's kicking all the time now, and I just want it to stop. We had to wait three weeks to get the test back, and during that time, whenever the baby kicked, I pretended it wasn't happening. I didn't want to bond with it, just in case. And now . . ." Her face scrunched up as she cried. "It's like I'm in this rage. I don't want it inside me anymore, but I don't have any control over it. Every time it moves I think how it hasn't asked for permission. Why can't it just die on its own, without me having anything to do with it? Then I wouldn't have to feel so guilty."

Marie looked stunned by her outburst. She glanced around the café, but nobody was staring. "I'll miss it too, you know," she added in a whimper.

The coffee grinder started up and drowned the sound of voices.

"What does Barry think of all this?" Elizabeth asked.

Marie moved to the edge of the loveseat. "Barry doesn't want the baby." She wiped at her tears. "And I really don't know . . ." She faltered. "I feel so selfish, like we're not willing to love this baby because it's not perfect. But who is perfect? We're going to talk again tonight, but unless he's had a drastic change of heart . . ."

"You make it sound like it's all Barry's decision," Elizabeth said. "Are *you* sure about this? What do *you* want?"

"That's just it, I honestly don't know what I want. And I don't feel like I have the time to figure that out. But I certainly don't want to lose my family."

Elizabeth put her hand gently on Marie's knee. "What makes you think you'd lose your family?"

Marie stared at the ceiling to keep more tears from falling. "It's got to be an awful strain on a marriage. Do you know how many marriages don't survive? What if Barry and I didn't make it? What would that do to the girls?"

"There's no guarantee that you'll make it anyway," Elizabeth said. "Ron and I almost didn't make it. We came close there. Isn't it more important to *agree* on the decision? Because if you do something that you don't believe in, for Barry's sake, how will you live together then?"

They sat silently for a moment. Elizabeth was the first to speak again. "It seems so black and white," she said. "Have the baby or terminate the pregnancy. Are you sure there aren't any other options?"

"None that make any sense," Marie said, steadying her hands on her knees.

"What about adoption?" Elizabeth asked. "I was adopted, and things worked out well."

"Yeah, but there wasn't anything wrong with you. Healthy babies always get adopted. I can't imagine waiting to find out if someone had adopted my baby yet. Plus, I couldn't very well explain that to the girls, could I?"

Elizabeth leaned back into the loveseat and sipped her coffee. She wasn't one to talk about adoption because she'd never wanted to adopt either. But Elizabeth couldn't compare her situation to Marie's because Marie had already had two children, which was something Elizabeth had never been able to manage. She tried to imagine what she would do in Marie's position but couldn't. There had been too many years of wanting a baby. Would I parent a child with Down syndrome if I knew in advance and had the choice not to? Would I take a child that I conceived, no matter what its condition?

Would I?

In the damp air of the coffee shop the question settled like mist over her skin, filtered into her blood cells, into her organs.

Would I?

She closed her eyes for a moment and felt the fire's heat. The sounds of the café gradually diminished. She felt herself drawn toward the heat of the fire, as if she were being gently guided. She was cradled in warmth. And in that solitary moment she felt a monstrous weight lifted from her. Her back straightened, her shoulders squared, her torso lengthened. She was light as a feather, her bones hollowed like a bird's. A sweet calm nested in her stomach, and tears spilled down her cheeks.

The heat coursed through her like an electric current. She opened her eyes and scanned the shop. The edges of the table looked sharper. The windows overlooking the street looked cleaner. The voices of the customers were more full of life.

Then she looked at Marie. Her head was bent down, and her dark hair spilled over her shoulders. Marie. She felt the hot breeze on her cheek, and the air felt humid like the summer afternoons they'd spent at the creek. She saw woven dandelion crowns. Tasted ripe Saskatoon berries on her tongue. Saw the dolls disappear in the fast-moving creek. Felt the coarse tree bark against her bare legs.

Words rose to Elizabeth's mouth unbidden. Her lips parted. "I'll take the child," she whispered.

Marie's head jerked up. Her eyes contained a mixture of confusion and fear. "What did you say?"

"I'll take the child," Elizabeth repeated more firmly, surprised by the words that her tongue had thrust from her mouth.

The colour drained from Marie's face. "What do you mean?"

"Let me raise her," Elizabeth said, more animated now. "I know this sounds crazy, and obviously you don't have to make a decision right now, but if you don't want the baby and you don't want to abort it either, give her to me. Let me raise her for you."

Marie looked as if the floor had opened up beneath her. She clutched the arms of the loveseat to keep herself from falling. Then she stood abruptly and grabbed her coat and purse. "This was not why I came," she said.

Elizabeth stood up too and placed her hands on Marie's shoulders. "Listen, Marie. Wait."

Marie fell back into the loveseat, her face white and fearful. Elizabeth reached out and firmly gripped her wrist. "Look, we're both kind of in shock right now, but think about my suggestion, okay? I'll take the child. I mean it. Or at least talk to Dr. Maclean before you make any decision. He was my doctor when I was young; he's an expert on Down syndrome. I remember going to his office and having the waiting room filled with children who had Down syndrome. He's done remarkable work; I think he's been a real pioneer . . . I could call him for you."

She stopped when she saw the panic on her friend's face.

"Marie? Are you okay?"

"No, I'm not." She put her face in her hands and sobbed. "I can't stay here," she said, pulling on her coat. "I have to go home."

Elizabeth stood up. "Wait. Marie! You've got more options than you think. I'd love . . ."

But Marie was already at the door, falling headlong into the driving rain.

THIRTY-FIVE

She heard Elizabeth's voice call after her but she kept on moving.

She'd come for sympathy, not for a solution. Elizabeth wasn't supposed to offer her another option. Didn't she know how to listen, how to pat a friend's hand and nod knowingly? Now there was yet another wrinkle in things.

The van was parked half a block down Jasper Avenue and the rain fell heavily onto Marie's hurrying figure.

Directly across the street was the General Hospital, ugly as a nuclear power plant. Why at every turn was there some sign of her predicament? Suddenly she hated everything about it, the crowded parking lot, the sad attempt at landscaping, the stone statues of mercy and grace.

Marie unlocked the van and ducked inside. The rain hadn't put out the fiery heat of her emotions. Elizabeth might as well have kicked her in the teeth or thrown her in front of a bus. *I'll take the child.*

A voice in her head said, Home.

She turned the key in the ignition and backed quickly from her spot and into traffic. Home. She needed to be home now.

I'll take the child.

Why hadn't Elizabeth just listened?

Let me raise her. That's what friends do, you know.

Her mouth tasted sour. Elizabeth knew nothing about being a friend. That was obvious now. Almost twenty years ago she'd taken Ron, and now she wanted Marie's child too?

She was driving too fast. She clutched the steering wheel, leaning forward in the afternoon's pale light to peer through the windshield.

Somewhere in a calm spot in her mind, she knew she wasn't being truthful or fair, but she couldn't help herself. She needed someone to blame.

Marie tucked her hair behind her ears and used the steering wheel to pull herself to her full height. Of course she would love the baby if it were born, but wasn't it a kind of love to protect someone from the pain of being different and excluded?

Sometimes love was available in life, and you chose it. But maybe sometimes you didn't choose it. If she had the baby, Marie didn't doubt that she'd love it. But if she didn't have the baby, then she'd be protecting her child from a life of exclusion. Wasn't that a form of love? Or was it just a big cop-out? Maybe what she was really wanting was to protect herself from the pain of loving a child that was now targeted as undesirable. If there was a test designed to weed these kids out, then who was she to go against that current? Hadn't skilled medical researchers worked years to isolate the ingredients that produced these children?

She turned the van into her driveway and parked it in the garage. Her girls would be home soon, and she needed to compose herself. This decision was likely going to be the biggest turning point of her life. She would need to live with herself afterwards, no matter what action she decided to take.

THIRTY-SIX

Elizabeth stared at the café door, certain that Marie would return, but after several minutes had passed she realized her friend had definitely gone. She replayed their conversation in her mind, looking to see where she might be at fault. She had blindsided Marie by saying she'd raise the baby, that much was certain. But it wasn't fair for Marie to be angry about her spontaneous offer. What *had* she said, anyway? That she'd raise the child as her own. It was the perfect solution. Marie didn't seem prepared to raise the child, but she also didn't seem keen on aborting it. With one simple decision, she could absolve herself of the responsibility of raising the child and erase her best friend's childlessness. Hadn't her own daughter, Nicole, once said that it would be a good idea for her mother to give Elizabeth a baby?

She stepped out into the rain and pulled her jacket tight to her neck. Dr. Maclean could help her. She stepped around the dirty puddles on the sidewalk. He would help convince Marie to let the child live.

When the light changed she crossed the intersection.

Why hadn't she been more persuasive? She hadn't said that she'd love the baby as if it were hers, but that should go without saying because Marie knew how much Elizabeth wanted a baby. Yet she hadn't rehearsed any of it. How could she have? She didn't know about Marie's test results. There was no way she could have prepared herself better.

She reached her shop and went straight to her office. The rest of the afternoon sped by, and soon she was in her car, heading home. In the stalled afternoon traffic, under the soft rays of the lingering sun, she picked her bottom lip until a thin strand of skin tore off and she tasted blood.

She wanted that baby.

Not since her last round of failed in vitro sessions had she wanted something so badly.

Yet here she was, placing her fate in another person's hands. Again. What if she didn't get what she wanted?

She gripped the steering wheel to erase the image of her own devastation. It was too much to contemplate. Now that Marie knew she had another option, that her best friend would raise the child as if it were her own, she wouldn't terminate the pregnancy. She couldn't.

Could she?

She licked her lips and tasted blood. A nervous giddiness lightened her stomach. Down syndrome. It wasn't so bad, was it? Certainly there were worse things. The girl would know she was loved and she'd return that love too. Elizabeth remembered the young mothers in Dr. Maclean's waiting room all those years ago when she'd still been his patient. One mother, in particular, had carried her baby in a sling and looked adoringly upon him as he lay in her lap. That kid would be almost thirty by now and probably still holding his mother's hand when he went for a walk.

She would phone Dr. Maclean and ask his advice. He'd made a career of studying people with Down syndrome. He would have wise words for her. But would he remember her? And how would she find him? He couldn't still be practising, could he? She did some quick math and decided he'd be almost seventy by now. She hadn't seen him since she'd gone for a prescription for birth control when she was seventeen. An irony, now.

The afternoon sun blazed on the western horizon. A car honked behind her and she inched forward in the heavy traffic on the High Level Bridge.

The small guestroom that was currently her study would be the nursery. She'd picked that room because the south-facing window brought in lots of light. She'd paint it, of course. Maybe she'd put some stencils on the walls too. Of teddy bears? Clowns? Balloons? There was so much to do in the next four months. And there'd likely be some legalities to iron out in terms of custody rights. But they had time to sort everything out.

And then she remembered Ron. She'd spoken as if he was in complete agreement with her. But if Barry didn't want the child, and it was his own flesh and blood, what made her think that Ron would agree to raise it?

The North Saskatchewan River shimmered in the sun's orange glow. The water levels had finally receded after the spring thaw. New islands of moist sand and silt dotted the north bank. A flock of seagulls bobbed sedately in the main channel, enjoying the lengthening days. She watched them and felt a twinge of envy for their simple lives.

She passed a stalled car at the bridge's south end and quickly picked up speed.

What am I going to tell Ron? she thought.

What is Marie going to tell Barry?

THIRTY-SEVEN

"She what?!" Barry said, his eyes wide with shock.

"Keep your voice down!" Marie hissed, rinsing lettuce in the sink. She cocked her head and listened for a moment. All was quiet downstairs.

"Is she nuts?" He paced the room. "I can't fucking believe this!"

"Calm down, Barry."

"Who does she think she is, Mother Teresa or something? She's supposed to *help* you, not make things harder. What did you say to her, anyway?"

"I didn't say anything! I just told her we got the results back and were having a hard time with our decision. She means well, you know."

"Oh, for God's sake!" Barry exploded. "Do you really think she's trying to help us? Do you feel better now, knowing that someone else would raise our baby while we can't wait to get rid of it?" He sat down abruptly at the kitchen table and put his hands over his face. "Christ," he mumbled. "What did you tell her?"

"I can't remember *what* I said. I was as shocked as you are. I *certainly* didn't tell her she could have it. Even if I thought it was a good idea, I knew I'd have to talk to you first."

"What do you mean 'even if you thought it was a good idea'? You're not actually thinking about it, are you?"

Marie turned back to the sink so Barry couldn't see her face. Of course she'd thought about it. How could she not? All the way home in the car she'd thought about it, alternately raging against the new scenario Elizabeth had introduced and then imagining her and Ron pushing a stroller.

She had also pictured the various scenarios involved in telling her children, her parents, and the rest of the family. *Auntie Elizabeth couldn't have her own children*, she imagined explaining to her daughters, *so we gave her our baby.* But wouldn't they later think it was strange that the child their parents had so generously given away was the one with Down syndrome? And then she'd thought about fabricating an even bigger lie. *Because she's my best friend and couldn't get pregnant, I agreed to carry Elizabeth's baby. So it was never ours to begin with.* That didn't seem so far-fetched. She'd read stories of people who'd carried children for friends or siblings.

Marie even briefly entertained the idea of going away for half a year, without the kids, telling the rest of the family that she'd terminated the pregnancy, and then delivering the infant to Elizabeth under a veil of silence. But she didn't want to leave her girls for four months, and her family would find it strange that Elizabeth had a baby that was exactly the same age that Marie's would have been if she hadn't terminated her pregnancy.

But the truth was no good either. *Dear kids, your parents didn't want a baby with Down syndrome, but Auntie Elizabeth did.* Absolutely not.

What, then? Terminate the pregnancy and tell Elizabeth she was sorry? Tell her if we can't have the baby, nobody can?

"Marie?"

"I thought about it all the way home," she said quietly, staring at her hands as they went numb beneath the cold water. "Just because we don't want it, does that mean that the baby has to die?"

Barry let his head fall onto the table.

The smell of frying onions and pork chops filled the kitchen.

Barry stood, reached into the cupboard above the refrigerator, and removed a bottle of scotch. Then he poured a tumbler full and quickly drank it.

"It would be one thing to give the baby up for adoption," he said, clearing his throat. "That would be hard enough. But to give it to your best friend? I just don't think we could do it. How would we explain that?"

"You were the one who said we shouldn't worry about what anyone thinks."

"Look, I'm not the bad guy here," Barry said. "I'm not pressuring you to do something against your will. We're supposed to be in this together."

Marie nodded. He was right.

"Plus, she's not even with Ron anymore, is she?"

Marie shook her head in disgust. "You never listen to me. I told you that she and Ron are back together again. Elizabeth moved back home."

"And I'm supposed to remember that? And even if she is living with him again, you can't exactly say that's a very stable home environment, can you?"

Marie tried to keep calm. Barry was slipping into his know-it-all stance. It irritated her when he pretended to be so sure of himself. What would it be like, she wondered, to live in a world where everything was black and white, where all the edges were sharp and never rounded.

"You don't know the whole story," she said with resignation. "I hardly think you're in a position to judge the state of Elizabeth's marriage."

"The hell I'm not. Judge and be judged, that's my motto. I can judge anything I want to. Like, for instance, what kind of friend she is. She thinks things come too easily for you, and now she wants to make something harder for a change. You call that being a friend?"

"Look, I'm not interested in debating my friendship with Elizabeth right now, okay? That's not the issue. We're supposed to be deciding what to do about the baby. Why don't you think about the baby for a minute, instead of yourself."

Barry sat quietly for a moment. "I can't believe we're even having this discussion. Do you honestly think that you could give the baby up once you've had it?"

Marie tried to imagine the larger picture. She saw her water breaking. Packing a bag for the hospital. The contractions, slow to start and then coming on like a train. The sweating, the vomiting, the rocking back and forth trying to calm herself. Searching for a better position of comfort. Waiting for the drugs to kick in to stop the pain that foreshadowed her own death.

She could hear, taste, smell, feel, and almost see the baby as it struggled to leave her body. The baby's head crowning, the burning, the burning, and the splitting open, before its entire length slipped out. And then the incredible relief when the pain ended.

For what? To swaddle the baby and hand her over?

But if she agreed to do this, then Elizabeth would be in the room with her, and perhaps even Ron, to watch their daughter's birth.

Marie reimagined it. Elizabeth holding her hand, scared and excited at the same time, encouraging her, telling her she could do it, that she was doing just great. Elizabeth's eyes widening with excitement when the head crowned, knowing her baby was almost there. Then Elizabeth's tears as the slippery bundle was placed into her arms and she stared down at her own little girl, loving its sweet face, its tiny fingers, its perfect toes.

"I don't know if I could give it up," Marie said softly. "But I do know that there's nobody else in the world that I'd do it for but Elizabeth."

Barry listened quietly. "I'm scared," he finally admitted. "We've pretty well always agreed on things, but what if we don't agree on this? I'm having a tough time imagining Elizabeth and Ron walking away from the hospital with our baby."

"I know."

"What would the kids do?"

"They love Elizabeth."

"Yeah, but do they love her enough to give away their baby sister?"

"That's hard to imagine, isn't it? But we'll still have to tell them something because either way there'll be no baby in the house."

They were silent for a moment as the weight of Marie's words settled into their bones.

The grandfather clock in the foyer chimed six o'clock.

"Maybe I'm just being a coward," Barry said a minute later, "but it somehow seems easier to explain why the baby wasn't born at all than why it's not living with us."

Marie nodded. "I know. But are we going for what's easy or what's right?"

Barry walked to the sink and put an arm around her. "We need to do what we think is best for us and the girls." He pushed her hair off her face. "No matter what we do, we'll probably have some regrets."

He was right. They had already talked. They would talk again. For now, she would do the next obvious thing—serve dinner. She walked to the top of the basement stairs and called down, "Nicole! Sophia! Dinner's ready." Then she moved back to the stove and began filling plates with food.

Elizabeth was seventeen and in love for the second time in her life. Her body felt exciting, and it pleased her that her boyfriend's hands could elicit such wonderful and exhilarating feelings; it was similar to how her stomach felt when the roller coaster ascended the rise to its highest point, slowing to a crawl just before it plunged down the steep slope on the other side. It was exciting and terrifying all at the same time. Her body was wanting more; she hadn't gone all the way yet, but when that time came, she wanted to be prepared.

Marie told her she should go to Planned Parenthood, for the anonymity, but Elizabeth thought that was a depressing way to begin one's sexual journey, "planning," as if parenthood was the only reason to have sex. Plus, everybody knew that women who went to Planned Parenthood were there because they *hadn't* planned and had gotten themselves into trouble.

She certainly didn't want to go to her regular doctor because what if she wasn't discreet and mentioned it offhandedly to her mother, who was also a patient? Elizabeth loved her mother, but there were times when she needed some privacy, some little bits of knowledge about herself that no one else could share. So instead of going to her family doctor, she looked Dr. Maclean up in the phone book and found he still ran his practice out of the University Hospital.

"Dr. Maclean's office," the receptionist answered.

"Hi, uh, I used to be a patient of Dr. Maclean's, and I'm wondering if I might be able to schedule an appointment with him."

"What is your name?"

"Elizabeth Crewes."

"And when did you last see the doctor?"

Elizabeth counted in her mind. "Uh, it's been about five years."

"Well, I'll have to ask the doctor. Can you hold, please?"

A few minutes later she was back on the line. "Dr. Maclean says he'll be happy to see you. Can you come on Friday at two forty-five?"

By the time Friday rolled around Elizabeth was embarrassed that she'd made the appointment at all. Once she stepped into his waiting room she remembered why she and her mother had stopped seeing him. There were three patients with Down syndrome who were waiting with their mothers. Two of the children were fairly young, under the age of ten, she guessed, but the third one was maybe in her mid-teens. She was bald and her scalp was covered with patchy bits of downy hair as if she'd come straight from chemo. Maybe she had. Elizabeth knew that some of the kids born with Down syndrome had other serious conditions. It hardly seemed fair; hadn't this girl and her parents been dealt a difficult hand already? Why wasn't that sort of thing spread around a bit more?

She took a seat across the room, beside a woman with a baby on her lap. Elizabeth picked up a magazine and glanced surreptitiously at the child—sure enough, it bore the tell-tale signs of Down syndrome. She glanced at the mother again and noted how young she was, maybe only a half-dozen years older than herself. The baby sucked its fist while the mother clucked her tongue encouragingly and caressed the baby's tiny, stockinged feet.

"Elizabeth Crewes," a nurse called, and she gratefully followed her into an examination room.

Dr. Maclean looked almost exactly the same as when she'd last seen him, except that his hair had a bit more grey in it and he had the slight beginnings of a paunch. Other than that, he looked good, although he was more nervous than she'd remembered him.

"Hi," she said.

"It's good to see you again, Elizabeth. It's been some time," he said, clicking his pen open and shut, open and shut.

"Yes, since I was twelve, I think."

"And now you're . . ."

"Almost eighteen."

"My, time flies," he said, continuing to click his pen open and shut. "You're finished school now?"

"I'll be going to university in the fall."

"Wonderful. What will you study?"

"I'm enrolled to do a Bachelor of Arts."

"How are your parents?"

"Good," she replied. "Nothing new to report."

He laughed.

Why was he looking at her like that? Had she forgotten something?

"Is something wrong?" she asked, suddenly self-conscious.

The doctor smiled and laughed. "No, of course not. My apologies, I've had a busy week. Now, what brings you in today?"

He'd known her since she was a baby. He'd treated her for chicken pox, measles, bronchitis, strep throat, and eczema. He'd also, she suddenly remembered, known her parents' secret that she was adopted.

She was glad she was sitting down because her legs felt unusually weak. For the first twelve years of her life, she'd believed she was her parents' daughter, but then, out of the blue, a new narrative was placed before her, and Dr. Maclean would forever be linked to that discovery.

A cough interrupted her musings. Dr. Maclean was staring at her, a prescription pad in hand.

"Oh, sorry," she said. "What was your question?"

"Are you already sexually active?"

Elizabeth felt her face redden. She knew it was silly. It was his job to ask personal questions.

"No, not yet." But soon, maybe. She was dating a nice boy, and he'd been hinting about wanting more, but given her personal history, she knew that a girl could get pregnant when she was young and have to make some hard decisions.

"Anything else?" Dr. Maclean asked, handing her the piece of paper and hanging on to it a bit too long.

She shook her head, suddenly eager to get out of the doctor's office. "No. Everything's fine," she said, standing and smiling. "Fine."

"Well, you know where to find me if you need anything," he said, extending his hand and smiling. "It was good to see you again."

She filled her prescription on the way home. Tiny pink and white pills housed in their own plastic wheel. One pill a day, every day. The seven white pills were for when she was having her period. Just to keep in the habit of taking the pill daily. And she did. Responsibly.

Religiously. Even when she'd stopped seeing the nice boy she kept taking the pill, just in case she met someone new. Then Ron came along and after their marriage they no longer needed them. Oh, happy day! She remembered flushing three months' worth of pills down the toilet.

Such glorious optimism.

THIRTY-NINE

2002

Elizabeth pulled the pasta from the oven. She moved with a nervous energy, wanting everything to be perfect. She tossed the salad and put the breadbasket on the table, along with some butter. Ron opened a bottle of red wine and lit the candles.

"You look nice," he said, coming up behind her and circling her with his arms.

She'd brushed her hair out after work so it hung loosely down her shoulders. Then she'd dabbed some perfume behind her ears before slipping into a pair of leggings and a long black silk shirt.

She moved her head to direct Ron's kiss to her cheek. "Sit," she said, motioning toward the table.

She turned the kitchen light off and let her eyes get accustomed to the semi-dark. The flames on the candles flickered back and forth with the invisible air currents that circulated in the room. Soft music filtered in from the stereo in the front room. It was their first quiet meal together since she'd moved back home.

Caught up in the festive mood, Ron lifted his wineglass. "To us," he said, smiling. They clinked glasses and drank.

"I had coffee with Marie today," she began tentatively.

"Oh yeah? That's nice." Ron finished a mouthful of lasagna and buttered another piece of bread. "How's she doing?"

"Not very well, actually."

He raised his eyebrows to show he was listening.

"In fact, she had some bad news to share. Remember how I told you she'd gone to have an amnio done? Well, she got her results back, and it turns out the baby has Down syndrome."

Ron looked up from his plate and stopped chewing. "You're kidding. That's awful."

"I *know*. And now they have this big decision to make and Marie's feeling terrible about it. She was talking as if they might terminate the pregnancy."

Ron shook his head. "God, I feel for them. That's a tough one, for sure. It's not a decision I'd want to have to make."

Elizabeth's mouth filled with saliva. She swallowed hard and watched Ron return his attention to what was on his plate.

"It's a little girl," she added.

Candlelight reflected from Ron's glasses. The lower half of his face was in shadow. From where she sat, Elizabeth felt as if she were looking directly into the flames. She picked up her wineglass and swirled the red liquid around. Then she took a big mouthful and enjoyed the feeling of the heat flowing down her throat.

"She was really in a state about things. She didn't feel that she had any options."

Ron nodded and continued eating.

"Either she has to terminate the pregnancy or have the baby. I asked her if there wasn't any other option, and she said she didn't think so." Elizabeth hesitated. Ron shook his head in sympathy, clearly imagining the pain involved with such a decision.

"I was feeling so badly for her. I shut my eyes and tried to imagine what she was going through. It was strange, actually. I felt as if I had left my body or something, and suddenly I had this thought. Without even knowing what I was going to say, I told her I would take the baby if she didn't want it."

Ron stopped chewing.

Elizabeth looked down at the food on her plate and felt the kitchen walls close in. When she looked up she saw Ron put his cutlery down and wipe the corners of his mouth with the thumb and index finger of his right hand.

"Say that again," he said.

"I told her I'd take the baby," she whispered.

Ron pushed his plate away and nodded as if he got it now, the special meal, the candles, the bottle of wine. She could tell he felt set up. "I see."

A minute passed in silence before he spoke again. "And were you planning on discussing this with me? Or doesn't it matter what I think?"

"Please don't be angry," she begged, reaching across the table for his hand. "I honestly have no idea where the words came from. I didn't even know when I went there that Marie had gotten her results back."

"And did you wish you could take them back once you'd said them?"

She looked directly into his eyes. "No. I didn't. It felt like the most right thing in the world."

"What did she say?"

"She didn't say anything. She was probably as shocked as I was. She just grabbed her coat and mumbled something about talking it over with Barry."

Ron shook his head. "Here we go again."

"But she didn't say no," Elizabeth added hurriedly.

"I really don't know what to say. You were never interested in adopting before. What's changed?"

"This is different. We've got all this shared history. Her kids are the closest thing I have to nieces—they're almost like my *own* family." Elizabeth struggled to make Ron understand the emptiness she'd always felt in not knowing any of her real family. She moved to the edge of her chair to minimize the distance between them. "I sat there and listened to Marie talk about how guilty she felt for not wanting the baby, and I thought, there must be another way. She shouldn't have to go through so much pain. And then it was as if I *knew* that I was supposed to have that child. I knew it was up to me to give her that choice."

Ron didn't look convinced.

"I guess in offering to take the baby I assumed that you'd be here with me."

He took a deep breath and then took her hand. "Elizabeth. Listen to me. It's not going to happen. They're never going to give up their baby. Please don't get your heart set on this. I've seen you so disappointed in the past."

"But if she does agree . . . ?"

His face registered a mixture of disbelief and compassion. "Do you honestly think she'll give us her baby? What would she tell her family? It's way too complicated."

Elizabeth felt a surge of anger. Why couldn't he just go along with her for once and imagine something positive? Couldn't he tell that she was excited by this? "You're avoiding the question," she said irritably. "If they agree to let us raise their baby, will you help me?"

Ron sat back in his chair and closed his eyes. "I'm kind of in shock, to be honest. Do you need my answer right now?"

Elizabeth felt the sting of disappointment. She tried to smile to hide her longing. After all, she had sprung it on him, and he hadn't reacted too badly. He just needed some time to get used to the idea. She reached for her fork and began eating again.

Best of all he hadn't said no, and in her mind that was as good as a yes.

FORTY

"Drs. Knowles and Podnosky's office. How may I help you?"

Elizabeth froze for a moment before finding her voice. Even though her office door was closed she felt as if the entire world was eavesdropping. "I'm actually looking for Dr. Maclean. He used to practise at your location I believe."

"He retired a few years ago, but Dr. Knowles has taken over all his files. Is there something in particular I can help you with?"

Elizabeth shook her head, forgetting that she had to speak. She didn't want to talk to just anyone, she wanted Dr. Maclean.

"Hello?"

"Uh, sorry, I used to see Dr. Maclean when I was younger, and I was hoping to see him again."

"Well, if it's important I can get a message to him. He is in contact with some of his older patients still."

"Yes, thank you," she said. How could she say please hurry without sounding like she was crazy? But she didn't have much time. Marie could be making her decision right now. "Does he still live in the city?"

"Yes, he does."

Elizabeth gave her name and both her home and work phone numbers. "It's not exactly an emergency," she added, "but it *is* very important."

"I'll be sure to tell him."

She hung up the phone and cursed herself. It *was* an emergency. A child's life was on the line. She opened her desk drawer and removed the phone book. If Dr. Maclean still lived here, then maybe his number was listed. She leafed through the thin pages until she found the Ms, then looked more closely at the incredibly small type for Maclean. There were a lot of listings, but only three Dr. Macleans. She should be able to figure it out by process of elimination. Since his office had been at the University Hospital for years, she guessed he likely lived on the south side. That eliminated one possibility.

Elizabeth scribbled down the two remaining numbers and put the phone book away. She felt as if she'd had a lifetime of thoughts in the last day. It was hard to believe she'd only met with Marie the day before.

She glanced at the phone numbers before her with some doubt. What would she say to Dr. Maclean? How would she explain herself? *Hi, doctor, it's been twenty years. The last time I saw you I wanted birth control. This time I want my best friend's baby because I was never able to have my own. But it's not just any baby, it's a baby with Down syndrome, a baby that will need even more attention. And I can do that! Since you're an expert in the field, I thought maybe you could help me . . .*

She dialled the first number.

On the fourth ring a man answered in a soft voice. "Hello?"

"Hi," Elizabeth said. "I'm looking for the Dr. Maclean who worked with patients who had Down syndrome."

"Well, you've found him. That would be me."

"I'm not sure if you remember me," she began slowly, "but I used to be a patient of yours many years ago. I just phoned your office and left a message for you, but then I thought I'd look you up in the phone book because I wasn't sure when you might get back to me and it's sort of an emergency."

"May I ask your name, please," the doctor inquired.

"Oh, yes, of course. Sorry. I'm Elizabeth Crewes."

There was silence on the other end of the line.

"Are you still there?"

"Yes," came the quiet reply.

"I know it's been a long time," she continued, "just over twenty years, to be exact, but I need your help."

"Go on."

"My friend just found out from her amniocentesis results that her baby has Down syndrome and I'm afraid she'll abort the baby."

"Does this have anything to do with your mother?"

"My mother?" she asked. "No, my mother has nothing to do with this and she doesn't even know I'm calling. I was hoping, given all the work you've done in the field of Down syndrome, that you'd talk to my friend and help her to know it's not the end of the world. I thought maybe you could help."

"Does your friend want to talk to me?"

Did she? Probably not. Elizabeth recalled the look of panic on Marie's face when she ran from the café. "I'm not sure, to be honest, but if she does, I wanted you to know she'd be calling. Is it okay if I give her your number?"

She gripped the phone tightly in her hand, aware that everything seemed to be moving in slow motion.

"Is there something you're not telling me?" he asked. "I find it hard to believe that you've called me out of the blue because of your friend."

He had seen right through her. "Well," she said slowly, "I told her that if she didn't want the baby I'd raise it for her."

Once again there was silence.

"Why?" he finally asked.

Three little letters that asked so much. One small world that begged a million replies.

"Why?" she repeated.

"Yes, why?"

"Because she's my best friend and I think she'd regret her decision."

"You think she'd be making a mistake?"

This wasn't what she'd imagined when she'd called. She wanted him to help her, not judge her. "I'm not sure . . . she might be. But if I'd raise the child for her . . ."

"Why would you offer to do that?"

She heard a whine creep into her voice that she couldn't control. "Because I've never had children of my own and this would be the next best scenario."

"The next best scenario?" he echoed. "Do you know what you're asking? Because I know a lot about the health issues of children with Down syndrome, and they can be numerous."

"Yes, but you're also an advocate for these kids. You must have had strong reasons for doing so."

"Yes, I did."

"Well, obviously it must have been rewarding to you. Your practice consisted almost entirely of people with Down syndrome, didn't it?"

"That's correct."

"And me," she added abruptly. She'd been the only healthy child in his waiting room for her entire childhood. *It makes you feel grateful, doesn't it?* her mother had always said. But why had she been there at all? Surely there were other doctors to choose from.

"Dr. Maclean, why were you my doctor when I was young? Were you just beginning to specialize with Down syndrome cases and were in the process of changing?"

"No, I started specializing right around the time you were born."

Elizabeth had the chilling feeling that someone was going through photo albums of her childhood without permission. "You remember when I was born?"

"July 10, 1963."

That same person was now looking at home movies of her childhood birthday parties.

"Why do you remember my birthday? You must have seen thousands of patients over the years, you can't know their birthdays."

"Let's just say yours was a memorable case," he said. "And I can't say anything more."

"There's more?" she asked. "How could there possibly be more?"

"Have you talked to your mother about any of this?"

"Any of *what*? I was phoning to ask if you would talk to a friend of mine about Down syndrome. That's all."

"I'd be happy to talk to her if she's willing. Feel free to give her my phone number. What is her name, in case she calls?"

"Marie. Marie MacPherson."

He repeated the name slowly, as if he was writing it out at the same time.

"Is there anything else I can help you with?" he asked. It was that same tone he'd used many years ago when he'd inquired if everything was good with her family. Even then she'd sensed some hidden meaning that he'd covered quickly when she'd looked perplexed. What did he mean that hers was a memorable case?

"What's going on here?" she asked. "I'm getting the feeling there's something that I should know but I don't."

"It was nice to hear from you again," Dr. Maclean said lightly. "Give my regards to your mother."

"My mother? Why are you so solicitous of my mother?" And which mother? If he remembered the date of her birth, maybe he knew who her real mother was.

"Which mother do you mean? My birth mother or my adoptive mother?"

"Your adoptive mother."

"But you know who my birth mother is, don't you?"

"Elizabeth, this conversation should not take place on the phone."

Why not? she screamed in her head.

"I would prefer if you spoke to your mother before coming to see me."

Was she going to see him? She hadn't planned on that. What the hell was going on? Obviously she'd been far too trusting her whole life. All those times when she'd felt something was amiss her mother had somehow smoothed things over. Like when Elizabeth had wanted to access the government records that would provide information about her birth mother, her adoptive mother had found a way to postpone the investigation. Not maliciously or anything, but deliberately.

"Perhaps when you talk with your mother you'll understand better your desire to raise your friend's baby."

She felt chastised, spoken down to as if she were a child. "I wasn't calling for a diagnosis, you know."

"I'm sorry if it sounded that way."

The silence was deafening. She could hear herself breathing heavily into the phone. Her life was going off the rails, and she wasn't strong enough to stop it.

"Tell your mother I still have the notebook."

The notebook? Outside her office door, bells announced a customer's arrival, followed by the high-pitched wail of a newborn.

"What notebook?"

"She'll know. I have to go now. Please tell your mother that I wasn't the one to contact you, although I must admit I'm happy you finally called. I'm seventy-two now. My days are numbered."

Maybe the doctor had dementia. But that didn't explain his knowing her birthday.

"Look, I have a very bad feeling that I've missed something here. You are referring to a notebook that has something to do with *me?*"

"Yes. It's basically my medical notes on you from the time you were born. I was the attending physician at your birth."

Her mother had told her this years ago, but Elizabeth had never put the pieces together or thought to follow up on that trail.

"Then you do know my real mother."

"I can't say any more now."

"I'm not a child," she said, almost shouting. "As you already know, I'm thirty-nine years old. I don't need to ask my mother's permission to find out something that concerns me!"

Neither one of them spoke for a moment. "You are absolutely correct," the doctor finally said. "I guess I'd always imagined your mother being involved in your discovery. Forgive me."

"Dr. Maclean, obviously there has been some crucial information withheld from me for too long. You know what it is, and apparently my adoptive parents do too. Don't you think it's about time that *I* know it?"

"Yes I do, but I'd rather tell you in person. Would you be able to meet me today sometime? I'll bring the notebook for you."

"Why don't I come to you," she said. "I can leave right away."

He gave her his house address and said he'd be expecting her.

It was ten-thirty in the morning and her day had taken a sudden U-turn. Seeing Dr. Maclean wasn't just about Marie anymore. She'd have to leave the store understaffed for a few hours. At least the young woman working today was friendly and competent. She'd manage okay on her own. Elizabeth pulled on her sweater and left the office. "Julie," she said when she entered the front, "I've got a slight emergency and I have to run out for a little while. I'll be back as soon as I can." She headed immediately toward the back door.

"I hope it's nothing serious," Julie called to her retreating back.

"Nothing I can't handle," she replied, feeling suddenly stronger by voicing that thought. "The sooner I go, the sooner I'll be back."

Elizabeth left the shop by the alley door. She climbed into her car and unfolded the piece of paper that she'd scribbled Dr. Maclean's address on. He lived just across the High Level Bridge in Garneau. She'd be there in ten minutes.

She put the car in gear and headed south, wondering if she should have called her mother. But what would she have said? *Mom, you know that stuff you've always wanted to keep from me, that stuff about my mother? Well, I'm on my way to Dr. Maclean's right now to find out what it is.* What would her mother do? Confess everything in a torrential downpour?

The traffic was light going over the bridge. She reached the top of the hill, passed the Garneau Theatre, and turned right a few blocks down. He'd be in the first block on the left. There it was, a dirt brown stuccoed two-storey house with a sloped roof line. She parked at the curb and turned off the engine. This was it. Her heart accelerated. She was about to learn something that might change her life. Did she really want to know?

Dr. Maclean opened the door almost immediately, as if he'd been watching out the front window for her arrival. He was thinner than he used to be, and his dark hair had gone completely grey and thinned considerably. When he gestured for her to come in, she noticed that his right hand had a pronounced tremor.

"Hello, Elizabeth. It's good to see you," he said, smiling. "Please come in. I've put the kettle on if you'd like some tea."

She stepped into the foyer. A wooden banister separated the stairs on the right. The living room was off to the left. It was tastefully decorated with an old matching couch and chair set. Landscape paintings hung on the wall.

"We'll sit in the kitchen. Follow me." He lead her toward the back of the house and into a bright kitchen that had been remodelled fairly recently. A grey-muzzled black lab ambled toward her and placed his snout in her palm. "That's Seamus number three," the doctor said. "I name all my dogs Seamus. It makes it easy to remember. He's an old boy now, with not much pep. We're quite the pair," he added with affection and scratched behind the dog's ear.

The dog sniffed her hand for a moment, gave it a quick lick, and then returned to his pillow in the corner.

On the desk by the phone were photos of Dr. Maclean's wife and children at various ages.

"Will your wife be joining us for tea?" she asked.

"Sadly, no. Joanne died ten years ago."

"Oh, I'm sorry to hear that."

"Me too," he said. "But I've gotten sort of used to it now, and my children all live in the city, so I'm not entirely on my own."

He carefully poured boiling water into a teapot and placed it on the table along with two cups, some milk, and a pot of sugar. "Please, sit down."

"Thank you for agreeing to see me," Elizabeth began. "I know this must be highly unusual, to have a former patient track you down so suddenly."

"I'd expect it from you," he smiled. "You've always been unusual."

"Well," she said, smiling, "I guess it's about time I know what you mean by that."

He reached behind him for a hard-covered black notebook that sat on the counter. It trembled in his hand before he managed to place it on the table before her.

"These are my notes," he said formally. "They begin the day I learned of your mother's pregnancy and end on your last visit, when you were twelve. Then there's a brief addendum when you came to see me when you were seventeen and wanted birth control. So obviously there was a five-year break. And the notes slowed down as you moved from infancy to toddlerhood and adolescence. It didn't take long for us, by that I mean myself and another doctor who were observing your case, to determine that you were a healthy child with normal to above normal development."

She nodded as if she were a journalist taking notes about someone else's life. "Can I interrupt for a minute?"

He stopped speaking and raised his eyebrows.

"Why wouldn't I have been a normal child?"

The doctor gazed down at his hand, the one trembling on its own, and didn't speak for some time. "I've thought about this meeting for years," he finally said. "And now that it's here I really don't know the best way to tell you this." He met her gaze and asked, "Are you certain you want to know? Much of what I have to say might seem hard to believe, and I'm not sure you'll find it entirely to your liking."

She nodded mutely.

"Okay. I will try to start from the beginning and I suggest that you don't interrupt me until I finish."

Again she nodded, aware that she felt sick to her stomach.

"In 1962, I was fresh out of medical school and looking for employment. My wife and I wanted to stay in Alberta because all of her family lived here and we were just embarking on our own family life together. I sent out inquiries to all the major medical institutions, but the only one to interview me and offer me a position was Poplar Grove Provincial Training Centre, a government-run institution for the mentally retarded." He paused for a sip of tea. Elizabeth kept her hands wrapped around her own cup, drawing in the warmth.

"Aside from maybe one lecture at medical school, I'd had no training when it came to dealing with severe mental retardation, so I took the position with much trepidation. You must remember that this was over forty years ago, and societal opinions and expectations of the mentally and physically disabled have improved tremendously since then. Some of the patients who were there when I first arrived had been there for decades. Suffice it to say there was much room for improvement in the conditions in which these people lived. A good portion of the patients who lived at Poplar Grove had Down syndrome, or what they then referred to as mongolism. In fact, they even had a mongoloid ward to house them together. Now here is the part that you might find hard to believe." He paused and ran his hand over his bare scalp before continuing.

"I first met your birth mother on the mongoloid ward. She had been institutionalized in 1947 when she was just two days old. Her parents were encouraged to put her in Poplar Grove because there were no other options offered back then to parents who birthed a baby with Down syndrome. I could go on, but there's really no need for me to go into the history of institutionalization now."

Elizabeth's tongue felt thick and she spoke with difficulty. "Are you saying that my mother had Down syndrome?"

"Yes."

She attempted to laugh. "I don't believe you. That's not possible, is it?"

"That's exactly what I thought, but she—your mother's name was Carolyn—was over seven months pregnant before the discovery was made."

The information was coming too fast now. Her mother's name was Carolyn. Was? "Is she still alive?"

Dr. Maclean shook his head. "She died in March of 1967. Her heart had always been somewhat weak, and while the pregnancy didn't kill her, it was a contributing factor."

"Can we stop for a minute?" Elizabeth said. "I'm having a hard time processing this." She tried to recap everything. "Okay. You're saying that my birth mother had Down syndrome. She got pregnant. Wait. How old was she?"

"Sixteen."

A mother with Down syndrome and a teenaged pregnancy. The obvious question to follow was one she was afraid to ask. "Who was the father?"

Dr. Maclean had difficulty meeting her eyes. "We don't know."

"Who *might* the father have been?" She couldn't bring herself to use the personal pronoun in this line of questioning.

"Believe me, I've thought about that extensively. An investigation was launched after the pregnancy was discovered, but we never found any concrete evidence. The father could have been an orderly, another patient, a member of another patient's family who visited, or even, I'm sorry to say, one of the visiting doctors."

"Are you telling me it likely wasn't consensual?"

Dr. Maclean held his hand up like a stop sign. "Stop right there. I know where you're going with this, and I want to caution you before you get there. Patients with mental retardation can still have healthy sexual drives. Because society in general tends to see these people as perpetual children, they often believe they should be prohibited from any sexual activity."

"Yes, but surely you're not saying a sixteen-year-old girl with Down syndrome should be sexually active?"

"No, I'm not, but what I *am* saying is that we don't know if it was consensual or not. In other words, I'm trying to keep you from going somewhere with this that would be more harmful for you. When Carolyn's own mother discovered the pregnancy, she had some difficulty dealing with the shock."

"Whoa, whoa whoa," Elizabeth said. "Her mother kept in contact with her?"

"Yes." He nodded. "She visited once a month until the pregnancy was revealed. She never visited again after that and she signed the papers that allowed you to be adopted."

"And this was when?"

"She stopped visiting in the spring of 1963. The year you were born."

"What's her name?"

"I'm afraid I can't give you that information. You'll have to go to the government registry to find that out."

Her extended family. She had an extended family that she'd never been in contact with. "My adoptive parents know all about this?"

"They don't know about any family, per se, but they do know about your birth mother's condition."

"And you were involved with my case because . . ."

He placed his hand on the notebook. "Because your mother was the first case in this country of a woman with Down syndrome becoming pregnant and, on top of that, delivering a healthy child. Initially we followed your case to determine that you *were* mentally sound. While I wanted you to be placed up for adoption immediately, others wanted to give the prospective parents the full assurance that they were indeed adopting a healthy child. This notebook contains my research notes as well as some information about your birth mother. I realized over time that should you ever want to know more about your origins, I might be the keeper of that information. Before I left Poplar Grove I photocopied some case notes about your mother, but I had to black out the identifying names to maintain confidentiality."

"When was that?"

"In 1967. The day after your mother died I handed in my resignation. I realized that the only thing keeping me there was my interest in you and your mother, and once she was gone I no longer had any desire to work in that environment."

"And so you went on to study Down syndrome."

"Yes. That's how my career took an unusual turn and how it was connected to you. And perhaps you might also understand now why your offer to raise a baby with Down syndrome might have some biological drive from your earlier life."

Elizabeth snorted. "You don't honestly believe that, do you?"

"That there might be a link between your attraction to a baby with Down syndrome and the fact that your mother had Down syndrome?" He spread his hands out, palms up. "Is that too far-fetched for you?"

"Yes, as a matter of fact. It is. I'm almost forty years old and I've just found out my mother had Down syndrome. You can't possibly believe that there's some biological trigger here, can you?" She looked down at the notebook resting on the teak table before her. What other surprises might be in store for her within those pages?

"Do you have a picture of her?"

He shook his head. "No. Not one. To be honest, it never occurred to me, and by the time it did, she had already passed away."

"Well," she said, laughing, rubbing her hands over her eyes. "This meeting certainly didn't go as I'd expected. You wake up and it's an ordinary day, and you go to bed and your entire life has changed."

The dog whimpered on its cushion in the corner; its front paws twitched involuntarily.

"Are you going to be all right?" the doctor asked.

She met his eyes. "I honestly don't know. I'm probably in shock. Now I have to go out and talk to my husband and my parents and my friends and decide what I want to tell them. Or maybe I just leave here and say nothing at all. I mean, does my life have to change? Does one little piece of information have to change everything? It doesn't, does it?"

Dr. Maclean put his hand over hers. "No, it doesn't. Your adoptive parents were the happiest people in the world when they got to take you home. None of that has changed. And everything you've done in your life is still your doing. Now you have the back story to your existence that had previously been missing. That can be a good thing or a bad thing, depending on what you do with it. But take it from an old man like me, life's too short to get hung up on a little bit of barbed wire."

She smiled, not convinced that his hardships were similar at all to her current situation. But she got his point—pick yourself up, brush yourself off, and keep on going.

"Before I go, what suggestions do you have for my friend and her baby? After all, that's why I came, remember? To help a friend."

"I don't have any advice, if that's what you're asking. What I do know is that most positive tests for Down syndrome result in termination. I can't advise on that because it's a personal choice. My role has always been to help the children who *are* born with Down syndrome, not to counsel parents one way or the other. In my brief career, treatment has gone through three stages. At the start of my career, babies born with Down syndrome were routinely institutionalized. Then in the late 1960s and into the 1980s, parents were encouraged to raise their babies at home. That was the great integration stage. But now that prenatal testing is available, the majority of fetuses with Down syndrome are terminated. I think the numbers might be as high as ninety percent. Maybe even higher. It can make a person feel like his life's work has been for naught."

He shrugged his shoulders. "That's why most of the people you see with Down syndrome these days are adults. The younger demographic that would have continued to be present has been severely reduced. Some advocacy groups believe the intentional eradication of persons with Down syndrome is a form of modern-day eugenics." He shrugged. "It's an interesting point."

The quiet afternoon sunlight fell through the small bay window over the sink. Dr. Maclean walked toward it and rinsed his cup in the sink. His hand trembled as he reached for a striped tea towel and gingerly dried the cup before placing it in the empty drying rack beside the sink.

"In my many years working as a doctor," he continued, "the greatest epiphany I ever had was the realization that compassion is not an innate trait. On the contrary, I now believe that compassion is a learned behaviour. So those contact moments, those moments when we see a child with Down syndrome, or in a wheelchair, are moments that elicit compassion. What happens to us, as a species, if we limit those moments of contact? There will be fewer opportunities to be compassionate. And if we think of compassion as a muscle that requires exercise to stay strong, then we could be in big trouble."

He raised his eyebrows so that his forehead was pleated with wrinkles. "Times change," he said, "but not always for the better. My profession has a lot to answer for. The quest for health at times turns into the quest to label certain conditions as unhealthy and therefore undesirable. Who knows," he chuckled as he held his hand out before him and watched it tremble uncontrollably, "maybe one day they'll weed out fetuses who test positive for Parkinson's disease. I know my death won't likely be a pretty one, but I'm hoping that I've contributed something positive during my lifetime. And I certainly hope that whoever has the lucky job of spoon-feeding me when I can no longer feed myself will have a strong compassion muscle."

Elizabeth's eyes filled with tears as she nodded.

"Overall, the families I've worked with over the past four decades have grown to accept Down syndrome in their lives. They simply adjust their expectations. They move away from a belief in perfection, and they broaden their ideas of what's 'normal.' That's something we might all benefit from, isn't it?"

He returned to the table and sat down. "I'm sorry if that sounded like a lecture."

"No apologies are necessary."

"I don't have many opportunities to share my views these days. I'm afraid they're not very popular; maybe I'm old school, but I think the more choices we're given, the more selfish we become." He pursed his lips thoughtfully. "I'm afraid that as science gives us the ability to pick and choose our children, we will become a much less interesting species, and I can't help but think the world will have less compassion in it."

Elizabeth drew the notebook toward her and fingered its hard edges.

"Your mother changed me," he said. "You wouldn't know this, but she loved being outside. I remember looking out my office window one afternoon and seeing Carolyn and her mother sitting on the bench by the pond. That was their favourite spot. It was a sunny day, and they sat with their eyes closed and their faces turned to the sun. It was a beautiful sight, and I think of it often, the way their hands were clasped on the bench between them. Carolyn's mother always brought her a rose. Carolyn loved roses. Roses and robins."

"I own a flower shop on Jasper Avenue, across from the hospital."

"And if I'm not mistaken, your middle name is Rose, isn't it?"

He didn't miss a beat.

She extended her hand. "Thank you for everything. I really don't know what else to say."

He clasped both of her hands in his and held on tight. "It's always been my pleasure," he finally said. "I'm not sure what I'll do with myself now. I've been waiting so many years for you to come and see me. What have I got to look forward to now?"

Elizabeth laughed. "Oh, I'm sure you'll think of something."

He returned her grin. "You're probably right. But I'm sorry to say goodbye." He cleared his throat and looked away. "Now I'll see you to the door."

Before she could say anything more, she felt his warm hand on the small of her back, guiding her firmly to the front hall.

Overcome with emotion, she kissed his whiskery cheek, tucked the notebook under her arm, and walked slowly down the front stoop to her car.

FORTY-ONE

Elizabeth sat in her car and stared out the window at the school playground across the street. Sunshine and laughter. It was recess time and children were running in the field in their usual chaotic fashion.

When she got home she'd tell Ron the sad story of her life, or rather, the sad story of her birth mother's life. The notebook sat on the passenger seat. What *was* that story? She picked up the book; her hands trembled as she opened the cover.

The first half-dozen pages contained photocopies of the early records of Carolyn's institutionalization. At two days old she was placed in the infant ward at Poplar Grove. She didn't walk until she was five. She wasn't toilet trained until she was eight. She was deemed to be "extremely dull-witted." When she was twelve she had an IQ of thirty, or, as was noted, the functioning level of an "imbecile." Notes were scrawled in poor penmanship and with infrequency. There was nothing about what Carolyn's favourite colour was, or whether or not she liked dolls. What was her temperament? What made her happy?

> May 16, 1963
>
> A remarkable event has occurred of which I'm trying to make sense. Today one of my patients' mothers stormed into my office with her daughter in tow. The cause of her rage was not immediately clear to me, but when she explained herself more fully I understood. It appears the girl is pregnant. What is remarkable here is that she's not one of the regular mental defectives (who are healthy in body but not in mind), most of whom, I believe, if they've reached sexual maturity, have been sterilized. In this case, Carolyn is a sixteen-year-old mongoloid who, after my examination, appears to be into her seventh month of pregnancy.

I will search for other cases, but to my immediate knowledge I do not know of other female mongoloids who have become pregnant. One article from an obstetrics journal published in 1960 did mention, however, that in terms of the reproductive powers of mongoloids with good physical development, one could well imagine that pregnancy would not be absolutely impossible.

Whether or not Carolyn will deliver a child remains to be seen. If she does carry to term, I can only assume that the child will also be a mongoloid.

May 18, 1963

I met today with Dr. Stallworthy, who is on the board of directors here at Poplar Grove. He focused mainly on the legalities of the situation and whether or not the staff were meeting the legal requirements for the patients. He wasn't keen to launch an internal investigation, but I said it was paramount in determining if this case of sexual activity is an isolated one or a common situation among patients. As so many of the women in our care have been sterilized, pregnancies are not the "normal" indicator to reveal sexual activity. It goes without saying that when dealing with mental defectives and imbeciles, there is much room for exploitation to occur. As the communicative skills of Carolyn are significantly below average, she will be of little help in revealing who the father of her child might be.

I requested permission to stay with the case and suggested I work with Dr. Cooper, a former colleague of mine who now works in the Pediatric Department at the University Hospital. Permission was granted but only if all of Carolyn's care was conducted here on site. In other words, Dr. Stallworthy disallowed the notion that Carolyn might be transferred to the university for care once she goes into labour. I believe this has more to do with his trying to keep the reputation of Poplar Grove intact. He also expressed a strong interest in

Carolyn's family and their likelihood to press charges. I told him that the mother had been suitably shocked upon discovering her daughter's state, but that she'd left the matters in my hands. Staff records show that Mrs. H., Carolyn's mother, only began to visit her when she was four years old. Monthly visits followed. Nobody but the mother has ever visited.

The seeds for an article have already taken root: Pregnancy and Mongolism. I have not been this excited in my studies for years.

Elizabeth closed the notebook and shook her head. How much medical literature had been written about her? She flipped ahead.

January 1967
Another six months have gone by and three-and-a-half-year-old Elizabeth appears to become more mature by the day. This morning she arrived in a new red velvet Christmas dress with white lace around the collar, wrists, and hem. She even brought her good black patent shoes to replace her snow boots once she arrived. What she seemed most pleased with, however, was the white fur hand muff into which both of her hands could simultaneously disappear. She played magician for a full five minutes, "Now you see them, now you don't!" before her mother could divert her attention to something new. Santa had been very good to her, she told me; he had given her everything she wanted but a kitten.

Elizabeth hadn't thought about that dress in years. He had known her then too. No wonder he had been so kind and attentive to her; he'd been keeping notes the entire time, holding a magnifying glass over her as he prepared for his next article.

March 12, 1967
This morning, Carolyn H. died of cardio-respiratory

complications, four months shy of her twentieth birthday. As is the custom at Poplar Grove, her body will be buried in the graveyard on the grounds.

The time of death is estimated at 3:30 AM. The nurse doing the morning rounds discovered Carolyn in her bed at 7:00 AM, curled into the fetal position. Her body was removed and an autopsy was performed.

Had I known her time was so near I would have held a vigil by her bedside so she would not have died alone. I could have told her that she'd brought love into the world. I could have told her that her daughter, now four years old, is a vivacious and precocious child who was adopted by loving parents and who will live freely in the world from which she herself had been barred.

Elizabeth's eyes burned with tears. In the middle of a lonely night on a dark ward, her mother's heart had stopped and she'd left this world virtually anonymous and unknown. And her own child, not even four years old, had likely twirled about in her red velvet dress while some stranger dug a grave for the mother she would never know. Of course it was too much to think a child would know when her own mother died, but to be entirely oblivious? Elizabeth was being introduced to a grief she'd never known belonged to her.

March 13, 1967
Today I hand-delivered my resignation to Dr. Stallworthy, who is on the board of directors. At first he tried to talk me out of leaving, saying that the longer I stayed the more I'd get used to the place. I informed him that after four years of full-time employment I would never become used to the dehumanizing behaviour that passes for "care" at Poplar Grove. Dr. Stallworthy virtually hurled the epithet "liberal" at me when I spoke of reforms in the care of mental defectives. Yet what does he really know about how this place works? He directs from a distance and does not witness the daily bedlam of life behind locked doors.

As much as I shall miss Carolyn, I cannot help but be relieved that her days of monotony are over.

I must go now and pack my desk.

A bell rang at the school and the children began to leave the playground. Elizabeth closed the notebook, acutely aware of the irony of her situation. Women her age were worried about *having* a baby with Down syndrome, not discovering they were the *product* of a mother with Down syndrome.

If she told Marie about her birth mother, would it have any effect on her decision? She imagined Marie thinking about her baby right now, its every movement a glaring reminder of its condition.

What was Marie going to do?

And how much longer could Elizabeth wait for Marie's decision?

She turned the key in the ignition and drove away from the doctor's house. The notebook occupied the passenger seat like a long-lost relative.

"Any news from Marie yet?" Ron asked during dinner.

"No, but you're never going to believe what happened to me today."

"Try me."

"This is big, Ron. I just found out something that makes our decision to raise Marie's baby even more complicated for me." Her eyes filled with tears and she wiped at them in irritation.

"When I was younger I used to want to know more about my birth mother. I figured I'd go to the government registry when I was eighteen and find my real mother, but my parents always found some subtle way to postpone or discourage my attempts. I never gave it much thought, but now I know exactly why they did what they did."

The flames on one of the candles hissed and a chunk of wax fell on the tablecloth. Elizabeth put her index finger onto the soft wax and pushed it flat to keep it from burning a hole in the fabric.

"Why?"

"I had a doctor when I was growing up named Dr. Maclean. I remember going to his office and being surrounded by people who had Down syndrome. When I turned twelve, we switched doctors." She stood up and retrieved her purse. "Here."

She handed Ron the black notebook.

He flipped through the pages with confusion. "What is this?"

"It's all his notes about my case. It seems I was a bit of a medical miracle." She tried to laugh.

"I'm still in the dark here."

"Well, here comes the unbelievable part. My birth mother had Down syndrome. She was institutionalized when she was two days old and she had me when she was sixteen." Her voice had begun to shake. "I was born at Poplar Grove Provincial Training Centre, an institution for the mentally handicapped." It was hard to say those words out loud.

Ron stared with disbelief, unsure if she was joking, but she didn't laugh.

"You're serious, aren't you?"

"One hundred percent."

He looked confused. "What happened? How did you find out now?"

"To make a long story short, Dr. Maclean used to work at Poplar Grove. He was on staff when they discovered my mother was pregnant. Her name was Carolyn, by the way. He was one of the attending physicians at my birth, and he did a lot of follow up after I was born. Most of the medical community believed that a child born from a woman with Down syndrome would also end up being mentally deficient. That I was apparently 'normal' was remarkable to them. Because of me, Dr. Maclean became a leading specialist in the field of Down syndrome."

Ron flipped through the notebook. "This is incredible."

"When Marie told me that her baby had Down syndrome, I wanted her to talk with Dr. Maclean. I thought he might be able to persuade her that it would be okay. He knows it's not all doom and gloom. So I tracked him down and called him. Once he realized it was me, he said he'd wondered when I'd phone him and stuff like that. At some point it occurred to me that we were talking about two different things and something more was going on than I knew. So I went to his house and we talked."

Ron flipped through the book. "I can't believe you never knew."

"Well, at least it's pretty clear now why my parents never wanted me to find out."

"I guess," Ron said. "It's a pretty difficult thing to explain . . . but still, it doesn't seem right that it was kept a secret for so long."

"I know. It's hard to wrap my head around it. I'm not sure what to feel. I'm sort of mad that my parents never told me, but now that I know I can see that they were only trying to protect me."

"Listen to this," Ron said, and he began to read out loud.

August 1967

Elizabeth occupies her world so entirely that it's a joy to watch. She is the centre of all activities in the waiting room, and the other children naturally gravitate toward her. Today I discovered her patiently attempting to teach two of the young children with Down syndrome how to play patty cake. She is only four herself, and her matter-of-fact singsong lisp was delightful. However, it was the laughter of the three children that I recall best.

Elizabeth embraces all of life's opportunities so fully it pains me to know that my adult sensibility is largely void of an immediate sense of wonder. Such is the gift of childhood—the ability to respond instantly without filtering or censoring one's emotions.

"He sounds like a good guy," Ron said. "He obviously cared for you."

Elizabeth nodded abstractly.

"Did Marie call him?"

"I haven't given her the number yet. I thought I'd give her a day before I call with it. I think I shocked her yesterday, and I don't want to scare her off."

She stood and reached to clear Ron's plate from the table; he caught her wrist and pulled her into his lap.

"This doesn't change anything, you know? That your mother had Down syndrome, wild as that seems, doesn't mean that it's meant to be that Marie gives you her baby. Right? She'll make her own decision, no matter what you do or don't do."

Elizabeth knew he was right.

And yet . . . She slipped from his grasp and took their plates to the sink.

FORTY-TWO

Thursday morning was hectic. Barry left the house earlier than usual for a meeting at work. Sophia remembered at breakfast that she had a book report due that day that she hadn't yet started. Marie lost her temper. "Fine time to remember, isn't it? Do I have to be responsible for *every* single thing in your life?"

By the time she calmed down, Sophia was in a state and threatened to not catch the school bus. In the end, it was Nicole who managed to get her sister out the door by offering her full control of the television for the night.

Marie watched the skills of her twelve-year-old with admiration and shame. Who was the adult here? Wasn't Marie supposed to be the one to set a proper example?

Finally the front door closed behind her daughters and the house was quiet. Marie picked up the phone with a trembling hand and dialled Dr. Cuthbert's number. She gave her name to the receptionist, said the doctor was expecting her call, and was put on hold.

Five minutes passed.

"Hello, Marie. It's Dr. Cuthbert."

"Hi."

It was a sunny morning. Likely the early rays were streaming across the doctor's desk and spilling onto the carpeted floor.

"My husband and I have made a decision," she said.

"That's good. What have you decided?"

"You said we needed to make our decision quickly," Marie began, hoping the doctor wouldn't make her spell it out entirely. "So you could make an appointment for us."

"Yes." Dr. Cuthbert's voice was neutral, neither supportive nor condemning. "If you're sure about this, then I'll schedule an appointment immediately. I'll phone you back as soon as I know, but right now I'm thinking, given your dates and that it's almost the weekend, we might be able to book you as early as tomorrow afternoon."

The words sounded as if they were coming from a great distance.

"So soon?" she whispered. Tomorrow was Friday. By the weekend the baby might not be in her body any longer. She felt an immediate need to protect it. She hadn't felt the baby kick since she woke up. Maybe it knew what was coming. Maybe she had listened to the conversation she and Barry had had the previous night, and she'd wrapped the rubbery cord around her neck, wanting to control her own destiny. Maybe right now she was floating peacefully—senseless and forgiving.

The doctor didn't hear her question. "If it is tomorrow, then you'd have to go in tonight for a small procedure, but if tomorrow doesn't work out, it would help to know if you could be available for any other day."

Marie gripped the phone until it felt as if her thin bones might crack. She closed her eyes. "Any day," she said quietly. "I can be ready any day." *Will I ever be ready?*

The clock above the sink ticked loudly. The faucet dripped once, twice, three times, big drops that echoed like shots in the stainless steel basin. Marie sat at the kitchen table and stared across the room at the sink. She watched four more beads of water drop and counted the time between drops as if she were counting the space between lightning and thunder and waiting for the big crash to come.

Everything she had ever wanted or dreamed about lived in this house. Barry, her girls, all of their things. How was she going to fit this event in?

Her foot tapped the metal legs of the kitchen table. The girls' breakfast dishes rattled as the table slightly bounced. The baby kicked. *I'm still here. It's not too late to change your mind.* She stood up, as if to distance herself from the movement within. What was she going to tell Elizabeth? Marie felt sick even imagining the conversation. *Hi, Elizabeth. Thanks for your offer to raise our baby. I certainly appreciate your generosity, but Barry and I have decided not to go ahead with the pregnancy. We like our family just the way it is. Sorry about that. Want to do lunch sometime?*

Yeah, right. Elizabeth wouldn't want anything more to do with her. So now she'd suffer two deaths—that of her child and of her lifelong friendship. Marie couldn't help but feel that her suffering at the moment was greater than Elizabeth's. It wasn't her fault Elizabeth couldn't have a baby. That didn't mean she had to give up her own, did it? Her mind reeled. She was giving up her baby anyway, wasn't she? But she couldn't phone and destroy Elizabeth's hopes. Plus, deep down, Marie knew that if she talked to Elizabeth, her friend might actually persuade her to change her mind.

The phone rang and Marie jumped. Was it the doctor's office calling to tell her today was the day, instead of tomorrow? *No,* she thought, *not yet.* She let the machine take the message.

"Hi, Marie, it's me, Elizabeth. Are you there? Pick up if you're there." Her voice echoed in the cavernous kitchen.

"I don't mean to bother you, and I'm sorry if I surprised you at the café on Tuesday, but I wanted to give you Dr. Maclean's phone number." She paused. "Remember I told you about him? He's the doctor who specializes in Down syndrome. Well, actually, he's retired now, but he still lives in Edmonton. I spoke with him yesterday and he said he'd be happy to talk to you."

Again there was an awkward pause.

"He took your name down, so he won't be surprised if you do call. Okay?" She recited the seven numbers slowly. "I'm sorry you're not home so I could talk to you, but given the time constraints with your decision I didn't want to wait. So, I guess that's it. Can you call me and let me know what's going on? You know how to reach me. At work or home, okay? Anyway, I'm thinking about you. Love you."

Oh, leave me alone! Marie thought as she sat at the table. I can't deal with this! Of *course* Elizabeth was trying to be helpful—she had her sights set on mothering Marie's baby. Would she be as helpful if she knew Marie would keep the baby? Marie hated even thinking that way. Of course Elizabeth would be happy for her. Despite Barry's belief that she only had her own interest at heart, Marie knew her friend wasn't that cold-blooded in her selfishness. She wrote the doctor's phone number on a pad beside the phone and then immediately erased the message. Barry did *not* need to hear it.

Her appointment at the hospital was likely already made. She and Barry had discussed it into the small hours of the night. How many more conversations could they have? Did she want to phone Dr. Maclean and open up a new discussion? What good would it do to talk to him? If he'd made a career working with children with Down syndrome then clearly he'd have a soft spot for them. If every mother chose the route she was about to take, the good doctor would have been unemployed.

Right now, she didn't want to hear how those children brought joy to their families. Obviously, if she *met* her daughter she'd feel love, but didn't it make some sense to choose *not* to have her now, before they even met? How many parents, after having a handicapped child, would confess to wishing it hadn't been born? And how many marriages didn't hold up under the pressure?

No. The decision had been made, and she wasn't going to muddy the waters by calling on some specialist. Why was Elizabeth making it so difficult?

At noon, Marie phoned Barry and told him what the doctor had said.

"When will you know?" he asked

"By this afternoon."

There was silence on both ends.

Ask me how I'm doing, Marie thought. She could hear Barry tapping his pen on the edge of his desk.

"Can you let me know as soon as you know?" he asked. "I'll need to shuffle a few things at work."

Say you want to be with me. Say you won't let me go through it alone.

"Marie?"

"I'll phone as soon as I hear," she said coolly, hoping he would hear the distance in her voice.

"Okay, talk to you then."

She held the phone long after Barry hung up. He'd survived the uncertainty and turmoil of her pregnancy, and now he was getting back on track, back to his schedules and precise routines, back to the Barry who had cereal, toast, coffee, and juice for breakfast each morning. Back to the Barry who believed he knew things about things he didn't know anything about.

At one o'clock, the doctor's office phoned. She was lucky, they said. There had been a cancellation. She was to come in tonight for a small, initial procedure. Her appointment was fixed for the following day: Friday at two o'clock. She was to pack a bag and check in after lunch. She would be released Saturday by noon.

Marie thanked the receptionist and phoned Barry. Then she went upstairs and crawled into bed, pulling her knees to her swollen belly, curling her hands beneath her chin. She had two hours before the girls came home.

The afternoon sun streamed in her bedroom window and fell in wide shafts onto the bed. Marie closed her eyes and positioned herself so the sun was on her face. Through the thin flesh of her eyelids she saw red. She regulated her breathing until it was soft and rhythmic. The sun's heat warmed her. She inhaled and exhaled and felt the tension leave her body.

In the dream, she swam underwater, able to breathe without scuba gear. Her arms pulled long, hard strokes in the translucent water. Her feet fluttered just so and her hair streamed out behind her like untangled seaweed.

The water was warm and salty; it did not burn her eyes. Tiny fish with electric colours circled the clear bubbles that came from her mouth and nose.

She swam closer to the surface, where sunlight streamed into the emerald water. The sun's heat penetrated through to her skin and into her bones. Something swam toward her and nestled in her out-stretched hand. It curled into her cupped palm and stretched to its full length—two legs, two arms, little nubs of fingers and toes, a short torso, and an enormous head. Blue veins mapped its skull; she saw the pink mass of brain pulsing beneath the translucent skin, *ba boom, ba boom, ba boom*. It climbed up her arm, onto her shoulders, and into the thick matting of her hair.

Both hands free now, Marie swam on, wanting nothing but to

please the small, clinging creature. She felt the power in her arms and shoulders as she pulled hard strokes to gain speed. They swam through great schools of slumbering fish, past mountainous rocks and coral reefs, and through beds of kelp that swayed and danced. She felt the pressure of the sea surging all around her, rising and falling as the waves at the surface built and built and finally crashed into the shore.

Small hands caressed her face. Marie gasped for air. Nicole and Sophia stood over her, smiling. "We're home, Mom," they chanted in unison. "We're home."

FORTY-THREE

Across town on that Thursday afternoon, Elizabeth stood in her flower shop in a heightened state of expectation. Every time a customer came in, her eyes darted to the door, hoping it would be Marie.

Two days had passed. Surely Marie and Barry had had time to talk things through. And now that Marie had Dr. Maclean's phone number, she'd be able to talk with him and possibly be reassured.

Elizabeth pulled her hair into a bun so that the stray pieces wouldn't distract her. The glass door swung open, the little brass bell jingled, customers streamed in and out. The day was the same as any other except she was the daughter of a mother with Down syndrome, waiting to see if she'd soon become the mother of a daughter with Down syndrome. When would Marie stroll in, her thick hair tucked behind her ears, her swollen belly arriving just slightly ahead of the rest of her?

Elizabeth was not sure how long the silence could go on. It seemed ludicrous that she and Marie should eat their meals and go about their days in separate spaces without actually speaking.

The phone rang. Elizabeth raced to the counter and tried not to let her disappointment be obvious in her voice. It was just another customer requesting flowers. She was breathless and tried to calm herself. A pang of hunger radiated outward from her stomach. She hadn't eaten breakfast. She'd felt too queasy. For Ron's sake she'd tried to nibble on a piece of toast, but her body hadn't been interested. She'd almost been ill watching Ron dip his toast into the runny yolk of an egg.

She'd been thinking about names for the baby and, given the nature of its predicament, two names had sprung to mind immediately— Faith and Hope. She said the names quietly to herself, marvelling how each one required a different movement from the tongue and lips. *Faith*. A deep exhalation of breath to form the *F*. All she needed was faith. Maybe she would have Faith in the end. Faith . . . She closed her eyes and saw little pink sleepers, tiny socks and shoes, soothers, and stacks of flannel receiving blankets.

Hope. Air pushed from her lungs for the *H*; her mouth formed an *O*, then her lips closed tightly and popped open to form the *P. Hope.*

The door to the flower shop jingled open. A middle-aged woman entered and headed straight for the cooler with the expensive flower arrangements. She was an attractive woman who looked well taken care of, as if she had enjoyed a facial every week of her adult life.

"Can I help you find something?" Elizabeth asked.

"Yes. Roses. I'd like a dozen roses, please."

"Certainly. Any colours in particular?"

"My mother's always been a fan of red," she replied. "But I'm partial to yellow. So perhaps just a mix of yellow and red. How about half and half?"

Elizabeth nodded and began pulling roses from their oversized vases in the cooler.

"Do you need them double-wrapped?"

"That would be good, yes," the woman replied. "I'm just going across the street to the hospital, but even so, it is a bit windy outside."

Elizabeth took the woman's credit card. Dr. Rebecca Harrington. Rebecca; that name had come up before. And she was buying roses.

"Are you from Montreal by any chance?"

The woman looked surprised. "Yes, I am. How did you know?"

"Your father comes in every week; we get talking sometimes, and he told me you were a doctor. He always buys roses," she added as further explanation.

She laughed. "I bet my father told you all about me, didn't he? Everywhere we go he starts a conversation with someone. I can't blame him, though, it's not like he's got a lot of people to talk to. He lives alone now." She stopped suddenly. "Look at me! I'm about to tell you all about him! I guess I'm my father's daughter, aren't I?"

Elizabeth completed the transaction and returned the credit card. "I enjoy visiting with your father. I never find he talks too much, I guess because he doesn't only talk about himself. I bet you'd find that he could tell you quite a bit about me if you asked him. I'm Elizabeth Crewes."

Rebecca smiled, revealing straight, white teeth, and extended her hand across the counter. "Nice to meet you, Elizabeth."

"How is your mother doing?"

"Well, she's definitely failing, but she could also go on in that state for years." She paused for a moment before adding more. "Even though I'm a doctor and I spend lots of time in hospitals, I have to say that Alzheimer wards are depressing places. But I guess I'm grateful that they exist because my father couldn't care for her at home anymore. She had started to wander, and a couple of times he woke up to find her gone and heading to a bus stop. I have no idea where she'd have gone, but I guess she was pretty determined."

"That must have been scary for him." She wanted to add that putting her in care must also have been difficult, but she didn't. This woman knew that helpless people at the mercy of strangers didn't always bode well. But then again, helpless people at the mercy of their own families didn't always fare much better.

"How old is your mother?"

"She was born in 1925, so she turns seventy-seven next month."

"That's not old these days," Elizabeth said.

"Yes, well, sadly my mother has been in decline for the past few years, although she's really gone downhill in the last month."

"Your father was worried she wouldn't recognize you."

Rebecca nodded. "Yes, he was pleased that she knew I was her daughter. But she keeps calling me Carolyn and saying how sorry she is. It's the strangest thing."

The hair on the back of Elizabeth's neck rose. "Does she have someone close to her, like a sister or best friend, named Carolyn maybe?"

"Not that I know of."

"That's odd. Does your father have any idea who Carolyn is?"

Rebecca shook her head. "He says he doesn't, but he gets a funny look on his face when he doesn't want to be interrogated, and that's what he looked like when I asked. Likely there's some story there, but I don't think he wants to talk about it."

Elizabeth nodded. "Well, we all have our secrets. I just found out that my mother's name was Carolyn."

Rebecca looked confused.

"Oh, sorry. That must sound strange. I was adopted, and I only recently, just yesterday, in fact, found out some information about my birth mother. Her name was Carolyn." Elizabeth shrugged, embarrassed by her sudden disclosure. "Are you here for long?"

"I'm going back to Montreal tomorrow," Rebecca said. "Although I might come back for my mother's birthday next month."

Elizabeth found herself doing some quick math, knowing that this moment was going to pass if she didn't seize it. "If you don't mind my asking, what year were you born?"

"1949. Why?"

That fit. But it couldn't be that easy. She taped the paper over the flowers and stole a quick glance at Rebecca. This time she noticed that her cheekbones were similar to her own—high and sloping at a dramatic angle. "You don't think your mother ever gave up a child, do you?"

Rebecca looked startled. "No," she said, shaking her head. "I'm sure she didn't. We would know about that, for sure. No, it's just my older brother and me." She shouldered her purse and gathered the wrapped flowers in her arms. "It was nice meeting you," she said. "I appreciate your kindness to my father."

"It's no trouble at all," Elizabeth said. "Maybe I'll see you again next month."

The bells jingled and echoed throughout the empty store. Elizabeth stood at the window and watched as Rebecca Harrington, wrapped flowers cradled in her arm, walked briskly down Jasper Avenue to the corner, where she waited for the light to change. A steady stream of pedestrians marched by, enjoying the more temperate spring weather despite the occasional gusts of wind. The light changed for Rebecca and she hurried across the street and was soon out of sight.

Carolyn H. Maybe the H stood for Harrington. If so, that would make Rebecca her aunt and Mr. Harrington her grandfather. Dr. Maclean had said he wouldn't be surprised if Mrs. H. had never told her other children about Carolyn.

Elizabeth's mind raced. Carolyn was born in 1947. Rebecca was born in 1949. And she had an older brother, so there was another child in between, in 1948. The dates were tight, but it wasn't unusual for women to have children so close together back then. Plus, there were twelve months in a year, and a January baby had the same birth year as a December baby, so perhaps they weren't as close as the dates made it sound.

She felt a thrill of excitement. Secrets didn't always stay secrets for life. It just took one person to find a thread and pull to unravel it all. Maybe she'd found that thread.

Dr. Maclean's notebook was more than a thread; it was a detailed narrative with medical records that provided dates and everything; it was a paper trail that could lead to the adoption agency. Papers had been signed. Whose signatures were on those papers? She could find out.

The bell jingled and another customer entered the shop. Elizabeth's heart gave a leap. Marie?

It was the mail carrier.

Elizabeth took a coffee break and escaped to her office and closed the door. She pulled the black notebook from her purse. She sat at her desk and opened to an early page.

July 12, 1963

I was entirely unprepared for the birth. Two days have passed since Carolyn delivered a baby girl and I have been able to think of little else. During my medical training I attended a number of births, so I was ready and scrubbed when Carolyn went into labour. However, Dr. Stallworthy, the head director of Poplar Grove, authorized the patient to be drugged senseless and a Caesarean to be performed. How lifeless Carolyn was even as a new life was taken from her. I don't believe I've ever attended a more joyless birth. What should have been a celebration felt more like a funeral, and I guess for Carolyn it was. She'll never see her child. The newborn was cleaned and swaddled and quickly sent away. I voiced an opinion that Carolyn should at least have the opportunity to see her baby, but my view was not considered. I believe someone said it would only do Carolyn harm as she would not have the opportunity to see her child again anyway. Dr. Stallworthy also said that Carolyn would never know what happened seeing as she'd been asleep and all. I felt a great shame for my profession and a greater

shame that I allowed the infant to be spirited away in
a shroud of secrecy.

Elizabeth dabbed at her eyes with a tissue. Now she knew the desolate details of her birth. Now she knew that her birth mother had never even laid eyes on her, let alone held her, or placed a kiss on her brow. Did the doctors believe she was incapable of experiencing wonder or joy? Did they believe any fetal movement she experienced was simply ignored or misunderstood? Did they for one second have any humanity about them at all?

Her sadness slowly turned to anger as she reread the passage.

And nobody standing up for her, not even Dr. Maclean.

FORTY-FOUR

Her mind moved in and out of clarity, like a cloud at the mercy of the wind on a blustery day. On a good day, like today, she knew she was in the hospital, and her past was as clearly detailed as numbers in columns in an accounting ledger.

But the bad days were more frequent and perplexing; she experienced them as a drowning of sorts, a panicked flailing about in the hopes that a strong hand would clutch the nape of her neck and guide her to safety. Sometimes she could feel solid ground, but more often now, she felt nothing but a vast openness beneath her feet.

The roses on her bedside table were fresh, not wilted. That meant Donald had visited recently. He'd been good to her for over fifty years; she didn't like to live away from him. Not in this place, anyway. She sympathized with the woman in the next room who repeated the same thing over and over again in a small, yet urgent voice: *Let me die. Let me die.*

The sounds and smells of this place triggered sordid memories of a place where furtive liaisons went unnoticed and unpunished and where regret burrowed deep. When she'd left there the last time, she'd prayed for her daughter to be freed from the indignities that must have occurred in her life in Poplar Grove. When Dr. Maclean's letter bearing news of Carolyn's death had arrived, she'd been relieved because the protection her child had not received was now no longer required. Death meant she was free. There were no institutions in heaven; Carolyn would be welcomed like anybody else. She would finally be equal, and she would forgive her parents for what they'd done. Margaret knew she would be with her soon. They would find another sunny bench and sit together, like in the old days, holding hands and listening to the robins' song, the sun warm on their faces.

The wind picked up. Margaret felt confusion enter her mind, dark clouds of forgetfulness forcing her concentration to the side. The woman in the bed beside her began to howl. Margaret squeezed her eyes tight as if that would block out the sound. She turned her head from side to side in bewilderment. What was this place? Who had put her in here? Fresh roses were on the table beside her bed. Carolyn must have brought them. She loved roses. Margaret reached out a bony hand and plucked a single red petal from one of the flowers. Then she rubbed the redness into her lips, just like her daughter had taught her. The petal began to pull apart into small bits. She licked her lips and then placed what was left of the petal into her mouth.

She closed her eyes and felt someone take her hand and pull her toward the door. "Yes, yes," she said. "We'll go outside, dear. The sun's hot. We'll go sit on the bench, shall we?"

Margaret knew where she was now. There was a large room outside her door filled with partially clad people in varying degrees of distress. That damned cement wall had pictures on it again, and the orderly with the floppy leather belt would be lurking somewhere, ready to pounce on the unwashed swarm that was hungry for attention. They'd be lined up in a row, waiting for some kindness. A kiss, maybe. Or a flower.

Down the hall an orderly would be force feeding that sweet boy in the wheelchair again, the one who didn't appear to be handicapped at all, despite his physical challenges. He was incapable of speaking, but Margaret had learned a thousand things about him just by meeting his gaze and seeing the fierce intelligence that shone there.

She stood shakily beside her bed and put on her cardigan. Lately they'd been taking to locking the door. She'd have to hurry if she wanted to catch the asylum bus. James and Rebecca would be waking from their naps soon, and the babysitter had a class to attend. What if she missed the bus? She found her slippers beneath the bed, slid them on, and shuffled to the door.

The hallway was relatively quiet as she made her way past the nurses' station and to the door she knew would lead outside. She pushed and pushed, but it would not budge. Where was that dishevelled orderly who constantly made mistakes? Why on earth had he locked the door? She always used this door! Her fists bruised as they pounded the cold metal surface. Why wouldn't anybody open it? She was going to miss the bus!

She glanced around her in a panic. There was a man walking toward her. He had red hair and a white stick body and looked like an unstruck match. She recognized his face. Who was he? He sauntered over and smiled with his perfect teeth. His breath was searing hot and outhouse foul. "Back so soon?"

Margaret screamed. She screamed and screamed and beat on the door before crumpling to the floor. She would not be silent this time. A woman in a white uniform raced toward her. She'd always been free to leave Poplar Grove, but something had changed. Had someone signed papers she didn't know about? She hugged an invisible being in her arms and fought hard as the nurse tried to take her baby.

"Carolyn!" she screamed. "Carolyn!" This time she wouldn't let them take her. She saw her old house in the distance, swaying in the shimmering heat like a mirage. If she got there, she'd be safe. She clutched her child to her chest and willed her legs to move.

A sharp pain as the needle found a home.

Then the freefall began.

FORTY-FIVE

The sparrows that hopped and darted about Marie's bird feeder outside the kitchen window looked permanently startled. Their movements were quick and jerky. What a tense little existence they had, Marie thought, and she wondered why she'd never noticed this before.

She put the casserole she'd just made into the refrigerator. Frances had agreed to arrive at three o'clock so she would be here when the kids got off the school bus. She would stay with them until Barry returned home from the hospital.

The night before, Marie had arrived at the Royal Alex Hospital to have something put inside her, some kind of a "tent," they called it, that would begin to dilate her cervix. Tent. Camping with her children. S'mores for a bedtime snack. Moving to avoid the smoke that constantly followed her around the bonfire. Tent? That word had always had happy connotations for Marie, but not anymore. Now it carried death and mourning, not adventure.

After the device had been inserted, the doctor cautioned that she might have complications once the termination was complete. Placentas don't always co-operate when the delivery is so early, he explained. Sometimes surgery is required. What could she do to get her placenta to co-operate? Bribe it with a treat? Offer it money? Beg? *Oh, please, not this too.*

She took a piece of paper from the drawer beneath the phone table and wrote a note to her sister. *Frances, there's a casserole in the fridge for you and the kids (yes, it's vegetarian). Heat it at 350 degrees for 45 minutes. There's also salad stuff in the crisper if you feel like a salad, and there are cookies in the cookie jar. Help yourself to anything. Thanks for doing this. Marie.*

On the corner of the paper someone had written a phone number without a name attached. Marie stared at it dumbly. It was her writing and yet . . . Her mind worked hard. Maclean. Dr. Maclean. She'd actually taken down the number when Elizabeth had left that message. She took her pen and pushed hard to scribble out the numbers until it was hidden beneath a series of dark lines.

There was nothing Marie could do, it seemed, without suddenly being reminded of Elizabeth. She glanced at her watch. If she phoned now, she could catch Elizabeth at work and tell her she was on the way to the hospital. She wouldn't have to spell it out, just say she was going to the Alex. Then Elizabeth would know. But what if she showed up with flowers? If she showed up Marie would feel guilty that her friend stuck by her no matter what, and if she *didn't* visit, then she'd know that her actions were unforgivable. Right now she couldn't handle knowing she'd lost her best friend too.

She wiped the counters with a fresh cloth and put the dishes in the dishwasher. There was no sense not keeping up her usual standards, even if she did feel like she was going off the rails. Upstairs, she took her overnight bag out of the closet. Normally she would have had her bag packed in advance, but she'd been avoiding the task. For every moment she did *not* pack, she remained uncommitted to her decision. But the hours had passed. Barry hadn't phoned to say he'd changed his mind. And she hadn't phoned him either.

She folded her nightgown into its smallest shape and tucked it into the case. What else? Something to read. A magazine maybe. A hair brush. Toothpaste and a toothbrush. Some pads for the bleeding. Face cream. Fresh underclothes. Tissue.

Barry was picking her up at one-thirty. He'd taken to biting his nails again, paring down layer after layer of nail as if he were trying to strip the last bit of chicken from the bone. It bothered her to see his fingertips raw and wet with saliva.

She wandered down the hallway and stood in the doorway of Nicole's room. Her daughter was at that age when she had one foot in childhood and the other stretching toward adolescence. Sometimes it was a precarious balance. She was still young enough to have a few stuffed animals propped up on the pillow of her made bed, but not for much longer. Her room decor was already changing. Two bottles of nail polish stood side by side on her dresser. Earrings were lined up on the mirror over her desk. A poster of some young female singer was tacked over her bed. Marie couldn't remember the singer's name. She should remember if it was important to her daughter. She resisted the urge to crawl into Nicole's bed and pull the covers over her head. Such a powerful love, parenting. It crept up on a body and could knock you down if you weren't careful. Nicole—her first-born child. The being that had thrust her into another dimension—mothering. Did Nicole know how fiercely she was loved?

Downstairs, she checked again to make sure she'd unplugged the kettle.

Then her eyes landed on the phone. Elizabeth. I should call Elizabeth. But it was too late. There was nothing to say.

Give her to me. I'll raise your baby.

She heard the front door open and close.

"Marie?"

Barry's voice sounded as if it were coming from far away.

The baby kicked, a soft volley of heels. She closed her eyes and breathed deeply, instinctively rubbing her hand in a slow circle over her belly.

"Marie?" Louder this time and inflected with worry.

She heard his feet on the tile floor heading toward the kitchen. They followed the sound of his voice echoing through the quiet house.

Marie turned away from the window as he entered the room.

"There you are," he said, obviously relieved. "Are you okay?"

She nodded.

He checked the time on his wristwatch. "Are you ready?"

"My bag is in the foyer."

Barry checked the time. "We should go."

We should go . . .

Marie nodded mutely.

You should call.

"What's wrong?" Barry asked, seeing the pained expression on her face.

Marie looked away. *Wrong?* she wanted to say. *What could possibly be wrong?*

"I should call," she whispered.

"Call who?" he asked, confused. "The doctor already knows you're coming, right?"

"I should call Elizabeth."

Barry looked afraid that she might change her mind. "We don't have time," he said. "It's now or never."

The statement hung heavily in the air and echoed off the walls. Was "never" an option? Barry moved first. He retraced his footsteps down the slate tiles lining the hallway and into the foyer. He picked up her bag firmly and called back to her. "Do you have everything?"

A siren blared in the distance. Ladybug, ladybug, fly away home. Your house is on fire and your children are alone.

Everything? No. She didn't. She was sure she'd forgotten something.

"Come on," he said. "Let's go."

Marie willed her feet to follow.

FORTY-SIX

By the following day Elizabeth's nerves were on red alert. Three days had passed since her meeting with Marie, and she still hadn't called even though Elizabeth had asked her to when she left Dr. Maclean's phone number. She didn't know how to interpret the silence and was afraid to delve too deeply into the possibilities. She had relived their conversation countless times.

Rush hour traffic was always heavy on Fridays, and today it was even heavier than normal. Elizabeth reached the south end of the High Level Bridge and thought how different her life was today than it was two days earlier, when she'd driven this same route to Dr. Maclean's house. She'd gone because of Marie's baby, but she'd come away with something for ·herself—a new life story. Had Marie ever called him?

A car honked behind her and she put her foot on the gas. She knew there were few guarantees in life, but she'd always believed that she and Marie would remain friends to their graves. Now she was having doubts. No matter how she tried to rationalize Marie's silence, she knew if the shoe had been on the other foot, she would have called Marie by now. Guaranteed.

The black notebook in her purse contained her entire history from birth to age twelve. The entry about her adoptive parents was particularly poignant. They had known her entire history—that she was an illegitimate child born to a mother with Down syndrome—and they hadn't balked. Instead, they'd wanted to know more about her birth mother.

> January 1964
> There could not be two happier people in the world than Frank and Cheryl Crewes, who were today granted custody of Carolyn's child. The infant now finally has a name—Elizabeth Rose. I must admit that I had some

influence in her middle name. The Creweses were given ample opportunity to ask questions regarding the background of their new baby. They know, for instance, that the mother had Down syndrome and that nothing is known about the father. But what touched me greatly was Cheryl asking about Carolyn. What did she like? she asked. Did she have any favourite colour, or animal, or joke? Was there any particular craft she enjoyed? I found myself flustered. How little they knew about the workings of Poplar Grove, where the patients had few personal objects and often sat staring at blank walls. But when I put my mind to it I remembered that Carolyn's mother used to bring her roses and take her out into the garden when the weather permitted. Apparently she enjoyed watching the birds, particularly the red-breasted robin. Yes, I told Cheryl, she liked roses and robins.

A van the same colour as Marie's pulled up behind her, but it wasn't her friend at the wheel.

The sun glimmered high in the sky, big and orange and heavy with a pre-summer heat.

She tapped her wedding ring on the steering wheel and felt it spin slightly at the base of her finger. Ron would be home soon, but the idea of sitting and talking about her day exhausted her. She wasn't up for it. No, she didn't want to go home. Not yet.

Elizabeth switched lanes suddenly and turned left onto Saskatchewan Drive. She drove on, following a rusty homing instinct that was still surprisingly powerful once she gave in to it. Most of the single-family dwellings that had looked out over the valley when she was a girl had been replaced with expensive high-rise condos that boasted of their view. The road curved around to a set of lights. She continued on, past the old Ritchie Mill that was now a pub on one floor and a real estate office on another. Frances still lived around here somewhere, didn't she?

She crossed 99th Street at the lights and drove into the Mill Creek neighbourhood. Suddenly, the pulse of heavy traffic was gone and she found herself in a quiet residential area, the streets lined with old elms.

The years slipped from her. These were the same trees she'd played under as a girl. These were the same streets her small bare feet had run down. Some of the houses were bigger and more affluent, but despite that change she could still see her young self running, and for a moment she felt lighter and more compact.

She drove after the image of herself, down a steep hill, and parked at the small cul-de-sac where the river valley trails began. It was peaceful when she turned the engine off.

She sat quietly for a moment, and then once again gave in to the pull of the black notebook nestled inside her purse.

March 1969
Today is the two-year anniversary of Carolyn's death. On my way home I will buy a red rose to place on her grave. It has fallen to me to acknowledge the occasion.

April 1969
Mrs. Crewes made a special appointment for Elizabeth today. Even though the child had a routine case of the chicken pox, I was pleased, as usual, to see her. When I asked Elizabeth to lift her shirt she happily displayed the dozen or so fluid-filled blisters that covered her torso. I gave Mrs. Crewes a tube of calamine lotion and told her to keep Elizabeth home until all the blisters had formed scabs. Until then, she would be highly contagious. And dear Elizabeth seemed to notice for the first time that all the children waiting with their mothers had a similar condition. With a seriousness that surpassed her five years she asked me if she could catch what those children had. I smiled and explained that they were born that way.

Elizabeth closed the notebook and listened to the birdsong from the woods: robins, blue jays, magpies, sparrows. If she listened hard she could isolate each song. Now she would never look at a robin without thinking of her mother.

She stepped from the car and onto the dirt path. Caragana and wild rose bushes lined the way. The air was heavy with spring scents: damp earth, grass, and new leaves. She could almost feel the energy bursting from the pods on the trees and bushes.

Gravel crunched under her low-heeled pumps. *Hope, Hope, Hope.* A squirrel reprimanded her from a wooded hollow, *Marie, Marie, Marie.* A cool breeze pulled at her collar. Where was Marie now?

The road disappeared behind her. Soon, the gravel path turned into dirt and opened into a large field.

She had skipped down this trail daily in her childhood summers, her hand linked with Marie's, their laughter swallowed by the wind. And Marie's little sister Frances had often followed them, believing herself to be stealthy and unseen.

Marie, Marie, Marie.

At the bottom of the hill, the trail intersected with the main bike path. Elizabeth crossed the path and followed the dirt trail alongside the creek.

Water trickled surely along the glistening rocks. Up ahead, the old railway bridge spanned the creek. When she reached it, her footsteps echoed dully on the wooden slats. The water was high. Below the bridge it had formed a dark pool, a large mirror reflecting the clouds in the sky.

The sun fell deeper into the woods. Only its top rim was visible over the stand of trees along the trail. The shadows lengthened.

Elizabeth reached into her pocket and pulled out some change. Five coins. Five wishes. Each silver coin dropped through the air like a tiny orb of light. Each coin carried the same desperate cargo. *Please give me the baby.* Plunk! *Please let me have the baby.* Plunk!

The coins disappeared into the water's darkness. The creek stared back at her: greedy, cold, and selfish.

Where are you, Marie? What are you doing?

FORTY-SEVEN

Elizabeth was moody that night at dinner. She felt Ron watching her from across the table as he ate, dipping a piece of bread into the creamy dill sauce beside his salmon and wiping his plate clean.

"Are you going to finish that?" he finally asked, eyeing what remained of her salmon.

She pushed her plate to his side of the table. "Go ahead."

When he had wiped her plate clean too, he said, "I'm going to say something that you might not like. Are you ready?"

She put her hands into her lap and nodded.

"I was relieved when you wanted to quit all the interventions to have a baby. I thought maybe we could move forward with our lives. No more tears. No more bitter disappointments."

"I know," she began, but he held up a hand to silence her.

"And then, presto! You pull Marie's baby out of a hat, and here you are again, desperate for a baby and spiralling into another depression."

"I've always wanted a little girl," Elizabeth whispered, feeling her chin quiver. Marie had little girls.

"Well, you're driving yourself nuts moping around and waiting to hear from Marie. It's been three days already. Why don't you call her?"

Elizabeth saw his point. Maybe Marie hadn't gotten her phone message. That happened sometimes, especially with kids in the house.

"Just call," he repeated more softly. "Isn't it better to know than to be left wondering? Then we can move on, find out more about your past, and just move on."

He squeezed her hand. What had he just said? Something about Marie. That she should be there for her, no matter what.

"You're right," she said, nodding. "I'll phone as soon as we finish cleaning up."

"I'll do the dishes," he said and pushed her gently out of the room.

Elizabeth took the phone to the bedroom. She closed the door and rested her forehead against it for a moment. Why was it so hard to phone?

She sat on the bed and stared at the phone in her lap. Seven numbers. That was all that separated her from Marie's voice. Seven little numbers. She recited the number in her head and willed her fingers to move. Do it. Do it now. Ask how she's doing, how she's feeling. Keep your voice light. Don't ask for any more information; wait until she offers it. Remember, you're concerned for her.

Her fingers dialled the numbers; her stomach clenched into a tight fist. She put the phone to her ear and listened as it rang.

"Hello?"

The voice wasn't Marie's. Had she dialled the wrong number? "Marie?"

"No, I'm sorry, she's not here right now. Can I take a message?"

"Frances? Is that you? Sorry, I was expecting Marie to answer."

"Elizabeth? Oh, hi. I thought you might be Marie, actually. Or Barry. I haven't heard from them yet and I'm getting a bit worried."

Elizabeth's body flushed with heat. She tried to keep her voice calm. "What's wrong? Is everything okay?"

"Oh, I'm sure it is," Frances said. "But Barry hasn't called yet from the hospital."

A soft rush of air escaped from Elizabeth's mouth. She put the phone beside her on the bed and placed her head in her lap.

"Elizabeth? . . . Elizabeth?"

She picked up the phone again. "I'm still here."

Frances's voice dropped an octave. "You did know, didn't you? I mean, Marie told you, didn't she?"

Elizabeth nodded, as if Frances could see her. She kept her voice even. "Yes, she did. We had coffee on Tuesday. She told me about her test results."

"Well, then you knew they only had a few days to make their decision. Marie's doctor scheduled her appointment for some time this afternoon or early evening. If all goes well, she'll be home tomorrow morning."

If all goes well.

The room began to spin. She took a small gulp of air. "Well, thanks for the news, Frances. I'll try Marie tomorrow. Say hi to the girls for me."

She put the phone down. A high-pitched wail escaped her lips. She curled into a ball on top of the covers. Her hands became fists as they nestled in the crook of her neck. *You stupid idiot*, she spat at herself. *You stupid, stupid idiot.* She rammed her fists into her eyes to stop the flow of tears. *As if she'd give you her baby! What on earth were you thinking?*

A mixture of rage, self-pity, and raw hatred vibrated through her body. It was hard to know which one was which, but they were all hard-edged and sharp, wanting to do damage. Any minute now she'd hear her adoptive mother's voice, as if responding to one of her frequent childhood rages. "Elizabeth Rose Crewes, settle down this instant." Or "Lizzie, contain yourself!"

But this was worse than a scraped knee or a rusted nail in the ball of the foot. This wound sliced right through her, and if she didn't get a hold of herself and stop the freefall, she might not surface again.

Elizabeth cried like she'd never cried before—for the baby, for her birth mother, and for her friendship. Did everything have to die?

Fifteen minutes later, the bedroom door softly opened. Elizabeth tensed and held her breath. The mattress dipped as Ron sat on the edge of the bed.

"What happened?" he whispered.

She kept her eyes closed. She felt Ron pull the moist hair from the side of her cheek. "Marie's in the hospital," she said dully. "She ended the pregnancy."

"Did you talk to her?"

The last glow of light filtered in through the white sheers on the bedroom windows.

"She wouldn't be there otherwise."

"How do you know she was there?"

Elizabeth didn't feel like explaining. Why couldn't he just leave her alone until she was ready to tell him?

"Don't shut me out, Lizzie. Please."

He was right to be afraid. People often had warnings when bad weather was coming, but sometimes the tornado never touched down. Just because you got a warning didn't mean it would actually happen.

She could hear him breathing beside her. He wasn't going away. Then she felt his hand lock fingers with hers. With his other arm he reached behind her back and pulled her into his lap. She remained limp in his arms and kept her eyes closed as he rocked her slowly back and forth as if she were a baby.

"I can't believe she didn't tell me," she sobbed. "She could have phoned and told me!" She felt a new emotion, hiding behind the anger: grief.

"If she didn't tell you, then how do you know?"

"I phoned her house. Frances answered and said she was worried because Barry hadn't called yet from the hospital."

"But are you sure that . . ."

"Yes! I'm sure!" she shouted.

He continued to rock her. Minutes passed.

"She should have told you," Ron finally said. "But knowing in advance wouldn't have made it any easier or hurt any less."

His hand stroked the back of her head and she resisted the urge to swat it away. She didn't want to be comforted. She had been wronged; she wanted to stay mad. She knew that if she opened her eyes right now and looked into Ron's she'd find relief in his eyes. Deep down she knew he'd been afraid all along that Marie would say yes.

"I read some of the notebook," he said. "It's all kind of hard to believe, isn't it?"

Elizabeth didn't reply.

"The conditions in that place sounded pretty horrific."

"Poplar Grove," she whispered.

"What?"

She cleared her throat. "The place was called Poplar Grove. Poplar Grove Provincial Training Centre. It's closed now."

"I've driven by there before," Ron said. "It's that big brick place just on the south end of the city, isn't it?"

Elizabeth nodded, fully aware that Ron was trying to direct her attention elsewhere, and she was grateful.

He was silent for a moment. "You know," he said. "If you wanted . . ."

"What?"

"I don't know if now is the right time to bring this up," Ron said.

"What?"

"Well, I was just thinking that one day soon we should drive out and see if we can find your mother's grave. Carolyn's grave, at Poplar Grove."

She looked into his eyes and saw his deep concern. He'd been caring for her for almost half her life. This was the same man who'd fished her out of that cold mountain stream and eagerly warmed her in his sleeping bag at night. And here he was again, catching her as she fell and bringing her back into her own life, into the new history that was hers to explore and interpret.

"Just flipping through the notebook I saw that Dr. Maclean visits every year on March 12, the anniversary of her death. I know we missed it this year, but you could be the one to visit now, and more than once a year if you want."

Elizabeth felt her body soften and she curled into husband's arms and turned her face into the warmth of his neck.

"Yes," she said. "I'd like that."

FORTY-EIGHT

Friday afternoon the doctor used an ultrasound to inject saline into her baby's heart; Marie had always known that too much salt could kill a person, but she'd never imagined how a baby's heart would stutter and stall when introduced to it. Numb. What else could she be but numb? After the injection, the nurse turned up the oxytocin drip that induced labour.

What followed hurt.

Barry stayed by her side; their lives were no longer neat and tidy, were they? As the pain increased, Marie requested some morphine. She didn't want laughing gas, the mask over her face, the floating sensation that brought joy. This was nothing to laugh about.

"One more push," the doctor finally said, and Marie felt the slick and lifeless limbs slip from her body.

Did they want to hold the baby? Did they want a photograph?

She was lucky, they said, for with some cajoling, her placenta co-operated.

Afterwards, Marie was wheeled back to her room and given a mild sedative. Barry sat beside her bed and stroked the back of her hand with his thumb until it felt as if he'd taken a layer of her skin off. She pulled her hand away.

Tears rolled down her cheeks and into her ears. She missed Nicole and Sophia. She wanted Elizabeth.

A pale blue curtain had been pulled around her bed for privacy, closing off the rest of the room. The nurses had said she was lucky to have a bed, but it was worse being here, behind that thin curtain, with Barry holding her hand. She couldn't see the rest of the room and its inhabitants, and they couldn't see her. But it was no kind of privacy at all because every cough and conversation was magnified in that sterile room and it was impossible not to eavesdrop. The woman in the corner whimpered quietly to herself. No one came to comfort her.

At ten-thirty she was still awake and Barry was still beside her.

"You should go home," she said.

Barry startled. "Pardon?"

Marie cleared her throat and spoke louder. "I said you should go home. I want you to be there in case one of the girls wakes up tonight." The girls knew something was wrong with the baby, but they didn't need to know everything. She would tell them later that the baby had not lived.

Barry nodded. "Are you going to be okay?"

I don't know. She smiled weakly. "Go."

He leaned forward and kissed her cheek. Then he rested his head on the pillow beside her. "I love you, Marie," he whispered, his voice catching.

She stroked the back of his head.

He pulled back from the bed. "It's going to be okay," he repeated.

Marie could see the uncertainty in his eyes. His statement was really a question. *Is it going to be okay?*

He cleared his throat and said more firmly, "Let's just try to put this behind us."

Marie nodded.

Finally, he left. She lay there wondering if she would ever sleep again. Only a week had passed since they had received the results. In that time, she had moved from one task to the next, putting food on the table, doing laundry, packing school lunches, planning meals. For the sake of her children, she had tried to carry on as usual.

She repeated all the arguments in favour of terminating the pregnancy to convince herself she'd done the right thing, that it was better this way, that her family would get on just fine. A cramp twisted her insides. When it passed, she sank back into her pillow. She had taken for granted that she would be okay.

What would Elizabeth think of her now?

Was it a bad thing to want an easier life?

She rolled slowly onto her side and pulled her knees to her chest.

When she closed her eyes, Elizabeth's face stared back at her. Once again she felt the heat of Elizabeth's hand on her wrist. She saw her lips move: *I'll take the child. Let me raise the baby.*

It was too late. Everything had seemed so logical at the time. But now . . .

It was enough that she had lost her baby. She might never recover from that. She couldn't lose her best friend too.

Marie fought the sleep that came suddenly upon her.

I did it for the children.

It's better this way.

Who would take care of her when she was older?

We were afraid.

FORTY-NINE

On Saturday morning Elizabeth got up early and made Ron breakfast before he left for the gym. She made an effort to be light-hearted, but she'd never been a good actor.

"Do you want me to stay home?" Ron asked, concerned.

"No, I'll be fine. It'll be good to be alone for a while." Men didn't understand the cathartic nature of crying. She needed to cry without someone telling her that everything would be okay.

When Ron left, Elizabeth lay down on her bed and stared up at the ceiling. The black notebook sat on her bedside table. She picked it up and let it fall open at random.

> Carolyn Jane H., age sixteen, went into labour spon-
> taneously on July 10, 1963. A low cervical Caesarean
> section was performed under spinal anaesthesia
> and a five pound, two ounce, apparently normal,
> female infant was delivered. Pomeroy sterilization
> was performed.
>
> The mother is a mongoloid and the father is
> unknown.

And later.

> Mrs. Margaret H., Carolyn's mother and only visitor,
> signed the requisite papers releasing the child to the
> care of a government agency.

Margaret? She hadn't noticed that before. An old man's voice spoke in her head, *I just hope Margaret recognizes her at least once.* Rebecca Harrington's face appeared unbidden. *She keeps calling me Carolyn and saying how sorry she is.*

Now that the waiting was over, Elizabeth felt as if she'd been holding her breath for a week, and she was left with nothing but a black notebook stuffed with information about a woman she would never know and the child she had once been. She squeezed her eyes shut to block out the daylight that was growing steadily in intensity. Darkness. That's what she wanted. Darkness.

Later, if she had the energy, she'd find out how to visit Poplar Grove. Even though it was closed, there must be somebody there who tended the cemetery. How much explanation would she have to give to find out where her mother was buried?

She picked up the notebook and flipped through until she found the entry she was looking for.

> March 1967
>
> It's the first day of spring. Driving onto the grounds again felt strange since I so recently officially left my employ at Poplar Grove. I felt like a free man driving away for the last time, but then I realized there could be no last time. What I wasn't able to do for Carolyn in her lifetime I shall be sure to do now.
>
> I chose the first day of spring to visit her grave. I remember that Carolyn loved to be outside and to sit in the sunshine. When spring came around her mother often took her to sit on a bench by the small pond. Even though I knew Carolyn's grave would be simple and unadorned, I was nonetheless disturbed by the massive number of white headstones lined up row after row with barely more than a foot between graves. Also, the older part of the cemetery is now being reused for burial. It's bad enough that most of the patients have been forgotten here, but to have the older graves dug up to make room for the newly dead? I could not help but shudder and count my blessings that I would no longer be affiliated with this place of monumental grief.
>
> Using the map I located headstone #982. It was simply engraved with her name, and her dates: June 15,

1947–March 12, 1967. I placed a red rose on Carolyn's still fresh grave and told her that her baby girl was doing just fine.

Elizabeth felt a new energy enter her limbs. She would go to Poplar Grove, get a map, and find her way to her mother's grave.

FIFTY

Barry parked the car in the driveway and raced around to open Marie's door. He held her arms as she took small steps up to the front door.

Frances opened the door before they got there. Nicole and Sophia stood beside her, wide-eyed and nervous. Marie allowed Frances to hold her elbow and pull her gently inside the house. Everyone was treating her as if she was made of china. She bent down and took each of her girls by the hand and pulled them into her embrace.

"Boy, did I miss you," she said, her eyes clouding with tears.

"We missed you too," Sophia said.

Nicole stared at her mother. "What happened? Is the baby okay?"

"Everything's going to be okay," Barry said.

"Is it?" Nicole persisted.

Marie's heart clenched. "No, it's not." Fresh tears ran down her cheeks.

Sophia started to cry. "I wanted to be a big sister."

"Did it die?" Nicole asked.

Marie nodded.

"Can we at least close the door and discuss this?" Barry said.

Marie hugged Nicole. "The baby wasn't well, sweetie. We're all sad."

"When's the funeral?" Nicole asked.

Marie and Barry exchanged glances. They hadn't foreseen this.

"I want to go to the funeral."

"Me too," Sophia said.

It would be days before the small urn they'd chosen would be filled with their baby's ashes and be ready for them to pick up.

What would they do with it?

Sophia whimpered in her mother's arms. Barry helped Marie to the couch and made sure she was comfortable.

"Come on, girls," he said. "We've got swimming lessons in half an hour."

Marie hadn't expected the normal routine to kick in so soon. But Barry didn't want to leave any open spaces. Clearly he thought if he kept the girls busy, then things would get back to normal sooner. He didn't understand that what Marie really wanted was to cuddle on the couch with her children and cry with them.

"Come on," he repeated. "Get your stuff together."

Then he turned to Frances. "Thanks for all your help." He corralled the girls and their things and left. Their sudden departure left a gaping silence.

"Sheesh," Frances said. "Why's he in such a big hurry to get out of here? Shouldn't he want to stick around for a bit?"

"He just wants to act as if nothing has changed," Marie said.

"Yeah, well it's a bit late for that, isn't it?"

Marie felt a dark rage rise within her. Everywhere she went she had to take care of people. Her children, her husband, and now her sister. It was a heavy load to carry. Didn't Frances see that all Marie needed was some peace and comfort? She was in no mood to mediate. "Stop it, Frances. I'm not in the mood."

It wasn't often that Frances was speechless. For a moment it almost looked as if she might apologize, but instead she said, "Would you like some tea?"

"No, thanks."

An awkward silence followed. "Where's Max?" Marie asked.

"He's sleeping," she said. "Are you going to be all right?"

Marie wiped her nose and nodded.

"Did the doctors say anything about counselling?" Frances asked.

"They suggested I come back in a few weeks to talk with someone."

"That seems a bit far off. Will you go?"

"I don't know," Marie said. "We'll wait and see. Barry might need it too, who knows."

Frances sat quietly and waited.

The neighbours' dog began to bark.

"You should really eat something," Frances said. "How about some soup? Or a fruit salad?"

Marie shook her head violently. Soup—that's what she'd been eating when the call had come. Salty soup that had later burned like acid in her stomach.

"The girls were quite concerned about you last night," Frances began again.

Marie wanted to draw a hot bath and lounge in it until the girls came spilling in, high-strung and energetic. She hadn't slept much the night before, even with the help of a sedative. A new bed, new noises, the strangeness of being in a room with other people, the heavy emptiness in her abdomen, the coarseness of the hospital sheets and blankets.

"I'd like to have a bath," Marie said quietly.

Frances wasn't listening. "Elizabeth was concerned too," she added.

The air in the room suddenly shifted. Marie focused on her sister with a new clarity. "What did you say?"

"I said Elizabeth was concerned too."

"What do you mean?"

"She phoned last night to see how you were doing. She seemed surprised to hear you were at the hospital."

Marie fought to maintain her composure. "What did you tell her?"

"She did know, didn't she?" Frances asked. "I didn't let anything out of the bag, did I?"

Marie closed her eyes and remained silent.

"You had coffee with her the day after you got the results, after you had lunch at my place. That's what Elizabeth said. You told her then, didn't you?"

"Yes, I told her."

"But she didn't know you'd gone into the hospital?"

"No," Marie said softly. "I didn't tell her that part."

Marie tried to block the image of Elizabeth's stunned face when she heard the news. "I don't feel so good," she said abruptly. "I'm going upstairs to lie down until the kids come home." She stood gingerly. "Thanks for everything you've done, Frances. I'll be all right now. You might as well go home."

She made her way through the kitchen and down the hallway to the stairs.

She knows, Marie thought, the realization almost buckling her knees. Oh, God, she knows. And she didn't hear it from me.

FIFTY-ONE

On Tuesday, Elizabeth arrived at her store with a heightened sense of urgency. The morning dragged by, but soon the lunch hour arrived and, along with it, Mr. Harrington with his slow gait and hunched posture. Elizabeth ran to hold the door for him and took his elbow as he made his way over the threshold.

"Whew, it's getting warm out," he said, removing his hat and mopping his brow. "It's about time it felt like spring," he added. "It's always been my favourite season."

"Yes," Elizabeth agreed, "it's my favourite season too. It's hard not to feel optimistic when all the colours are coming back."

He nodded and leaned against the counter.

"Let me guess," Elizabeth said. "You want roses." Carolyn's mother gave her a love for roses. It made sense that roses would be her own favourite flower.

Mr. Harrington smiled. "You're very perceptive," he said. "A mind reader."

"I met your daughter, Rebecca, when she was in town," she said as she reached into the cooler behind her. "She seems very nice. Talkative, like you. I like that."

"Yes, she is. We're quite proud of her, my wife and I. Rebecca said you'd had a nice discussion."

"And how is your wife doing? Her name is Margaret, right?" She needed to be sure.

"That's right." He nodded.

Elizabeth pricked a finger on a thorn. She placed her hands on the counter to hide their shaking. Obviously Mr. Harrington knew he had fathered a girl with Down syndrome, but at some point he'd begun to believe that Carolyn had died. He certainly didn't know that she'd ever become pregnant and delivered a child.

Elizabeth put some roses in paper and began to wrap them. When she looked up she saw an old man standing before her, an old man whose wife was dying a slow death. On bad days she barely remembered she had a husband and she didn't know her own children. Yet she remembered Carolyn and she said she was sorry. Did he need to have his world upset even more?

"Rebecca said your wife recognized her. That must have been nice; you had been worried about that."

"Yes, she even called her by name."

Elizabeth plunged on. "She also said your wife kept asking about someone named Carolyn. Did you ever figure out who that was?"

She counted out six red roses, three yellow . . .

He pursed his lips thoughtfully.

Elizabeth willed him to continue.

"Children believe they know everything about their parents," he said softly, "which of course they don't. In our case, we never told them that we'd had a baby who'd died before they were born."

She didn't die!

"How sad," Elizabeth said. "If you don't mind my asking, how did she die?"

"Carolyn was born with Down syndrome. Our doctor said she likely wouldn't survive and suggested we put her into an institution. Sometimes that feels like yesterday." He sighed. "My wife never really did get over it, I think. I certainly see that now."

Your daughter was almost twenty when she died. And your wife visited every month for twelve years! She only stopped visiting when she discovered that Carolyn was pregnant. She had a baby girl who was put up for adoption and . . .

"I'm sorry," she said. "I shouldn't have asked."

"No, it's all right. It's good to talk about it. I wish now that my wife and I had talked about it more. I think we erred by not wanting to upset each other."

"Do you think you'll tell Rebecca?"

"I don't know. If Margaret keeps going on about it I suppose I'll be forced to at some point. Alzheimer patients often get fixated on earlier parts of their lives. Obviously giving up the baby affected her more than she ever let on."

"What about you?"

"What do you mean?" he asked.

"Giving up a child must have been difficult for you too. Wasn't it?"

He studied his fingernails intently for a moment. "It was difficult, yes. Certainly it was, but my entire focus at the time was to keep Margaret whole. I was afraid of losing her to grief, so I expect I proceeded as if nothing had really changed in the hopes that our lives would return to normal somehow. Our son, James, was born a year later, and that helped. Margaret had been nervous throughout the entire pregnancy, and I think we were both a bit surprised that our son was healthy when he was born." He chuckled for a moment. "The doctor had said lightning doesn't strike twice in the same place, but we weren't at all convinced. I can't tell you how relieved we were to be able to bring a baby home."

Elizabeth finished wrapping the flowers, taped the paper together, and delivered them to the man across the shop. "These are on the house today, Mr. Harrington. For being one of my most valued customers." *Grandfather.*

She helped him stand and gave him a quick hug. "Give my best to Margaret."

"Thank you, Ms. . . ."

"Elizabeth. Call me Elizabeth, or Lizzie."

He nodded and smiled. Then he put his hat firmly on his head and stood up, cradling the flowers like a newborn in the crook of his arm.

She opened the door for him. "See you next week," she called to his retreating form.

"If all goes well," he replied as he walked steadily to the corner.

After work Elizabeth crossed Jasper Avenue, passed the two stone statues, and walked toward the entrance of the hospital. It looked more like an office building than a hospital, with its many storeys with small windows running in straight lines across the old stone.

The glass doors slid open automatically when she approached the main entrance, and she walked directly to the information desk on the right. Behind the glassed window a plump, grey-haired woman in her early sixties greeted her warmly. "Can I help you, dear?"

"Hi, I hope so. Can you tell me how to get to the Alzheimer's ward?"

"There are Alzheimer patients throughout the hospital, dear. Are you sure she's in the Alzheimer's ward? You need to give me a name."

"Margaret Harrington."

She searched through her files. "Oh, yes, here we are. She's on the tenth floor. Ward Y. The elevators are just down the hall." As she spoke she gestured to the group of elevators in the middle of the lobby.

"Is there a nurse's desk there? I haven't visited before, but I'm family."

"Yes, the desk is just inside the ward. They'll be able to direct you to the right room."

"Thank you."

Elizabeth stood in front of the elevators and stared at her distorted reflection in the metal doors.

The air carried the smell of food from the cafeteria, flowers from the gift shop, and disinfectant from the cleaning staff's mops and rags. The air also held hope, despair, relief, and grief. Lives were saved here and lives were lost. Miracles and misfortunes.

Elizabeth stepped out at the tenth floor and followed the signs to Ward Y, hugging the flowers to her chest. If she met Mr. Harrington, she'd say she was delivering some flowers for a customer, as a personal favour, but she was hoping he didn't spend the entire day with his wife.

At the end of the hallway were a set of doors with a sign overhead reading WARD Y. To the right of the door was a green button to push for entrance. Elizabeth pushed it and heard a click as the door momentarily unlocked. She stepped inside and the door swung heavily shut behind her. A combination code was on the wall beside the door, but for now she was effectively locked in.

She experienced a moment of panic immediately followed by shock at the powerful smell of disinfectant on the ward. Obviously it was supposed to mask the unpleasant odours of bodies kept in captivity. Holding tanks for people past their prime. What was it about humans, she wondered, that made them lean toward caging things?

The nurse's desk was directly in front of her. A reed-thin woman with curly black hair was talking on the phone.

"Can I help you?" the nurse inquired when she finished her call.

"Yes, please. I'm here to visit Margaret Harrington. I'm her grand-daughter." How strange it felt to say it out loud.

"She's in Room 7," the nurse said. "Bed 2. It's down the hall on the left."

"Can I ask why the door's locked?"

"For security. This is the lockdown area. The patients here tend to wander off. This way we know none of them are finding exits. We'll let you out when you're ready."

Elizabeth thanked the nurse and walked slowly down the hall that branched out into an open recreational area with rooms on the outer walls in a circular pattern. Several patients sat watching television by the potted ferns. One woman with hair white and sparse as a dandelion sang bits of a song to herself over and over again while the man on the couch kept telling her to be quiet.

The room numbers were on the door, and as Elizabeth passed she peered in to find two beds per room. "Is that you, Gertrude?" a woman called out. "Is that you?"

Mrs. Harrington's room would be almost at the end on the left side. Most of the patients were bed-ridden, but two were wandering up and down the aisles as if searching for something.

Elizabeth stopped outside Room 7, peered inside, and was relieved to find no visitors. A vase of fresh roses sat on a table beside Bed 2. The woman in the bed was sound asleep, her mouth hung slack. The other bed was unmade but empty. Elizabeth stepped quietly to her bedside and looked at the photographs beside the roses. One was an old wedding picture. In another she recognized Rebecca, who posed with her family. The third photograph was of a man (Margaret's son?) and his family. Tucked into the frame of the wedding picture was a small photograph of a golden retriever in full flight after a ball.

Now that she was here, Elizabeth wasn't sure what to do. She looked more closely at the sleeping figure in the bed and noted how papery thin Mrs. Harrington's skin looked. Small blue veins around her temples looked as if a child had taken a ballpoint pen and drawn them there. Her sparse white hair held the look of a fresh styling. Her dentures had been removed and her mouth had sunken into itself, leaving her chin to jut sharply from her face.

Elizabeth sat down in the chair beside the bed. This woman had allowed her husband to believe that her first-born child had died. This woman had secretly visited that child every month and then had disowned her when she'd discovered her daughter's pregnancy. This frail woman, fragile as a newly hatched robin thrown from its nest, had lived with the weight of her decision all these years. Had she ever inquired after Carolyn's baby to see if it had found its way to a good home?

Elizabeth's mind raced with questions and various scenarios, but she felt calmly separate from any blame or anger. Maybe it was the newness of discovery that allowed her to be self-controlled. Whatever the case, Elizabeth knew she'd had a good life. That she'd never had a child wasn't the end of the world, despite the dark years of trying. There were greater darknesses out there, and this late discovery about her own life seemed pointless in a way. It could just as easily be the narrative of someone else's life, an interesting one that would make for a good story, but not one that resulted in shattered lives.

Wait until she told Ron that she'd just visited her maternal grandmother.

Just then Mrs. Harrington's eyes opened and fixed on Elizabeth's face. She had startling blue eyes with a faint milky haze on them. She stared and stared without blinking and without changing expression. Elizabeth felt trapped by her gaze. Who was she to be here?

Her granddaughter. That's who she was. She lifted her chin slightly and smiled.

Then Mrs. Harrington reached out an icy hand and gripped Elizabeth's arm with a surprisingly firm hold. "I knew you'd come," she said in a small, shaky voice. "I've been waiting for you."

Elizabeth placed her hand over Mrs. Harrington's and allowed the warmth from her youthful body to spread into the chilled hand of the woman who had been expecting her for forty years.

FIFTY-TWO

On the Monday following Marie's release from the hospital, she watched from the front window as her parents' car pulled up to the curb. Her father stepped slowly from the car, looked toward the house, and smoothed what was left of his grey hair back into place. Then he walked slowly around to her mother's side of the car and opened her door. Fay stepped briskly from the car and gathered her floral skirt in her hands as her husband closed the door behind her. Fay had always been great in a crisis, and she'd been through this once before with Frances.

Fay's omnipresent black purse hung from the crook of one arm while a bouquet of flowers was wrapped and cradled in the other. She turned and said something to her tanned husband, who promptly opened the back door of the car and emerged with some grocery bags. Then the two of them began a quick ascent up the cement path and rang the doorbell.

Marie took a deep breath and opened the door. Her mother's head tilted to one side when she saw her daughter and her eyebrows lifted onto her forehead in a severe gesture of sympathy. Then she passed the flowers to her husband and opened her arms as she stepped over the threshold. Marie walked right into them, as if she were eight years old and had just fallen from her bike.

"You did the right thing, dear," her mother said, patting her on the back. "Everything's going to be okay."

The right thing? Fay didn't know that Elizabeth would have taken the child. What would she have said about that?

No! she told herself fiercely. Barry and I spent hours looking at both sides. It wasn't an impulsive decision!

Somehow she got through the visit with her parents—her mother's well-meant clichés and her father's sorry eyes, sad as a basset hound's.

Then the long weekend came and Marie packed her family's belongings for the trip to Jasper. Barry had made reservations for the family at Jasper Park Lodge. He said they needed to get away and have some fun, and he was probably right. Barry had ignored that she rarely made eye contact with him and that she had little to say. He didn't understand that their lives would never be normal again. You didn't just end a pregnancy and carry on as if nothing had happened. Some grieving had to take place, some acknowledgment that she and Barry had played a part in ending a life. It wasn't right for him to simply move on to the next item on his agenda.

He hadn't been the one to give birth; *his* body hadn't changed in the least. The bleeding had finally stopped, but that didn't mean her body had entirely forgotten its ordeal. At least ten extra pounds circled her waist, and she still found that her hands instinctively went to her belly and rubbed the excess flesh that no longer needed tending.

Every morning prior to leaving town she had awoken saying, *Today's the day. Today's the day.* And every day her resolve diminished with the weighty knowledge of her deed. She knew the longer she waited, the harder it would be, but something kept her from picking up that phone. Guilt. Shame. Fear. Grief. A whole host of emotions.

The buds on the trees sprang to life overnight with their shiny green leaves. For a few days the entire city looked as if it were blanketed in electric green.

Marie threw another load of laundry into the washer and transferred one to the dryer. Barry didn't realize how much work it was to go away. He made reservations, put gas in the car, and thought his job was done. Meanwhile, Marie took care of everything else, and lately she found herself resenting all the lists she prepared to make sure everyone had what they wanted for the next few days. God forbid she forgot something one of the girls needed. *Where are my goggles? You know I need goggles when I swim!* And what about amusements for the car to keep the kids occupied? It was only a four-hour drive, but unhappy kids could make that seem like a lifetime. *Are we there yet? I'm hungry. She's touching me.*

She climbed the stairs from the basement holding a clean basket of laundry in her hands and sat down at the kitchen table. Four piles grew on the glass tabletop, one for each of them: Barry's underwear, socks; Nicole's underwear; Sophia's undershirt, socks; her own bras. Marie's hands moved on autopilot. She had completed this task hundreds of times in the past dozen years. No, thousands. But since coming out of the hospital she'd been in a constant state of irritation. It didn't have much to do with the kids, or even Barry for that matter—he just happened to be an easy target. Her mind was elsewhere. She hadn't called Elizabeth.

The silence between the two friends had stretched far longer than Marie had believed it could, and she now wondered if their friendship could remain intact. She'd never been good at playing games, and now she had no idea whose move it was. But if it was a contest over who was hurt more and needed comforting, Marie figured she should be the one on the podium. Gold medal to Marie. Silver medal to Elizabeth.

She picked up one of Barry's white undershirts by the empty shoulders and shook it hard, flapping its corners like a whip. Then she folded the arms behind the back and tucked the shirt in half. She folded it over onto itself and kept on folding until his shirt got smaller and smaller and her hands looked larger and larger.

This time last week I made the appointment . . .

Despite her irritation at preparing for the trip, Marie was glad they were going away for the weekend. She looked forward to being surrounded by complete strangers who had no idea what she'd just been through. She didn't want anyone feeling sorry for her, searching to find the right words of condolence. For the most part, everyone had been wonderful. Her mother, for instance, had been surprisingly sympathetic. Marie sat at the kitchen table, encased in a fortress of piled clothes.

The May long weekend proved to be as nice as the weather announcers had forecast.

Despite the sun, the mountain air was cool and pungent. It smelled of pine trees, glacial runoff, hidden valleys, and naked earth. A couple of male elk ambled slowly by, their necks covered in shaggy brown fur. New racks poked from the nubs in their brows, covered in a soft velvet, mere suggestions of what they would become by fall. She stared with wonder, trying to imagine velvety bone pushing up from a hard skull. Did it hurt? Was it the equivalent of enduring teething pains on a yearly basis? How could they possibly sleep at night with so much force gathering inside their skulls?

The girls had wanted to take the tram up Whistler Mountain; they were excited, but Marie couldn't fake the enthusiasm to go with them. The skin on her face felt heavy as lead. She was entirely joyless, so Barry took the girls without her. Bathed in full sunshine in a lawn chair on the deck of Jasper Park Lodge, Marie watched an elk lower its head to Lac Beauvert and drink deeply. Water dribbled from its velvety lips when it lifted its head. Another elk followed slowly behind, waiting for her new calf to follow. Calving season had just ended. The clerk at the front desk had warned them not to get between a mother and her calf because the instinct to protect was so pronounced. Barry had abruptly asked about the pool hours to change the subject, and Marie had pretended not to notice.

A train whistle blew long and low and echoed down the valley. In the distance, Mount Edith Cavell broke the skyline with its snow-covered peak. Its flat rock face looked like an open palm issuing a command. *Halt! Take stock. Notice the beauty!*

The grey rock, the white snow, the blue, blue sky.

Closer, and off to the right of her vision, a tramcar slowly ascended Whistler Mountain, swaying in the wind. She regretted not going, now that her family was gone. Children didn't understand an adult's need for solitude. *But why?* they'd asked when she told them she wanted some time alone. *Why?*

Marie's eyes filled with tears. This was yet another moment of regret to add to her list of bad parenting moments. She should be with her girls now, feeling the tram swaying in the wind, laughing light-heartedly. Instead, she'd allowed her own grief to keep her alone and at ground level. There'd been many such missed moments over the years, when her need to be alone outweighed her desire to be a good mother. A child late at night, excited to tell her one more story while she chastised her and sent her back to bed. Missed moments when her children wanted to be with her, confide in her, make her laugh.

The tramcar looked tiny on its metal cable. From that height, they must be able to see everything, she thought. For a moment she imagined the tramcar disengaging from the wire and plummeting to the valley below with her family inside. She played the whole tape and felt the anguish of losing her daughters. Barry's death would be hard too, but her daughters'?

Stop it, she told herself. Stop.

She shifted against the hard wood of the Adirondack chair and let her gaze fall once again on the tramcar as it ascended the mountain's peak. If Elizabeth only knew how much she'd wanted to call her before . . . But what would she have said? *Thanks for the offer, Elizabeth, but we've decided against it.*

And what would Elizabeth have said? *Oh, well, it was worth asking. Thanks anyway.*

She watched as another tramcar swayed precariously on its metal cable. Whistler Mountain looked suddenly forbidding with its dark patches of trees thinning and thinning as they gained altitude, their roots becoming more unstable, clinging desperately to the shallow soil that eventually turned to sheer rock.

Another train whistle sounded and echoed throughout the valley. Behind her, the door from the lobby opened and a large guided group emptied onto the deck, exclaiming and gesticulating wildly at the sight of the elk, rushing to get pictures. Marie closed her eyes and tried to re-enter her silence without success. Finally, she stood and turned back to the lodge. What now? A swim in the salted pool that spilled out into the open air? A massage? More food? Another cup of tea? There were too many choices.

Loss brings a certain exhaustion to the body, powerful as the urge for bones to grow, for tides to rise and fall. A grieving body needs sleep. She glanced at her watch. If she hurried, she had just enough time for a nap before her family returned.

She walked quickly through the lodge trying not to notice a group of well-dressed women in their thirties. How many of the other women she saw also carried dead babies slung around their necks like scarves? She tucked her chin into her chest to hide her tears and hurried toward her cabin.

FIFTY-THREE

Elizabeth leaned her full weight into the shovel and turned the moist soil in her small patch of garden. Dark mounds of dirt in perfect rows marked her progress. On the grass beside her back deck sat the boxes that housed her summer's ambitions: seed packages of peas, carrots, beans, spinach, onions, and beets. Bags of peat moss and fertilizer were stacked neatly alongside the boxes. Beside them, a dozen tomato plants were hardening off.

The first time she'd heard that phrase was at the farmers' market. As she paid for her purchase, the farmer told her to be sure to harden off the plants before putting them in the ground. He said it as if it was the most obvious thing in the world.

"Harden them off?" Elizabeth tried to visualize the process but couldn't.

"Yes, before you plant them leave them outside during the day for a couple of days. Bring them in at night, though. They've been in a greenhouse the whole time, so they need hardening off."

Don't we all, she'd thought at the time. That's what childhood was, a hardening-off period to prepare you for the real world. Something her mother, Carolyn, had never had—exposure to the *real* world. Yet she'd been hardened off too, hadn't she? In the worst way possible.

The dirt turned easily; its dark underside glistened. Elizabeth adjusted her gardening gloves; already she could feel blisters forming on the soft flesh of her palms. Next to her shovel, moist black beetles scuttled for cover.

The dank smell of things fermenting hung heavily in the air. She surveyed her garden, calculating how much time this manual roto-tilling would take, and then took a deep breath and began again. The shovel lifted and fell in her thin arms. Sweat gathered on her brow, in the hollow between her breasts, in her armpits, in the small of her back. She paused when her shovel hit something hard. A large stone had made a home in her potato bed. She bent down and threw it over by the compost heap.

It was not yet noon and already the day was hot. Loud shouts of glee filled the air from the neighbours' backyard. The children had the sprinkler on. She could see small flashes of nakedness through the boards of the fence. In the alley, a group of young boys in baggy pants swerved their trick bikes around the potholes, their heads dwarfed by large helmets.

Last year's giant sunflowers came out easily in her hand, roots and all. Elizabeth was always amazed that their shallow root systems supported such height. When she was a child she'd sat in her mother's backyard to see if the sunflowers really did follow the sun's path. She never managed to stay still long enough to find out.

From seed, to adolescence, to old age, the sunflower did all that in a brief season while always reaching for the sun. It was so life affirming and beautiful.

A robin sang from a tree branch nearby. She imagined her mother reaching for the song. The sun's heat intensified. Elizabeth kept turning the soil and with the rhythmic motions her mind's attention moved to the new family she was beginning to discover—her grandparents, Mr. and Mrs. Harrington, and her Aunt Rebecca and Uncle James and their families. Granted, she hadn't made a full introduction yet, but she soon would. Dr. Maclean had agreed to help her. He said he'd talk to Mr. Harrington and fill in the gaps in his knowledge.

"I'm only doing this because it's you, Elizabeth," Dr. Maclean had said when she called. "You know I've always had a soft spot in my heart for you."

"I know." She'd laughed. "I'm reading all about it in your notebook."

Elizabeth bent down and transferred the pile of weeds into a garbage bag. A person should never want something so much, she thought. Ron had been right about that. When she'd latched on to the idea of raising Marie's child, she'd lost her bearings. And when Marie had left her in suspense long after her decision had been made, well, it was like discovering someone you loved had been betraying you for years and the entire relationship was a sham and you didn't really know your lover at all. Betrayed. Yes, that was how she felt. Betrayed and abandoned.

Except she couldn't deny that Marie's baby had been the reason Elizabeth had contacted Dr. Maclean again in the first place. If not for Marie, then Elizabeth wouldn't have access to her new family. And given that Mrs. Harrington didn't have long to live, she was grateful to have the opportunity to meet her, even if her mind was clouded. So, in effect, Marie had given her a family, indirectly, but a fresh start nonetheless.

"You know," she'd told Mr. Harrington on his most recent visit to the store, "I have a friend who worked at a place called Poplar Grove. He's a doctor, though he's retired now. His time there overlapped with your daughter's."

It was a risk speaking to him, she knew, because if he got mad he might leave forever. But it was almost as if his wife, by talking about Carolyn, had given him permission to ask all the questions he'd never asked before.

"I could ask him about Carolyn and see what he says. Is that okay?"

Mr. Harrington had nodded wordlessly. Week by week she would feed him information. Dr. Maclean was waiting in the wings until he received his cue.

A soft breeze blew through her backyard. It combed the blades of grass and flicked through the weeds before swirling around Elizabeth's compact, bent figure. She caught the scent of creek water and fermenting leaves and mud and freckles and scraped knees and the undercurrent of childhood summers.

A cloud passed before the sun. The sweat cooled on Elizabeth's skin. The neighbour children squealed and laughed.

I would have loved that baby, she thought. I could have given her all the love my mother never received.

FIFTY-FOUR

The three-storey red brick building at the end of the wind-ing drive retained its imposing presence. Elizabeth nervously took in the surroundings as Ron navigated the car up the paved driveway and parked beside a path with a sign that pointed to the gardens. Goosebumps sprang to life on her arms and she experienced a sense of vertigo. Dozens of small windows looked out like eyes onto the world. In the centre of the building a tall brick chimney reached for the sky like the arm of an eager child, desperate to ask a question.

Elizabeth hadn't expected the building to be so big. In her mind she'd imagined that her mother's case was somewhat isolated, but seeing the size of the building made her understand that there were many people like her mother who had also been locked away.

Each red brick represented one word in the sad narrative of her mother's life: one brick for birth, another for farewell. But those bricks, strong though they were, couldn't contain her story. Finally someone listened, and wrote the story into a black notebook, and held it for almost forty years before it was, at last, delivered to her, the perfect reader for an imperfect tale.

"Are you ready?" Ron asked.

She nodded. They left the car and walked hand in hand down the gravel path to the trailhead where a small commemorative plaque gave a brief history of Poplar Grove. At the trailhead there were two signs: one pointed to the gardens on the left and another pointed to the cemetery on the right.

Elizabeth squeezed Ron's hand and scanned the cemetery and the grounds. Sparrow song filled the air. A magpie made its presence known. Elizabeth took it all in. She closed her eyes and imagined a young Mrs. Harrington, her hair freshly done and her nails impeccably filed, sitting on a sunny bench, holding her daughter's hand, not able to entirely let go of her first-born child. And she imagined the child,

Elizabeth's own mother, gratefully turning her dished face to the sun and drawing the heat into her pale, hungry skin.

Some stories are just too heavy to carry alone, she thought, and she was grateful for Ron's solid presence beside her.

They found her grave marker in a modest patch of spindly prairie grass that somehow stretched to cover similar plots, and they stood motionless before the humble grave of Carolyn J. Harrington. June 15, 1947–March 12, 1967.

Elizabeth bent down to rest her vase of red roses against the white headstone.

The sun shone brilliantly in the cloudless sky. Elizabeth tried to picture the woman she'd never met before, but she only managed to envision blunt brown bangs framing a round face with eyes that, she hoped, had at times flashed with laughter.

She raised her face to the sun and closed her eyes. This was the kind of day that Carolyn would have loved. It contained the three key ingredients that brought her joy: sun, flowers, and birds. Oh, yes, and a fourth ingredient—family, for Elizabeth didn't doubt that Margaret's visits had brought Carolyn great joy.

Elizabeth felt the sun on her face. The wind blew across the open field in the distance that would be beautiful when the canola bloomed. Birds sang in the trees around her. She squeezed Ron's hand and smiled as she realized that these four ingredients—sun, flowers, birds, and family—were enough to bring anyone happiness.

FIFTY-FIVE

It was after nine, but nightfall was still almost an hour away. The long nights of summer were just around the corner. Marie looked forward to eating ice cream cones and walking in the park, to wearing sandals and shorts, and to spending time with her kids once school was out. Especially now. The girls had seemed a little nervous lately, unsure of how to behave at home. They didn't quite understand what had happened, but they were intuitive, and without knowing why, they wanted to spend more time with their mother. They understood that an urn filled with ashes was all that was left of their younger sibling, and they knew that a family discussion would soon determine the resting place for those ashes.

Marie's bare feet padded soundlessly on the thick hall carpet. She closed the door to her room and perched on the edge of her bed. The cordless phone sat on her bedside table. She picked it up; it was a dead weight in her palm.

Long shadows covered the floor. A slit of white light poured beneath the bedroom door from the hallway. She closed her eyes and listened to her heart beating. It was no longer the drum against which her baby grew.

When she opened her eyes again, they had become accustomed to the semi-dark. The room was bathed in a soft grey light. She could make out the silhouette of the old mahogany dresser, the cedar hope chest pushed beside the dresser, the shuttered closet doors, the antique chair where Barry threw all of his clothes, the white wicker laundry basket overflowing, the full-length mirror next to the window. Shadows danced along the wall from the branches of the mountain ash outside. It swayed as if a child were swinging up into its branches, or as if a flock of waxwings had descended to strip it of its berries.

She stared down at her hands, took a deep breath, and closed her eyes again.

Marie filled her lungs with air and exhaled slowly. Courage. Her heart hammered and her hand shook as she dialled Elizabeth's number. The familiar tune sang from the touch-tone pad.

What if Elizabeth refused to talk with her?

What if she hung up?

What if she yelled at her or even cried and called her names?

Marie gripped the phone and bit her lip. Her insides felt all watery. From far off, she heard the phone begin to ring.

Elizabeth unpacked the grocery bags that lined the floor in front of the sink. To gain access to a cupboard, she shifted one of the bags with her foot, and cursed as oranges spilled out and rolled under the table. It had been a long day and she was tired. She'd sat with Mrs. Harrington for an hour and hadn't wanted to come right home afterwards, so she'd grabbed a quick bite to eat and decided to get some groceries too. What she really wanted now was to curl up beside Ron on the couch and watch a movie. She bent quickly to reach for the oranges, tucked three under her arm, and dumped the rest of the bag into the glass fruit bowl on the counter.

Somehow, the days were passing. She could move forward now. She had read the entire notebook more than once. Nothing was shocking anymore. She had thrown away the last baby sleeper that she'd kept hidden in a hatbox on her closet shelf. She'd hardened off, and she'd planted her garden. Now she would tend it and watch it grow, weeding around the small green shoots that would soon press their way through the dark soil. In the coming months she would focus more on work. Business was good. In fact, spring sales had been the best yet. And she would spend more time with Ron. Maybe they'd go to the mountains, do some more hiking.

Marie's face surfaced unbidden in her mind and she pushed the image away. It disappeared immediately. There, she thought. That wasn't so bad. She could train her mind to erase Marie's face whenever it infiltrated her brain. All good things came to an end, she reminded herself. Friendships too. She had to accept that. She'd try harder to meet new people. Maybe she'd join a club or something. Start playing squash again. Join a league. She turned back to the sink and began to wash some grapes. The kettle announced its boil on the countertop. She reached to unplug it. The phone rang.

Marie held her breath. One ring. Two rings. Her hand shook. She could hang up. It wasn't too late.

No. There had to be a way to get through this. She nestled the phone against her shoulder to steady her hand. Maybe she should have sent flowers first, or a letter. Something to prepare her. Maybe it wasn't right to surprise her with a call.

Three rings. One for each decade of friendship.

Come on, Elizabeth. Please pick up the phone.

Elizabeth answered the phone.

"Hello?"

Oh, God. Marie's stomach heaved at the sound of her friend's voice. She tilted her head back and closed her eyes. Her mouth opened silently. No words came out. She fought the impulse to hang up.

"Hello?" Elizabeth's voice again, irritated now. She didn't have all night. "Hello?"

"Elizabeth?" Marie said softly, her voice a small cry.

Silence.

Marie squeezed her eyes to slow the tears that were falling. What if Elizabeth had the strength to go on without her?

"Elizabeth?" she repeated, her voice gaining strength. "It's me."

Silence.

Marie licked her lips and stood up, needing to move. She walked instinctively toward the light spilling from beneath her bedroom door. Her hand rested on the doorknob. She turned it and the door swung open. She winced with a momentary blindness.

"I'm sorry, Elizabeth," she whispered and walked into the empty hallway.

She saw herself as if from above, one arm folded protectively over her tender breasts, her still-puffy figure standing alone in a bare hallway that looked like a road stretching out forever and ever before her.

Elizabeth heard the whisper come through the phone line, soft as a breeze.

Marie.

She sat down abruptly at the kitchen table. The water continued to run in the sink, trickling softly down the drain. She had imagined this moment many times and thought that, by so doing, she'd be prepared, but now that she was in it, she didn't know what to do. Marie's apology echoed in her ears. Elizabeth didn't know if she could forgive or if she even wanted to. Was she supposed to say, *It's okay*, and give Marie the freedom to carry on?

"Elizabeth?" Marie closed her eyes as if in prayer. *Please, please.* "Are you there?"

A hundred years passed. Marie's stomach hovered, ready to drop as she waited.

She leaned her back against the wall and slid slowly to the floor.

The phone pressed hotly against her ear. She cradled it with her shoulder to hold it in place. *Please, please.* Then she wrapped her arms around her bent knees and rocked herself from side to side.

"Can we talk?"

Elizabeth moved to the sink and turned the tap off, then stared out the kitchen window. The clouds in the night sky glowed eerily, backlit by a sliver of moon. No matter the outcome of the call, the sun would rise the following morning. So many things could be counted on. The sweet peas would bloom fragrantly in summer. The tomato plants would bear fruit. The carrots would burrow deep into the earth to grow. Fall was just four months away. What use was suffering? *Are you there? Can we talk?*

"You didn't even call," she said softly. "You didn't even call."

Marie opened her eyes. Above her, the hall light shone like a distant star.

"I'm sorry," she repeated. "I wanted to tell you, but I didn't know how."

Elizabeth was tired of apologies. Her voice shook with restraint. She measured each word carefully before she spoke. "I want you to know what it's been like for me. Every day I waited for you to call. I stood in my shop like an idiot, expecting every customer who walked through the door to be you. But you never showed up. I got the news from Frances instead, and only because *I* called. You didn't even have the guts to tell me yourself."

Marie received each word like a blow. She pressed her spine into the wall and braced herself against the hard truth. Elizabeth was right. How many times could she say she was sorry? "I'm sorry."

Elizabeth felt the anger leave her body as if each word carried its own cargo of rage and resentment. Her shoulders dropped to their usual place and she realized she'd been walking around for weeks with them tucked close to her ears. She heard Marie apologize again and imagined the tears running down her face. Now Marie was the one who was waiting, the one who didn't know if she'd be forgiven or not. Elizabeth had an entirely new history that Marie knew nothing about. And maybe she never would. Maybe Elizabeth would keep her own secret, holding the memory of the girl tight to her chest, the little girl born with Down syndrome in 1947 who'd been locked away.

Nobody spoke. Neither woman hung up.

Elizabeth heard the television in the other room and knew that Ron was waiting for her to join him. Steady Ron. Her real foundation.

She heard Marie's soft breath as if a seashell was pressed firmly against her own ear.

Her childhood echoed back to her. The railway bridge and the dolls staring blankly as the current pulled them north. The hours spent aloft in trees, silently watching.

"Are you still there?" Marie asked.

Elizabeth nodded.

The grapes glistened on the counter like dozens of individual planets. She understood now that no matter where she went in life, Marie would always orbit around her. There was no way clear of it.

"Yes," she sighed.

And again, after a moment, "Yes," she repeated.

Her voice was firmer now. She had stepped into another part of her life, the after part, and now she meant what she said.

"I'm still here."

ACKNOWLEDGMENTS

Many people helped me to write this novel. In no particular order, I wish to thank for their incisive comments and unfaltering enthusiasm: Gloria Sawai, Ruth Krahn, Norm Sacuta, Cathy Condon, Kate Kidd, Hanae Kiyooka, Renie Gross, and Shelagh Wildsmith. Thanks, also, to Tim Bowling for always supporting my need to write, and to my wonderful Mill Creek community.

For financial assistance, I acknowledge the Alberta Foundation for the Arts and the Leighton Colony at the Banff Centre for the Arts. I'd also like to thank the editors of *Alberta Views* for publishing an excerpt in their magazine.

Thanks, as well, to Ruth Linka at Brindle & Glass for believing in this book. I am especially grateful to Lisa Martin-DeMoor for her generous and insightful editorial comments.

And, finally, I'd like to dedicate this book in memory of my father, Bill Shea (1938–2012), and my dear friend and mentor, Gloria Sawai (1929–2011).

THERESA SHEA has published poetry, fiction, essays, reviews, and articles in a number of Canadian magazines and journals. Born in Maryland and raised throughout the United States, she moved to Canada in 1977 and now lives in Edmonton with her husband and three children. Having come to motherhood relatively late, Shea has always been particularly sensitive to the technological and moral issues surrounding women's choices regarding childbirth. Follow Theresa on Twitter at @SheaTheresa.